"You're one of a kind, Maggie Harper," Shep said.

As Maggie lifted her head to meet his mouth, something wonderful broke loose in her wildly beating heart. Closing her eyes, she leaned against him.

When his mouth tenderly grazed her lips, a sigh rippled from her. It was that dichotomy about Shep that always threw her. He looked like a warrior: big, hard-looking and so very powerful. Yet she was privileged to know this other side of him, too, so it was easy to yield to him completely. With him, she was safe. She knew he would care for her as if she were a priceless and fragile treasure.

She slid her arms against his broad, tense shoulders. Maggie wanted him. And as his lips moved in a claiming gesture against hers, she knew that what they'd shared so long ago was alive today. That he wanted her now just as much as he had in the past.

Maybe even more.

A SOLDIER'S MISSION

NEW YORK TIMES BESTSELLING AUTHOR

Lindsay McKenna

&

Carol Ericson

**Previously published as *The Untamed Hunter*
and *Bulletproof SEAL***

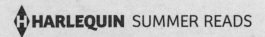 **HARLEQUIN** SUMMER READS

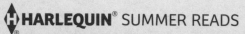 HARLEQUIN® SUMMER READS

Recycling programs
for this product may
not exist in your area.

ISBN-13: 978-1-335-45515-4

A Soldier's Mission

Copyright © 2021 by Harlequin Books S.A.

The Untamed Hunter
First published in 2000. This edition published in 2021.
Copyright © 2000 by Lindsay McKenna

Bulletproof SEAL
First published in 2018. This edition published in 2021.
Copyright © 2018 by Carol Ericson

This edition published by arrangement with Harlequin Books S.A.

For questions and comments about the quality of this book, please contact us at CustomerService@Harlequin.com.

Harlequin Enterprises ULC
22 Adelaide St. West, 40th Floor
Toronto, Ontario M5H 4E3, Canada
www.Harlequin.com

Printed in U.S.A.

CONTENTS

The Untamed Hunter   7
by Lindsay McKenna

Bulletproof SEAL   183
by Carol Ericson

Lindsay McKenna is proud to have served her country in the US Navy as an aerographer's mate third class—also known as a weather forecaster. She was a pioneer in the military romance subgenre and loves to combine heart-pounding action with soulful and poignant romance. True to her military roots, she is the originator of the long-running and reader-favorite Morgan's Mercenaries series. She does extensive hands-on research, including flying in aircraft such as a P3-B Orion sub-hunter and a B-52 bomber. She was the first romance writer to sign her books in the Pentagon bookstore. Visit her online at lindsaymckenna.com.

Books by Lindsay McKenna

Shadow Warriors
Running Fire
Taking Fire
Never Surrender
Breaking Point
Degree of Risk
Risk Taker
Down Range

The Wyoming Series
Out Rider
Night Hawk
Wolf Haven
High Country Rebel
The Loner
The Defender
The Wrangler
The Last Cowboy
Deadly Silence

Visit the Author Profile page at
Harlequin.com for more titles.

THE UNTAMED HUNTER

Lindsay McKenna

To Emile and Patricia Daher,
who serve the best food in Sedona at Shugrue's.
It's a joy to come and relax, laugh and share
pleasantries and friendship.

Chapter 1

"You could die on this mission, Maggie. This one is no walk in the park." Dr. Casey Morrow-Hunter drilled Dr. Maggie Harper with a hard look hoping to convince her of the danger she'd be facing. The world-renowned virologist sat on the other side of Casey's huge oak desk at the Office of Infectious Diseases.

Maggie raised her eyebrows slightly at her boss's huskily spoken warning. Sighing, she lifted her long, artistic-looking hands. "I risk my life every day in the hot zone. So what's new?" With a shrug of her shoulders, she gave her a challenging grin. "Tell me *what* in our business *isn't* dangerous, Casey."

"Touché," Casey muttered. She tapped her pencil on the top secret file that was open on her desk as she studied the woman before her. Maggie's red hair, which was almost always captured in a chignon at the nape of her long neck when she went into the lab to work with deadly viruses and bacteria, flowed across her proud, thin shoulders. Casey had caught Maggie and pulled her into her office for this discussion before the doctor had a chance to suit up for hot zone work scheduled later that morning.

Maggie pulled the tea bag out of her flowery cup and placed it on the white china saucer balanced on her crossed legs. "So," she murmured, giving Casey a knowing look, "what little special assignment have you cooked up for me this time? You know how bored I get. It must be a field assignment? To Africa?"

Casey smiled at her assistant. Maggie was only five foot three inches tall, but she was a firm one hundred and twenty pounds and an all-around athlete. Despite how small she was, Maggie had a seventeen-hand-high Thoroughbred that she raced in cross country events whenever OID issues didn't take her weekends away from her. Twelve miles and twenty or so challenging jumps at top speed didn't faze Casey's friend of many years. Maggie could break her neck at any time. More than once, Casey has seen her limp into the OID after a brutal weekend of competition. And now, at the thought of a new assignment, Maggie's hazel eyes inevitably were sparkling with life. She liked living on the edge.

As if that wasn't enough, Maggie was not only on the OID sharpshooters' team, she was leader of it, being more than a little handy with pistols and rifles. Which was why Casey had pulled her for this dangerous mission. Maggie thrived on competition and adventure. When in danger, she was coolheaded, and didn't allow her emotions to interfere with the steps a doctor on a mission for OID often had to take to save her life.

More than once, Casey and Maggie had had a good chuckle over Maggie's trauma-junkie attitude toward life. It served her well in their dangerous field missions to epidemic outbreaks around the world.

Tapping the file, Casey said, "I'd take this one myself, but as you know, I tested positive for pregnancy a week ago."

Glowing with genuine joy, Maggie sipped her tea. "I know. I'm thrilled for you and Reid. Is he still walking on air?"

Chuckling, Casey nodded. "Yes, and he's having hissy fits over me working with all these microbes, saying I've got to be extra careful now."

"Yeah, like in our business, we're sloppy." Maggie burst into laughter.

The room rang with their black humor that only those in the medical field could truly appreciate. Behind Casey through the slats of the venetian blinds, the sun sent blinding light into her pale pink office, drawing her eye momentarily to the peaceful landscape paintings on three of the four walls. "Oh, he's like any expectant father. A worrywart," she murmured softly.

"That's why you took yourself off the hot zone list." Maggie nodded and squeezed a tad of lemon juice into her tea. Delicately, she placed the lemon wedge on the side of the saucer. "Wise move. Have you had morning sickness yet?"

Rolling her eyes, Casey said, "I'm only six weeks along. And no, no morning sickness—yet."

Sitting back in the expensive leather wing chair, Maggie sighed. "You've got a wonderful guy. But I think you know it."

Casey's eyes grew soft. "Yes, I do. But he knows he's got a wonderful woman, too."

Grinning widely, Maggie said, "With that kind of respect for one another, a marriage is sure to last."

"Humph, unlike these two-to-five-year throwaway marriages I see littering the landscape everywhere I look."

"Well," Maggie said, "those people marry too young. They don't take the time to get to know the other person—or themselves." She grimaced. "I almost made that mistake back in college. I learned my lesson, believe me." She took another sip of tea. "I'd rather be single than make the same mistake twice."

Casey nodded. She knew Maggie had come close to getting married a couple of times in the seven years she'd worked at OID. Both relationships had fizzled. And both times the reason had been that the man wanted to control Maggie, who, being a very modern woman, wasn't about to kowtow to any man. It had to be an equal partnership or she wasn't going to even think about getting involved. Too many men still felt it was their right to tell a woman what to do. Fortunately, Maggie had the grit, the confidence in herself to know better. Still, Casey held out hope for the brilliant, courageous medical doctor. Someone would come along who truly appreciated everything she brought to the table.

"So, what's this dangerous mission?" Maggie inquired.

"This is *really* dangerous, Maggie. It's not like you gallop pell-mell down a steep hill to a four-foot jump, believe me."

Leaning forward, she said, "Tell me more."

Seeing the glint in Maggie's eyes, Casey knew she'd

chosen the right person for this mission. "Okay, here's the skinny on it." She flipped open another page of the top secret file. "I got a call from Perseus last Friday. They are a supersecret government entity that works deep behind the scenes with our national security agencies. Morgan Trayhern, the head of Perseus, asked me for a volunteer from OID because there's a bioterrorist group active in the United States right now. Some of Morgan's people just captured one of their top people, a professor who possessed genetically cloned anthrax bacteria. They've found out from this professor that the terrorists are trying to get more anthrax because Morgan's people captured their only supply."

Maggie nodded and finished off her cup of tea. "We have it here, in our lab. The only material known in the U.S.A."

"Right, which is why the spotlight has shifted to the OID." Casey frowned. "Black Dawn isn't a wasted word on you."

"No…it's not." Maggie set the cup and saucer on Casey's large desk. "Don't tell me they're involved in this?"

"Up to the gum stumps," Casey muttered unhappily. "They are the slickest, most professional and dangerous bioterrorist threat in the world today."

"Ouch." Maggie stood up and slid her hands into the pockets of her lab coat. "So, how do we figure into this odd equation?"

"In a very interesting way, believe me," Casey said admiring the tall, proud way Maggie carried herself. There wasn't an ounce of spare fat on her frame. Maggie was the picture of bravery and steadiness, in

Casey's opinion, and she would need all of that—and then some—if she took this mission.

"Morgan is setting a trap for them. Well, several traps, to flush the rest of Black Dawn's operatives in the United States into the open. I've approved his plan. What Morgan needs is a decoy from OID to tip their hand."

"Hmm, sounds fascinating," Maggie said, slowly walking to the windows and looking out through the blinds. Outside the OID building were long, sloping green lawns and huge live oaks. Maggie often looked out to the huge, centuries-old oak trees when faced with a new challenge at work. The sight of the trees comforted her, as they typified the South, where she was born.

"Well, let's see if you continue to think that," Casey said, glancing over her shoulder. She saw Maggie's oval face grow pensive. Even though she was a risk taker of the first order, when things got serious, Maggie could walk her talk. She wasn't irresponsible when the chips were down.

Fingering the file, Casey turned another page. "Here's the plan. Morgan wants to draw Black Dawn out. The only way we can do that is to set up a decoy situation. We know they've lost their genetically altered anthrax, because the FBI found it on Kauai, Hawaii. Black Dawn will want more. Morgan will rig a call that we know Black Dawn has bugged, alerting them to the fact that OID is sending a vial of it north, up to the army base in Virginia. That's where you come in, Maggie. You will be the official courier responsible for getting this vial up there."

"That's really interesting," Maggie said, turning and

studying Casey. "And then Black Dawn will descend upon me to get the vial, right?"

"That's what we're hoping." Opening her hands, she added, "Of course, you'll be well guarded. I don't want you to think we're throwing you out to the terrorists like a bone to a dog."

Chuckling, Maggie walked back and sat down in front of Casey. "I figured as much. So, you need my shooting ability because Black Dawn plays hardball, right?"

"Yes," Casey said unhappily. "I tried to persuade Morgan to send a policewoman, or a woman from the military, but he argued that Black Dawn might not go for the trap because they'd know a member of OID was not involved. We *always* send along one of our virologists with any shipments in transit from OID."

"SOP," Maggie said. "Standard operating procedure."

"Yes." Casey tapped her fingers against the file. "This is going to be *very* dangerous, Maggie. I don't like the plan. I understand it, but I don't have to like it. Putting you in danger is my biggest worry. Black Dawn plays rough. The FBI has promised full cooperation with Perseus on this mission. You'll be well guarded, but that's no guarantee. I told Morgan of my concern over this. They can't just put you in a car with the case containing the vial and tell you to drive from Atlanta to Virginia by yourself. He agreed. So he's sending his top mercenary with you."

"Ah, company," Maggie said with relief. She rolled her eyes. "At least I'll have company on this trip."

"You always have a sense of humor," Casey muttered worriedly.

With a short laugh, Maggie shrugged. "Hey, listen, I've been in some pretty dire circumstances when I ride that wild horse of mine. And I've felt some serious pressure while trying to win a pistol shooting award for OID. Either way, no matter what the stakes, it's pressure. I thrive on it. You know that."

"Well, how's the mission sound so far?"

"Okay," Maggie said. Her hazel eyes narrowed. "Frankly, I'd like to flush some of those bioterrorists out of the woodwork. If I can be of help, I'm volunteering. I'm sure the FBI is going to shadow us."

"They will, but they can't shadow you so close as to scare off Black Dawn. It's going to be dicey, Maggie. They could strike at your hotel room, or when you're driving on the interstate…anywhere. You've got to be on full alert a hundred percent of the time."

"As long as you give me a flak jacket to wear—not that I like those things, they are so uncomfortable— and a Beretta pistol to carry, I'm game."

Drilling her with a searching look, Casey asked, "You're sure about this? You do want to take the mission?"

"Why not? What else am I doing, anyway? I'd like to think my life counts for something, and if I can help bag the bad guys, that will make me feel like I'm doing something worthwhile for humanity."

"You've got a big heart, Maggie. I don't know about your logic, though," Casey said, scratching her brow nervously.

Reaching across the desk, Maggie shook her finger at Casey. "Listen, big mama hen in the sky, I'll be fine! I'm an OID sharpshooter, remember? Our team is number three in the U.S. We've got a shot—pardon the pun—at the next Olympics. I intend to keep leading the team. I'd love to try for gold."

Grudgingly, Casey nodded. "I think you're a twenty-year-old inside that thirty-six-year-old body."

Laughing heartily, Maggie got up. She was never one to stay still for long. Circling the office, hands stuffed into the pockets of her lab coat, she chuckled. "I'm a big kid at heart. And okay, so I take a lot of chances riding my horse in those events. I know what I'm doing, Casey. I'm *good* at what I do." She turned and looked at her supervisor, who was more like a big sister to her. "I'm right for this mission and you know it or you wouldn't have asked me to volunteer for it." With a shrug, she said, "Besides, I don't have a family. I'm single. No kids. I'm the perfect person for it."

Turning another page in the file, Casey nodded. "You're right," she conceded. "Morgan was hoping you'd take it. Black Dawn knows who our best virologists are. You're listed as number three here at OID. That's as good as it gets. If Black Dawn knows you're the courier, Morgan is sure they'll make a play to capture you and the anthrax vial. There's no question in his mind."

"For once," Maggie said, "my list of credentials will really impress someone."

With a sour grin, Casey joined in with her laughter. Maggie had graduated from Harvard University at the head of her class. She'd brought millions of dollars in grant money with her when she decided to make the OID her home. In the world of virology, Maggie had more than made her mark. She was known around the world for her abilities and for her pioneering work in the field.

"Well, now that you've decided to take the mission, this is your escort." Casey handed over an eight-by-ten color photo of a man. "He's one of the top mercs at Perseus. A specialist in undercover work."

Still smiling, Maggie reached out and took the photo. When she turned it around, she gasped. The photo tumbled out of her hand.

Casey saw Maggie blanch. "What is it?" She watched as the photo fluttered from Maggie's frozen fingers to the carpeted floor, saw Maggie's eyes widen with shock and then pain. Automatically, Casey got up and moved around the desk. She picked up the photo. As she stood to her full height and her gaze locked on Maggie's, she saw tears in her friend's eyes. But just for a moment. The tears quickly disappeared and Casey saw anger in those hazel eyes, instead.

"What's going on, Maggie?" She held the photo out to her.

"Oh, Lord," Maggie croaked. She took a step away from Casey and the proffered photo. "You aren't serious, are you?" She jabbed a finger at the photo. "Do you know who that is? Do you have *any* idea?"

Nonplussed, Casey looked helplessly at the photo. "Well, yes… Shep Hunter. He's Reid's older brother."

A strangled sound issued from Maggie's throat. She wheeled away and moved over to the windows. Jamming her hands into her pockets once more, she muttered defiantly, "Get that bastard's photo out of here, Casey. I want *nothing* to do with him! Not a damned thing!"

The obvious hurt, the trembling in her voice, shook Casey. She took a look at the photo once more and then studied Maggie's drawn profile. Maggie had compressed her full lips into a hard, thin line and suffering was written on every square inch of her features. "Maggie, I'm sorry. I didn't mean to shock you. I know you told me that you'd known Shep a long time ago..." Casey grimaced. "I guess there's a lot more to this than you'd told me before?"

Turning coldly, Maggie stared at her across the office, the tension thick. "You could say that." She saw the shock and concern on Casey's face. It was obvious she didn't realize what was going on. "I knew Shep a long time ago," she said in a whisper. "At Harvard. He was going for a degree in engineering. He was a member of ROTC, which led him eventually into the Air Force, to become a pilot." She waved her hand in irritation. "But that was *after* us. After a relationship that lasted my entire freshman year there at the university."

"Oww," Casey murmured, beginning to understand. "So, you two had an affair?"

Her shoulders had drawn up in sizzling tension, and Maggie forced herself to try and relax. Her heart was pounding wildly in her breast. She couldn't control her breathing yet. It hurt to think of Shep. It hurt to remember. Their relationship had ended so many years ago. How was it he could still affect her like this now? With a groan, Maggie turned to Casey. She deserved the full story.

"It was more than that. We fought like cats and dogs, Casey. He wanted to control me. I fought him every inch of the way. We were both independent types. Both bull-headed as hell. He always thought his way was best and my ideas were second best to his. We fought...brother, did we fight. Of course, making up was a lot of fun, too..." She sighed, some of the anger in her voice dissolving. "I've never been in such a wildly passionate relationship before or since. He was everything I'd ever dreamed of in a man, but he treated me like an idiot with no brains. He never thought I had an *equal* idea to his, much less a *better* one. Of course," she fumed, "more times than not, my ideas *were* better than his. But he had so much damned pride he'd never admit it. And on top of that, he was the strong, silent type."

Casey groaned. "Oh, one of those Neanderthal throwbacks, eh? Pride *is* a problem with the Hunter men, from where I stand."

"He was so arrogant," Maggie said, a hard-edged rasp in her voice. "So full of himself. He always thought he was smarter than everyone else. Maybe he was, over in the engineering department, where he pulled straight A's and was on the dean's list. But in my world, he couldn't shed that egotism and arrogance, Casey. He could never relax with me, let go and just be an ordinary human being who had good days and bad days, who *needed* someone else. He was such an icon! He reminded me of Mount Everest—always proud, unapproachable, needing no one and nothing."

Casey moved over to her side after placing the photo back into the file. "So you broke up because he couldn't really be intimate with you? Is that the bottom line?"

Miserably, Maggie nodded. "Yeah, Case, it was." She wiped her eyes. "Damn him. After all these years, I still feel so much for him! My heart is stupid. My head knows better now." She pursed her lips and glared out the venetian blinds. "If he could have said 'I need you' just *once*, Case, I'd have jumped up and down for joy. But he never did."

"Did you need him?"

"Sure I did," she said bitterly. "Oh, he liked that. He wanted to feel needed by the weaker sex. Well, weak nothing! I was his equal. And he knew it. And he would never acknowledge that. He treated me like a twit."

"Ouch," Casey murmured. "Neanderthals have that proclivity, don't they?"

Maggie raised an eyebrow. "You ought to know. You married one of them. But I can't really believe Reid is like Shep. You wouldn't have married him if he was."

Casey chuckled. "You're right. I'd have told him to get lost."

"Maybe Reid's different because he's the youngest of the four," Maggie said in a hurt voice. "He must be. I mean, I've met a lot of men in my life, and Shep Hunter takes the cake for the glacial Neanderthal type, believe me."

"I met him," Casey said slowly, "about six months ago. He was coming off a mission for Perseus, and he dropped by to see us here in Atlanta."

Maggie peered up at her. "And he hasn't changed one bit, has he?"

Hearing the hurt and pain in her voice, Casey shrugged. "He *tried* to be friendly when he met me. I could tell he was making an effort."

"Maybe life's changed him a little, after all," Maggie whispered. "With age comes maturity, right? Don't answer that."

Casey stood there, in a quandary. "Maggie, if you take this mission, you take Shep, too. It's a done deal. Everything is set up. Morgan feels that Shep will give you the best chance of surviving."

Bitterly, Maggie folded her arms against her chest. "Yes, that's one thing Shep Hunter is very good at—

survival. He won't let you into his heart, that's for sure. He'd just as soon walk away from a woman who loved him, really loved him. He's a coward, Casey. Such a coward…"

"Men who can't be intimate are scared," Casey agreed softly. "It takes a lot of courage to share our feelings with one another."

"Women do it at the drop of a hat. You can't tell me men can't. It's just that they *won't*. That's a big difference. They're made just like us. They have hearts that feel." Making a strangled sound once more, Maggie turned and said, "Don't get me started on this. I used to have this argument every day with Shep. I'm surprised our relationship lasted a full year before we agreed, mutually, to walk away from one another."

Casey could see the pain in Maggie's large hazel eyes. "You walked away because it was destroying you. I'm sure Shep walked away out of relief because he couldn't take the pressure of your demands for him to open up and be emotionally accessible to you."

"You should have been a shrink, Case. Yes, that's hitting the nail on the head."

"Well," Casey murmured, looking back at her desk, where the file lay, "what are we going to do? I won't be able to change your guard dog for you."

"I don't *want* him on this mission, Casey. Anybody but him. Please…"

Casey studied her friend's strained features, wishing it wasn't too late to grant her desperate request.

"Well, Shep, what do you think?" Morgan tried to gird himself for Hunter's reaction to the mission. More than anyone in his organization, Shep Hunter was a loner. Morgan knew why and understood Shep's demand for solo missions. Morgan studied the man standing before his desk in the war room of Perseus, which was hidden deep in the Rocky Mountains of Montana. Shep was a giant at six foot six inches tall, and the thirty-six-year-old ex–air force pilot was one of Morgan's best mercenaries. Shep was heavy-boned and muscular, and even dressed in jeans, cowboy boots and a denim long-sleeved shirt with the cuffs rolled up to his elbows, he looked dangerous. Maybe it was his square face and that jutting, rock-solid jaw that gave Shep such a hard look, Morgan thought. With his short black hair and thick, black eyebrows, which emphasized his frosty blue eyes, Shep Hunter reminded Morgan of a mighty eagle ready to swoop in an attack and gut the quarry he had his sights on.

"Humph," Shep said as he sat down in the chair across from Morgan's desk and continued to read the mission proposal rapidly. "OID, huh?"

"Read on…there's more to this," Morgan warned him briskly. He was prepared to see Shep refuse the mission once he read page two, which identified the OID virologist who would be on the mission with him. Every time Morgan tried to pair Shep up with a partner, he'd refused. They'd had hellacious shouting matches over the subject from time to time, in this very room. And Morgan knew Shep would walk out and quit rather than be assigned a partner. No, ever since Sarah had died on that fateful mission with him, Shep had closed up tighter than an proverbial clam. He absolutely refused to be partnered up again.

And yet, as he tried to appear at ease as Shep devoured the mission brief, Morgan gathered his argument points as to why, if Shep wanted this mission, the OID decoy must be part of it. He just hoped Shep would take it. No one was better suited for this task than Shep, Morgan knew.

Glancing at the photos of his family on one side of his desk, Morgan felt some of his tension easing. The fraternal twins in Laura's lap were smiling. How simple and beautiful life could be. He loved his wife and four children more than anything in the world. Looking up at Shep once more, Morgan realized he saw a lot of his former self in him. Morgan had once been as hard and icy as this merc sitting in front of him. It would take a woman who had metal, who had courage to probe the depths of Shep's fear of intimacy, to help open him up. Morgan acknowledged even today that Laura had had more courage than he'd ever had back then. She'd taken him on—and won. But Morgan was the real winner as far as he was concerned.

When Shep rapidly flipped the page, Morgan steeled himself.

"I'll be damned."

Morgan leaned forward in the chair and put his elbows on his desk. He saw surprise in Shep's normally hard, unreadable features. "What?" he asked tentatively.

"I'll be damned. I don't believe this," he said in a deep tone. He held the file pointing to the photo. "This is the woman I'm supposed to guard? Dr. Maggie Harper? Are you sure?"

Puzzled by Shep's unexpected reaction, Morgan said, "Yes. Why? Is there a problem?"

With a shake of his head, Shep uncoiled to his full height. Tossing the folder on Morgan's desk, he turned and walked around the large, silent room with his hands on his hips. "I'll be go-to-hell, Morgan. Life really is full of surprises and twists."

Morgan scooped up the file and looked at the photo of the doctor. He didn't understand Shep's reaction. He'd never seen Shep act this way about a mission. And Morgan wasn't sure if Hunter's response was a good or bad one. Usually, Shep would throw the file at him and tell him to go to hell if there was a partner involved. This time, the man's face was softening. Morgan could see a glimmer of something warm and tentative in his icy blue eyes. And his mouth, usually a thin line, had the corners turned up in a slight smile.

Stymied, Morgan held up the file. "Clue me in, will you, Hunter?"

Turning, Shep gave his boss a measured look. Though his fingers were draped casually across his narrow hips, tension thrummed through him. He felt his heart beating hard in his chest. And he felt happiness threading through him. The feeling was completely unexpected, but beautiful. It made him breathe in deeply—as if he were coming alive after a long, long sleep. How long had it been since he'd felt *any-thing*? Especially happiness? Oh, he'd felt happy for his younger brother Reid when he finally met Casey Morrow. And he was overjoyed that Ty and Dev had finally found women they wanted to spend their lives with, too. Yes, everyone in the family was married now—except him. And each time he'd met the woman one of his younger brothers had chosen to marry, he'd felt sad, too. Sad because he knew no one would want him. He was one mean son of a bitch who didn't give an inch in a relationship. But after what had happened to him, how could he?

That was life, Shep decided. Life had been cruel to him. And torturous. After Sarah… He quickly snapped his mind shut, like a bear trap. Pain suddenly intermingled with the quiet joy pumping through him with each powerful beat of his heart.

"That *is* Maggie Harper?" he demanded. "She is a graduate of Harvard Medical School, right?"

Floundering because Shep never reacted this way to a potential partner, Morgan quickly flipped to the back page of the mission folder and glanced at her bio. "Yes, Harvard." Looking up, he narrowed his eyes. "Just what is going on here, Shep? Tell me what I don't know. Usually you blow up when there's a partner even mentioned. This time you're standing over there like a raccoon grinning over a crawdad you just caught."

Shep smiled a little more widely. "Maggie Harper was my first real relationship. We met in our freshman year at Harvard. What a hellion she was." He shook his head in fond remembrance. "She had guts to take me on."

Tentatively, Morgan murmured, "I see…"

Allowing his hands to slip from his hips, Shep moved back toward the desk where Morgan still stood with a confused look on his face. "I'll take the mission, Morgan."

Stunned, Morgan held the younger man's stare. Shep wasn't one to smile often. He wasn't exactly smiling now, but the corners of his broad, generous mouth were pulled slightly upward. Morgan saw something else in Hunter's eyes that he'd never seen before: happiness. And hope. He stared back at the color photo of Maggie Harper.

"Does she… I mean, have you had contact with Dr. Harper—"

Chuckling, Shep said, "Nope, haven't seen her in—let's see—almost twenty years. I think I'm going to find this interesting, Morgan. It says she's on a sharpshooting team. Third best in the U.S. She hasn't changed at all. She was riding eventing horses before she went to Harvard. Looks like she's still doing the same thing—taking risks."

"Well," Morgan began, completely shocked by Shep's behavior and his agreement to take the mission, "it's yours, then."

Rubbing his hands together, Shep said, "And I can hardly wait to meet Maggie again. This is going to be some homecoming…"

Chapter 2

Maggie rubbed her long fingers together. They were ice cold. They got that way when she was nervous. She stood in her office at OID, waiting. According to Casey, Shep Hunter would arrive at 0900, and after Casey talked to him, Maggie would be buzzed on her desk monitor to come to Casey's office for a wrap-up on the final details of the mission.

Why, oh why, had she agreed to take the mission? In her angst, Maggie paced the length of her rectangular office, jamming her cold hands into the pockets of her white lab coat. Outside, the day was beautiful. The bright sun and dark green grass and lush trees made her yearn to be astride her Thoroughbred and galloping through the countryside. The sky was so blue it almost made her squint as she looked out the venetian blinds. Her heart and mind swung back to Shep. What a fiery relationship they'd had, each of them bullheaded, each so very sure their own way was the right way.

Maggie ran her fingers through her hair, which she wore loose today because she wasn't going to be working in the lab. No, today was going to be spent arranging details for a very dangerous mission. Maggie told herself she had agreed to the mission because she understood the impact of anthrax bacteria being dropped by bioterrorists on some unsuspecting city. She couldn't stand to think she would refuse a mission because the man working with her was an old boyfriend. Actually, Shep had been much, much more than that. Maggie had fallen helplessly in love with him all those years ago. He'd been a star football player while keeping his straight A average at Harvard. He was keenly intelligent, competitive, and he'd loved her with a passion that Maggie had never experienced since.

Sighing, she ran her chilled fingers through her shoulder-length hair once more. "What have you done, Maggie?" she whispered through tight lips as she ruthlessly perused her desk, which looked like a tornado had hit it. Restlessly, she picked up some papers and tried to concentrate on them.

The phone on her desk buzzed. She jumped. The paper fluttered out of her fingers and wafted to the tile floor.

"Oh!" Maggie whispered, scooping up the letters. She was jumpier than a kangaroo. Her heart was throbbing at the base of her throat. She knew it was Casey buzzing her. It was time. Reluctantly reaching for the phone, Maggie wished she was anywhere but here right now. She was actually afraid to meet Shep once again. Gulping, she picked up the phone.

"Maggie?" Casey asked.

"Yes?"

"It's time. Come on down so I can give you two the final briefing on this mission."

Shutting her eyes, Maggie whispered, "Okay... I'll be right there..."

Placing the phone gently back into the cradle, Maggie tried to steady her breathing. It had been so long since she'd seen Shep. Had he changed? Had life softened him at all? Was he more inclined to listen to other people now? Or was he still arrogant and self-righteous? A chill swept through her. She felt fear—raw, unbridled fear. Chastising herself mentally, Maggie automatically touched her hair. Taking a look in the ornate, gold-framed mirror that hung in her office, she saw that her eyes looked huge. Like a rabbit about to face a starving wolf.

Her fingers were so cold they almost felt numb. She was unhappy with her reaction. She was acting like the freshman she'd been when she first met Shep. Back then, Shep always seemed to have the world by the tail. It was as if he knew what would happen next, planned for it and then executed it so easily that Maggie felt like an idiot in comparison. Hunter was always calm, cool and collected. Right now, as she swung out her door and into the highly polished hall that lead to Casey's corner office, she felt disheveled, unprepared and scared.

Giving herself a stern talking to as she slowly walked down the hallway, she greeted her lab cohorts who passed, feeling comforted by the sight of familiar faces. The people at OID had some of the best minds in the U.S. They were at the vanguard of the attempt to keep people safe from killer bacteria and viruses.

Shep was a virus, Maggie decided with mirth. She was infected by him and hadn't built an immunity to him yet. That was why she felt vulnerable right now. But wouldn't eighteen years be an immunity in itself? Time was supposed to heal everything, wasn't it?

As Maggie reached for the brass doorknob that led to Casey's office, her heart beat hard in her breast and she quickly ran a hand over the maroon slacks she wore beneath her lab coat. Mouth dry, she closed her fingers around the doorknob. Inside that office was Hunter. She felt hunted, all right. Taking a deep breath, Maggie jerked open the door and forced herself to move quickly into the office.

Shep contained his surprise. The woman who walked resolutely through the door into Casey Morrow-Hunter's office was even more beautiful, more poised and more confident than he could recall. Despite her small stature, Maggie carried herself proudly, that small chin of hers leading. The years had been kind to her, Shep realized with pleasure. He rose from his chair at the corner of Casey's desk as Maggie closed the door quietly behind her.

Their eyes met for the first time. Shep felt his heart thud hard, like someone had struck him full force in his chest with a sixteen-pound sledgehammer. He struggled for breath as he studied Maggie's oval face, her high, smooth cheekbones. The freckles across her nose and cheeks—those delicious small copper spots—were still there. He saw her nostrils flare. That was something she'd done when he knew her years earlier—something she'd done when she was afraid. Her eyes widened incredibly. He saw every nuance of every emotion she was feeling in her gaze. The fear was there, the uncertainty, the desire…yes, desire. He knew he hadn't wrongly read what she was feeling. That made him feel good. Damn good.

"How are you?" he said, his voice deep and unruffled. Stepping forward, Shep offered his large hand to her. He saw Maggie recoil. It wasn't so much her posture or any outward shrinking away from him; rather, it was in her jewel-like, hazel eyes.

Forcing herself to lift her hand, Maggie croaked, "Fine…just fine, Shep…" As her fingertips slid into his proffered hand, she was once again reminded how large he was. She felt like a midget in comparison. To her right, she saw Casey stand, a smile affixed to her face but trepidation in her eyes. Maggie knew she had to make this work for Casey's sake and for the OID.

"Your hand is cold," Shep murmured, stepping closer and placing his other over the one he'd held captive. So much was flooding back to him about Maggie. Oh, he'd never forgotten that whenever she was nervous and uptight, her hands would turn freezing cold. As he covered her hand with his now, he also remembered how small and delicate and feminine her hands were compared to his huge, hairy paws. Shep strangled the desire to pull Maggie into his arms and hold her. What would she feel like? As warm and fragrant as he recalled? A hint of honeysuckle wafted into his nostrils and he drew the scent deep into his chest. He knew it was Maggie's skin and the delicate perfume she wore. He saw her face turn a dull red as she tried to pull her hand from his.

Panicking, Maggie jerked her hand free from Shep's. She stood there, looking up at him and thinking that life had made him even more ruggedly handsome than before. Those ice-blue eyes of his, so wide and filled with intelligence, now burned with a tender regard for her. His mouth curved in a slight smile of welcome. Hunter rarely smiled. She felt special. She felt enveloped by his intense interest in her as a woman. There was no doubt Shep was all-male. Very male and very dangerous to her wildly thudding heart. Rubbing her hands together, Maggie managed to murmur, "You haven't changed at all, Shep."

The corners of his mouth turned upward even more as he watched Maggie nervously rub her cold fingers together. "Eighteen years has done nothing but make you more beautiful, Maggie." And that was the truth. He remembered the soft, young Maggie of before. This was a woman standing before him, mature and confident. He liked that. He saw her arched red brows dip momentarily in reaction to his compliment.

"Have a seat, you two," Casey invited. She pointed to a second chair at the opposite corner of her desk, gesturing for Maggie to sit there.

Relieved, Maggie sat before she fell down. Just the way Shep perused her—with that raw, naked look that was so male—made her knees go weak. She gripped the arms of the chair, relief sheeting through her. Once more she felt Shep's amiable inspection of her, but she refused to look at him. He was so damned intimidating when he wanted to be! Nervously smoothing her lab coat across her thigh as she crossed her legs, Maggie devoted all her attention to Casey. Shep's sincere words echoed through her head. He thought she looked beautiful. Maggie wasn't any cover model, that was for sure. She felt attractive, but not beautiful in the way Shep had suggested. Yet she sensed he was being sincere. That explained why her heart was galloping away within her breast.

People who knew Shep Hunter were often repelled by his glacier look, but Maggie knew the real Shep. Having gone with him for a year, she knew his expression was a façade to purposely intimidate others. He was afraid of being hurt, so he threw up this nearly impregnable don't-even-approach-me kind of demeanor. It worked on everyone except her. She had gotten inside Shep's considerable armor once. She knew the sensitive man who hid behind it, but his ego made him unapproachable. As she sat rigidly in the chair, her hands clasped, she wondered if Shep had kept his sensitivity. Or had life robbed him of that, too?

Maggie painfully remembered that when they broke up, Shep had left Harvard. He'd managed to get an appointment to the Air Force Academy, instead. She knew why: he couldn't stand being at the same school with her. The pain of their breakup had been too much for him to deal with. Stealing a look out of the corner of her eye, Maggie marveled at how wonderful Shep looked. He was dressed in a pair of dark blue chinos, a white, short-sleeved shirt and a pair of jogging shoes—very California-looking compared to the more businesslike dress of the East Coast inhabitants at OID. He was deeply bronzed and obviously spent a lot of time out in the sun. His hair was still ebony with blue highlights, the short length and neat cut shouting of his military background. But it was the thick, black hair on his lower arms and the tufts of hair peeking out the top of his shirt that shouted of his masculinity.

Shep was still in superb athletic condition, Maggie realized. He had always been strong and sturdy. She recalled his football days, and decided he looked just as firm and fit now. She wouldn't be surprised if he regularly worked out with heavy weights at a gym. Her mind continued to wander as Casey riffled through a number of papers on her desk. Was Shep still in the Air Force? Maggie had heard he'd become a pilot of some of the hottest fighter jets available. Was he married? She didn't see a gold band on his left hand, but that didn't mean anything. He could be living with someone. A twinge of jealousy shot through her. Surprised at her emotional reaction, Maggie felt very unhappy with herself. Why couldn't eighteen years erase what Shep had meant to her?

"Okay, here we go," Casey murmured, giving them both an apologetic look. Lifting out the mission brief, she said, "Morgan e-mailed this to me last night over a secure line. He wants you two to pretend that you're a married couple from Atlanta going on a minivacation to Savannah. You will stay there, at a bed and breakfast near the heart of the city, and then, the next morning, continue your automobile journey to Hilton Head Island in South Carolina. You will stay at a time-share overnight, and the next morning continue on to Charleston. From there, you will go due north to Fairfax, Virginia, and the USAMRIID facility. The reason he's outlined his route is that it will make the best use of FBI help and protection. The roads you'll be traveling are all interstate and therefore, easier to drive and easier for them to get to you if something goes down."

Maggie opened her mouth and then shut it, realizing Casey wasn't done as she continued to read from the document.

"Again, you are to pose as husband and wife. Morgan will leak out the entire scenario to Black Dawn one hour after you leave here. Black Dawn will know you are couriers in disguise. These routes will give them ample opportunity to strike at you. Morgan has given them your itinerary, route and time of arrival at these places. There will be satellite fly-bys to keep tabs on your vehicle. Each time the satellite orbits the earth, it will make a check on your location. You'll drive an unassuming dark blue sedan. Nothing fancy. He wants you to blend in and look like tourists on a vacation."

Casey flipped the page. "Maggie, you will carry the aluminum suitcase, which is small and portable. It will contain the fake anthrax. The vial will be marked to make Black Dawn think it is the real thing, but it's not. But they won't know that they have nothing until they test it out for three days in a petrie dish."

"Let Black Dawn get close to that suitcase." Shep growled. He glanced over at Maggie. Did she know how very dangerous this mission really was? The thought of bullets ripping into her flesh made his stomach contract with agony.

Maggie nodded. "I'll hand it over when the moment arrives, don't worry," she muttered. Just meeting Shep's gaze sent her heart skittering. Why did he have to be so good-looking in his rough kind of way? He was no male cover model, that was for sure. The crow's feet at the corners of his eyes attested to years spent living under harsh conditions. The slash marks at the sides of his mouth were deep with time—and the result of too little smiling. His prominent nose had obviously been broken several times. Maybe it was the squareness of his face and that granite chin that made him look like the untamed Rocky Mountains where he'd grown up.

She knew he'd probably shaved in preparation for the meeting, but even now the shadow of returning growth gave him a decidedly dangerous countenance.

Casey nodded and flipped the page. "You will both wear flak jackets beneath your civilian clothing. You'll get Beretta 9 mm pistols to carry on your person. The car will have bulletproof windows."

"But not bulletproof metal?"

"No," Casey said. "They're doing what they can to protect you, but this is no armored car."

Shep nodded. "I'll do the driving."

"No, I will." Maggie straightened up, her anger surfacing. "I'm the courier. You're the guard dog. Remember?"

Casey held up her hands. "I think there will be plenty of driving for both of you. This is going to take all your attention, your concentration. Each of you can drive for a couple of hours and then switch off. It will keep you fresh and alert."

Maggie bristled. How like Shep to just walk in and take over. He was beginning to treat her like that little freshman he knew so long ago. Well, she'd grown up. She was damned if he was going to start making decisions without consulting her first! Glaring across the space at him, she saw him scowl. Too bad. He was going to find out that she wasn't the weak little girl he'd met back at Harvard.

"Please understand," Casey said, looking at Maggie, "that just because the FBI is working with us doesn't mean they can protect you twenty-four hours a day. They are human. And so are you. There will be surveillance, but technically, you two are on your own. The cell phone has an emergency number you can dial if they attack. It may take fifteen to thirty minutes to get to you if something happens, depending upon your position when an attack takes place. The FBI can't tail you or Black Dawn will pick up on the fact. They will be stationed at certain points along the interstate, on alert, if you do need help. That's the best we can do."

Maggie squirmed. "I understand that, Casey. But why have us married? Why can't we have separate rooms?"

"Because," she said patiently, "Morgan wants Black Dawn to think we're stupid enough to use such a ruse. We want them to think we're inept."

The news that she would be staying in the same room with Shep was a shock to Maggie. She'd never fathomed such a thing happening. It was simply too much for her to imagine. "But," she protested, opening her hands in appeal, "I don't see the wisdom of it."

"There's safety in numbers," Shep said as he met and held her widening hazel gaze. His conscience pricked at him. It was obvious Maggie wanted nothing to do with him. Her file said she was single, but it didn't give him a wealth of information about her private life. Maybe she was living with a man? That thought didn't set well with him. Silently chiding himself, he realized he was still just as protective about her now as he had been then!

"Safe?" Maggie's voice was laced with sarcasm. "There's nothing 'safe' about you, Hunter."

His mouth worked and a corner lifted. "That was a long time ago, Maggie. I think I can control myself for your benefit."

Flushing deeply, Maggie refused to look at him or Casey. She was making a fool out of herself and was old enough to know better. Knitting her fingers together, she said in a raspy tone, "I *still* don't think it's a good idea to stay together in the same room. If we had separate rooms next to one another, we'd at least have a chance if Black Dawn tries to blow us away. It would make it harder for them to get to the two of us."

Casey nodded. "That's the point. We want to make it *easy* for Black Dawn to get to you."

Chagrined, Maggie saw the simplicity of Morgan's plan. "I see…"

Casey stood. "Here is your wedding band set."

Stunned, Maggie took the box. Casey went over and gave Shep one. Opening hers, Maggie saw it contained a gold band and a solitaire engagement ring.

"Don't worry," Casey said with a laugh as she stood between them, "it's all fake. Plate gold and zircons, Maggie."

"At least we don't have to stand in front of a preacher," she groused as she studied the bands.

Shep rose easily. "Here, let me put them on you, Maggie."

Casey smiled down at Maggie. "Great idea."

Stunned, Maggie watched Shep approach. "No thanks, I can do this myself." She quickly shoved the rings on the proper finger. There was no way she wanted Shep to touch her. Already her flesh was begging for his touch. Would it be the same as she recalled? Better? Worse? Why did he have to move with such a boneless grace? For all his size, he reminded her of a lithe African leopard. She saw the disappointment in his eyes as she refused his help. Well, he'd better get used to it. She had a mind of her own and he might as well learn that now.

Shep stood watching Maggie. Her cheeks were

stained a bright red as she jammed the rings on her hand. It occurred to him that he'd never met another woman even remotely like her. He felt an old ache from a wound that still scored his heart from their breakup. Only flying his jet, when he was in the Air Force, would assuage some of the loss he'd felt when they'd parted. But it had been a necessary parting. He and Maggie never saw eye to eye on anything.

Looking down at her, he met her challenging gaze. "Casey suggested we have lunch, go over the details and then start the mission tomorrow morning. How about it?" He saw her thin brows draw downward in protest and knew nothing had changed between them. She was nervously fingering the fake wedding ring set on her left hand, as if it were a germ infecting her. As if giving in to him on any point would kill her.

"Oh…all right. There's a cafeteria in the basement. We can go there." She looked at her watch. It was only nine-thirty. "Besides, it will be practically deserted now."

"I had a nicer place in mind," Shep said.

Rising smartly, Maggie glanced at Casey and then drilled him with a look. "The cafeteria is fine. This isn't pleasure, Shep. It's business. I want it kept that way."

The warning growl in her voice made his gut clench. Did she hate him that much? Distaste was clearly written in her expression. But Shep thought he saw fear edging her gaze as she moved robotically toward the door. She kept rubbing her left hand against her lab smock. Fear of him? Why? He had a helluva lot of questions and no answers.

Following Maggie out into the hall, he told Casey they'd be back later. In his hand, he carried a black leather briefcase. As Maggie walked briskly ahead of him, a number of people said hello to her. He watched her face thaw as she cheerfully engaged them in conversation. Damn. This was going to be hell, he told himself as he entered the elevator with her.

Maggie punched the basement button and then made sure she stood opposite Shep. He looked very unhappy. Clasping her hands, Maggie internally rebelled against the wedding ring set. She kept running the bands around and around on her finger. The elevator felt claustrophobic to her. Shep Hunter filled it with his size, and with the incredible quiet charisma that radiated from him like a thousand glowing suns.

As soon as the doors whooshed open, Maggie strode confidently out of the elevator. Choosing a table and chairs near the window, on one side of the cafeteria, she sat down. Shep sauntered over and placed the briefcase on one of the empty chairs.

"Can I get you some coffee?" he asked. "If I remember right, you like it sweet and blond."

Maggie sat very still. She looked up at him. She saw the struggle in Shep's normally inexpressive face. His voice was low and intimate. Her flesh prickled. Oh, how tender a lover he could be! All that hard invincibility melted away to leave a man with breath-stealing sensitivity in its wake. Maggie found herself aching to be with that man once again. Stymied, and afraid of her own heart, she muttered with defiance, "Yes, coffee would be fine, thank you."

He smiled a little at her petulance. "And if I'm reading you correctly, a shot of brandy in it to quell your nerves?"

Shutting her eyes, Maggie felt her heart blossoming beneath his gentle cajoling. No, Shep was still the old Shep she knew. Oh, how was she going to survive this? She was more afraid of him than the damned assignment!

Opening her eyes, she fearlessly met the warmth that now filled his blue gaze. "Right now, a shot of whiskey would be my choice."

Nodding, he said, "I think I understand why. I'll be back in a minute."

Just watching him saunter over to the serving area, Maggie sighed. She was being nasty to him when he didn't deserve it. Yet he seemed to be taking her in stride and not letting her attitude get to him personally.

When Shep arrived back at their table, he held a tray filled with food. He set a cup of coffee in front of Maggie, and then a saucer that contained a huge pecan sticky bun. He placed a second plate, piled high with fluffy scrambled eggs, six slices of bacon, hash browns and grits, on his side of the table.

"I'm not hungry," Maggie said, pushing the plate with the sticky bun toward him as he sat down.

"I remember it was your favorite pastry," he told her, unruffled, as he settled into the chair. The look on her face was one of puzzlement and heartbreaking sadness. With a one-shouldered shrug, he murmured, "But look, if you aren't hungry, I'll eat it."

Not hungry? Maggie was starved for his touch. Even the briefest of ones. But Shep could never know that. "Thanks...you can have it."

Scooping up a forkful of the eggs, he gazed across at Maggie as she wrapped her fingers around her coffee mug. "You still get cold fingers when you're upset."

Nodding, she took a sip of the coffee. "I switched

to drinking tea a long time ago, Hunter. Being around you makes me want to have coffee again."

His mouth curved in a slight smile. "So, is this good or bad, Dr. Harper?" he deliberately teased her. For a moment, Shep saw her shoulders, which were gathered with tension, begin to relax slightly.

"Being around you is like a bad cold returning."

"Thank you."

"Only *you* would take that as a compliment, Hunter!"

Chuckling, he spread some strawberry jam on his toast. "You haven't changed at all, Maggie. I was wondering if you had, but I can see you haven't."

"Well," she said under her breath, leaning forward so only he could hear her, "you haven't, either."

Gazing at her was like looking at a delicious dessert to him. "So, where does that leave us?"

"At odds with one another. As usual."

"Eighteen years is a long time, Maggie."

"And it's like a blink of an eye, because you were the same then as you are now."

"Thank you—I think."

"Don't start preening, Hunter, because it wasn't a compliment and you know it."

"How's your coffee? Did I get the right amount of cream and sugar in it?"

Flushing, she refused to meet his gaze. Hands gripping her cup, she looked down at it. "Like I said, nothing has changed."

"We're older, if that helps?"

"Just more stuck in our same old patterns and personalities as far as I'm concerned," Maggie retorted. She saw his gaze thaw considerably. When she realized he really wasn't taking anything she said personally, she was stunned. Back then, he had. They'd fought all the time. Fought and made up. And the making up had been incredibly delicious.

"Maybe," he said. "Life has thrown me a couple of curves. I hope I've learned from them."

She sipped her coffee, feeling rebellious. Hunter always brought out her feistiness. Only he could. She wasn't explosive like this with any other man she'd ever had a relationship with. Only around him. "Whatever the reasons, Shep, you bring out the worst in me. All we did then was fight, and from the looks of it, it's starting up all over again." Her nostrils flared. She hated it when her voice quivered with emotion as it did now.

Shep ate slowly, thinking about how he was going to handle Maggie on this mission. There was much more at stake here than she realized. He had to be the boss on this venture whether she liked it or not. At this moment, he wasn't ready to tell her that. They had a day to get ready. One way or another, Maggie was going to have to bend to his way of doing things. Or else...

Chapter 3

"I'll drive," Shep said, heading around the car they would be using. The vehicle was parked in the underground garage of the OID building. The July morning was warm and humid, hinting of the high temperatures and humidity to come in the sultry afternoon hours.

"Hold your horses, Hunter."

He turned, surprised at the warning in Maggie's voice. As she stood near the passenger side of the car, Shep had a tough time keeping his gaze from devouring her, because to him, she looked beautiful in the comfortable khaki slacks and dark blue blouse she wore. The sleeves of the blouse were decorated with a touch of lace, giving her a very feminine look. Beneath the silk of the blouse he knew she wore her flak jacket, mandatory on this mission. He was wearing his beneath his white shirt and sport coat. Already the thing was beginning to chafe him, but he knew the wisdom of wearing it.

"What?" She was looking at him with her eyes narrowed. Shep knew that look. Halting, his hands on the top of the car near the driver's door, he said, "What's the problem?"

"How can you ask?" Maggie demanded. She tried mightily to ignore how handsome he looked this morning. His black hair was damp and gleaming from his recent shower. His jaw was scraped free of the shadow of beard that would inevitably appear in the afternoon hours. His eyes were bloodshot, and she wondered if he'd gotten much sleep last night. She sure hadn't; too much of their tortured and passionate past had kept resurrecting itself before her closed eyes while she lay in bed. "Shep, this is *not* a replay of eighteen years ago. You think you know everything. You think that, as usual, I'm a hothouse violet incapable of being your equal."

"Wait a minute—"

"No," Maggie said coolly, locking her gaze on his frosty one, "it's different this time, Hunter. And *you* are going to have to be a lot more flexible than you were two decades ago. Or else!" She held up the keys to the car and smiled a little. "I'm driving."

"I suppose you've taken evasive driver's training?"

"Yes."

"And terrorist evasive training, as well?"

"I can see the surprise in your eyes right now, Hunter." She gave him a smile that dripped with honey. "Yes. And just in case you ask me when, I'm certified for the next year. I just passed the two courses, for the fifth year in a row."

One corner of his mouth flexed upward. "Maybe you *have* changed," he admitted sourly. "Okay, you drive for two hours, and then we'll trade off in shifts. How's that sound to you?" He decided to concede to her on this point, knowing there would be tougher battles ahead— things he couldn't allow Maggie to do herself, for fear she'd get killed. Like Sarah.

Maggie was pleased that he was thinking in partnership terms right now. "That sounds fair and equitable, Mr. Hunter. Thank you for your consideration." She saw his blue eyes glimmer with unease. And the slight downward movement of his hard mouth made her openly grin in triumph. "Nothing has changed at all with you, Hunter, through all these years. You are the same guy I knew way back when."

"Some things don't change," he agreed grumpily. Shep moved around the rear of the car. As Maggie passed him, their hands brushed. How he ached to really touch her, to be able to slide his fingers knowingly up that smooth, warm flesh. He recalled how wonderful she had felt in his arms as they made torrid love to one another.

Once inside the car Shep forced his mind back to business, taking note of the special equipment in the vehicle. An onboard computer showed the map of the area where they would be driving, including all the rural routes and all the country roads. Georgia was full of country roads, and if they got into trouble, they would have to know which one to take to try and escape their pursuers. There were two different radios, one connected to the state police and the other a direct line to the FBI van, a mobile headquarters that would shadow their journey. After testing each instrument to make sure it was operational, he glanced over at Maggie as she strapped in with a special seat harness and adjusted the mirrors.

"I hate flak jackets," she griped as she scratched beneath her right arm.

Shep nodded and shut the door. "They're necessary." He strapped himself in, turned on the computer and opened a laptop, which was plugged into the car lighter. The laptop was mounted where the glove box should have been and sat on a small movable table in front of him, fitting comfortably above his thighs. "Part of the game we're entering," he warned her, in case she had any thought of ditching it because it was uncomfortable.

Glancing at Maggie once more, he felt his heart beat hard, underscoring how much he still…still cared about her. Nightmarish visions of Sarah's death suddenly filled his mind. Blinking hard, he removed the specter. No, he wouldn't let Maggie meet Sarah's tragic end. It had been his fault that his one and only partner at Perseus had been killed in the line of duty. His fault. Only his. Shep would be damned if Maggie got caught in the line of fire because of him. No, he had to control this mission from the get-go—whether Maggie liked it or not. Her life was at stake. He'd lost one woman he'd loved to a bullet. He wasn't about to lose Maggie, too.

"Everything up and running?" Maggie asked as she switched on the car's engine. The sedan purred to life.

"Roger that," he said, doing a double-check on their computer map. "I'll give you the directions to get on—"

"Never mind," Maggie said briskly, "I memorized the route to Savannah last night." She proceeded to verbally give him the details of where they were supposed to drive. Their route had been set up by the vigilant FBI, and there would be cars with agents placed along certain milepost markers, where other roads intersected the freeway, so that the FBI could give them help sooner rather than later, if they called for it. The unmarked white van would always be on the freeway, ten miles behind them, to relay such information to the awaiting agents.

She saw his face darken as she reeled off the routes in perfect order. What was the matter with Shep? He should be pleased with her preparation for this mission. Instead, he was looking at her oddly. And he seemed more controlling than she last recalled. Not that Shep had *ever* been Mr. Sharing. Nope, not him. Smiling a little, she put the car in reverse and backed out of the space.

"I take that look to mean I got it right. So, let's go, Colorado Cowboy."

Taken aback by her confidence and aplomb, Shep snapped to the business at hand, though hearing her old nickname for him warmed him unexpectedly. His heart swelled with feelings that he brutally squashed. If anything would put them in danger, it would be a lapse of concentration on his part. It was too easy to look at Maggie and drink her in like a tall, cool liquid. She could always quench his fire, satisfy his needs—every last one of them. In some ways, they'd been made for one another. They fit together in a special way that Shep had never experienced since Maggie. He had loved Sarah but she'd been different in many ways. Sarah didn't have those qualities of self-confidence and inner strength that glowed in Maggie like the sun itself.

As they turned onto the road that led to the OID, a redbrick building on a knoll surrounded with manicured green lawns, Shep automatically began to sweep his eyes from right to left. To him, surveillance was a mental game of sorts: look for the cars, memorize their color, their style and how many occupants in each. If they were being tailed by Black Dawn, this was the only way to sort it out. The Mac laptop was hooked directly into police computers, so they could run license plates. A set of binoculars rested between the two front seats, so he could read the numbers from a safe distance.

"I felt you go into alert mode," Maggie said. She pulled the visor down and put on a pair of gold-framed sunglasses. They brought out the highlights in her hair, which she'd gathered in a chignon at the nape of her neck. Already too warm due to the high humidity that was common in the South for this time of year, she adjusted the air-conditioning.

"Yes, you did." Shep studied her profile. She expertly wove the sedan into morning rush hour traffic. Maggie had always been a good driver, he recalled from his days with her at Harvard. More memories poured back about her and her family. Her father bred race horses for the major tracks in the United States. He was a speed freak and Maggie had certainly inherited those genes. "Your father still racing horses?"

Chortling, Maggie nodded and said, "Yes, Dad is still trying to breed that Triple Crown winner. And Mom continues to go to her bridge parties every week."

Nodding and continuing to look around Shep asked, "What about racing sprint cars? Does he still do that? He's pretty old now, I'd think."

Pleased that he remembered so much about her family, Maggie briefly met his thawing blue gaze. When Shep let his guard down—which wasn't often—he was open and approachable. The hard line of his mouth had softened, too. This was the old Shep she knew from Harvard. How she desperately wanted him back! Not the hard, controlling warrior who thought he was in charge of this mission.

"Dad stopped racing sprint cars about ten years ago. Mother pressured him into realizing that as he got older, he needed to start taking better care of himself. She wanted to enter old age with him intact, not in tatters." Maggie chortled at the thought of her mother. "My prim, steel-magnolia Southern mother had a real plan of attack to get my dad away from the sprint car races. I watched her apply that so-subtle pressure on him over a year's time. It was like watching an army general plan strategy and tactics—and win." She smiled fully as she saw Shep's mouth turn up in as wide a smile as he ever gave.

"Southern women have their ways," Shep agreed. He knew Maggie's father was a Northerner, her mother a Southerner from Atlanta. "Does he still have his horse farm in Kentucky?" Because Maggie's father was also a computer manufacturing tycoon, Shep knew the man never wanted for money. He was a billionaire. That status had afforded Maggie the best colleges in the country. But then, she'd earned the right to attend because she was a brilliant woman.

"Yep," Maggie said. She kept most of her attention on the traffic in front and behind them as they moved out of Atlanta, heading in a southeasterly direction toward beautiful Savannah, near the Atlantic Ocean.

"And what about you?" Shep's heart beat a little harder. He really wanted to find out about her life. Had she married and divorced? That information wasn't available in the file he'd read on her. Did she have someone she loved now? Was she in a live-in relationship? In his heart, he didn't want the answer to be yes. Getting to see her again like this was such an unexpected yet wonderfully sweet surprise. Shep found himself jealous of her attention, and confounded by his emotions and reactions. He'd never thought that he could feel now what he had at eighteen years old.

Maggie felt heat stealing up her neck and into her face. Blushing again… With an internal groan, she realized that no matter what her age, she would always be a blusher. Maybe it was because of her red hair; she wasn't sure. Hands tightening momentarily on the wheel, she said flippantly, "Me? I'm up to my rear in bugs at OID. I love my work. I like going into the field and hunting down and identifying an epidemic virus."

"Just like your daredevil father, only you're not racing Thoroughbreds, you're doing something even more dangerous—looking for bacteria and viruses that kill people."

"Are you griping? Or making a statement?"

He chuckled. The sound came from deep within his chest. "You haven't lost your sense of humor, either."

Smiling a little, Maggie moved the automobile into the fast lane and set the cruise control at sixty-five. "My sense of humor has kept me alive, Hunter." She gave him a knowing glance. "Living with you for a year, I had to have a real sense of humor."

Nettled a little by her wry comment, he dropped his brows slightly. Pretending to be checking their route on the onboard computer, he muttered, "It wasn't all thorns and thistles, you know. Or is that all you remember?"

"What do you recall?" Maggie wasn't about to step into *that* trap. No way. She was too frightened of her own feelings, too afraid her clamoring emotions would make her tell Shep how she *really* felt. Maggie didn't want to put herself into that kind of vulnerable position with him. Besides, he'd never give her the same satisfaction. Shep was hard to read. And getting him to talk about how he felt—well, she might as well be a dentist pulling teeth!

Should he tell her? Shep wondered. He wanted to. No, he didn't dare. "I have a tendency to remember the good things we shared, Maggie. Not the bad."

"I don't consider being opinionated bad," she pointed out smartly.

Groaning, he perused the traffic and then used the rearview mirror to once again check the cars around them. "Bullheaded was more like it."

"Are you telling me that in all these years you *still* haven't changed your feelings one iota about women who are smart, savvy and confident? Do you still think we're all stubborn and refuse to bow to your greater intelligence, oh great one?"

"Here we go again!" he growled, giving her a frosty look. "You talk about not changing. Neither have you. In fact, you're worse than I recall."

Maggie's mouth blossomed into a full smile. "Oh, Hunter, you are so archaic. You're worse than that Neanderthal younger brother of yours, Reid. It's a good thing he married Casey. She'll straighten him out."

Shep nearly groaned again as he stole a glance at her. She looked delicious. With her dark glasses on, that red-and-gold hair highlighted by the sun behind her, she looked more like a Hollywood starlet than a virologist in that moment. Maggie was not stick thin like those television actresses who looked positively on the brink of starvation. No, she was firm, filled out and supple looking. Although she was short in comparison to him, she had a strong body. Remembering how that body had felt beneath him, he decided to move to a safer subject.

"Tell me, are you still riding hell-bent-for-leather on those eventing horses of yours? Or did you give up the desire to die on one of those jumps, like your dad gave up sprint car racing?"

Laughing delightedly, Maggie wagged a finger at him. "You're good, Hunter. I'll give you that. This is called let's change topics in midstream so Maggie is thrown off the scent. You never did play fair."

"And neither did you."

"You're gloating, Hunter. I can see it even if you don't change the expression on that iceberg face of yours."

He warmed to her teasing. Their repartee had always been like this. He knew she wasn't being mean or nasty, just teasing him to get him to respond. Granted, he wasn't the most spontaneous person in the world, but life had taught him not to be. In his job, spontaneity could get one killed, and Sarah had died because of just such a spur-of-the-moment decision on his part. Some of the warmth cascading through his chest was doused with sadness over Sarah's untimely death.

"What's wrong?"

Lifting his head, he stared over at Maggie. "What?"

"You're sad."

"I am?" How the hell could she know that? Unsettled, he shifted in the seat.

"Oh, Hunter!" she griped. "You never gave me credit for sensing what you're feeling. Not eighteen years ago.

Not *now*! Do you know how *frustrating* that is?" She made a strangled sound in the back of her throat.

"No," he said primly, and began to look around. The traffic was thinning. Along the freeway, roughly a couple of hundred feet on either side of it, grew kudzu, a weed from Japan that had been brought to the States as an ornamental bush and, due to the humid conditions in the South, had spread like a plague. He studied it now, trying to gather his thoughts after her attack.

Maggie gave him a dirty look. Shep seemed impervious to her emotional response. Well, that was just like him. But something was different. Before, he would open up a little bit, show some of his vulnerability to her. Now he had snapped shut, like a proverbial clam. "So, why are you so closed now?" she wondered softly, and sent him a direct glance he couldn't dodge.

Caught. Yep, Maggie had zeroed in on him. Moving uncomfortably and tugging at his flak jacket beneath his shirt, Shep muttered, "Life does it to you, Maggie. You know that."

"Tell me when you started to work for Perseus. I always thought you loved to fly more than breathe. What took you out of the Air Force and into a merc job?"

Sighing internally, Shep was relieved her questions weren't of a more personal nature. Maggie was too often personal. Feeling edgy, he replied, "I flew Falcons around in the sky until seven years ago. Morgan made a pitch to me that I couldn't resist. I liked the idea of helping people more directly. He used my flying skills for a number of years. I flew one of the Perseus jets for him. I also flew small, single engine planes like the Cessna, too. I was usually involved in missions that required a getaway aircraft on a very short dirt runway. I did a lot of work like that in Africa."

"Interesting we never ran into one another," Maggie said, "because I've spent almost a third of my professional life over in Africa. Many times, with Casey, on outbreak situations. There, or in South America, in the Amazon region."

Shep almost said, "I wished we had," but he snapped his mouth shut before the words could blurt out. Traffic was lessening now as they left the sparkling buildings of downtown Atlanta behind them. Ahead of them, he could see both the wide-open grassy flatland and gently rolling hills welcoming them into rural Georgia. Groves of tall, spindly pine trees began to line the freeway like a green wall. Georgia was a pine tree state, there was no doubt, and the lumber industry was going strong, a result of perfect soil and weather conditions for trees to grow fast and tall.

The sky was a bright blue. He could see a few cumulus clouds beginning to form. With the high humidity, cloud formation was inevitable as the sun rose higher in the sky. And then, later in the day, thunderstorms would pop up unexpectedly here and there across the state, but especially along the coast where the mix of warm, humid air created constant instability.

"So…" Maggie said in a low voice, "how has life treated you in the personal department? Did you ever marry? Do you have kids?" She held her breath. Shep hated these kinds of questions and she knew it. But she had nothing to lose and she really did want to know his status. Maggie didn't look too closely at why, however.

Frowning, Shep felt a sharp pain in his chest region. "You haven't lost your touch, have you?"

"What?" she demanded impertinently.

"Oh, come on, Maggie. You always went for the jugular."

"If asking a personal question is the jugular vein for you, Hunter, then something is wrong!"

He saw a pink flush spread across her freckled cheeks, but there was laughter sparkling in her eyes. If anyone but Maggie had asked him those questions, he'd have told them to go to hell in a hurry. "My private life is private. You know that."

"Oh, right. As if mine isn't. You've asked me personal questions and I've answered them, haven't I?"

"Yes."

"Well, it's tit for tat, Hunter. Now you get to answer mine."

"Where's the logic in that?"

She knew he was baiting her. She could sense it. Besides, one corner of his mouth flexed. "Logic dictates that if you ask personal questions of a person, you're basically saying it's okay to have them asked of yourself. It's one of those nonverbal understandings. You know?"

"My questions to you were not *that* personal. Yours are."

Rolling her eyes in frustration, she nailed him with a dark look. "Being evasive, are we?"

"My stock and trade, brat." Oh, damn! Where had *that* come from? Groaning, Shep held up his hand. "Sorry, I didn't mean to call you by that name."

Shaken by the warm intimacy of his endearment for her, Maggie's hands tightened around the steering wheel. Brat had been his intimate name for her, a term used with love. Licking her lips, she carefully felt her way through what he'd just said.

"Are you *really* sorry you used it, Shep?" Again, she briefly met his gaze. She saw such sadness in his eyes. And longing. For her? For what they'd had, even if it had been rocky, argumentative and imperfect at times? Maggie was unsure of what to make of his slip.

"Well, yes…no… Hell, it just slipped out, Maggie. I'm sorry. That's the past. I guess some things just don't die."

"They live or die because you want them to."

It was his turn to feel deeply uncomfortable. Now the car felt claustrophobic. "Don't make too much out of it, okay? I have a long memory. Some things I just don't forget."

"Why did you remember my nickname?" Maggie asked more gently. "Because you hated me? You're still angry because we broke up instead of getting married? What, Hunter? Is this multiple choice? Do I get to pick?"

"Maggie," he pleaded, holding up his hands, "stop running circles around me. You can outtalk me, I agree. But shooting three or four questions at me isn't going to get any more of a response out of me than one will and you know it."

She grinned a little. "Just like old times, ain't it, Hunter?" And in many ways, she enjoyed their verbal sparring. Sensing the feelings around him, Maggie saw that on one hand, Shep was uncomfortable, but on the other, she was a known entity to him and he knew she would never ever deliberately wound him with her words. That was part of the dance, the cement of their relationship. Their sparring was teasing, but never hurtful.

"Yes," he sighed. "You haven't changed that much, Maggie. You know that?"

Her grin widened. "Thank you. I'll take that as a compliment. As I told you before, neither have you, Hunter."

"So, did you ever get married?"

She stared at him, her mouth opening. She quickly snapped it shut. "What *is* this?" she demanded. "You can ask me highly personal questions, but you don't have to answer mine? Oh, no, Hunter. That's not how this relationship of ours is going, this time. You might have gotten away with these little tactics then, but not now. No way."

"Relationship?"

Groaning, Maggie said, "Wrong word. I didn't mean that. Just because we have to pretend we're married and stay in the same room at night does not a relationship make, okay?"

He grinned. Maggie rarely used the wrong words to describe herself or how she saw the world. The flush across her cheeks had deepened to a delicious strawberry color. It made her hazel eyes look like dancing emeralds set in gold, with a bit of cinnamon brown in the background. She was so alive to him. More alive than any other woman he'd ever met. She was so much like Sarah, and yet Sarah had been a pale shadow to Maggie's ebullient, sunny personality. Shep found himself starving for Maggie's quick wit and the playfulness that she automatically extended to him. In some ways, Maggie was the same as before. In others, she was better, more polished and poised. That made him desire her even more.

"For a dyed-in-the-wool wordsmith, Dr. Harper, I don't think you're in the habit of using wrong words.

So—" he looked at her "—you see what we have here as a relationship?"

"Hunter, you're not getting one more word out of me until you answer my questions first. You're not in control of this situation like you think. I'm your equal this time around. I'm not some starry-eyed eighteen-year-old you can intimidate. Does that compute? Once it does, then I think we can talk and share more. Yes? No? Tell me how you feel about it."

With a shake of his head, he muttered, "Maggie, you can run circles around people with that beautiful mouth of yours. You always could. Maybe you missed your calling. Instead of a doctor you should have been a lawyer. Right now, I feel trapped, as if my arms and legs were tied to steel spikes so I can't move."

Chuckling and rather pleased with herself, she said drolly, "Oh, suffer eloquently, Hunter. It's what you do best, as I recall. You always gave me that puppy-dog look of hurt in your eyes so I'd ease off. Not this time. Uh-uh. I'm older and wiser. Nope, the stakes stay in and you're trapped. So you have a choice to make— put up or shut up."

Checking the traffic one more time, Shep picked up one of the radios and made the obligatory call. Every hour on the hour they were to check in with the FBI and give their location by mile marker, and a status report. He watched Maggie drive as he spoke to the agent at the other end. She was smiling broadly, as if she'd just won a chess game with him. Well, hadn't she? Hanging up the microphone, he slid his arm across the back of her seat. His arm barely touched her proudly thrown back shoulders.

"Because I don't like icy silence for the next hours

we have to drive," he began in an amused tone, "I'll answer your questions. No, I'm not married. No, I don't have any children."

"That's all?"

"What do you mean, 'that's all'? Didn't I answer your questions?"

"Geez Louise, Hunter, you're just so wordy with your answers. You'd think you were in the DA's office being grilled by detectives before your attorney arrived!"

He couldn't help but laugh. "You know what?" he said, meeting her gaze, "I've *really* missed being around you. You're the only one that can pry anything out of me whether I want you to or not."

Gloating, and warmed by his too rare laughter, Maggie said, "So, are you in a relationship now?" A huge part of her hoped not. She saw him hesitate, open his mouth and then close it. He looked away for a long minute before turning his head and meeting her glance once again.

"I was… But I'm not now." He removed his arm from behind her seat, his hand resting in a closed fist on his thick thigh.

There was pain in his voice, as much as he tried to disguise it, Maggie realized. There was no mistaking the anguish that he tried to hide in his eyes, either. She lost her smile. In that moment, she reached out, her hand covering his. The gesture shocked her as much as it did him. Maggie found his hand felt just as strong as she remembered from decades ago.

"What happened, Shep? I can see it really hurt you."

Glancing at him again, she saw his stony expression and knew he had closed her out once more.

Chapter 4

They reached Savannah in the early afternoon. Maggie was glad she knew how stubborn Shep could get because he was closed up so tightly ever since she'd asked about his past that patience was the only answer in dealing with him. He would never give up personal information easily. Maggie knew, as Shep drove them alertly down Interstate 16 toward what she considered the most beautiful city in the South, that Shep was still chewing on the question she'd asked hours earlier.

For just a moment, she allowed her gaze to sweep the antebellum architecture that Savannah was so famous for. From the freeway, she could see the gold dome of city hall. Nearby was the riverfront district, lined with old cotton warehouses now turned into restaurants and gift shops.

The Savannah River, wide and slow moving, had been a main traffic route in the nineteenth century for ships taking cotton grown in Georgia overseas to English textile mills. Yes, Savannah had a very rich history. The city was semitropical, as it sat seventeen miles from the Atlantic. Hurricanes were the only threat to it. Offshore, as the river opened into the ocean, lay many islands, such as Tybee, Wilmington and Skidaway. The Low Country, as it was referred to, was a busy tourist destination for visitors from around the world.

Off to her left, Maggie could see the world-famous architectural wonder, the Talmadge Memorial Bridge, which spanned the Savannah River and linked Georgia with South Carolina. In her mind, Maggie had always called it Harp Bridge because its structure reminded her of harp strings, strung as it was with thick, strong, white steel cables from a central girder. Sighing softly, she realized she felt at peace, as she always did when she came to Savannah.

Their itinerary called for them to eat at the Olde Pink House Restaurant and Planter's Tavern. A Georgian-style mansion that had been turned into a restaurant, it had a rich and varied history, having been built in the late 1700s for James Habersham, Jr., a wealthy merchant. In the 1800s it had been turned into the Planter's Bank.

As they turned down Abercorn Street, Maggie sighed again. "I can't help it. I think Savannah is the crown jewel of America. Look at the pastel colors of all these beautiful old mansions. It reminds me of driving down the street and looking at prettily colored Easter eggs."

"I like the way you see the world, Maggie," Shep replied casually, though he remained on guard, his gaze sweeping the area as they pulled into a parking lot. Shep knew the reason for this location. It was in the open, not cramped or crowded. He knew FBI agents would be inside and outside, watching them and making sure they were safe. "Easter eggs..." He shook his head, gave her a quick glance and turned off the engine. As he removed his seat belt, he smiled a little. "Only you would see three- to five-story mansions as colored Easter eggs."

The softness of his gaze touched her deeply. Profoundly. Maggie lowered her lashes as she nervously fiddled with her safety belt. "I'm the idealist, Shep. You were always the hard-core realist. All you probably see in these incredibly well-kept mansions is their architecture, not necessarily their outer beauty." She tried to keep her eyes off him. He looked lean, professional in the dark blue sport coat, the white, open-collared shirt and khaki-colored slacks. He was comfortable, but sharp looking, in her opinion. And she knew why he was wearing the sport coat: to hide the weapon he carried. Otherwise, she was sure he'd have shed it long ago in this heat and humidity.

Getting out of the car, he rearranged his sport coat so that the pistol he carried beneath his arm in a holster was hidden from the public as well as the prying eyes of their enemy. Moving around the car, he opened the door for Maggie. She gave him a surprised look.

"I've always been a gentleman," he reminded her archly, holding out his hand to her.

"I'm so used to opening my own doors that I forgot," Maggie said with a sudden laugh. She slid her hand into his. Shep's grip was warm, strong and welcoming. Her fingers were still cool from the nervousness of being around him all these hours.

"Hmm," he said as he pulled her gently upward, "you're not icy feeling anymore."

Without meaning to get so close, Maggie found herself pressed against his tall, powerful frame momentarily. It was shocking. Wonderful. Only their clasped hands remained a barrier between them. But just as quickly, she stepped away. Not before seeing the amusement and longing burn in his eyes as he looked down at her, however. His lips had parted, and suddenly, Maggie knew Shep wanted to kiss her. She stood trapped between the car door and him.

"Easter eggs," Shep murmured as he lowered his head, keeping his hand around hers so she could not escape him. "You know, you're one of a kind, Maggie Harper. Even if you're the most headstrong woman I know, I can't help myself…" And he couldn't. Throughout the drive to Savannah, Shep had been aching to kiss her. To feel Maggie's soft, wide, smiling mouth once more captured by his. Well, they *were* married, weren't they? And if Black Dawn was watching, wouldn't they expect a newly married couple to do things like steal a kiss in a parking lot? Of course. Shep wasn't going to disappoint them. He needed Maggie too much. He'd accepted this assignment because she had been thrown tantalizingly in his path once again. Shep had forever regretted their breakup. Oh, he'd had women and affairs after her, but none of them ever matched Maggie, with her fire and verve.

Maggie's breath caught as she saw the predatory look come to Shep's narrowing eyes. She felt his hand hold hers a little more firmly. Without thinking, she let him gently pull her toward him once again as his head descended toward hers. He was going to kiss her! Stunned, she felt her mind blank out momentarily. It was the last thing she'd expected from him. But then, as she leaned bonelessly against him and felt the hard-

ening of his muscles as he took her weight, her heart
burst open with a longing that left her literally breath-
less in the wake of it.

All the sounds of downtown Savannah—the cars,
the horse-drawn buggy clip-clopping nearby—were
drowned out beneath the heat in his eyes, the intent
clearly written in his face. Yes, this felt right. So very
right… Maggie didn't struggle. As she lifted her head
to meet his mouth, something old and wonderful broke
loose in her wildly beating heart. How much she had
missed Shep! Maggie hadn't been aware of it until this
precious, unexpected moment. Closing her eyes, she
stretched upward as she leaned against him. She felt the
moisture of his breath against her cheek. She sensed his
nearness. It was a good feeling. So fertile…so desperately needed by her.

When his mouth grazed her parting lips, she quivered. She felt him remove her hand from between them.
In moments, her arm was wrapping around his narrow
waist as his slid across her shoulders. He brought her
gently and fully against him. A sigh rippled from her
lips as he grazed them tenderly again. It was that dichotomy about Shep that always threw her. To look at
him was to realize this man was a throwback to war-
riors from the past. In Maggie's heart, she'd always
seen him as a crusader from the twelfth century: big,
bruising, hard-looking and so very, very powerful. Yet
she was privileged to know the other side of him, too,
so it was easy to yield to him completely. With him,
she was safe. She knew he would care for her as if she
were a priceless and fragile treasure.

Moaning, she whispered his name and slid her arm
up across his broad, tense shoulders. Maggie wanted

him. She didn't care who was watching. In this moment, she realized how much she had ached to touch Shep once again. What they'd shared so long ago was alive and vivid now. That surprised her, but she wasn't going to apologize for it, either. As her fingers slid through the short, sleek hair at the nape of his neck, she felt his mouth settle powerfully against hers.

His lips moved in a claiming gesture. His breath was hot against her skin. She opened to him, yielded to his superior strength because he was tenderly sliding against her, exploring her and reveling in the renewal of something that had begun so long ago. Another quiver coursed through her as she felt his arm move more commandingly down her arched spine, his large hand settling comfortably against her hip. Yes, this was the old Shep she knew so well! And she couldn't get enough of him and that teasing, heated mouth of his. The roughness of his beard caused a delicious, prickling sensation against her skin. The male odor of him entered her flaring nostrils as she responded strongly to his pressure upon her mouth. Fingers sliding provocatively through his hair, she felt him shudder. As she drowned in the sunlit offering of his mouth, she felt him opening to her on all levels. Maggie felt the controlled power of him as he ravished her lips. This was heaven. *He* was her heaven. Oh, why had they broken up so long ago? It seemed so silly now.

Maggie didn't want the exploratory kiss to end…and she moaned a little in frustration as his mouth lifted reluctantly from her wet, slick lips. Slowly looking up, she drowned in the dark, stormy color of his eyes as he studied her in the intense moments after their kiss. Her mouth curved recklessly. "You've gotten better with age, Shep."

His returning smile was filled with mirth. "Why did I ever leave you, Maggie?" And with a shake of his head, he eased her from the safety of his embrace. She was soft and curvy in all the right places. He liked a woman with some meat on her bones. Stick women never turned him on. Maggie was well built, firm and in tremendous athletic condition. It made him burn with desire for her, with the urge to consummate what he knew was theirs to take with one another.

"I don't know..." She said softly, captured in his burning gaze, which scorched her like a delicious, sweeping fire. But she did know. The passion had always been strong between them. That hadn't changed. But she also knew there were things about this man that drove her crazy. How he hadn't always trusted her abilities. Or seen her as an equal. And yet, she'd seen the respect in his gaze for her today during his unguarded moments and that made her feel good about herself.

Running her fingers up the sleeve of his jacket, she whispered, "Maybe being eighteen-year-olds with no maturity or experience behind us made us act a little too rashly?" She was still thunderstruck by the power of his kiss—and the feelings in her it had aroused.

Capturing her hand, Shep forced himself to step back. The late sun beat down on them, and sweat trickled down his rib cage. He hungered for Maggie, who had the sweetest look on her upraised face. In her hazel eyes, he saw desire for him alone. It made him feel strong and good about himself. "Maybe so, brat..." He hesitated, then took another step back, with a slight smile of apology. "Damn, I can't seem to kick the habit of calling you by my favorite nickname. Sorry." And he was. Moving to the rear of the car, he opened the trunk and lifted out the aluminum suitcase containing the fake anthrax. He handed it to Maggie, because she was the official courier.

"Why?" Maggie moved aside and allowed him to shut and lock the door. "I *liked* my nickname. I earned it, remember?" She felt the weight of the suitcase in her left hand and remembered why they were together. And the danger they were in. It washed away some of her euphoria. If Black Dawn were here, she and Shep could be taken out in two shots. Both of them could be dead. Suddenly, she rebelled at the danger. She'd just found Shep again! Why couldn't they have met some other way? Somewhere safer? Less intense? All at once every touch of his hand on hers she absorbed fully, feeling the importance of every second, every minute spent with him.

Chuckling, Shep held her hand as they walked toward the front door of the restaurant. "So, if I slip again, you're not going to throw a book at me or something?" On guard once again, he was checking out pedestrians on either side of the street, which was clogged with traffic and cars at this time of day. He was looking for anything unusual or out of place. Shep knew that from rooftops around this restaurant, FBI agents in battle gear, with sniper's rifles, were discreetly watching them through their scopes.

"Of course not," Maggie said with a laugh. "Granted, I was a hothead back then, but I've mellowed a little since."

"Really? You could have fooled me." He grinned sheepishly and added in a confidential tone, "That's good to know." He opened the door for her and allowed her entrance into the restaurant. He smiled a little as he remembered how, when they were younger, Maggie had more than once sent a book sailing across the room at him when she got really angry. Of course, Shep acknowledged as they were led up to the second floor of the restaurant, he'd probably had it coming, because he would mercilessly provoke her sometimes just to see that redheaded anger of hers explode. Making up was always such a delicious reward, and that's why he usually did it. Shep gazed around the remarkable, historic restaurant. There were oil paintings of the residents of old Savannah. Even one of George Washington, and of course, the owner of the mansion, Habersham, in gaudy-looking shoe and knee buckles.

As Maggie sat down and accepted a menu, she glowed. "This is the best window in the place, Shep." After giving their drink orders of iced tea, they were left alone. "Look," Maggie said excitedly as she pointed out the window. "There's Reynolds Square. Isn't it beautiful?"

"What I'm looking at is beautiful," Shep murmured as he closed his menu. Maggie flushed. Beautifully. He ached to reach over and undo that chignon at the base of her long, lovely neck. Though he told himself that it was bad timing, he enjoyed seeing how his flattery made her glow even more.

"Shep…"

"Well, it's the truth, Maggie." He glanced out the window. The tree-covered square was one of many in the heart of downtown Savannah. Each square was unique and beautiful in its own right. Around each were the antebellum mansions—the Easter eggs, as Maggie referred to them—that brought such rainbow colors to this incredible city. "I think the maître d' brought us to the most romantic table in the restaurant."

"He did," she said. Maggie looked around. At this hour, after the lunch-hour crowd, there were not many diners, which was good as far as she was concerned. It meant less people to keep tabs on while they ate. "This is one of my favorite places to dine. It's so rich in history."

"And you always loved history."

"Yes," she said softly. "I still love it."

"We have a lot of ancient history between us, you know. Dinosaurs, maybe?"

She chuckled. "So, we're two ancient people."

"I'd never say you looked like a dinosaur, Maggie. You look beautiful and fresh to me. History helps us understand the past. What we did right…or wrong. The good or bad decisions we made."

She arched inwardly at his gruffly spoken words, allowing his compliments to touch her opening heart, wanting desperately for him to kiss her once again. She struggled to maintain some decorum in the restaurant. He looked sad after he spoke the words. But she didn't get a chance to ask him about them, as the waitress brought iced tea with fresh sprigs of mint in it and bright yellow crescents of lemon on a doily-covered plate. Maggie sighed. "I'm going to enjoy my meal, Hunter." She looked up at the waitress and said, "I've *got* to have your wonderful she-crab soup laced with sherry, and that to-die-for Caesar salad with cornbread oysters as my main course."

Shep absorbed Maggie's gusto for living. Everything she did she did with passion, with excitement and intensity. Her eyes were sparkling like jewels as she gave the order to the blond waitress attired in a white cotton blouse and black slacks.

"And you, sir?" the waitress inquired.

Shep looked at Maggie. "You know this place. What would I like to eat?"

Thrilled, because they had done this long ago with one another, Maggie laughed and looked up at the waitress. "This guy will eat half a steer in one sitting if you don't watch him. Give him a 'welcome to the South' meal of sautéed shrimp with country ham and grits. He'll take the she-crab soup, too, and a small dinner salad with blue cheese dressing on the side."

Shep leaned back, feeling pleased. Maggie hadn't forgotten one thing about him…even his favorite salad dressing. Amazed and still a little dazed over their kiss, their rekindling of what he'd thought had died long ago, he felt a new determination sweep through him. He'd lost Sarah. He wasn't about to lose Maggie. No…he just couldn't. Remembering that terrible day doused much of Shep's current happiness. If only he'd kept a better eye on Sarah. If only he hadn't let the situation get out of hand, Sarah might be alive today. Well, that wasn't going to happen now. Maggie was here and she was alive. And his heart shrank in terror at the thought of having a terrorist's bullet rip through her vital, beautiful body and steal her away from him.

As he gazed around the room out of habit, he wondered why he was being given a second chance with Maggie. Her kiss had been wonderfully revealing— soft, feminine, strong and sweet. Wherever she had touched his body with her own, he could still feel the tingles, the yearning.

"Why are you looking so sad?" Maggie asked as she sipped her iced tea.

Startled, he stared at her momentarily. And then he remembered just how well Maggie could read him, no matter how he tried to maintain a poker-faced expression. "Can't hide much from you, can I?" He played with the silverware absently. "Yeah," he finally responded, "I'm a little sad."

Tilting her head, Maggie asked, "Why?" She saw grief in his eyes, combined with a hard determination.

"After we broke up," he began in a low tone, "I swore off women for a long time." He moved the fork around in his fingers and stared down at it for some moments. "And then, gradually, over time, I got back into socializing more. I never met anyone like you, so I never got married...until...later, when things changed." His brows drew together. "When I went to work with Perseus, Morgan teamed me up with a partner. That was his mandate—everyone had to have a partner. Well, I rebelled on that one, but if I wanted to work for him, I had to go along with company policy. So I did." He lifted his gaze to hers. "My partner was a woman named Sarah Collier. She was an ex-marine sniper and damn good at what she did. We were partners for three years, until I did something very stupid that I'll pay for forever."

Maggie placed her elbows on the table and cradled her chin on her clasped hands. Raw anguish burned in Shep's eyes. She felt a terrible sense of grief and guilt surround him as he restlessly rolled the fork back and forth across the white linen tablecloth in front of him. "What happened, Shep?"

"I got her killed in the line of duty," he answered flatly. He stopped rolling the fork around. Forcing himself, he looked across the table at Maggie. "We were in Macedonia on an undercover assignment to find this little girl who had been kidnapped by the Serbs. There were thousands of mines all over that area. Maybe a million. I don't know." He shrugged his shoulders painfully in remembrance. "We'd found the girl. She was alive. Unharmed, thank God. We were being pursued by her captors and we came upon this open farm field. Sarah said we should go around it. She warned me about the mines. I made a command decision to cross it. I had the six-year-old in my arms and we started running because we could hear the enemy in hot pursuit. All we had to do was make it across that field, to the trees, and we'd be safe." His mouth hardened and he looked away, the memory fresh and hurting.

"In my hurry to cut off a minute of time because I didn't feel we had it, I risked all our lives. I knew there were mines all over the damned place. I knew it..." He gripped the fork so hard that his fingers whitened around the utensil. "Sarah was leading the way. I was running and bringing up the rear. She was two hundred feet ahead of me, being the point person, paving the way for us. She was the one taking the risks..."

Maggie closed her eyes when she saw tears gleam momentarily in Shep's slitted gaze, his mouth forced into a suffering line. "Oh, no... Don't tell me she stepped on a mine?"

He nodded, the words choked in his throat. The look on Maggie's face made him want to cry. How easily touched she was! How wonderfully sensitive she was to the human condition...and to him. "Don't feel sorry for me in this," he growled. "I was the stupid bastard who was in a hurry, remember? If I hadn't been so damned much in a hurry that morning, she'd be alive today…"

"And were you or the child hurt?"

"No…"

Gently, Maggie said, "Shep, I think Sarah knew what she was doing. She understood the risks. And who is to say that the minute you cut off by going through the field instead of around it *didn't* save your lives? Can you be really sure that your decision wasn't sound, under the circumstances?"

Painfully, he lifted his shoulders. "It was more than that, Maggie. Over the years, I had fallen in love with Sarah. I finally figured what life was about. I had finally found a woman somewhat like you…" He gazed at Maggie fiercely. "But she wasn't you. She had some of your attributes…"

"I'm sure you loved her for all the right reasons," Maggie whispered. Without thinking, she reached over and captured Shep's left hand. "I'm so sorry, Shep. For both of you. Sarah sounded like a very, very brave, competent woman."

Gripping Maggie's warm fingers, he gave her a measured look. "I'll tell you one thing, brat, I'm *never* going to allow that to happen again. After Sarah died, I came off that mission and told Morgan that I was either going solo on missions from that time onward or he could fire me. At that time, I didn't care, I was so full of grief and guilt. As it was, I hit the bottle. I drank the pain away. It took me more than a year to pull myself out of it, and to be honest, if Morgan hadn't been there to kick my butt all over the place, I'd probably still be in a dark bar somewhere drinking away my guilt."

Her heart twinged with grief. Maggie saw that the

guilt was still there. "Listen to me, Shep—you saved that little girl's life. Two people walked away from something that might have killed all of you. Have you looked at it from that angle?"

He release her fingers reluctantly. "Sure I have. But SOP—standard operating procedure—said to avoid open fields. They were well known to have mines planted throughout them. I disobeyed. I was arrogant. I thought I knew what was best for all of us…"

Tenderly, she moved her fingers across his outstretched hand. "You are a little arrogant. But many times, you know a lot, Shep. That doesn't mean you don't listen to good people who know things, too."

"As you pointed out long ago," he muttered, "that was one of my failings, one of the things that broke us up."

Chuckling slightly, Maggie said, "How well I remember. You had all the good ideas and I had none." And now she saw how that attitude had gotten him tangled up in the mission with Sarah. Maggie would never know what the right answer had been on that mission. She hadn't been there and there was no way to judge if Shep had really made a wrong decision or not. But he believed he had. Obviously.

"On this mission," he warned her gravely, "I'm not going to lose you. I swore I'd never take on a partner again and Morgan knew that. But when he showed me your photo, told me that you were volunteering to set yourself up as a decoy to try and capture Black Dawn terrorists, my heart got ahead of my head and my past experiences didn't matter. I told Morgan I wanted it. I wanted you as my partner. He about fell off his chair. I think he thought he was going to have to argue long and hard for me to take this mission with you—but he was wrong. You're too beautiful, Maggie, too alive. You deserve the best protection in the world on this top event. If I'd known ahead of time, I'd have talked you out of it. This mission is lethal. You could be killed."

Shep shifted uncomfortably in the chair. "I came because I want you to walk out of this mission alive and in one piece. I've learned a lot since Sarah's death. I'll control this situation completely this time. I'll make sure you survive it."

Uneasily, Maggie studied him, heard the steel resolve in his deep baritone voice. "Shep," she begged gently, "don't say you're going to control this situation. That's what probably got you into that position with Sarah. If you *had* listened to her, things might have turned out differently. Don't you see? You *were* controlling her and the decisions at that time. Frankly, I would hope that you'd listen to my input. Granted, I'm not up on stealth tactics, but I've got two eyes, good intuition and a fair amount of practicality. I'd hope you'd listen to me. We're a team on this, Shep."

Shaking his head, Shep growled, "This isn't up for discussion, Maggie. I'm keeping you safe on this mission. There's no way I'm putting you in jeopardy like I did Sarah. I lost one woman I loved. I'm not about to do it twice. No way in hell."

She opened her mouth and then closed it. What was Shep really saying? That he couldn't trust her? That she was a mute partner in this deadly dance they were on? That her input didn't matter? Bristling internally, Maggie capped her emotional reaction. Right now, Shep was raw with guilt over Sarah's death. He'd loved her. Well, Maggie was sure his reaction didn't mean he loved *her*.

Maggie and Shep had a past history with one another and with his overprotective nature, she was sure he couldn't help taking charge on this mission.

Out of the corner of her eye, Maggie saw the waitress approaching with their soup. "I'm tabling this discussion for now," she warned him in a low voice, "but once we get to our bed and breakfast later, we need to talk more. Okay?"

The resolve in Maggie's tone shook him. This wasn't a soft, willowy eighteen-year-old talking to him. No, it was a mature, confident woman. It brought back vivid memories of Sarah's confidence. She had been rock solid as a warrior and could always be relied upon to give her best. She'd never let Shep down in the three years they were paired. Not once. It was *he* who had let *her* down. Well, Maggie thought she could be like Sarah, but she couldn't. Not on this mission. No, Maggie needed his protection and experience. Whether she agreed with him or not, Shep was going to fully control their situation. Every minute of it. Somehow, if he could complete this mission successfully, he knew that he could assuage some of his guilt where Sarah was concerned. If he could get Maggie safely through this gauntlet, maybe some of this terrible guilt would stop eating him alive and life would look a little more hopeful to him than it did now. That was all he asked for.

Chapter 5

Just as they were leaving the restaurant, Shep's cell phone, which he carried in his sport coat jacket, beeped. Reaching out, he pulled Maggie aside in the lobby. Automatically, he placed himself in front of her and the doors of the restaurant—just in case.

"Yes?" he growled into the phone.

Maggie felt tension sizzling from Shep. His eyes narrowed and became icy with only a bare hint of blue in their depths. Understanding that the FBI had just phoned, she figured the call was more than likely a warning. Maggie's focus shifted from her personal thoughts to the dangers that surrounded them. Gripping the attaché case in her left hand, she kept her right hand free in case she had to pull out the pistol she carried in her purse. Though the traffic outside looked normal, Maggie knew the terrorists' best cover was their ability to fade into the fabric of the world around them. A professional terrorist never stood out like the proverbial sore thumb, she thought grimly as she watched Shep click off the cell phone and jam it back into his pocket.

"Trouble?" she guessed.

"Yes. They've spotted a black luxury sedan that has gone around this block four times in a row. Two men are in it. The feds are running the plates right now. A sniper on the building across the street noticed them." Shep glanced down at her. "We're staying put until we know more."

Maggie felt his tremendously protective nature now; it flowed around her powerfully. The fact that Shep had automatically positioned his bulk in front of her, in case bullets came flying through the glass of the doors toward them, wasn't lost on her. He stood slightly slouched, his feet apart like a boxer waiting to receive a blow. She was getting a taste of the warrior in Shep. Right now, her heart was beating hard in her breast and she was scared. Gulping, her throat dry with the adrenaline coursing through her, she whispered, "Do terrorists always drive such fancy cars?"

"Not necessarily," he said, his gaze fastened on the slowly moving traffic on the street in front of them. It was rush hour now, five o'clock, and the traffic had increased substantially. "They usually don't use high end, expensive cars because they stand out too much. This is probably nothing to worry about, but I'm not in the business of taking chances." Especially with Maggie at his side.

Somehow, Shep told himself, he was going to have to get her through this in one piece. At the other end of this mission, he wanted—no, demanded—time alone with her. More than anything, he realized suddenly, he wanted to reestablish a personal connection with Maggie. His lips tingled hotly in memory of her soft, yielding kiss against his mouth. She'd kissed him back. She'd wanted to kiss him as eagerly as he had. After all these years, a spark had exploded between them like a candle lighting the darkness of his wounded heart. For him, Maggie symbolized a freedom he'd found only with her. Now, as he stood with his knees slightly bent, prepared for an attack, he wanted that brass ring. He wanted Maggie. All of her. To hell with consequences.

The cell phone rang again. Shep pulled it from his pocket and flipped it open. His features were grim as he said, "Yes?"

Maggie gazed tensely out the restaurant doors. This was downtown Savannah, and at rush hour it was always better to walk in the beautiful squares rather than drive. Her gaze moved from one building top across the street to the next. She couldn't see any of the FBI snipers who were hidden up there for their protection. They were doing a good job of staying out of sight.

"I see… Thanks…"

Maggie turned her attention to Shep. He put the cell phone away. "Trouble?"

"No. A false alarm."

"Probably tourists looking for a parking spot to come here and eat at rush hour. Bad combination," Maggie said with a slight smile. "This time of day, you can circle a square for half an hour before you find a parking spot."

Shep nodded. He moved forward and opened the door for her. "Let's go. And let's stay on alert. I don't have a good feeling about this."

As they walked down the street, Shep moved to the curb side, his arm going around Maggie's waist. He drew her close in a protective gesture. The sunlight was hot and intense, the humidity still high. Above the buildings Maggie could see cumulus clouds thickening into mighty thunderheads. She wouldn't be surprised if it stormed tonight, judging from the size of them.

Shep's long stride was making her take two steps for his every one. He suddenly sensed she was having to almost skip to keep up with him, and he instantly slowed his pace. Liking the curve of his hand around her waist, Maggie smiled to herself. How wonderful it had been to simply talk to Shep. For once he was forthcoming and not as closed up as usual. Or maybe life had made him more accessible than he had been in his younger years? Maggie fervently hoped so.

"I'll drive," Shep said, opening the door.

"No, it's my turn."

"Maggie—"

"Hey, it's my turn, remember?"

Tensely, Shep gazed around the parking lot which was now filled with people arriving to eat at the famous restaurant. Every one of them was a potential terrorist threat as far as he was concerned. Losing patience as Maggie moved to sit in the driver's seat, Shep gripped her arm and stopped her.

"Not now, Maggie. We'll fight some other time."

Jerking her arm out of his grasp, she glared up at him. "Use your head, Hunter. I *know* this city. You don't. If we get attacked, who is going to know the ins and outs, the back alleys and the best ways to avoid the attack? It sure won't be you."

Frowning, he watched as she disregarded his orders and sank belligerently into the driver's seat. He almost reached out and pulled her out. *No.* Now was not the time to get into one of their squabbles. This was just like before, when they were living with one another. Didn't she realize that he should have control because he knew best in this situation? Frustrated, he stalked angrily around the car, jerked open the passenger door and got in.

Maggie started the car after closing her door. She felt anger radiating from Shep. She saw it in the hard, unhappy line of his mouth. "I know where the Crescent Bed and Breakfast is located."

"I've changed my mind," he told her gruffly, and pulled out his cell phone. "We're not going there. I have a bad feeling and I don't like it."

Maggie stared at him. "But…the FBI are there. We'll be safe…"

"The FBI don't guarantee a damn thing, Maggie." He got his contact, Agent Caldwell, on the phone. "Yeah, we're going to avoid the bed and breakfast. I want to change our plans. We'll head up toward Hilton Head Island and pick a random place to stay. It's only an hour from here. If we're getting tailed, this will throw them off. If we act like we're easy targets, they might get suspicious and think it's a trap. We've got to make them think otherwise. If we seem likely to escape, Black Dawn will get bold and strike."

Rolling her eyes, Maggie sat back and waited until he was off the phone. "Just because you don't get to drive, you're going to blow a place that's protected by our side?"

"That's not the reason," he said as he looked around. "Let's go. You know how to get to Hilton Head via the freeway?"

"Of course I do." With a shake of her head, Maggie backed the car out of the slot. Once on the street, she made the necessary turns to head back onto the interstate. It was five-thirty, with plenty of daylight left. The drive to Hilton Head was on a four-lane freeway, through rolling countryside. It was a relatively untraveled route, so they could easily spot a tail.

Once on the freeway, they found the traffic still congested for the first couple of miles, with commuters heading home for the evening. The sky ahead was dotted with thunderstorms that were building up and looming menacingly. Maggie wondered if they'd get the storms as they moved in a northeasterly direction toward Hilton Head. Since it was off the coast of South Carolina, and there was so much ocean humidity and warmth, she knew the chance for storms increased proportionately.

Shep continued to gaze around and keep track of the cars nearby. His tightened gut eased only a little. Something was wrong; he could feel it. He couldn't say *what* it was; he only knew he felt stalked by the terrorists. His gut feeling had saved his life too many times before for him to question his decision now. He glanced over at Maggie's set profile. He knew she thought he was being controlling again—a know-it-all. Well, he wasn't.

"I really think this is a mistake, Shep. You blow a perfectly good place that's protected and throw us out in the unknown." Maggie pointed to the clouds ahead. "And on top of that, we're going to get nailed tonight with a lot of thunderstorms up in the Hilton Head area. That's not good. You can't hear anything coming with the thunder bouncing around. Rain could play a dangerous part if we can't hear terrorists approaching."

"Your protest is noted," he said heavily. "You can put it in your after-action report when we get through this mess in one piece."

"I don't like your sarcasm. You're belittling me—

again. Just like you did when we were together." Her fingers tightened around the steering wheel. "Damn, some things just don't change. I was hoping you'd be more reasonable."

"Maggie…don't start…"

Glaring at him for a moment, she returned her attention to the traffic. "You didn't even bother to consult me, Shep. That's what I don't like. You couldn't care less what I think, and that really makes me angry. Well, I'm not some airhead eighteen-year-old, all right? I'm thirty-six and I damn well have some experience of the world. You should be taking advantage of my knowledge, not canning it like it doesn't count."

Her nostrils flared and she tried to shake the anger she felt toward him, but to no avail. "A leopard never changes his spots. That's *you*, Hunter."

Holding up his hand, he watched the traffic thinning dramatically now. Ahead of them the freeway was nearly empty as they drove toward Hilton Head. "Look, I made a military strategy decision. You've got to *trust* me during times like this. I had a gut feeling on this, Maggie." He drilled her with a dark look. "I suppose you're going to tell me that women's intuition counts for something, but if a man has intuition, it doesn't work the same way?"

"You're so good at holding ground and arguing your points as to why your decision is the best one, Hunter." Maggie met his gaze sadly. "I'm disappointed in you, that's all. And if you think for a moment you're going to keep this up without my input, you are dead wrong."

Wearily, he said, "Let's use our energy, our alertness for the enemy. Let's not be taking pounds of flesh out of each other, okay? We agree to disagree. Let's leave it at that."

How could she enjoy kissing him so much one moment, and then have him backhand her like this when it came to such an important decision? Maggie knew she wasn't being overly dramatic. Shep's call could mean life or death. Her reaction wasn't irrational at all. But he didn't get that. He never did. "Some things never change," she told him bitterly. "Fine, I'll shut up. But if I see something or feel something about this mission, I'm going to be in your face, Hunter. And next time, I'm not going to be sweet or yielding about it. You got that?"

Now he was tasting Maggie the warrior. He could tell the way her hazel eyes blazed with controlled anger that she damn well meant every word. "Fine," he muttered. "I'll try to listen to you."

Well, that wasn't going to happen. Shep knew best. His thoughts moved ahead. Calling up the computer maps of the area, he studied them in tense silence. Soon the light changed. Looking up, he saw ragged gray-and-white cauliflower-shaped clouds blotting out the sun. He hoped it wouldn't rain. Rain and thunder, as Maggie had rightly pointed out, could benefit the terrorists, allowing them to approach without detection. It was a dangerous situation.

Shrugging off his apprehension, Shep took a deep breath. He felt better being on the road again. Moving targets were harder to take out than sitting ducks in a bed and breakfast. So the FBI had to scramble now, trying to tail them and get ahead of them. That was part of their job. Shep was in charge. He made the final calls on this mission. If the FBI team was upset, then so were the terrorists. And that was just what Shep had intended. Black Dawn would never suspect a trap—they'd be too busy trying to keep up.

Fuming, Maggie kept her attention on her driving. Taking Route 278, they made a wide, looping turn over two arching bridges that spanned salt marshes, taking them to the posh Hilton Head Island, where the rich and famous lived. The island was shaped like a human foot, quite literally. Maggie had friends who lived on the island retreat. It was surrounded by dark green tidal wetlands, home to many different types of shorebirds and waterfowl, including the magnificent great blue heron, whose wingspan was seven feet wide.

"Do you have *any* idea where you want to stay?" she demanded icily. Above them, the skies were turning turbid and threatening. Soon, the first approaching thunderhead would hit the island with well-known summer fury and power. The unstable, humid air of the coast bred some of the most violent thunderstorms Maggie had ever seen. The traffic was thickening again. It was 6:20 p.m.—time for tourists to be leaving the island and residents to be trying to get home. Traffic on Hilton Head was terrible, in her opinion, confined to two-way streets for the most part, except for two main arteries that were blessedly four lane.

"I have several options, according to the computer list."

"Well, why don't you ask me? I've lived in this area. I know this island like the back of my hand. See, Shep? Even now you'd rather rely on a damned computer than ask me what I know."

Rankled, he glanced over at her with apology in his eyes. "Okay, you're right. So what do you suggest?"

Frustration ate at Maggie. "I think we should stick close to 278, the only main route off this island if things go bad and we need to run. I think we should go to the Hilton Head Plantation area. There are a lot of time-share resorts down there and there's bound to be a last-minute cancellation at one of those villas. It's summer, so it's peak season here." She gripped the wheel nervously. "We'll just have to take our chances. It might mean stopping at a few time-share offices."

He shrugged. "Sounds good to me." Shep knew the FBI could locate them at all times. There was a device in the car that constantly transmitted their position to a satellite, and then to their mobile computer base. He knew there were four technicians in the white van, plus a driver and guard. It was, quite literally, headquarters for this operation. From the van, which he knew was probably ten miles behind them, any and all law enforcement could be called in to assist them at a moment's notice. The thought was comforting.

"I'm going to try and situate us at Skull Creek Marina, on the north side of the island. If things get dicey, we can always jump into a boat and escape. I don't think Black Dawn will have a boat around here, do you?"

"It's a good idea, having a second type of transportation to rely on," he agreed. He saw Maggie arch beneath his compliment. She was right: he really needed to bring her into the loop on this mission a lot more than he had. As usual, he was thinking that his partner didn't know the area—but she did. Shep pointedly reminded himself to take advantage of her expertise.

Maggie turned off onto Whooping Crane Way. The traffic was stop and go. She felt better with Shep taking her advice. Finally, after fifteen minutes, they reached the Skull Creek Marina. It was on a deep, quiet inlet guarded by several small islands. The marshy islands reminded Maggie of a series of stones set in a necklace. A much larger island beyond—Pinckney Island Wildlife Refuge—afforded thousands of migrating birds a roost at different times of the year.

Maggie saw the marina ahead. Everything from million-dollar yachts, to bass boats, and even a few aluminum fishing boats with outboard motors on back, made this harbor their home. With the threat of thunderstorms, the smooth, mirrorlike water looked like black marble.

"There's a nice time-share known as the Great Blue Heron Resort just down this street."

"Let's try for it."

Pleased, Maggie made a right turn. "This particular time-share is right on the water, and the marina is steps away from it. I'm trying to strategically situate us so we have more escape options, if it comes to that."

"Good thinking," he exclaimed. Why in hell didn't he consult more with her? Maggie had her head on straight.

He knew why. Sarah. The mistake he'd made with her. Rubbing his jaw in discomfort, Shep watched as the tightly packed houses, each worth millions, he was sure, opened up to a three-story, blue-gray building that had a sign with a great blue heron carved on it. Maggie turned in.

"Nice looking."

"It is." She pointed to the marina, which was truly within walking distance. "Hope it has a cancellation."

"We'll find out soon enough," Shep said.

"I think this is Maggie Harper luck," Shep said as they drove back to the isolated time-share. They'd been fortunate; a family of six had canceled and a second-floor villa was open for the taking. Shep typed in their location on the laptop computer, gave their room number and sent off the e-mail message. The mobile HQ would pick it up. The FBI would then, within the next hour, establish a new perimeter of defense to wait and watch.

Pleased, Maggie smiled as she parked the car in the garage below the villas. "It's nice to be here. I like being near the ocean." As she opened the door, the first carom of thunder rolled across the area. It sounded like someone was pounding a huge kettledrum above their heads. She and Shep quickly removed their luggage from the trunk and headed to the stairs at the side of the building. Palm trees, cypress, pecan and live oak surrounded the place. High hedges also promised privacy. Hurrying up the stairs, Maggie was relieved to get to their villa.

Once inside unit 214, Maggie saw two bedrooms off to the left and one down at the end of a long hall on her right. The decor was cheery, the bamboo furniture covered with cushions in bright, tropical prints. The kitchen was painted a warm yellow, and there was a bar where people could eat, as well as a formal dining room that had a large bamboo-and-glass table.

"Nice place," she murmured, and started down the hall to the right.

"Hold it," Shep cautioned. He held up his hand, locked the door behind them. Motioning to the left, he said, "Let's stay together. You take one of these two bedrooms. If something happens, we don't want to be separated, okay?"

Hesitating, Maggie stood in the living room, her luggage in hand. "Okay…" She turned and walked down the teak-floored hall which gleamed golden-brown beneath the lights. The bedrooms were for children, with two twin beds in each one. Maggie chose the dark green bedroom and wearily put her luggage on a bed. This room, too, had a tropical motif and thick, cushiony bamboo chairs.

Poking her head out, she said, "I'm going to take a quiet, hot shower, Hunter. Don't disturb me unless they come smashing through the front door, okay?"

He ambled down the hall and stood just outside her door. Each room had its own private bathroom. Maggie looked drawn and tired. He could see slight shadows beneath her beautiful green-and-gold eyes. "Yeah, go ahead. I'll play watchdog. When you get done, it's my turn."

Maggie entertained the thought of sharing a shower with Shep. It had been one of their favorite activities after making love. And many times it resulted in making love all over again beneath those wonderful streams of warm water. She saw a gleam in his eyes and sensed he was thinking the exact same thing. Heat rose in her neck and flowed into her face. Damn, she was blushing. Turning away, but not before she saw the corners of his mouth lift a little, she muttered. "Why don't you call for pizza delivery or something? We had a late lunch, but there's no food in this place. I don't want to go to another restaurant. I'd just like to sit and rest."

Nodding, he said, "It's a good idea. But let's discuss it later?"

The shower was her way of unwinding from her dangerous job at the OID.

Maggie quickly rubbed a dark green cloth with some jasmine-scented soap. Outside she could hear thunder rumbling again and again. The stained-glass window above her, which depicted a great blue heron standing elegantly in a marsh, was splattered with rain pouring from the sky.

Shep was sitting on the bamboo couch, several maps spread out on the glass table in front of him, when Maggie emerged. She had changed into a pair of comfortable jeans, dark brown loafers and a short-sleeved pink blouse with shell buttons and some lace around the Peter Pan collar. Running her fingers nervously through her damp hair, she absorbed the powerful intent in his eyes as he looked up. Maggie felt his desire for her. It was a wonderful discovery. She reveled in the sensation. Her body tightened and she ached once more to kiss him. The situation didn't merit such a possibility. Right now, Maggie understood how volatile a game they were playing. Lightning flashed nearby and she watched the sky light up outside the double glass doors that led to a spacious screened-in porch.

"Looks like we're in for it," she murmured, moving to the bar and sitting on one of the stools.

In more ways than one, Shep thought. How provocative Maggie looked, her face flushed from the heat of her bath and her hair mussed from the humidity. Even without makeup, she looked incredibly beautiful. Maggie had a charisma that drew him powerfully to her. The soft, flexible way her lips moved entranced him. How desperately he wanted to taste the honey, the sweetness of her once more.

"I'm going to go get that pizza you suggested," he said. "I'll fetch it now, while it's still light. I don't want anyone coming to the door, Maggie. Your idea about getting some food for later is good." He jabbed a finger at the local map of the island. "I see there's a pizza parlor at the marina. It's close and handy. Now that you're out of the shower, I'll go pick one up." He lifted his head. "You still like anchovies on your pizza?"

She grinned. "Always. Half with anchovy, half with pepperoni, right?" Her eyes gleamed with laughter, with tenderness.

It was like old times to Shep. He disliked anchovies. Maggie loved them with a passion. Their tastes were just like everything else in their relationship—opposite. Rising, he shrugged on his sport coat to hide his weapon. "You don't forget a thing," he told her in amazement. Moving toward the door, he said, "I'll knock three times and give you the code for the day. Then you let me in. Otherwise, don't answer this door—or the phone—for any reason while I'm gone." He drilled her with a dark look. The set of her lips told him she didn't like being told what to do. "Please?"

Softening a little, Maggie said, "Okay, I won't answer the door."

"This should take about twenty or twenty-five minutes," he said as he opened the door and checked the hallway.

"You're going to get rained on, Hunter."

He grinned slightly. "Yeah, well, just deserts for my bullheadedness, right?"

Laughing, Maggie slid off the bar stool and sauntered to the foyer, where he stood with the door open. It was pouring outside. "We could be at the bed and breakfast in Savannah enjoying a nice, comfy evening, you know."

"This is a better way to go," he assured her confidently. As he moved out into the hall, Shep decided not to tell Maggie that the FBI had been delayed by an accident on the highway leading into Hilton Head. He didn't want her worried or upset that they were without protection right now. What she didn't know wouldn't hurt her. Besides, as long as she followed orders and kept the door locked, she'd be fine for the twenty minutes he'd be gone. "I'll see you in a little bit," he promised, and left.

Maggie made sure the door was locked in his absence. Turning around, she decided to watch television. At least she could catch the national news. Sitting down after adjusting the television, she sighed and pushed off her shoes. Wriggling her toes in the thin, white cotton socks, she stretched out on the couch. Closing her eyes, she promised herself she wouldn't fall asleep. But she did within moments. The stress and danger of the day had taken its toll.

The banging at the front door jerked Maggie upright. The pounding was fierce. Outside, the thunderstorm still rumbled. Flashes of lightning danced nearby. Instantly, Maggie was on her feet. Disoriented from the druglike sleep she'd fallen into, she glanced at her watch. It was thirty minutes since Shep had left.

"Open up!" a deep voice called. "FBI! Dr. Harper! Open up! This is the FBI!"

Hesitating, Maggie ran to the door. Should she open it? Where was Shep? He was late. Oh, Lord, why had she fallen asleep?

"Dr. Harper? Open up! This is the FBI. We've got a situation. You're in danger! Open the door now!"

Her heartbeat tripled in time. Dry mouthed, Maggie started for the bedroom, where her pistol lay, but looked out the peephole of the door as she passed. She saw a man dressed in dark blue clothes, a baseball cap that had FBI printed in yellow across the front. He was older, around forty-five, his dark eyes narrowed with tension. Should she open the door? Shep had told her emphatically not to.

"What situation?" Maggie yelled through the door.

"Ma'am! Your partner, Shepherd Hunter, is down! The terrorists got him. Open up! You're in danger! We have to protect you!"

Shep! With a moan, Maggie grabbed for the brass doorknob. Wait! Was she crazy? She wasn't following procedure! Jerking her fingers, she shouted, "What's the security code?" The FBI had a code set up if something went awry and they needed to talk to one another. Anyone could claim he was an FBI agent and Maggie wouldn't know the difference. Knowing the code ensured that the players were actually who they said they were. Breathing hard, she waited, her hands pressed against her breast.

"Alpha bravo whiskey!" the man shouted. "Now come on! We've got a man down. We need you *now*, Dr. Harper!"

The code was correct. Shakily, Maggie jerked back the dead bolt. Next came the chain. She twisted the knob. Before she could open it, the door was smashed inward by the weight of a man's body. With a cry, Maggie was thrown to the foyer floor, her breath knocked out of her. Stunned, she saw two men leap into the villa. One was dressed in a dark blue FBI uniform from the waist up. The other man was in civilian attire. Panicked, Maggie tried to scramble to her knees to avoid his outstretched hand snaking toward her.

"No you don't, Dr. Harper." The man had a British accent, she noted numbly as he drew a gun and pointed it in her face. "Now be a good girl and get up. Now!"

The other man ripped off the baseball cap, shrugged out of the dark blue shirt and turned to them. Beneath the uniform he was wearing a short-sleeved, crimson shirt. His hair was black, with gray at the temples, his eyes dark green. He looked familiar, Maggie thought, as he smiled savagely in her direction. "How trusting you are, Dr. Harper." His accent was thick now and sounded Russian.

Confused and scared, Maggie watched as the one with the Russian accent hurried to her bedroom, where the aluminum attaché case sat in plain view upon the bed. "What? Who are you? You're not the FBI! How did you know the code?" And then, suddenly, Maggie recognized the man standing tensely at her side. He was a scientist she knew from conferences she'd attended for the OID. She'd heard him speak on anthrax epidemics a number of times. "Wait…you're Dr. Bruce Tennyson. From Britain. I—don't understand. What are you doing here?"

Chuckling, the man drew out a pair of handcuffs and pulled Maggie's hands behind her. "No, Doctor, we aren't the FBI and yes, I'm Bruce Tennyson. At your service."

"Shep?" Maggie asked, her voice cracking. "How bad is he wounded?"

"That was a lie, too, Doctor. Come on! You're going with us." He jerked a look over his shoulder at his friend. "Romanov?"

"Got it!" Alex Romanov called triumphantly from the bedroom. "Everything's here. The vial is here."

"Are you *sure*?" Tennyson snapped tensely as he pushed Maggie toward the door, his pistol jammed between her shoulder blades.

"Absolutely!" Romanov ran out to where they stood, grinning from ear to ear. "We got it!"

"Don't gloat yet, old chap," Tennyson said as he thrust Maggie ahead of him. "We've got to get out of here first. Let's go, Dr. Harper!"

Maggie jerked a look over her shoulder. The door of the villa was standing wide open. *Shep!* Oh, Lord, she'd done what he had said not to do! She'd opened the door! Now she was kidnapped. But how had they known the code? She'd never have opened that door if they hadn't given her the correct password. The pain arcing between her shoulder blades was intense as Tennyson jabbed her again, forcing her at a trot down the deserted hall toward the front of the building.

Romanov chuckled as he jogged beside her. "This is too sweet! We get the vial and the doctor. The FBI are going to be angry, eh, my friend?"

Tennyson grinned tightly as he jerked open the door that led outside to the stairs and the underground garage. "More than a little, Dr. Romanov. More than a little. Did you leave our calling card?"

"Of course," the Russian replied, hurrying down the stairs. Wind and rain whipped around them, the water making spots upon the crimson shirt he wore. "They'll know Black Dawn got to the anthrax and Dr. Harper," he gloated. "That other agent is going to be angry and in a lot of trouble. He left her wide open for the plucking…"

Chapter 6

Maggie sat shivering in the rear seat of the white van. The material of her blouse clung to her chilled flesh. She had gotten soaked in the downpour as they made a dash for the van, a vehicle, she noted, that looked exactly like that housing the FBI mobile headquarters. Her head spun with a hundred questions and no answers. She had to think!

She tried to steady her breathing. The driver and passenger side windows were tinted, making it impossible for those who passed by to see inside. Fear zigzagged through her as she studied the man who had joined them. Small and lean, he looked to be of South American descent. Something about his demeanor told Maggie he was a killer, not a doctor like she knew both Tennyson and Romanov to be. She still couldn't believe that Tennyson, who five years ago had been considered

a leading expert on anthrax epidemics, was now stealing what he thought was DNA-altered anthrax for a far
more deadly purpose.

Shaken, Maggie tried to see out the windows. The
thunderstorm was gathering in fury, the rain sleeting
almost horizontally, so she would see almost nothing. They passed the marina at a crawl, probably so
they wouldn't garner attention. Where was Shep? Why
had he been delayed? Her mind spun drunkenly and
she glanced to her left, where the South American sat
dressed in military fatigues, a pistol at his side. His
feral-looking black eyes regarded her as if he were a
hooded snake and she the prey, she noted, a shiver of
terror running down Maggie's spine.

"Can't you at least uncuff me now? I'm losing circu-
lation in my hands and arms," she pleaded to Tennyson,
who sat ahead of her in the passenger seat. Romanov
was driving, all his attention on the wet, flooded surface of the road as they headed toward the main route
off Hilton Head Island.

Tennyson turned his head. "Juan, take the cuffs off
Dr. Harper and put them back on when she's got her
hands in front of her."

Maggie gulped as the man unwound like a lethally
coiled snake. She leaned forward and turned her back
toward him so he could reach the cuffs more easily.

"*Señorita*, do not think this is an invitation to try and
leave," he warned her in a smooth tone.

Trying not to jerk away from his rough, hurtful
hands as he unlocked the cuffs, Maggie groaned, then
slowly eased her arms forward. As soon as she slumped
wearily back in the seat, Juan loomed over her grasp-

ing her wrists to cuff them once more. When he had finished, he sat back down and smiled at her.

"You are a pleasant surprise, *señorita*. Dr. Tennyson did not think we could capture you alive. But here you are."

Trying to think coherently, Maggie watched as the van turned onto the main route off the island. The thunderstorm was abating, the rain reducing in fury. Ahead, she could see the arc of the bridge to the mainland. Shep would come back to an empty villa. He wouldn't have a clue as to what had happened. Swallowing hard, she rasped, "Bruce, how did you get the FBI code?"

Chuckling indulgently, he relaxed, turned in his seat and gave her the kind of fond look a father might give an ignorant child. "Dr. Harper…may I call you Maggie? You and I were always on pleasant terms as colleagues at those conferences around the world."

Instinctively, Maggie realized the only way out of this situation was to lull them into thinking she wasn't going to try an escape. She was; at first opportunity, she planned to try and get away from them. But they didn't need to know that now. "Yes…of course…call me Maggie."

Smiling genially, Tennyson twisted his head toward Romanov. "See? I told you so. She's one of us. She just doesn't know it yet."

Romanov shrugged. "We'll see…" he said tensely as he pressed on the accelerator. They sped out of the storm and back into sunlight and a dry highway as they drove across the causeway.

Turning, Bruce smiled triumphantly. "Well, it was rather easy, Maggie. What the FBI doesn't know is that we've got a mole inside their bureau. We have been given the daily change of codes ever since we started tailing you to get the DNA anthrax."

"A mole?" she gasped. "Who?"

"*Señorita*, surely you do not think we're so stupid as to tell you?"

"She's just naive," Bruce chortled. "My dear Maggie with the beautiful red hair, we aren't going to divulge any names to you."

"Is that because you're going to kill me sooner or later?" she demanded. Fearing that they would, she turned her mind to escape plans. The van had three exits: the front passenger's and driver's doors and a double door at the rear. There were no side doors. It made escape impossible. Plus, her hands were cuffed, but Maggie knew she could manage with them bound if the opportunity to escape occurred.

"Oh, my, no," Bruce said in exaggerated horror. "Maggie...you're one of the world's top virologists." He preened a little and patted his chest confidently. "I'm the best in my country, Britain. Alex, as you well know, is at the top if his game in Mother Russia."

She glanced at the lethal-looking Juan. "And him?"

"Captain Juan Martinez is from Brazil, my dear. He's a part of Black Dawn, as well. You might think of him as your bodyguard and our protector." Smugly, Bruce smiled at his companions. "Although I must admit, we've all been through mercenary training over in Afghanistan with some of the best bioterrorists in the world. We pulled off a coup by getting you and the attaché case."

Sitting there, Maggie felt her heart ache, but not out of fear. She was thinking about Shep, what might have been and would probably never be, now. Despite their bickering and their problems, she loved him. She had to admit it to herself, because chances were she would soon be dead. It was just a matter of time. If there was any solace to the situation, it was that Shep had been gone when Black Dawn attacked. At least his life had been spared.

"And if my partner had been there when you came," she asked, "would he be here with me?"

"Him?" Bruce wrinkled his long, narrow nose. "Of course not. He's just a mule. A soldier. He doesn't have your knowledge, Maggie."

"No," Alex said with undisguised pleasure, "he would be dead."

Cold terror worked through Maggie and her stomach clenched painfully. Once more she tried to think, but it was so hard. She watched as Romanov took a route north on the mainland once they had crossed the two arcing spans of the bridge. "Where are you going?" she asked.

"You'll find out," Bruce said.

"You're kidnapping me. Why don't you release me? You've got the anthrax. Isn't that what you came for?"

Bruce gave her a grin. "Maggie, if I have my way, I want to extend an invitation to you to join us."

Stunned, she felt her mouth drop open. "What?"

With an eloquent shrug, Bruce said, "Why not? Think about it, Maggie. Black Dawn has fifty of the best and brightest academicians from around the world, all of whom are at the top of their game as virologists, microbiologists, physicists and biologists. We really aren't the threat I see written all over your face, my dear. We are a band of people who see our world sinking into absolutely destructive ways. We want to change that. And we can. We have amassed more brain power than any one nation could ever think of having. We've developed a plan, a global one, to get rid of this rotten, infected environment we are forced to live in. We want a peaceful world, Maggie. Not the world we live in now, which is full of hatred, prejudice and murder, attackers who get off from death sentences or well-earned prison terms. No," he said, his smile disappearing and his eyes narrowing as he gauged her response, "we want to cleanse the world and start over. And we've got the knowledge and the means to clean our house."

Her heart thumped in terror over his words. He was insane. They all were, as far as Maggie was concerned. But she didn't dare show her disdain for his ideas. "By releasing the anthrax you intend to wipe out several populations?"

"Yes, worldwide," he murmured in a pleased tone. Waving toward the front window of the speeding van, he added, "We tried it on Juma Indian Village in Brazil. It was a success. Fifty percent of the population died." His brows knitted. "The only problem was that our anthrax lab exploded, attacked by a secret U.S. government force, and we lost all our hard work. The professor heading the project was also captured. Unfortunately, he's in U.S. custody at a prison near Washington, D.C." He pointed to the attaché case next to Juan's right leg. "That's why we needed the freshly altered DNA anthrax. We had none of our own. Well, now that we do, we'll take it to our new lab facility over in Albania, which is well hidden in the mountain country, and we'll produce a lot of action in a hurry. Then we can move forward with our plan to try it on a major U.S. city. When that is successful, we'll have all our members fly to different cities around the world and start the epidemic."

The fact that they did not currently have any anthrax to use on a city provided Maggie with some relief. She knew how fast anthrax could be made, however. Little did they know that what they had in that vial was only E. coli, not anthrax. But it would take them days after smearing it on petri dishes to find that out, and that bought her time. As well as Shep and the FBI. *Shep!* Her heart twinged with pain again. How vital he was to her. Why hadn't she told him how she really felt about him? She was just as stubborn as he was when it came to waving a flag of truce and letting her real feelings be known. Meeting him again had undone her in the sweetest of ways. His kiss had opened up the beautiful treasures they'd shared before, treasures Maggie wanted now—and forever. But those hopes were now dashed. She was captured by a band of international terrorists who saw the world as one big infection that needed to be eradicated.

"So, you're going to fight fire with fire?" Maggie demanded throatily. "You see the world dominated by bad things, so you're going to let loose a bad bacteria to kill them off?"

"That's putting it crudely, my dear. Like cures like, does it not?"

"Not exactly," Maggie murmured tautly. "I agree we've got a lot of rotten qualities in the world today, but think of how many *innocent* people you're going to kill to get rid of those others."

"That's the price of a new world order, Maggie. We don't like it, but we can't separate out the rotting apples."

"Children are innocent!" she exclaimed hotly. "You

three can sit here and condemn babies and children to a horrible, lingering death from this anthrax and say it's all right?"

Tennyson lifted his long, spare hands. "Maggie, my dear, don't become upset over this. Look at the larger picture. The racial hatred, the prejudice, the murderers, thieves, rapists, the pedophiles—scum of the earth— will die, too. We want a world cleansed of such vermin." Tennyson's voice grew deep with conviction. "I don't know about you, but I'm sick and tired of seeing our collective legal systems let off the damned criminals. Who gets hurt? We, the victims of crime, do. Criminals are given more rights than we are! Our systems of law stink. They have swung too far to protect the rights of cold-blooded murderers. Well," he said with satisfaction, "that's all changing now. Members of Black Dawn have sworn a pledge to eradicate them all. We want a world order where people will be free from such vile and infectious trash!"

As she watched his green eyes glitter with fervor, Maggie tried to appear sympathetic. She had to somehow lull Bruce into thinking she was on his side. "You know, you have a point."

"Yes," Alex crowed, "we do!"

"My own children," Bruce told her fervently, "were here in U.S. schools for two years while I was working with your government. I was shocked at how degraded your public schools have become. My little Lisa was kidnapped by a local gang and held for ransom." He squeezed his eyes shut for a moment to get a handle on his emotions. Voice cracking, he said, "And my boy, Christopher, who is only nine, was pistol whipped by another gang of boys after school as he waited for his bus."

Anger shook the scientist's voice and he glared at Maggie. "Is it any wonder I feel the way I do? I paid the ransom and our daughter was returned to us, after being held for three days. She has changed so much since it happened. She was such a bright, beautiful ray of sunlight in our lives before. Now…" He lowered his voice, the pain obvious "…she is hyperalert, she trusts no one. She truly distrusts males—not that I blame my daughter—and worst of all, she shrinks away from me when I want to give her a loving squeeze or a hug to let her know I love her."

Sadly, he looked away. "My children have suffered gravely in your rotting country, Maggie. The worst thing is that, in both instances, no one was held accountable. The police to this day have not arrested anyone for those crimes. The experiences my children had are what drove me into working with Black Dawn. I want a *better* world for my children to grow up in. I want it free and clear of vermin. My wife is in anguish over what happened to our children. She is angry. And so am I. Those gangbangers got off scot-free!"

"I'm sorry," Maggie whispered. "I truly am, Bruce. I know our legal system isn't perfect—"

"Not anywhere near it," he snarled under his breath. Eyes glimmering, he said, "But now there's a way to change all this. I'm proud to be a part of Black Dawn. I feel badly that some innocents will lose their lives, but in the long run, we can eradicate the killers, the drug addicts, the thieves, the rapists and those who would stalk our children and abuse them. No, I want this new world order. My children have suffered enough!"

Maggie played along. She *did* feel for Bruce's children. What a terrible experience they'd had in the U.S.

"You're right, Bruce, this is terrible. And your children... I can only imagine how hard it was on you and your wife at the time the incidents happened."

Miserably, Bruce nodded. "Now you see why I'm backing Black Dawn. We *must* eradicate these inhuman species from the face of the earth. Black Dawn's mission is to create a sane world once more. Not like this world we live in." He jabbed his finger at the aluminum case. "*This* is our way of doing it. When it's all over, we can begin again. Laws can mean something. An eye for an eye. None of this coddling of prisoners. The death sentence will be imposed, and believe me, it won't take twenty years to send one of them to their rightful death, either."

Maggie nodded sympathetically, playing the game. As they drove north, she had noted, sunshine and blue sky had taken over once more. Traffic was at a minimum. She had to escape. How? Bruce was now treating her like she was already a member of Black Dawn. "You know, what you say makes a lot of sense," she forced herself to say. "Maybe you could tell me more about Black Dawn, about your goals, as we drive?"

Heartened, Bruce grinned. Alex perked up. Juan gave her a distrusting look, however; he obviously didn't believe her change of heart. The two scientists did, but the Brazilian military officer saw right through her. Maggie forged ahead anyway. She knew that no help, no rescue was coming for her. It was up to her to devise her own plan of escape.

"Maggie?" Shep's voice rang hollowly through the villa. He dropped the pizza at the door, which he had found wide open. Instantly, he pulled the gun from the holster beneath his left armpit. His heartbeat tripled in time. Thunder caromed around him, shaking the building in the aftermath. With his hand wrapped firmly around the butt of the pistol, he moved swiftly across the foyer, pointing the gun first right and then left. Nothing! No one. *Maggie! Oh, no. What happened?*

Breathing hard, Shep moved toward the left, where the two bedrooms were located. The attaché case was gone! Hurriedly, he searched the rest of the villa. Maggie was gone! Moving quickly back to the door, he examined the wood on the door frame. It showed no signs of a forced entry.

Jerking the cell phone out of his pocket, he made a call to the FBI. In a few minutes, they would come running to the villa, fully armed. Studying the entryway, he wondered what had happened. Maggie knew better than to open the door. Black Dawn had struck, he was sure. Walking back to Maggie's bedroom again, he rapidly searched it. On the dresser he saw a business card. Peering down at it, he felt his heart stop for a moment. On it was printed a caduceus—two snakes entwined around a staff. Only instead of the wings appearing in the symbol for physicians, the top of this caduceus held a globe of the world.

Shep's mouth went dry. He didn't dare touch it, for fear of smearing fingerprints that might be on it. It was Black Dawn's symbol.

Spinning around, he felt a cry of terror working up through his chest and into his throat. He wanted to scream out in rage, but forced himself to walk back to the living room and wait for the FBI to arrive. His heart hurt. Terror ate at him. He'd failed Maggie—just as he'd failed Sarah. Closing his eyes, he sternly ordered himself to stop letting his wildly escaping emotions take over. He had to think! And think clearly.

Hearing the thud of booted feet coming down the outer hall, he met the FBI contingent at the front door.

The FBI team was composed of six men and women, all snipers carrying M-16 rifles that were locked and loaded. They were dressed all in black, including flak jackets and protective helmets. Their leader, Agent Bob Preston, halted. In his late thirties, he was about six foot tall, lean like a whippet, with sharp, alert eyes and a long, narrow face.

"Black Dawn has taken Dr. Harper and the attaché case," Shep told him. The looks on the faces of the FBI contingent told him they were all crushed by the news.

"But, how—" Preston began in a strangled tone.

"Maggie let them in," Shep breathed savagely, pointing to the doorjamb. "For whatever her reason, she let them in."

Preston studied the wood along the lock for only a moment, then he straightened and turned. "Bayard, Mitchell and Connors, do a door-to-door search. Canvass the area, starting with this floor. The rest of you, spread out. See if you can find anyone who might have seen something in the last thirty minutes around this building or the underground garage. Call the instant you hear anything."

The FBI agents scattered like a dark cloud of startled ravens, moving in all directions. Shep walked back into the villa, shoulders slumped with guilt and anguish. Preston followed him into the quiet confines and shut the door. He shouldered the rifle, his face grim.

"Dr. Harper knew not to let anyone in unless they had the code. That code was changed daily."

Unhappily, Shep nodded. "I was gone thirty lousy minutes. I didn't think Black Dawn would know where we were, because we changed our plans at the last moment." Raking his fingers through his dark hair, Shep cursed softly at his own misguided rationale. He led the agent to the bedroom. "There's a business card there, on the dresser. It needs to be dusted for fingerprints."

Nodding, Preston put on a pair of latex gloves, picked up the item and placed it in a secure plastic Ziploc bag. "No sign of a struggle?"

Looking around, his brows locked downward, Shep muttered, "Nothing's been knocked over. There's no evidence of blood splatters anywhere. Nothing else seems taken. Just Maggie and the attaché case…"

Preston sighed and moved back to the kitchen, where he laid his rifle down and took off his helmet. He pulled a radio from inside his flak jacket. "The good news is they couldn't have gotten very far."

"We need a lead. A break," Shep muttered, more to himself than to Preston. *Damn!* He'd left Maggie alone and unprotected. What was wrong with him? But, he had been *sure* she wouldn't open the door to anyone but him. Some kind of ruse had to have been used. She had to have been thoroughly tricked, because she wasn't a fool. And he was sure she'd have used the code. Rubbing his jaw, he waited until Preston got off the phone.

"Only your mobile HQ knows the daily code, right?" Shep demanded.

"Only them. I'm the one who chooses the password. We then send it out to you at 0800 each morning."

"*How* do you send it?"

"Scrambled. If you're thinking someone picked it up on the airwaves, there's no way it could have happened.

That scramble is solid. No one to our knowledge has broken the encoding."

"Unless…" Shep began thinking slowly out loud. "Unless one of your people is a mole and slipped Black Dawn the code."

Preston's dark eyes sharpened. His mouth turned tight. "A mole?" he demanded scathingly. "I think you're feeling guilty over screwing this up, Hunter, and you're trying to pin Dr. Harper's kidnapping on the FBI. That isn't going to wash with us. Your theory is DOA."

Wrestling with his anger, Shep growled, "*No* agency is foolproof and you know it. The FBI has had its share of moles in the past, so don't try and sanitize that possibility with me. It won't work."

Preston's face whitened but before he could say anything, his cell phone squawked. Flipping it open, he growled, "Preston here…"

Shep saw the expression on the agent's face turn hopeful. Tensely, he waited until Preston was off the phone.

"What have you got?"

"Good news. Mitchell just interviewed a tourist staying here. She reported seeing a plain white van with tinted windows near the underground garage roughly twenty minutes ago."

"Did she see anyone?"

"Yes," Preston said triumphantly, "two men and a woman. She described the woman as having red hair."

Shep's heart squeezed. "Was she all right?"

Preston nodded. "Yes, she said the woman had her hands bound behind her in what looked like handcuffs, but she appeared okay. She said they opened the rear of the van and hurriedly climbed in. The van left—"

he looked at his watch "—around 6:45, give or take a few minutes."

"Did she see the make of the van?"

Preston shrugged. "No, she didn't. You know how women are about that. They never notice the make of a vehicle, just the color."

"Damn!"

"Hold your horses, Hunter, we might have another break." Preston smiled a little. "Did you know the bridge leaving the island has a camera trained on outgoing traffic? I'm going to contact the highway department and tell them to hold that piece of videotape for us. If there was a white van going across that bridge, then we know for sure they're on the mainland instead, and we can mount a search."

Heartened, Shep said, "Let's keep our fingers crossed."

"You get down to the bridge," Preston suggested. "There's a road on the right that leads to a small blue building where a security guard and the camera are located. Call me if you find anything?"

"In a heartbeat," Hunter promised, already out the door. As he hurried down the stairs, he barely took note that the thunderstorm was over. It was 7:00 p.m. They had another two hours of daylight, more or less, to try and spot that white van. The air was pungent with the odor of freshly washed pine trees as he loped through the underground garage to the sedan. Sliding in, he focused his mind as he drove out into the slanting, evening sunshine. First he had to contact Perseus. He had to let Morgan know what had happened. Shep's conscience ate at him as he punched in the Perseus number on his cell phone. What would they think of him botching this top event? Even worse, if Maggie was still alive, what would *she* think of him? He'd let her down, just as he'd let Sarah down.

As he sped along the rain-washed black asphalt, houses and trees sped by him in a blur. Once out on the main route, Shep stepped on the accelerator. Speed was of the essence now. If that videotape revealed a white van going to the mainland, that was all he needed.

"Lookie here," the security guard, Jameson Curtis, said in a soft, Southern drawl. Dressed in dark blue pants and a short-sleeved, light blue shirt, he sat in his chair pointing to one of the television monitors as he ran the last hour's videotape on it. Scratching his balding head, he said, "Here's your suspect, Mr. Hunter." He punched the stop button on the VCR. Squinting his gray eyes, Curtis added, "And you can see the license plate on that van plain as day." He wrote the number down for Shep.

Nodding his thanks, Shep reached for his cell phone.

"We've hit gold," he told Preston, giving him the van's make, model and plate number. He heard Preston repeat the information into another phone plugged into the FBI agency, where the numbers would be run and the owner located.

"Wait one minute," Preston said.

Impatiently, Shep waited, staring at the television screen as he did so. The white van, which looked like an ordinary workmen's truck, had some scrapes and a dent on the right rear side, he noted. Slightly dusty, slightly used, it would blend into a stream of traffic with no problem.

"Hunter?"

"Yeah?"

"The van is registered to an auto rental place in Savannah—secondhand vehicles mostly. The man who signed the five-day rental is Bruce Tennyson. Does that ring any bells with you?"

"Hell, yes!" Shep exclaimed softly. His heart beat hard. "Dr. Bruce Tennyson is a British virologist who used to work for the U.K. on top secret projects that involved creating viruses for biological warfare situations. He disappeared, literally, five years ago after coming back from a two-year stint here in the U.S.A."

"And he's in Black Dawn?"

"The list I've got says he is. A Professor Valdemar identified him as one of the key leaders in the movement."

"Jackpot," Preston whispered.

"Send out a statewide APB on him. In the meantime, I'll rent a single-engine airplane from the Hilton Head airport and try and locate them from the air. A plane flying a hundred and fifty miles an hour can cover a lot of terrain in a hurry. Do you have any aircraft available?"

"Negative, we don't. That's a good idea. Rent a plane and keep in touch. We still don't know which way they went once they hit the mainland."

"I know. I'll start a search grid. I'll let you know more about it when I'm airborne so we can coordinate."

"Fine. Preston, out."

Flipping the phone case closed, Shep thanked the security guard and hurried to the car. Looking up at the sky, he eyed the thunderheads all around the island. Flying could get dicey in a small, fixed-wing aircraft without state-of-the-art instrumentation. It would certainly be seat-of-the-pants flying. Climbing into his car, Shep sped off toward the airport. On the way, he called Perseus again to keep them updated.

At the airport, he hurried to a small office that had Cessna printed on the door. Pulling out his wallet, Shep took out his flying license, the first thing they'd demand in renting him a plane. As he entered the small, cramped office, which reeked of cigarette smoke, a gray-headed man with a goatee and glasses looked up. He was tall and spare and dressed in a red T-shirt and jeans.

"Can I help you?"

"Yes," Shep said, laying his license on the counter between them. "I need to rent the fastest plane you've got."

Chuckling, his eyes crinkling, the man studied the license. "Well, Mr. Hunter, the only planes we have are Cessna 150s. We use 'em to teach folks how to fly."

"Are any available?"

"Just one."

"I'll take it."

"How long will you need it?"

"Twenty-four hours. I intend to do some flying in the local area—maybe as far north as Charleston or down into the Savannah area."

The man shrugged and pulled out an order form. "You got a lot of thunderstorms right now, young fella."

"I flew jets in the Air Force," Shep told him. "I think I can handle some thunder bumpers." He was in a hurry, and the man seemed interminably slow. Shep tried not to convey his sense of urgency. He didn't want to cause a panic with the locals by alerting them of any danger in the area.

"Yes, sir, I guess you can."

Just then, Shep's phone rang. He instantly opened it and answered, "Hunter here."

"Preston. We got another break. We sent out the APB, and a South Carolina state trooper just reported seeing a white van of that description going north on Interstate 95, heading in the direction of Charleston."

Hurriedly, Shep grabbed an air map and spread it out on the counter. Fixing their position, he intently studied I-95 north of Hilton Head. "I see the route."

"There's a lot of hill country covered in pines up that way. And a lot of back roads. Dirt roads."

"That's okay, it gives me a direction."

"Listen, I'm coordinating for a helicopter out of Charleston, but the place is socked in with thunderstorms and they're grounded for now."

"That's okay, I'll be going up into that area real fast." Shep glanced over at the old man, who was painstakingly filling out the form.

"Good. Once you get airborne, stay in touch."

"Don't worry, I will," Shep promised.

Chapter 7

The light, airy movements of the Cessna 150 felt good to Shep. Almost nurturing. He was always at his best when he was in the air. As he guided the white aircraft northward after taking off from Hilton Head Island, the blazing western sun momentarily blinded him. He pulled aviator glasses from his shirt pocket and put them on. In the copilot's seat to his right lay his cell phone and an opened map of the area. Shep had been in a hurry to get into the air and had done a cursory walk-around of the airplane before leaping on board and taxiing straight to the takeoff point.

Checking the radio, he found to his dismay that it wasn't working. Cursing softly he glanced over at his cell phone. At least he had that. He wouldn't be completely out of touch with Preston, who was now coordinating the entire search and capture effort from the Hilton Head police station.

Though grateful for any backup, Shep planned on being the one to bring these terrorists in. Grimly, he swung the aircraft over the I-95. It was thick with traffic between Hilton Head and Charleston. He took out his binoculars and checked out anything that looked white from his flying altitude of one thousand feet. By federal aviation requirements, no aircraft could fly lower than that unless landing or taking off. Shep had pushed the throttle of the single engine to the redline position. The Cessna 150 wasn't a racehorse. It puttered along in the turbulent blue sky that was gathering clouds and threatening more thunderstorms. The air was unstable due to the humidity and warmth coming in off the ocean. The Cessna attendant had warned him that another cold front was coming like a freight train from the west, bringing with it a thirty-degree drop in temperature. That was why the sky around him was suddenly alive with angry-looking stormclouds.

A little Cessna 150 couldn't take the wrenching updrafts and downdrafts of a thunderstorm, and Shep would be forced to fly around the huge formations or under them. The Cessna couldn't climb over ten thousand feet, so trying to rise above one of these huge, forty-thousand-foot cumulonimbus clouds was out of the question. No, he'd have to dodge and dart between the mountainous masses instead. That, or fly real low, in which case he'd have rain to contend with, as well as fierce air pockets. If he got too close to the ground and got slammed by one of these big fellows, he'd be history. Downdrafts had knocked airliners out of the sky at Dallas International Airport, and hundreds of people had died. Such a force would take his little aluminum Cessna and bend it like a pretzel in a matter of seconds, smashing him and it like a fly beneath a flyswatter into the muddy earth below.

Trying to keep the plane stable was nearly impossible, Shep found. Air pockets kept swatting the game little aircraft about, lifting or dropping it a hundred feet at a time, like a roller coaster. Anyone not used to flying would have been thrown long ago, but not Shep. He was used to powering hot chargers like the F-15 Falcon fighter, the premier jet of the Air Force. This constant bouncing around in the evening sky didn't bother him at all. It did make looking through binoculars tougher, however.

As he flew northward along I-95, his gut kept nagging at him. What if Tennyson didn't stay on the interstate? Shep knew he wasn't a stupid man. Tennyson would realize he would be safer and less likely to be spotted if he took a rural, less-traveled route. Playing his hunch, Shep grabbed at the open map and spread it out across the yoke in front of him. He devoted intense seconds to determining his present position. To his right was the Broad River and Port Royal Sound, a rectangular inlet on the South Carolina coast. North of the river mouth was Parris Island, the Marine Corps boot camp. There was also a marine air station on the island. To Shep's left was the small town of Switzerland.

How fast could the van be traveling? Shep tried to project the situation in his head. Speeds were supposed to be no more than sixty-five miles per hour, but just by eyeballing the traffic, he knew most cars were probably averaging around seventy-five. His little Cessna was pushing ninety-five miles an hour, which was close to its top speed. Calculating things in his head, he studied the map again. Tennyson would probably use a side

road, if he could. Where was the man going? What
was his target objective? Who was he going to meet?
And where?

Blowing a puff of air from between his lips, Hunter
devoted half his time to flying the plane and the other
to studying the map of the area beneath him. He tried
to ignore his anguish and guilt over allowing Maggie to
be kidnapped. Was she all right? Was she dead? What
would Tennyson do to her? All the ugly thoughts that
came up only scored his aching heart more deeply.

Cursing softly, he shoved his terror for Maggie aside.
He had to in order to think clearly. He barely had an
hour and a half's worth of light left. Trying to search
for the van at night would be impossible. They would
have to rely solely on the highway patrol, which greatly
lowered the possibility of finding Maggie at all. Being
in the air was a huge advantage, but the willing little
Cessna simply didn't have the technical gear aboard to
accomplish night hunts like a military aircraft could.

Thirty minutes later, Shep diverted to a rural route,
Highway 17. It paralleled I-95 going north, but was far
less traveled. The sun was dipping closer to the western horizon, the streamers of light now caught by the
gathering thunderstorms, which looked like orderly soldiers marching determinedly toward the South Carolina
Low Country. Feeling panicked because he knew he
couldn't dodge the massive storm front, Shep notched
up the throttle to a hundred miles an hour. Below him,
the traffic on Highway 17 was sparse. His gaze swept
the route relentlessly. It was fairly flat country beneath
him, but thick with pine trees. He had reached the Ace
Basin National Wildlife Refuge, drained by the Combahee River.

The whole area was a huge marsh, Shep realized. The place must be alive with alligators, not to mention cottonmouth snakes that loved swimming in brackish water among rushes and reeds. The basin was ringed with millions of pine trees. It would be an excellent place to hide or meet someone.

Banking slightly to the left, Shep tipped the wing enough to see the highway ahead. Wait! His heart slammed against his rib cage. There! A white vehicle! Could it be them? Pulse pounding, adrenaline beginning to pump wildly through him, Shep tightened his hands around the yoke. He wanted to push the aircraft faster. The vehicle was miles ahead on a straight stretch and was heading for the bridge across the Combahee River. Wiping his mouth with the back of his hand, Shep glanced warily at the line of stormclouds, now looming closer. In another fifteen minutes he either had to turn back toward Hilton Head or fly a helluva lot lower than a thousand feet. The massive black-and-gray, churning cumulus were almost upon him. Dark sheets beneath the clouds promised heavy, almost blinding rain. Either way, he could crash if he wasn't careful.

The aircraft inched closer and closer to the white vehicle. Taking the binoculars, Shep raised them to his eyes, his heart thudding violently in his chest. It was a white van! It *had* to be Tennyson! His hunch had been correct!

A violent updraft struck the Cessna. Shep instantly released the binoculars to take hold of the yoke to steady the plane. The aircraft was lurched to the right like a toy in the sky. The binoculars struck the opened cell phone lying on the copilot's seat.

"Damn," Shep snarled as he wrestled with the plane.

Once he rode out the air pocket, he released the controls and reached out with his right hand. He shoved the heavy binoculars off the fragile cell phone. Picking it up, he pressed in some numbers. The screen did not light up. He tried it several times.

"Son of a bitch!" Again and again he tried it. Holding the yoke with one hand and opening the cell phone's battery case with the other, he checked to see if it was all right. It appeared to be. Once more he tried punching in the numbers to raise Preston. Nothing happened. Anger surged through Shep. The binoculars must have hit the device hard enough to loosen something inside it. Now there was no way to tell the FBI of his discovery.

Grimly, Shep thought about his options. There weren't many. He could land and try to find a phone to place the call. But where? Scanning the immediate area, he realized there was no airport available. Nor any suitable fields. He couldn't land in the marsh and he sure as hell couldn't land among the pines. Did he dare to stop following the van that he knew had Maggie on board? Tennyson could duck off the highway onto a lesser road and Shep could lose them completely. It was going to be dark in another half hour, at the most. What the hell could he do? Helplessly, he wondered how Maggie was doing.

"Bruce," Maggie said as sweetly as she knew how, "I have to go to the bathroom. Is there any chance we can stop?" She'd been able to lull Tennyson into thinking she was interested in joining Black Dawn. As a result, he'd ordered Juan to remove the strangling handcuffs. She now sat free and relaxed in the seat. Juan, however, did not trust her, and Maggie felt the soldier's dark, hooded eyes continuing to burn into her. She smiled as the doctor turned in his seat. It was nearly dusk, and they were surrounded by woods on both sides. It was a good place to try and make an escape. Maggie was scared. She wondered if they could hear her heart pounding raggedly in her breast.

There had been lightning and thunder around them for the last five minutes. Rain was starting to pound down upon them. It would be good cover if she got away. The thick stands of pines were less than a hundred feet from the highway and would provide enough cover for her if she was fast enough and smart enough. The rain, the whipping wind and the thunder would camouflage the noise of her escape *if* she made it to the trees. Maggie had no doubt that they'd track her down if possible. Still, they had to meet another contingent of Black Dawn in Charleston, so Tennyson might be torn between finding her and making the scheduled appointment.

Maggie knew that if she didn't escape they would take her with them—to Charleston and then overseas, to Albania. That was all she'd been able to get out of him thus far. She also knew that if she refused to join Black Dawn, he'd put a gun to her head and shoot her. It was clear to her now that Tennyson was a fanatic. Anyone who didn't join him was dead.

"Look at this!" Alex cried, and promptly slammed on the brakes. The van skidded slightly on the rain-slick asphalt.

Maggie peered through the windshield, past the beating wiper blades. The rain was so heavy that the blades couldn't do the job of helping with visibility. And suddenly, as if out of nowhere, dairy cattle were standing in the middle of the two-lane highway! To her left, she saw where a board fence had broken down, allowing a herd of at least forty Guernseys to escape. They ambled contentedly about munching roadside grass or chewing their cud.

With a curse, Tennyson said, "Juan, you and I will get them out of the way. I don't want you blowing the horn, Alex, and alerting anyone. They're dumb animals, they'll move if we shout and wave our hands."

Braking to a stop, Alex nodded.

Juan quickly moved to the rear of the van, opened the doors and hopped out.

This was Maggie's chance! Swallowing against a dry throat, she waited until Tennyson and Juan had covered their heads with their jackets and started running toward the disinterested dairy cows. Looking around, she spotted a piece of pipe, about two feet in length and big enough to do damage, lying near her feet. The attaché case was there, too. Hands growing icy cold, Maggie watched Alex. His attention was fixed on the action taking place on the highway, which seemed to stretch endlessly across the flatland. There was no other traffic in sight.

Maggie tried to quell her fear. With a jerk, she reached awkwardly down for the pipe, grabbed it and straightened.

Alex turned at her sudden, unexpected movement. "Hey!"

It was the only word he got out of his mouth. Grasping the pipe with both hands, she swung it as hard as she could. The blow caught him just above the nose with a sickening thunk. Romanov groaned and slid against the door unconscious. Blood spurted from a cut across his brow where the pipe had connected.

"Oh, Lord!" Maggie grabbed up the attaché case and scrambled on shaky legs toward the rear of the van. Escape! She had to escape! The instant her feet touched the wet asphalt, she ran from the van toward the trees at an angle that would hide her from the terrorists line of sight. How long would it be before Tennyson found her gone? Seconds!

The rain slashed at her face. She ran openmouthed, hoping the harsh sound of her feet on the pavement wouldn't be picked up by them. No one was coming to her rescue. Maggie knew that. Slipping, almost falling, she leaped for the berm. Steadying herself, she saw the trees, less than fifty feet away. Oh, Lord, let her make it! Let her make it to safety! It was so hard to see where she was going! The rain pummeled her brutally, the drops icy and huge. Her hair quickly became a soaked mass around her neck and shoulders.

"Stop!"

Tennyson's shout was drowned out by a roll of thunder.

Maggie involuntarily flinched, but kept running. She heard the zing of bullets. Pistols were being fired—at her. Only twenty-five feet to go! The grass was slick. She nearly fell twice. Gasping wildly for breath, she stretched her short legs as far as they could go. Lightning flashed so close that it made the hair stand up on the back of her neck. Instinctively, Maggie dove for the trees.

There! Safety at last! Looking around wildly in the graying light of dusk, the rain slashing violently at her face and eyes, Maggie kept on running. Her lungs burned. Her breath was coming in ragged gasps. She again heard Tennyson's voice. Close! He was so close! Maggie knew he was strong and athletic and had a much longer stride than she. It would be no time before he caught up with her.

The trees swallowed her up. Brush grew in clumps here and there, and thick brown pine needles carpeted the forest floor. Because sunlight didn't reach the earth in these massive groves of pines, the undergrowth was nearly nonexistent. She heard pistols being fired. Bullets sang by her head once again, some striking pines nearby. Flinching, she tried to shield her eyes with her free hand as she ran. Like shrapnel, the splinters could easily wound her or enter her eyes and blind her.

Running, her knees weak with fear and exhaustion, Maggie felt the attaché case numbing her wet, slick fingers. It was slowing her down. She had to get rid of it! Up ahead, she suddenly saw a clearing. What was it? Barely able to make it out through the thick veil of rain and the buffeting wind, Maggie tried to quicken her pace on the slippery pine needles. As the trees thinned ahead of her, she realized she'd reached a river. *A river!*

A plan came to mind. She jerked a look over her shoulder. The rain was so heavy that she couldn't see her pursuers. If she couldn't see them, they couldn't see her. Changing direction, she headed toward the muddy-looking ribbon of river. As she neared the marshy bank, she tossed the attaché case into the tall, dark reeds growing there. It promptly disappeared, swallowed up. Good!

Turning on her heel, Maggie headed back into the relative safety of the trees. She heard Tennyson shouting to Juan. They were to her left. *Good!* Somehow she'd evaded them, but Maggie knew it wasn't over by a long shot. Somewhere she had to find a place to hide. The land was becoming slightly hilly. Black rocks jutted out here and there. She had to hide! She knew Juan might find her. A trained mercenary, he was probably a ruthless hunter.

As she ran, Maggie thought of Shep. She loved him! She'd never stopped loving him, she realized. Would she be given a chance to consummate her love with him? To let him know how she felt about him? Running raggedly now, because she was out of breath and not used to this kind of physical stress, Maggie knew she had to push on or die.

Alex Romanov groaned. His hand went to his bleeding forehead. What had hit him? Blearily, he sat up and looked through the windshield soaked with rain. The dairy cows had gone back through the broken fence. Where were Bruce and Juan? Looking over his shoulder, he remembered that Dr. Harper had struck him and knocked him out. She was gone! *No!*

Thunder caromed around him. Reaching for his pistol from his shoulder holster, he realized that his friends must be out trying to find her. Just as he prepared to open the door, he heard a strange noise. It wasn't thunder. And it wasn't lightning. What the hell was it? Stymied, he peered through the rain-washed windshield. His mouth dropped open. There, coming out of the slashing, wind-whipped rain, was a small white-and-red airplane! To his amazement, it was trying to land on the highway where they were parked! It wasn't more than half a mile away from the van. What the hell was going on?

Gripping the pistol, Alex stared at the aircraft. What should he do? Was the pilot having engine trouble? Was it the U.S. government? An enemy? He wasn't sure, but he wasn't going to take any chances. Even if the pilot managed to land in this frightening thunderstorm, he was a dead man.

Sucking in a breath through tightened lips, Shep held the Cessna as steady as he could. Drafts from the thunderstorm were trying to wrench him up and down. For every downward pressure against the plane, he had to instantly compensate as he guided the lightweight aircraft toward Highway 17 below. And he knew that with every hundred-foot drop in altitude toward that wet, slippery asphalt, the chances of him being killed were tripled. The storm raged around him. As it pummeled the aircraft the Cessna shuddered and bucked from side to side.

Shooting a glance at his altimeter, Shep saw he was less than two hundred feet above the roadway. A half mile ahead, he saw the white van. Grimly, he used his feet on the rudders to keep the plane on the glide path. The rain became worse. He could no longer see the van. He was trying to land this thing in the worst possible conditions known to pilots. It might work in an airliner, but not in one of these little aircrafts. The small plane was too lightweight, too responsive to every blast of wind, to every purging veil of rain that avalanched around him.

One hand gripping the yoke, the other on the throttle, Shep slowly cut his speed as the plane came closer and closer to the pavement below. Sweat popped out on his wrinkled brow. Shep's eyes narrowed to glacial ice. The road suddenly loomed up in front of him.

At the last second, a gust of wind slammed into the plane. It bobbled. The nose thrust upward.

No!

Jamming the yoke down to compensate, Shep saw the highway suddenly lunging upward at him. *Damn!* He'd overcompensated. Instantly, he yanked the nose up again. The asphalt still came at him, the Cessna's fixed landing gear crashing into the pavement. The plane bounced back into the air. Shep sucked in a breath. He steadied the plane and cut the engine. He jammed the throttle downward, shutting off the fuel supply.

The Cessna settled on the asphalt with a loud crunching sound. This time it didn't leap back into the air. The wind shoved it to the left, so Shep applied a strong left rudder to stop it from being blown off into the grass. He was down! Ahead, the veil of rain began to lift. Pushing on the rudder tips, he braked the plane, which came to a shuddering stop. Quickly grabbing his cell phone, he placed it beneath his jacket, then drew the Beretta out of its holster. As the rain curtain moved on past him, he saw that less than a quarter of a mile away the white van was parked in the middle of the road. Eyes narrowed and intense, Shep spotted a man in the vehicle.

Heart beating hard, Shep waited a moment to fix his position. There was no doubt that it was the Black Dawn van. So why was it parked there? He saw the dairy cows off to the side and the broken fence. Rapidly putting things together, he wondered where the other Black Dawn members were. This didn't look good. Had Tennyson stopped the van, taken Maggie out and shot her in the head, leaving her body in the woods that surrounded them? Heart aching, Shep wanted to deny that possibility. Maybe the cows had blocked their path? If so, why was the van still parked? It didn't make sense.

A flash of lightning overhead made Shep wince. The driver in the van still hadn't moved. The hair on Shep's neck went up in warning. If Shep got out of the airplane with pistol in hand, the man would know he was an agent or someone who recognized the van. That was a giveaway. Yet Shep didn't like the odds. He saw another curtain of heavy rain approaching from his left. The tree line there was about a hundred feet away. He would use the cover of the thunderstorm to make it to the woods. And then he could watch and wait. Or at least try to buy time until he could figure out what was going on.

As the rain struck, Shep waited until the van disappeared behind its fury. Scrambling out of the plane, he launched himself toward the trees. All the while, as he sprinted, he listened for gunfire. Nothing. The rain soaked him instantly. Wiping the water from his face once he got inside the woods, Shep tried to steady his breathing. As the veil of rain lifted, he saw the van again. Only from this angle, he realized the back doors were thrown open and there was only one person in the vehicle. So what had happened to Tennyson? The woman who had seen Maggie taken had said there were two men.

Panicking at the thought that two of them had taken Maggie into the trees to kill her and leave her body, Shep turned and began jogging alertly toward the river, which he knew was less than a quarter of a mile away. As he jogged, he took note of his surroundings. The forest floor was covered with a thick mat of slick brown pine needles. He heard shouting—a man's voice. And then gunfire ahead of him.

Dodging behind one of the slender pine trees, Shep halted. He breathed through his mouth, the rain washing across his frozen features. Blinking rapidly, he looked around the trunk. Frantically, he tried to fix the sounds, but they were blurred and distorted by the thunderstorm rolling violently across land.

More gunfire. *To the left! Yes!*

With a curse, Hunter shifted and dug his toes into the soft, muddy soil littered with pine needles. They were chasing someone! He heard two male voices drifting toward him from time to time. They seemed to be moving away. If only the storm weren't roaring around them! Other sounds were muffled so that Shep couldn't get a good fix on where they were coming from.

Running hard, he kept his gaze fixed to his right. Somewhere in this pine grove were two Black Dawn members. And if he was right, they were chasing Maggie down like a dog. Had she escaped? She must have! But how? His hopes skyrocketed. He held the gun high in his hand as he raced among the trees. Suddenly he tripped and fell. Slamming into the ground, Shep groaned, rolled once more and leaped back on his feet, barely missing a stride as he headed at an angle toward the voices of the terrorists.

Inside his head, inside his wildly beating heart, he prayed that Maggie was still free. He prayed that she could outsmart them in this brutal thunderstorm, use it to hide in, use whatever was around to keep her safe from the murdering thugs. Because, as Shep knew too well, if Maggie had escaped, and Black Dawn found her, they would kill her on the spot. There would be no mercy for the woman he knew he loved with a passion that had never died.

As he continued to sprint through the grove, he wasn't sure any longer if his eyesight was blurring because of the slashing rain or because of his own tears at discovering that he had never stopped loving Maggie through all this time. He wanted a second chance with her. Yet they were up against one of the top terrorist groups in the world, one of the best trained. Maybe Maggie's event riding would give her a better sense of how to use the terrain as a friend, as camouflage, than most people would. Maybe her superb athletic condition could give her the edge she needed to outrun these terrorists who wanted her blood and her life.

Swallowing hard, Shep tried to steady his breathing and keep up his ground-eating stride. When lightning suddenly sizzled above him, the entire area lit up like a million-watt lightbulb. Blinded momentarily, Shep hit the ground hard. Air woofed out of his body as he struck the earth. The thunder that followed milliseconds after the nearby lightning strike pounded his body like a pugilist's punishing blow. Stunned by the nearness of the strike, Shep slowly got to his feet. Damn, that was too close for comfort. Raking his face free of the water, he looked around, trying to separate sounds of nature from the sounds of the terrorists.

Shouts! To his right. They seemed to be following the course of the river. His gut told him to stay among the trees and work at an angle away from the terrorists. If Maggie was escaping, she wouldn't use the riverbank. Maybe she'd plunged in and tried swimming downstream? Shep was uncertain. Wiping his eyes again, he headed off through the darkening pines. Somehow, he had to pick up on Maggie before Black Dawn found her. It was an impossible task, yet Shep knew he had to try. He had to try because he loved her, and he couldn't even think of life without her vivid, vibrant presence lighting the darkness of his unworthy soul.

Chapter 8

Ragged gasps tore from Maggie's mouth as she labored to cross a stream that fed the river. The thunderstorm was violent, the rain slashing against her like icy, pummeling fists. Holding one arm up to protect her eyes from the furious wind whipping through the pines, she stepped into the stream. Maggie slipped. With a cry, she threw her arms outward, caught herself and then plunged forward. The bottom was muddy. How close were her pursuers? Gasping, she splashed drunkenly across the knee-deep stream, which was lined with tall green rushes. She grabbed a handful of them to steady herself. Instantly, they cut into her palm.

"Oww!" Maggie knew the reeds had to be handled carefully or they would lacerate her skin. Plunging her hand back into the water momentarily to wash away the blood, she wished she was taller. The rushes swatted heavily against her as she clambered up the bank on the other side.

A flash of lightning sizzled overhead. Maggie crouched, then dropped to her hands and knees. It had been so close! Almost instantly, thunder followed in its wake, reverberating through her as if she were a drum being struck. Hanging her head, the water dripping off her nose and chin, she tried to orient herself. Tennyson was probably still hunting for her along the river, but she couldn't be sure. She *had* to find somewhere to hide. Lifting her chin, she peered through the darkening forest. The flatland was swelling gently in a series of knolls, with more rocks jutting out here and there. Maybe, in the coming darkness and the overhang of one of those large, black boulders, she might be able to wait out her pursuers.

Rising on rubbery legs, Maggie realized she'd pushed her body to its limits. She desperately needed a fifteen minute rest to fuel back up for another run. The sheets of rain eased as she cautiously looked around. *Wait!*

A cry nearly tore from her. Was she seeing things? The dusk was deep, and there were so many shadows, so many things that resembled a stalking enemy. She quickly knelt down in order to be less of a target. Eyes narrowing, she gulped in unsteady breaths of air. Maggie gripped the wet, needle-covered ground to steady herself. *There!* Yes, she saw movement! *But, who?* It wasn't near the river; quite the opposite. Was one of the terrorists scouting inland for her? It was growing so dark. If only she could see better!

Just then, another bolt of lightning lit up the dusk, and Maggie's eyes widened enormously. There, no more than two hundred feet from her, moving from tree to tree, pistol held up and ready, was Shep! How could it be? Was she seeing things? Was she making this up because she knew she was going to die? Her mind froze and her heart swelled wildly. It *had* to be Shep! He was real. He *had* to be!

Rising unsteadily, Maggie wanted to call out to him, to get his attention, but she didn't dare. If Shep could hear her, so could her enemy. Sliding unsteadily away from the stream, she finally found purchase and broke into an erratic trot in his direction.

Something told Shep to look to his right. His lips parted as he saw a dark figure running toward him. Maggie! It was Maggie! She looked like a drowned rat, her hair a sleek dark ribbon against her skull, her clothes muddy, soaked and clinging to her skin. Her eyes were huge with terror, her mouth open in a silent scream. But she was all right! Shep turned on his heel and headed directly toward her with long, loping strides.

Lightning flashed as they drew close to one another. Shep controlled his desire to forget the dangers and just hone in on Maggie. He knew he couldn't resist touching her, though. Reaching out those last few inches, he curved his left arm around her sagging shoulders.

"Oh, Shep!" Maggie sobbed as she fell against his tall, hard frame. "You're here! You're here!" She gulped unsteadily and felt him press her hard against his chest in a protective gesture. Clinging to him, she found herself half crying, half laughing.

"Shh!" he rasped against her ear. Shep had dragged her against him and located a large pine tree to hide behind. Maggie felt so warm and soft against him. He felt her fingers digging convulsively into his shirt and chest as he guided her down between his opened legs.

They crouched together, using the tree as a natural cover and support, protecting them from prying, unseen eyes.

Bringing his other arm around her, and making sure the pistol was pointed away, he embraced her closely and just held her. She was trembling badly and shivering from cold and shock. Pressing kiss after kiss against her wet hair, ear and cheek, he whispered harshly. "It's going to be okay, Maggie. Lord, I thought you were dead. I thought the worst… I'm so glad you're alive, so glad…" He was blinded momentarily by a wave of emotion surging up through him as Maggie's hands moved around his neck. When she raised her chin, however, he saw the terror, the need, in her haunted hazel eyes. Shep would do anything to ease the fear from Maggie's eyes. Leaning down, he groaned her name and put the pistol aside. In one movement, he framed the cool, wet skin of her face, and kissed her. As his mouth closed over hers he felt her quiver beneath his warm, exploratory onslaught. Their mouths met hungrily. Almost violently. She tasted warm and alive. She tasted of life. He could feel her shivering in his arms, her mouth eagerly taking his and returning his wild, unexpected kisses with equal ferocity and need. Maggie was here! In his arms! She felt so damned good in his arms, like a wet, trembling puppy ecstatic at seeing his favorite human once again.

Tearing his mouth from hers, Hunter gazed deep into her tear-filled eyes. She looked so helpless in that moment, but Shep knew differently. With shaking fingers, he tried to wipe some of the rain away from her forehead and cheek. It was then that he realized she was crying. Probably out of sheer relief that she had not been abandoned by him, after all.

"How—" Maggie sobbed. She slid her hands over his face, the prickle of his beard feeling wonderful to her chilled fingers. "How did you find me?" Her voice cracked again, and she couldn't help sobbing openly. The sense of relief was profound within her. "I didn't think anyone would find me…"

Gently, he smoothed the rainwater from her flushed cheek. "I wouldn't stop until I did, brat. Not ever…" His deep voice shook with emotion. Picking up the pistol, Shep angled his back against the tree. For a moment they were safe. They were talking low, and the rain, wind and thunder would certainly hide their whisper as they huddled for warmth in one another's arms. Absorbing her presence, his long, powerful thighs like brackets supporting Maggie in the downpour, he felt some of his guilt dissolving.

Choking back her tears, Maggie pressed her cheek against his shoulder. "Just hold me, Shep! Oh…just hold me. I'm so tired…so weak…" But he was feeding her with his incredible strength, she knew. Just being able to cling to Shep as the darkness fell was wonderful. The way he soothed his hand across her shaking shoulders made her feel hope. Finally, after a few minutes, Maggie lifted her head and looked up at his dark, familiar features. Though he held her closely, his gaze was darting alertly around them. She felt tension sizzling through his body and knew he was doing what he did best as a mercenary. Never had Maggie felt as safe, as protected, as now.

"How…" She managed to croak, her fingers sliding against his hard jawline. "How did you find me?"

He glanced down at her for just a moment before continuing to scan the forest. No place was safe as long as those three Black Dawn members were hunting them. "A lot of luck. A woman going to her car in the garage at the villa saw you being taken away by two men. She described the van. We got a real break when we found out there's a highway camera at the bridge leaving Hilton Head. The security guard ran the video back, and we got the van's make and license plate number."

Amazed, Maggie sank more deeply against him. She felt Shep take her full weight. How good it was to be held by him! "And you followed us?"

He smiled grimly. "I rented a plane from the island airport and flew north. A highway patrolman saw the van and reported it. I flew north following I-95, until I found you."

Her eyes widened. "You were in a plane? In this storm?"

His mouth flexed. "I landed that sucker on the highway a quarter of a mile from where the van's parked."

Amazed, Maggie stared up at him. "That must have been right after I escaped! Did they shoot at you?"

Tightening his arm around her, Shep kissed her cheek. Very slowly, the storm was moving to the east. The rain was lessening, too. His lips near her ear, he said, "No. There was one man in the van, just sitting there. I used the rain as cover to leave the Cessna and make a run for the woods."

"Oh…" Maggie sighed and closed her eyes. "I brained him with a piece of pipe. His name is Alex Romanov, Shep. I knocked him out and escaped out the back of the van. There was a whole bunch of cows on the road. That's why we stopped. Bruce Tennyson and a Brazilian soldier named Juan left the van to shoo them off the road. I took a chance…" Maggie shivered violently at the memory of her bold escape. Pressing her face against his damp clothing, she sobbed, "I was so scared... I knew if they caught me, they'd kill me. Tennyson's a fanatic. I lulled him into thinking I'd join Black Dawn. That's why he took the handcuffs off me. I had to take a chance to get away when we got stopped by the cows." Opening her eyes, Maggie looked up at him. "I've never been so scared in all my life, Shep. This made event riding look like pabulum in comparison. I was sure they'd find me and shoot me."

Grimly, he grazed her wet hair with his fingers. "You're the bravest woman I've ever met, brat. There's not many that would have risked what you did."

Sniffing, Maggie wiped her nose and tried again to remove the tears from her eyes. "I just kept thinking, Shep...remembering the kiss we shared in Savannah, remembering all the good times we had together...and I didn't want to die. Tennyson is planning to meet another contingent of Black Dawn in Charleston, at a place known as the Kemper Plantation. And then we were all going to board a plane at the airport and fly to Albania. There are ten other Black Dawn members waiting for Tennyson to get to Charleston."

Nodding, Shep smiled warmly down at her as he slid his hand behind her head. "Maggie, what we have together, as flawed as it is, is good. You just hold on to that, okay? I'll get us out of this or die trying."

Trembling, Maggie absorbed his tender touch and the undisguised warmth and love she saw glittering in his narrowed eyes. *Love! Yes.* She wasn't going to lie to herself any longer about how she felt toward Shep—had always felt but had denied it—until now. Gulping, Maggie whispered, "We've got to get out of this jam, Shep. I want a second chance with you. You hear me?"

His mouth twitched in a bare smile. "Brat, you're my life. No matter what happens from here on out, we're going to work as a good team. I'm going to try and listen to you and not just take over like I usually do. I've learned my lesson. Okay?"

How wonderful those words sounded to Maggie! Jerkily, she nodded. The evening was cool in the wake of the storms and she shivered every now and then even though she was in Shep's powerful and protective embrace. "You're probably mad as hell at me for opening that door to the villa," she whispered apologetically. In bits and pieces, she told him what had happened. She saw Shep's brows move up in surprise.

"They had the *code*?"

"Yes!" Maggie whispered fiercely. "Believe me, that's the *only* reason I opened that door, Shep! Tennyson said there was a mole in the FBI feeding them information. That's how they got their hands on the password."

Shep cursed softly. He moved slightly, his legs starting to grow numb. "Preston needs to know this," he muttered darkly.

"How? I mean, we're literally out in the middle of nowhere here, Shep."

"Not quite, brat. When I was flying in to land on the highway, I spotted a dairy farm off to the right, about a mile from here. It's on the other side of the road where they parked the van. I hate to involve the locals in this mission but we haven't much choice. If we could get to the farmhouse, I could make the necessary calls."

"But…what about Black Dawn? How are we going to get across that road?"

Easing upward and taking Maggie with him, Hunter

rasped, "Very carefully." Pushing against the tree, he stretched to his full height. Maggie seemed diminutive against him, yet she had the heart of a courageous fighter. How many other women would have done what she had to escape? "Maggie the Lionhearted," he whispered in her ear. "Come on, let's go. Follow me closely. Keep your hand on my waist belt, okay? If I suddenly drop to my knees you drop, too. Understand? And if you hear something, jerk on my belt and we'll go hit the deck together. This storm is moving on. Pretty soon it's going to be very quiet, and that's when they'll hear us moving around."

Her heart beginning to beat hard with fear once more, Maggie nodded. But she also felt a warm glow at Shep including her, asking for her help on this mission. Now they were really a team. The words *I love you* were almost torn from her lips as she wrapped her fingers around his belt.

Shep had been right. Within minutes, the storm moved toward the coast. In its wake the darkness was so thick they had to move slowly from tree to tree, their hands outstretched to find the next one. More than once Maggie tripped over unseen rocks and stumps. Her grip on Shep's belt stopped her from pitching onto her nose. He kept his stride short for her sake. She was amazed at how silently he moved. His body seemed boneless in comparison to her awkward, stumbling movements. Maggie tried to tell herself that he was used to such danger and had overridden the adrenaline rush to think clearly. She hadn't.

From time to time, she heard Tennyson's voice echoing eerily through the woods. And each time, they'd drop to their knees and wait. Each time, Tennyson's furious voice seemed to come from the river. As they neared the highway, Maggie heard Alex's thick Russian accent calling out for Tennyson. She and Shep both froze, slowly kneeling on the wet needles. Frightened, Maggie realized suddenly how close they'd come to the van! Gulping, she tried to get a grip on her escaping terror. Her night vision had adjusted now, and she could just make out the outline of the van against the dark specter of pine trees on the other side of the highway. When she saw the stabbing beam of a flashlight, she froze. Her breath jammed her lungs.

Shep gripped her hand and pulled her up. "Come on!" He saw the man with the flashlight heading away from the van toward the river. Now was their chance to cross the road!

Surprised, Maggie was wrenched upward. She hurried to keep up with Shep's lengthening stride. He was going to cross the highway in plain view of Alex! Was he nuts? She didn't have time to ask. They ran hard, down the slope to the berm and then quickly across the wet asphalt. On the other side, Shep led her to the break in the fence the cows had made earlier.

Gasping, her heart wildly pounding in her chest, Maggie felt herself pulled up the slight incline. They were once more inside the relative safety of the pines. *Good!* Her terror subsided a little as they slowed their pace. With night vision, now, they could see the silhouettes of trees so they wouldn't run into them. Shep kept his hand wrapped tightly around hers. Within minutes, they broke out of the pines into a meadow, where the dairy cows were contentedly munching grass or lying down for the night.

"There!" Maggie gasped, and pointed to their left. "Lights!"

Shep halted. He was breathing easily, but he heard Maggie's noisy gasping and knew he had to wait and let her catch her breath. Taking her in his arms, he realized they were targets standing out in the middle of the grassy meadow. "That's the farmhouse," he told her raggedly. Giving her a gentle squeeze, he said, "Can you walk? We've got to keep moving."

Nodding, Maggie absorbed strength and warmth from his embrace. "Yes, let's go…"

Sometimes they walked through the short, wet grass and sometimes they jogged. Maggie kept staring at the lights of the farmhouse in the distance. It appeared so far away! A mile? Or more? She often glanced across her shoulder as they moved silently from one pasture to the next. Each was rectangular and fenced off with white board fencing. They would crawl beneath the lowest board to avoid detection. The cows would lift their heads, stare at them and then return to eating, as if they instinctly knew Maggie and Shep did not pose a threat to them.

The farmhouse was on a knoll surrounded by stately, ancient live oaks. As they hurried up the graveled roadway, a dog began barking. Maggie's heart thudded with fear. She felt Shep's hand tighten momentarily around hers to reassure her. When the front door of the house opened, Maggie saw a man with silver hair come out and look in their direction. The dog at his side appeared to be a collie. It was barking nonstop.

Shep mounted the steps of the porch and halted in front of the man, who appeared to be in his sixties. He had a pinched face, weathered by outdoor life and hard work. Dressed in a pair of coveralls, his spectacles resting low on his narrow nose, he put his hand on the dog to silence her.

"What do you want, stranger?" the old man demanded.

Shep had already put his pistol away because he didn't want to frighten the man. "I'm Shep Hunter. I work for the FBI." He drew out his badge case and held it up for the man to appraise. "We're in urgent need of a phone. May we come in and use one?"

"Elmer?"

The woman's voice drifted out the opened door. Maggie moved to Shep's side.

"Eh? Oh, it's some police people out here, Trudy…" Handing the badge case back to Shep, he asked, "There's trouble out there?"

Shep nodded. "Yes. We won't stay long. We just need a phone, Mr. …. ?"

"Elmer Hawkins." He turned to his wife, a thin woman with short gray hair, wearing jeans and sweatshirt. "This is my wife, Trudy. Trudy, let 'em in. These young folks are in trouble. They need the use of our phone."

Shep nodded his thanks as the farmer told them to follow him. Standing out on the porch made them all targets. He breathed a little easier when the door closed behind them.

Trudy clucked her tongue. "Ya'll are soaked like a bunch of river rats." She smiled warmly and said, "Come on, come to the kitchen. Let me get you something warm to drink?"

"No, ma'am… Thanks, but I need to get to a phone," Shep said.

Trudy pointed off to the right of the shining cedar foyer. "Right in there, in the living room, on the lamp table next to the couch." She turned her attention to Maggie. "You look cold to the bone. Let me get you a coat?"

Maggie smiled weakly. She had wrapped her arms around herself, but her teeth chattered no matter what she did to stop them. She knew she was slightly hypothermic. "Yes. That would be wonderful, Mrs. Hawkins. Thanks so much…"

"Go join him," Elmer said. "Trudy, I'll get these young people some dry jackets. You go make 'em some hot tea. This ain't a night fit for man or beast."

Grateful beyond words, Maggie walked quietly into the old, antique-filled living room. The furniture was all Victorian. Fresh flowers sat on a sideboy. The television was turned to a game show, but the sound was muted. Shep was using the phone, his voice low as he spoke intently to the person on the other end. Maggie didn't want to sit down on the furniture, upholstered in a lovely floral fabric, and get it sopping wet. No matter where she walked, she was leaving footprints. Her shoes were soaked. Shivering, she stood close to Shep and listened to him talk to Preston.

Elmer came back first. "Here," he told her in a whisper, "put this on. This is Trudy's warmest jacket."

"Oh, thank you," Maggie said with a broken smile. It was a fleece-lined, dark blue garment with a waterproof outer shell. The moment she shrugged into it, she felt a modicum of returning warmth. Elmer put a black, rainproof jacket over the couch near where Shep stood talking.

"Here you go, my dear," Trudy said quietly as she

brought in a tray holding two mugs of hot, steaming tea. "I put a little honey in it for ya'll. Hope you don't mind," she set the tray on the coffee table. Picking up the rose-colored mug, she handed it to Maggie.

"Thanks so much," Maggie whispered, sliding her icy fingers around the warm, sleek surface of the mug. "You have *no* idea how wonderful this feels to me." Her teeth had stopped chattering now and she blew across the surface of the steaming, gold-colored tea to cool it a little. Sipping it, she felt fingers of warmth stealing down her throat and loosening the tightness in her stomach. The tea was herbal, and the sweetness made her smile. "This is wonderful," she told Trudy gratefully.

Pleased, Trudy touched her short, gray hair with pride. "It's my grandmother's recipe, you know. Chamomile with hops. You look a little shaken, dear. I thought a tea that would soothe your nerves was in order."

Laughing softly, more out of relief than anything else, Maggie felt some of the terror leaking away with each sip of the tea. "You're so sweet, Mrs. Hawkins. Letting us come in, two strangers out of the dark of the night…that's so very kind of you."

She nodded and fussed over Maggie, saying, "You're going to catch your death of cold, my child." She touched Maggie's limp, wet hair. "Can you stay here?"

"No," Shep said in a growl as he placed the phone back into the cradle. He glanced apologetically at the farm couple. "We need to keep moving."

Shep saw the terror in Maggie's eyes return as she gripped the mug to her breast, her hands wrapped tightly around it. Picking up his own mug, he sipped the hot tea with relish. "All the law enforcement authorities have been alerted," he told Maggie. Then, turning to the couple, he continued, "What I need now, Mr. Hawkins, if you've got it, is a vehicle and a cell phone. We need to get out of here and head toward Charleston. Do you have a car we could borrow?"

Trudy smiled and slid her arm around her husband's waist. "Why, we have a truck you could use, Mr. Hunter. Would that do?"

"Anything will do," he assured them fervently. "And if there's any damage to it while we use it, the government will pick up the tab for any repairs."

"Oh," Trudy said, "that's good. Hold on, I'll get the keys…" And she hurried from the living room.

"What should we do, Mr. Hunter?" Elmer asked worriedly. "Any possibility this trouble that's obviously stalking you might make its way here?"

"I doubt it. But if anyone comes around asking questions, pretend you know nothing. Chances are, no one will harm you. They're looking for us. If they can't find us within a certain amount of time, I'm sure they're going to leave to get to their next destination. If they do come, just play it cool and dumb."

Elmer smiled a little and rubbed his lean jaw. "Dumb I can appear."

Maggie laughed a little. "You are far from dumb, Mr. Hawkins."

Chortling, Elmer said, "Well, now, you know how city folks look down on us dumb-as-sticks country folks." His blue eyes sparkled with mirth. "Don't worry about us, little lady, we'll be fine." He turned when Trudy came back into the living room, holding a set of keys toward Shep.

"Which one did you give 'em?" he asked his wife.

Trudy smiled a little. "The three-quarter-ton truck. You think that tank will get them safely to Charleston?"

With a pleased chuckle, Elmer nodded sagely. "That truck is five years old, Mr. Hunter, but like my wife sez, it's a tank. That thing is the closest you'll come to protection. It will withstand a lot of damage and give better than it gets if you folks get into a jam."

Shep nodded. "I've got more luck than I deserve, Mr. and Mrs. Hawkins." He held up the keys and smiled in their direction. "When this is all over, we want to come back and thank you for your help. Without it, we'd be in big trouble." He also told Elmer about his cows breaking down the fence near the highway. "Right now, they're back inside your pasture and bedded down for the night. But I would look to repair that soon."

"Thanks for letting us know," Elmer said.

Trudy traded a smile with her husband. "Go out the back, through the kitchen, Mr. Hunter. Put this coat on first. You need to get warm, too. The garage is attached. Just go down the steps to the right. The truck is in there with our sedan."

Maggie reached out and gripped Trudy's long, thin hand. "You're both lifesavers. Thanks *so* much!"

"Ya'll just be real careful out there," Elmer drawled.

Shep shook the man's hand and thanked both of them for their courage and help. Without them, they'd still be shivering cold, with nowhere to turn.

Maggie hurriedly followed Shep, taking the concrete steps two at a time. A light automatically came on as they entered the garage.

"This is good," Shep growled. The huge, bright red truck stood there looking like a warhorse in full armor.

"We got lucky. This truck can take a helluva beating and keep on running."

Climbing into the passenger side, Maggie met his eyes as he made himself comfortable. "Do you think there will be trouble?" Her fingers shook as she fastened the seat belt.

Slamming the door shut, Shep started the engine. The truck growled to life, trembling around them. "I don't know. This truck has a big engine. We might need it." He glanced over at her as he prepared to back out of the garage. "If we get into trouble, you get down on the floor, understand?" Shep was damned if he was going to lose Maggie now that he'd just found her.

Licking her lower lip, Maggie whispered, "Don't worry, you won't have to tell me twice." She saw the set look of Shep's features. This was the man she loved. Would they be able to make it out of here? To escape Black Dawn? Shivering, she wrapped her arms around herself as Shep eased the big, hulking pickup carefully out of the garage.

"Are the police on their way up here?" Maggie demanded.

"Yes, but it's going to take time. We're thirty miles from the city." Moving the truck down the graveled driveway in the dark, he turned toward the highway. "Until then, brat, we're on our own…"

Chapter 9

Shep drove without lights as they crept down the muddy, dark road toward the highway. All around them, they could see flashes of lightning from storms that had gone by and were heading toward Charleston, and those that were still looming over them to the west. He glanced at Maggie. She was making sure her seat belt fit snugly, for safety reasons.

"Take my pistol," he said, handing it to her. "I'll do the driving, you do the shooting. You're the pistol expert."

At last Shep was treating her like an equal, as if she was a valuable part of their team. Quirking her lips, Maggie grinned widely and teased, "Wise choice. Between the two of us, I'm the pistol shooting champion here." She glanced at him as she checked the gun and snapped off the safety.

"In this bag," he said, pointing between them, "are extra clips of ammo."

Shep's eyes narrowed as he studied the road ahead, which disappeared between the two stands of pines. "Be on guard," he warned her in a deep voice. "Those terrorists could be waiting for us down there." Tightening his hands around the wheel of the growling truck, he forced himself to breathe in and out. It was only a quarter of a mile to the highway. Elmer had said the road joined the highway near the bridge. That meant they were behind the van and the Cessna. Were the terrorists still looking along the river for Maggie? Had they returned to the van? Had they already left for Charleston? Hunter knew his and Maggie's lives hung in precarious balance and there were no ready answers.

Maggie's eyes widened as they crept forward. Her fingers were icy cold on the cool metal of the pistol. The thought of using it to kill someone sickened her. She loved target shooting precisely because it was sport and didn't kill or hurt anything. Feeling the tension reverberating through Shep, she spontaneously reached out and gripped his forearm.

"Listen, no matter what happens, Shep, I want you to know—"

Bullets suddenly hammered the truck. Maggie screamed and threw up her hands to protect her vulnerable eyes from the shattering windshield. Hundreds of pieces of glass blew in on them.

"Son of a bitch!" Shep jammed his foot down on the accelerator. The pickup truck roared like a wounded bull, its rear end slewing from side to side on the slippery mud of the road, until it gained purchase and lunged forward. He saw winking red-and-yellow lights of gunfire from both sides of the road. Aiming the nose of the truck through the fiery gauntlet, he saw Maggie begin to fire back. More lead slammed into the truck. The bullets sang past his head. He ducked and kept his gaze glued on the road.

The instant the pickup hit the asphalt of the highway, Shep jerked on the lights and swung it heavily toward the bridge. All the firing was behind them. *Good!*

Gasping, Maggie jerked an empty clip out of the pistol and jammed in another one. "You okay?" she cried. The wind was shrieking in through the windshield, which now had three huge, gaping holes.

"Fine. You?"

"Yeah…okay…"

Shep drove like a madman. They careened up on the bridge that crossed the river. The pavement was still wet, and the pickup, thanks to its superior weight, held the road even though she could see they were shrieking along at a hundred miles an hour.

Maggie twisted around. She saw lights suddenly switch on behind them. It was the van, she realized with a sinking feeling. "They're following us, Shep. Oh, Lord…"

"Get on the cell phone," he ordered her tightly. "Punch in this number…"

With trembling hands, Maggie did as she was told. Once it rang, she handed it to Shep.

"Yeah, Preston, it's me. Listen, we're in trouble. We're heading toward you. We just crossed the bridge over the river." He gave the make and model of the pickup. "The van with Black Dawn is in pursuit. What can you send our way to help us? We've got one pistol against the semiautomatic and automatic weapons they're carrying."

The lights from the truck stabbed the darkness. It

was a lonely road with no traffic to speak of, hemmed in by pines on each side. It was a corridor to Shep, another gauntlet. He kept his gaze peeled for any back roads he could take to throw Black Dawn off their trail.

Maggie heard the tightness in Shep's voice as he spoke into the phone. She kept looking back, but didn't see the van's headlights—yet. The set of Shep's face scared her. Despite the darkness, the illuminated panel on the dashboard outlined his hard, rugged features like glacial ice. She heard the disappointment in his tone. He flipped the phone closed and handed it back to her.

"Preston is going to try and get a helicopter out of the Marine Corps air station on Parris Island. No promises, though, because they're ringed by thunderstorms. Damn…"

"How far until the state police can meet us?"

"Another twenty miles," he said flatly. Up ahead, he saw a dirt road. "Hang on," he warned her, and he slammed on the brakes. The tires squealed in protest, and the truck swung heavily from side to side as they slowed.

Maggie was holding on with both hands, gripping the seat and the door. "What are you doing?"

"Trying to lose them," he grunted, and swung the truck to the left. They bounced wildly over the roller coaster bumps at the beginning of the dirt road.

"Do we know where this road leads?"

"No, haven't a clue," he said, his voice harsh with tension. Shep kept both hands on the steering wheel. He couldn't race down this road. It was so pitted and torn up. "Call Preston again. Tell him where we made our turn. The closest mile marker was 54."

"Right," Maggie said, punching the numbers into

the cell phone. Her heart was pounding in her chest. While she explained their situation, Preston reviewed a map of the region.

Relief sheeted through Maggie at his response. "Preston says this road rejoins the highway about two miles down. It makes a loop."

Nodding, Shep said, "Good. Maybe the van will pass us by…"

Closing the cell phone, Maggie gripped it and the pistol. It was slow going down the muddy, bumpy road. The lights stabbed up and down with each hole they bounced into. Looking over at Shep, Maggie said, "Hunter, if we get out of this alive, I want a chance to get to know you again under less stressful circumstances. How about it?"

Giving Maggie a quick glance, he grinned a little. "That's one promise I intend to keep with you, brat." But would they survive this deadly chase? Shep couldn't promise Maggie anything.

Grimly, Maggie kept looking behind them. "I know we fight like hell. I know we're both stubborn."

"Bullheaded."

"Yes, that, too."

"I love you anyway."

Her heart slammed into her ribs. She stared, open-mouthed, at Shep's icy profile as he drove relentlessly. With each bump and shudder, glass would sprinkle into the cab from the shattered windshield.

"What?" she whispered disbelievingly. Had she heard right? Had she imagined what she had just heard?

Slowing down, Shep reached out with his right hand and gripped her left one. "I said I love you, Maggie

Harper. These last twenty-four hours have proven that
to me. How do you feel about it?"

His fingers were strong and warm over her cold
flesh. Gripping his hand briefly, because she knew he
needed both hands on that steering wheel to keep the
truck on the slippery road, she said in a choked voice,
"Yes, I love you, too, Hunter. Don't ask me why. I never
realized how much I missed you until you blasted back
into my life."

His mouth curved into a satisfied smile. Releasing
her fingers, he concentrated on driving. "Maybe what
was missing before, what broke us up was my not treating you like an equal?" They had gone a mile now,
and the road was curving to the right, back toward the
highway.

Nodding, Maggie bowed her head momentarily. The
humid, chilly wind tore through the broken windshield
and made her eyes water. "Yes…that's true. Before, you
treated me like a dumb bunny."

Chuckling, the sound rising up through his chest,
he assured her, "No, never a dumb bunny." How badly
Shep wanted to pull over, haul Maggie into his arms,
kiss her senseless and make love to her. He ached to
love her, to show her just how much she meant to him—
and always had.

Smiling weakly, Maggie studied his hard, expres-
sionless face in the dimness of the cab. "Do you think
we'll get out of this alive?"

Shrugging, Shep slowed down and flicked off the
headlights. They were within a quarter mile of the road
rejoining the highway. "I'm planning on it," he told her
with a growl. Maggie didn't need to know the odds
right now. She was scared enough. He could see it in

her blanched features. There were spots of blood here and there on her face where broken glass had struck her. It hurt him to think of her soft, firm flesh marred with those cuts. He hadn't planned on this happening. It served to tell him how dogged Black Dawn really was.

Maggie craned to see if there was any traffic on the highway ahead as thcy crawled cautiously forward. Unfortunately, pine trees blocked her line of vision.

"I'm getting to hate pines," she griped. "I can't see a thing to the right, Shep."

"It's okay," he soothed, and the moment the truck's tires found purchase on the asphalt, he sped up and turned toward Charleston.

Almost instantly, bullets rained around them again. To Maggie, the screech of metal, the pinging sounds, were like hailstones striking. Flinching her arms over her head, she cried out. Headlights suddenly flashed on behind them. Jerking a look over her shoulder, she yelled, "It's them!"

Damn! Shep shoved the accelerator down. "Fire back at them! Try to hit their tires. They're going to try and hit ours!"

Maggie unsnapped her seat belt. She turned around, pistol in hand, and began firing at the van racing up behind them. The headlights were on bright, blinding her. Maggie plantcd both her knees on the seat, her arm thrust out the broken rear window, the pistol aimed at the van. She had to steady the gun! Wind was tearing in around them. It was so cold. Icy cold. She concentrated. Bullets pinged and whined. She heard one sing past, inches from her ear. That was too close! Squeezing off shot after shot, she saw the van leap toward them.

"He's going to ram us!" she shrieked. Before she

could do anything, the white van smashed into them. Maggie cried once and was thrown backward. She struck the dashboard and crumpled between it and the seat.

"Hold on!" Shep roared. He worked to keep the truck steady. Again the van slammed into them. Bullets were being fired at them from the passenger side window. More glass shattered. He felt a hot stinging on his face. Eyes riveted on the road ahead, Shep pushed the pickup to a hundred and twenty miles an hour. Gripping the wheel hard, he yelled to Maggie, "Are you hurt?"

Clambering up from her pretzel position on the floor-boards, Maggie gasped, "No…" and she thrust the pistol back out the rear window and methodically began to fire once more.

Suddenly she heard another sound, like a pop. The van suddenly swerved to the right. The tires screeched.

"I hit 'em!" she shouted. She watched in amazement as the van slowed down and swerved to the right, off into the berm.

"Good," Shep exclaimed. "Now turn around here and get buckled up. We've got about ten more miles to go before we reach the police coming our way."

Her heart soaring with triumph, Maggie belted herself in. No longer were they being pursued. She'd punctured a tire on the van and rendered it useless! She felt her heart pounding like a hammer in her chest. Adrenaline was making her shaky in the aftermath of the wild, dangerous ride. "Are you okay?" she demanded, releasing the clip and putting another in its place.

"So far, so good," Shep said. He caught sight of a light to the right of them, up in the sky. "What's that?"

"What?" Maggie followed his jabbing finger. She

looked in that direction. There were red and green lights flashing above a stand of pine trees. "It's got to be a helicopter, it's so low. It must be the chopper from Parris Island!" she cried excitedly. Maggie couldn't see much in the darkness. Only when lightning from a nearby storm illuminated the night sky could she see anything. "Yes!" she shouted over the shrieking wind whistling through the cab. "It's a military helicopter for sure! It's black. All black!"

Scowling, Shep took his foot off the accelerator. "Get on the phone. Tell Preston that the helo has arrived…"

Smiling with relief, Maggie punched in the number. "Preston, this is Maggie. Hey, the helicopter from Parris Island is here!"

"What helo are you talking about? The one at the Marine Corps station is grounded. There's a thunderstorm overhead and it can't get airborne."

Puzzled, Maggie lifted her head and looked at the swiftly approaching aircraft. It was skimming the tops of the pine trees, heading straight toward them. "Shep…" she held up the cell phone "…I don't understand this. Preston says the Marine Corps helo is grounded at Parris Island due to a storm advisory. Who is this, then?"

His brows dipped immediately. "Son of a bitch, Maggie. That's *got* to be a Black Dawn aircraft! Tennyson must have been in touch with them all along!" He instantly sped up and kept his eyes on the swiftly approaching helo, which was now coming at them from the right, the side where Maggie was sitting. "Hang on!" he warned.

Confused, she gripped the door handle. "What?"

Before he could answer, Shep saw the winking of

red-and-yellow lights at the sides of the helicopter. "Get down!" he roared.

The scream never left Maggie's throat. She saw the winking fireflies beneath the aircraft as it dipped directly down upon them. Maggie heard a thunk, thunk, thunk along the earthen berm. The lights were bullets, she realized belatedly. They were being strafed. Frozen in terror, her mind refused to operate for a second. Shep slammed on the brakes. The truck groaned and halted, the rear end fishtailing around. Jamming his foot back down on the accelerator, Shep got them out of the line of fire.

The black helicopter roared over them, less than a hundred feet above the truck. Instantly, it banked sharply, turned and came back at them, below the treetops this time. The barrels of the guns fired at them directly as Shep sped back toward the white van.

"Hold on," he yelled. Again he slammed on the brakes. The truck slid sideways for a hundred feet, then wobbled violently to a stop. Again he hit the accelerator. The truck reared forward. Now they were headed toward Charleston once again. The helicopter overshot them because of his defensive driving. But Shep knew his tactics wouldn't buy them much more time.

"Maggie, get a fresh clip in that pistol!" he yelled over the screaming engine and the wind shrieking through the broken windshield. Keeping his intense concentration on the road, he gripped the wheel hard. Out of the corner of his eye, he saw Maggie drop the used clip and jam a new one into the butt of the pistol. *Good!*

Before he could speak, he felt the truck shudder drunkenly. It was being hit by fifty-millimeter ammunition! Nothing could withstand that kind of attack. Swerving and slamming on the brakes, he heard two of the tires blow simultaneously.

Maggie screamed as the truck flew out of control at the high speed. One moment they were on the highway, the next careening in wild circles off into the muddy berm and down its slope toward a stand of pines. More bullets rained up on them. Metal tore. It shrieked. She threw her hands over her face. The gravitational force of the truck turning round and round ripped at her. They were going to die! That was the last thing Maggie wanted. But she saw no way out of this. They were going to die!

The truck lurched drunkenly to a stop only a few feet from the pine trees. From overhead, the strong wash of the helicopter rotor blades buffeted them. Shep jerked off his seat belt.

"Maggie!" he roared, "get out of the truck! Get out! Now!" He knew it was only a matter of seconds before one of those gutting, fifty-millimeter bullets found the gas tank and blew them sky-high. He saw Maggie struggling with her seat belt in the darkness. Blinding light from beneath the helicopter's belly blasted in on them. There! Shep pulled her free of the belt. Reaching across Maggie, he shoved the door open. "Get out!" he cried, and pushed her with all his might.

Maggie sailed out the door. Her knees struck the embankment. The grass was wet as she landed with a thud on her hands and knees. Bullets continued to eat at the truck. Maggie looked up, terrorized, as the helicopter calmly hovered no more than a few hundred feet away, pouring hot metal into the vehicle.

Shep landed beside her. Gripping her upper arm,

he jerked Maggie to her feet and pulled her toward the trees. "Run!" he roared. "Run!"

Her feet felt like concrete. She slipped a number of times on the wet grass. Shep's steadying hand kept her upright. The blast of the rotor blades, the puncturing sound, tore at her eardrums. More bullets careened into the truck. She saw Shep slow, then place himself behind her. Trying to run as hard as she could, Maggie knew he was positioning himself as a shield between her and the enemy helicopter.

She heard a whoosh. Seconds later, she felt the shock wave from the truck exploding. The huge blast knocked her off her feet and sent her tumbling to the ground. Heat followed. Rolling over and over, Maggie flailed to a stop. As she crawled to her hands and knees, her eyes huge, she saw that the truck was a mangled, fiery wreck. *Shep!* Where was he?

Maggie crawled around, searching desperately for him. She saw him fifty feet away on the ground, unmoving. *Oh, no!* Was he wounded? He'd shielded her from a blast he knew was coming. He'd done it because he loved her. Tears stung her eyes as she swayed unsteadily to her feet. Maggie lurched toward where he was lying.

Above them, the helicopter began to move—toward them. Dropping to her knees, Maggie saw Shep open his eyes. He looked confused momentarily. And then his gaze sharpened and held hers. "Shep?" She reached out shakily, touching his hard, bloody face. "Talk to me…" Maggie pleaded hoarsely. "Are you okay?"

Nodding, he forced himself to sit up. The terror in Maggie's expression made him wince. He'd never expected this. Not a Black Dawn helicopter shadowing them. It only underscored their determination to get the attaché case they believed Shep and Maggie still had. Launching himself to his feet, Shep grabbed Maggie and dragged her against him. The noise of the helicopter as it slowly approached, hunting them, assaulted their ears. The nose lamp was moving back and forth, trying to locate them. Shep put his mouth close to Maggie's ear.

"Give me the pistol."

She held it up to him. Her hand was trembling badly.

Gripping the weapon, Shep guided Maggie to a very large pine tree. "Stay here. Whatever you do, don't run. Use this tree as cover."

Before she could ask why, Shep ran toward the helicopter, which was slowly approaching them in a methodical fashion. The high, intense beam of light swept the ground relentlessly. Sobbing for breath, Maggie wondered what Shep could do against such a powerful enemy. They'd be hunted down like dogs. A bitter taste coated her mouth.

Breathing hard, Shep zigzagged among the pine trees. The beam of light from the aircraft made it easy for him to see where he was going. He knew what Black Dawn was going to do. They would hunt them down, kill them and then land in hopes of finding the attaché case that contained the phony anthrax. Grimly, he continued to run. Well, that wasn't going to happen. He loved Maggie. And he damn well wanted a chance to love her once more—only this time, the right way—as a partner.

He hoped she would obey him now, though. She would be safer behind the thick, stout trunk of that pine. The rotor blade wash buffeted him. He was almost directly beneath the helicopter. Still not where he needed to be, Shep tried to anticipate the aircraft's next move. Running hard, he slipped and fell. With a curse, he rolled. Almost without missing a beat, Shep rolled to his feet, launched himself upright and dug his toes into the soft, muddy pine needles. He had to be at a precise spot in order to carry out his plan of attack. The pine trees were a hindrance. Would his strategy work? It *had* to!

Sobbing for breath, his lungs burning with exertion, Shep skidded to a halt. Yes, he was in perfect position! Lifting his arms, he used a nearby pine to steady his aim. Near the top of the fuselage was a red, blinking light. Every time it turned, it flashed on the rotor assembly. That was his target: the assembly. That was what he would have to try and put a bullet into. If he could do that, it would bring the helo down. Sweat ran down his face, stinging his eyes. Blinking harshly to clear his vision, he waited tensely. The tops of the pine trees were whipping violently back and forth from the rotor wash. He'd have only one chance to make the shot. Slowly, ever so slowly, the helicopter eased toward him. As the rotor appeared above the tops of the pines, Shep took aim. He'd have mere seconds to fire off the pistol at the assembly unit.

The flashing red light illuminated his target. His finger brushed the trigger as if it were a lover in need of a caress. The pistol bucked in his hands. Shep saw the bullet hit within inches of the assembly. Sparks flew. If the pilot heard the pinging sound, he'd hightail it out of there and Shep would lose his opportunity.

No way... Shep systematically pumped all eight of the bullets, one after another, into the assembly unit. He saw the bullets walking toward the rotor mechanism. Satisfaction thrummed around him. At least one would kill this machine.

Suddenly, there was a flash of light. It was followed almost instantly by the terrific thundering sound of an explosion. The helicopter nosed up, shrieking like a wounded being. Fire engulfed the entire rotor assembly. The aircraft sagged, then nosed down violently. In seconds, the aircraft crashed into the thick pines below. Shep leaped behind a tree as the wildly flailing blades struck limbs and earth. Metal cracked and shattered, filling the air with shrieking sounds as bits of shrapnel screamed through the darkness like lethal scimitars, slicing through everything in their way.

The tree he crouched behind shook and shivered as it was struck by the flying metal again and again. Shep doubled over in a tight crouch. The entire area shook with several more explosions—from the jet fuel catching on fire, he knew. Peering from behind the tree, he saw the liquid spilling like a river of fire all around the downed aircraft. There was no way anyone was going to survive this crash.

Standing, he realized the danger was past. Part of the blade had lodged itself only three feet above where he'd been crouching. When he touched the sheared-off metal, it felt hot to his fingertips. That was how close he'd come to death. His thoughts, his heart, turned to Maggie. Was she safe? Had she listened to him and stayed where he'd told her to?

Worriedly, Shep trotted toward where he'd left Maggie. The roar of the fire continued. There was no sense in trying to shout above it. Tucking the pistol into his belt, he hurried forward, winding among the trees.

Maggie looked up as someone came out of the shadowy darkness. At first she didn't realize it was Shep. She thought one of the Black Dawn members had found her. The scream died in her throat when she realized it was the man she loved, instead. With a cry, Maggie launched herself upward and threw her arms around Shep's neck. His arms came around her immediately, like steel bands, crushing the air from her lungs.

"You're alive!" Maggie sobbed, holding him as tightly as she could.

Placing a rough kiss on her hair, her cheek, he sought and found her mouth. Lowering her to the ground, he leaned over her, cradled her head in his large hand and guided her mouth to his.

"I love the hell out of you, Maggie Harper," he rasped, meeting her beautiful, tear-filled eyes. And he did. Now he was going to show her just how much. Their mouths clashed together, hungry, hot and needy. Just the way her body fit against his, her soft breasts pressed against his chest, her fingers digging into his massive shoulders as they deepened their kiss, was all he wanted. She tasted sweet against the specter of death that surrounded them. Her hair was damp and tangled, but he didn't care. She tasted of life in a way he'd never realized until this past twenty-four hours. He knew now he needed her for the rest of his days…

Chapter 10

Maggie sighed softly as she felt the fingers of sleep easing their grasp. She didn't want to move. She felt warm and languid as she slowly came awake, became aware of the fact that Shep's arms and his body were curved around hers. Sunshine peeked in through the cracks where the hotel drapes weren't tightly drawn. Where was she? Oh, yes... As she lay there, the memories trickled back.

Shortly after the downing of the helicopter, Agent Preston had arrived on scene. Maggie was shaken deeply by the unexpected turn of events. Never had she imagined that the aircraft would attack them from out of the sky, or that Shep would shoot it down. Life was so precious...

She moved her fingers down the length of Shep's hairy arm. His hand was wrapped protectively across her waist. She felt very safe compared to earlier. After they both had been looked at by paramedics, Shep had demanded that Maggie be taken to Charleston, to one of the best hotels, where they could get cleaned up, shower and sleep. They were both beyond the point of exhaustion. Never had Maggie been more grateful for Shep's leadership, direction and protectiveness than at that moment. She had literally been swaying with fatigue.

A soft sigh escaped her lips now. Looking toward the clock on the bed table, she saw that it was 6:00 p.m. She'd slept a long time. How wonderful it was to have taken a hot bath after they'd arrived at the hotel. Shep had hovered nearby, ordered in some food—breakfast—while he waited for her. After he had taken a shower, they had shared the table in the suite and eaten. Food had never tasted so good after their nightmare experience with Black Dawn.

Right now, Maggie was glad to be alive. She felt the rise and fall of Shep's chest as he slept, his head nestled beside her own on the goose-down pillow. Just listening to him breathe filled her with an unparalleled joy. After last night, Maggie understood as never before how much life with Shep meant to her.

Turning over, she saw that his face was heavily bearded. He hadn't shaved last night and now he looked positively dangerous lying there, naked, at her side. She was naked, too, and she relished the thought of sharing a bed with Shep like this. They had agreed that they were simply too exhausted to do anything last night other than fall into bed and sleep in the safety of one another's arms. Sleep was healing. Sleep gave them peace from the violence that had hovered over them from the start of the mission.

Maggie moved her fingers gently through his short, dark hair, massaging the tips over his smooth, broad brow. In sleep, Shep looked far less dangerous. Normally, he was a man of action. He always would be, Maggie mused, her mouth curving softly in a smile. His lashes were thick and spiky against his ruddy cheekbones. The thick, black hair across his chest tickled and teased her breasts as she moved lithely against him. The urge to love Shep was overpowering. Maggie no longer questioned the fact that her love for him had never died. Moving her fingers in a massaging motion behind his neck, she felt the thick cords of muscle meeting his heavy, broad shoulders. There wasn't an ounce of fat on Shep. A provocative, pulsating heat pooled deeply within her body. Rising up on one elbow, she leaned over him and placed her lips against his sandpapery cheek. He smelled of the lavender soap they'd used to bathe with last night. And then there was the very male odor of him, a heady fragrance to her flaring nostrils as she inhaled deeply.

With the delicious thought of kissing Shep Hunter awake and out of the arms of sleep, Maggie eased her lips against the parted line of his mouth. She felt him come awake in an instant, a knee-jerk reaction to possible danger. Leaning back, she smiled down at him, watching as the remnants of sleep fled from his icy blue eyes and were replaced by an alert, predatory look.

"Shh...everything's okay," Maggie whispered, still smiling. She moved her fingers in a lacy pattern across his arm and over his shoulder. "We're safe... I just woke up and decided to wake you..."

Shep gazed up at Maggie. Her red hair was in disarray and she reminded him of the wild British queen

Boudicca. Her cheeks were a rosy hue, her hazel eyes simultaneously sparkling with mischief and smoky with desire. He knew that look well enough to know that she wanted him, and his body responded powerfully to her touch.

"Everything might be okay," he growled as he eased her on her back next to him, "but you aren't safe, brat."

Soft laughter gurgled up from her throat and escaped her smiling lips as Maggie settled easily next to Shep. Just the touch of his flesh, warm and dry, was evocative. As he slid one hand in a possessive motion across her right hip, she felt his strong fingers range upward across her rib cage. When he caressed the curve of her breast, Maggie sighed and closed her eyes in pleasure.

Sleep had been torn from him, but he didn't mind. He placed his weight on his left elbow as he leaned across Maggie. How beautiful and willful she looked to him. And she was here, with him. She was his. That realization made him feel strong and good as never before. As he leaned down and teased her ripening nipple with the warmth of his tongue, he felt her tense. A whisper of pleasure rippled from her. Suckling her, holding her, became his only focus. How badly he wanted to make love with her. She was his life. And last night had proven that beyond any doubt. As Shep caressed her, sucked her, he remembered starkly how he had raced back through the woods after the helicopter had fallen out of the sky like a flaming, wounded bird, to see if Maggie was still alive.

When he found her, he had needed to hold her, to reassure himself that she really *was* alive. And now, as he heard her moan with pleasure, her body arcing and sliding hotly against him, Shep savored life fully. Her fingers trailed languidly down his neck and dug deeply into his tightened shoulder muscles. She smelled of a woman's sweet fragrance laced with the clean scent of the lavender soap she'd used last night to wash the stench of their nightmare mission from her flesh.

Helplessly caught by the thudding of her wildly beating heart beneath his chest, he felt her ease her leg over his, drawing him across her. Leaning on his elbows, he kept his upper body weight off her. Opening his eyes, he drowned in the gold and green of hers. "You're so brave," he rasped as he bent down and captured her mouth.

Maggie smiled beneath his male onslaught. She felt him grind his hips, his male hardness, against her, opening her legs. She felt the gruff hair of his thighs brushing the soft firmness of hers. Moaning, she felt his maleness pushing demandingly against her moist, beckoning entrance. Without hesitation, as he took her mouth, she moved her hands down the length of his torso, settling them on his narrow hips. Guiding him, Maggie arched upward, for she wanted to claim him, to love him and welcome him deeply into her womanhood.

The instant he thrust into her, Shep groaned. His entire body trembled from the raw pleasure that she was gifting him with. He felt Maggie's slender legs wrap around his. The moment she arched shamelessly against him, he felt himself sucked into the hot, golden light of life itself. Grasping the bedsheets on either side of her head, he lifted his chin, his lips curling away from his clenched teeth. Her body was hot now, slightly damp, pulling him into a vortex of scalding heat and promise. The rocking motion of her hips increased and he was helpless to do anything other than move in the primal rhythm with her. Joy spiraled with unfettered desire as Shep lost touch with the world around them. Maggie—her scent, her soft, firm touch, the heat of her fingers raking across his tightened back muscles—was his only focus.

The hunter became the hunted. Shep felt himself spiraling completely out of control as she slid her tongue across his lower lip. Her fingers wreaked fire upon his chest, his nipples, and her hips moved in demand to take him even more deeply into herself. This was the primal Maggie he knew. In those moments just before the explosion of white-hot heat flowed out of him, he knew that he loved her with a fierceness that had never died in all those years of separation. This was the woman he wanted at his side forever.

Shep's animal groan rippled through Maggie. She tensed with him. The powerful release of her body in tandem with his made her cry out. Clutching him hard against her, she buried her face against his dampened shoulder. The pummeling crash of his heart against hers, their wild and chaotic breathing, the taste of him on her lips, all combined. She floated aimlessly, locked in his arms as they shared the greatest gift of all.

For the longest time afterward, Maggie lay in Shep's arms. She didn't want to move. She wanted to savor the satiation she felt only with him. Time meant nothing. When she finally opened her eyes, she realized the slanting sunlight had shifted and the room was gray, but she felt like a vibrant rainbow inside. Her heart sang. Her body was fulfilled as never before. Shep's fingers grazed the damp lock of hair against her brow and she gazed up at him, her eyes soft.

"I love you, did you know that?"

Shep smiled down at her, placed his mouth against her wrinkling brow and whispered, "I'd have never guessed by the way you attacked me. You always wake a sleeping man up to get what you want out of him?"

Chuckling indulgently, Maggie sighed luxuriously as he moved his fingers down the side of her face, her neck, to capture her breast. Moving her hand upward, she slid her fingers against the roughness of his jaw. "With you, yes. That's the only thing you understand—a frontal assault."

It was his turn to chuckle. Gazing down at her, Shep lost his smile. "I'm lying here beside you wondering why the hell I ever left you in the first place, brat."

"Stupid, huh? On both our parts."

"Yes," he agreed quietly. Moving his hands tenderly down her ribs, Shep captured her hip more tightly against him. They remained within one another, the intimacy strong and incredibly beautiful to him. "What I share with you now, I've never had with another woman, Maggie. Not ever."

Sobering at his honesty, Maggie realized she had never felt her femininity more strongly than in this moment. Shep was very male, but tender in his own masculine way. He knew how to be intimate with a woman; he always had. "I don't know which of us was crazier, you or me. What we share is so good, Shep. I've never experienced what I have with you with anyone else, either."

Moving his hips reflexively, he watched her eyes close with pleasure. Her lips parted. "You're so easy to love," he murmured. "You make me feel good and strong, Maggie. You always did."

Maggie gave a shuddering sigh. It was tough to talk when he moved so provocatively within her. He knew his power with her, and she enjoyed savoring him. "So what are we going to do, Hunter? Keep talking in past tense or make what we have present and future tense?"

Grinning a little, Shep eased reluctantly from her warm, inviting form. He didn't want to, but there were other things to talk about. When making love to Maggie he didn't want any interruptions. No, when he loved her, he wanted her full, undivided attention, and right now, he knew there were other topics that had to be talked out between them.

He sat up, the sheet and blanket pooling around his waist. "Come here, brat," he told her gruffly as he leaned against the bed's antique brass headboard. Gathering Maggie into his arms, he pulled her up beside him. She lay against him, her head nestled in the crook of his right shoulder, her arm curved languidly across his torso. Pulling the sheet up around her, he shut his eyes and savored having her against him. "Now, isn't this better?" he rumbled near her ear. With his left hand, he moved his fingers lightly across her small shoulder and down the smooth indentation of her spine.

"Being with you at times like this is always better," Maggie murmured contentedly.

"So you want a present and future with me? Or did I hear wrong?"

Opening her eyes, she gazed up at him. His icy-blue gaze had thawed and she absorbed the warmth that he kept so carefully closeted from the rest of the world. Threading her fingers through the hair on his chest, she said, "You didn't hear wrong, darling."

"I think we're mature enough to handle our differences now, Maggie," Shep said quietly as he eased his own fingers through the soft strands of her hair. He felt her tremble and completely relax against him. "I can see what I was doing back then. I wasn't treating you, or what you brought to the table, with respect. I always thought my way was best."

"And it isn't, not always."

"No," Shep agreed as he pressed a kiss to her cheek, "it's not." His eyes narrowed as he looked around the dim room, filled with antebellum antiques. "Last night I thought I might lose you. We survived because we worked together, as a good team should."

"You listened to me," Maggie agreed gently. "And I listened to you, too. We each brought strengths to one another, Shep. And thank goodness you listened! When you were younger, you wouldn't have."

"I know," he said miserably. He struggled with the words and the feelings. "Damn, Maggie, I feel sad. When I stop and realize my arrogance, how my know-it-all attitude kept us apart all these years... And seeing now what we have and what we missed, it makes me miserable." His hand stilled on her cheek, and Shep looked down at her. "I really screwed up. And I'm sorry. I'm not good at putting how I feel into words, brat, but I want you to know that I want a second chance with you. It will be different this time around. You're my equal. We don't need to fight and argue like we did before. I think those twenty-four hours of hell proved that we're pretty good at listening and taking direction from one another, don't you agree?"

Nodding, Maggie threaded her fingers between his. Kissing his large, skinned knuckles with small sips from her mouth, she whispered, "So, when are we going to get married, Hunter?"

That was his Maggie: bold and beautiful. A rumble

of pleasure reverberated in his chest. His skin tingled where she was placing delicate, tiny kisses across his badly bruised and lacerated fingers. Did Maggie know how healing her touch was to him? He didn't think so.

"Do I have time to call my family? Could you stand getting hitched at my parents' home in Denver? Say, maybe in a week or two? It would give my other three brothers a chance, I hope, to make our wedding."

Eyes glimmering with tears, Maggie looked up at him. "Hunter, I've waited all these years for you to get your head pulled out of the sand. I don't think a couple more weeks are going to stress us out, do you? Besides, I need to call my family and tell them the good news."

His mouth pulled into a deprecating grin. "No, my redheaded woman, I don't think it will hurt anyone."

A knock on the door startled both of them. Instantly, Shep went into his mercenary mode. He slipped from the bed and reached for his pistol, which lay on the bed stand. Locking and loading it, he gestured for Maggie to remain where she was. Her eyes were wide with terror. Grimly, he went to the door, the pistol held high.

"Yes?" he called.

"Hunter? It's Preston. I need to talk with you."

Looking out the peephole in the door, Shep could see that it was the FBI agent.

"It's okay," he told Maggie. "It's Preston. Go get that hotel robe on?"

Maggie nodded and scooted out of the bed. She picked up a robe and then hurried over to him and handed him one.

"Just a minute," Shep told him through the door.

Maggie belted the thick, white terry cloth robe, pulled the covers across the bed and smoothed them out and then hurried to the windows and opened the drapes. Late-evening sunlight flooded the room. Turning, she saw Shep had put the pistol away and was already in his robe and heading into the other room of the suite, which had several chairs, a couch and a coffee table. Maggie followed him.

Preston nodded in greeting as he stepped inside. "I was hoping you two were awake by now."

Shep looked down the hall both ways, then quietly shut the door behind him. "You're looking a little better around the edges, too," he told the agent.

Maggie ordered coffee from room service as the men made themselves comfortable in the living room of the suite. She closed the entrance to their bedroom and came and joined Shep on the couch opposite Preston.

"You're both looking better," the FBI agent said.

Maggie smiled and slid closer to Shep. Slipping her arm around his shoulders, she tucked her knees beneath her, content to remain close to him. "Sleep works wonders," she agreed, smiling at the agent, who was wearing a dark blue suit, a starched white shirt and red paisley tie. He looked like an FBI agent, Maggie decided. There were still dark circles beneath his eyes and the stress was still apparent in his features.

"So, what brings you to our neck of the woods?" Shep demanded. He slid his hand across Maggie's robed thigh and savored their natural intimacy.

"I had some good news I wanted to share with you," Preston said, smiling a little.

"We can use it," Maggie whispered, and traded a smile with Shep. She saw contentment in his eyes. He was at peace, all the tension from moments ago dissolved. Absorbing his closeness, she liked the fact that his large, thick arm was draped across her lower body. Preston's eyes had widened a little at the gesture. Perhaps he didn't know of their past with one another and was astonished at their intimacy. Shep could clue him in later.

"It's about Black Dawn?" Hunter guessed.

"Yes." Preston sat up and gloated a little. "You're going to be very pleased to know that we've captured one-quarter of the entire Black Dawn contingent. What we didn't know was that six other operatives were here, waiting in Charleston, to hook up with Dr. Tennyson and his group. The people you took out when you shot down that helicopter were four in number, and were all DOA at the scene." Holding up his hands, he said, "In total, we've captured ten members of Black Dawn." He smiled even more. "And Tennyson is singing like a canary. He's agreed to spill his guts on the upper echelon of Black Dawn in exchange for immunity. He's giving us names, addresses and countries where other Black Dawn terrorists are living or hiding."

"Wonderful!" Maggie breathed. She grinned at Shep. "We're a pretty good team, aren't we?"

Just the way Maggie flushed, Shep found himself smiling in return. The triumphant look in her shining gold-and-green eyes made him go hot with longing for her all over again. He wanted to capture that smiling mouth once more. He wanted to hold her spirit, her vibrancy in his arms while he loved her.

"Yes," he admitted, "we're a damn good team."

"Couldn't have done it without you two." Preston sobered. "Maggie, I'm sorry you got kidnapped. That was no one's fault."

"How did Tennyson get the code from you? He told

me that there was a mole in the FBI feeding him the information."

"Yes, that's true. He's already given up the name of the mole," Preston told her grimly. "The man is under arrest. And he did know the codes on this mission."

"I would *never* have opened that door without the code," she told them. "I really wouldn't have."

Shep patted her leg gently. "We believe you, brat. You followed protocol."

"Well," Preston murmured, "I'm *really* sorry, Maggie. I had no idea we had a Black Dawn mole in our midst. It explains in part why we haven't, over the last couple of years, been able to trap and capture them. This agent has been feeding them information all along."

"When my brother Dev found that lab on Kauai with the help of Kulani Dawson, this whole thing broke open. It forced Black Dawn's hand," Shep said.

"No doubt about it," Preston agreed. "If it hadn't been for Morgan Trayhern, or Perseus, we would never have cracked this case. It goes to show us how private enterprises like Perseus are worth bringing in under the government tent. I'm glad Morgan works *with* us. He has incredible people."

Maggie brushed her fingers delicately against Shep's thick, corded neck. "Yes, he has incredible people who are completely committed to him," she agreed.

Preston cleared his throat. Rising, he adjusted the knotted tie at his throat. "Well, I've got to get back to the Charleston office. You have our thanks." He shook their hands. "I'll be talking to Morgan, too. Dr. Harper, your heroism may never be known publicly, but for what it's worth, I think you're one of the most courageous women I've ever run across."

Maggie flushed beneath the agent's sincere praise. "Thanks, Agent Preston."

"I know," Shep growled, "and that's enough."

"I'll let myself out. You two enjoy the night and get some rest."

"Couldn't you stay and at least have coffee with us? I've got it ordered," Maggie offered.

Preston smiled tiredly. "I'd like to, but I have to get back to the office. Thanks anyway. You two enjoy a well-deserved quiet evening together."

As the door quickly closed, Maggie turned her attention back to Shep. "How about that? A happy ending."

Shep patted her calf and slid his fingers around her dainty foot. "A partial victory," he warned her. "Terrorist groups will always exist. In this case, it sounds like we chopped off the head of the snake. Black Dawn may be gone, but that doesn't mean there aren't other factions out there waiting to take its place."

"Humph," Maggie said, her skin tingling where Shep touched her, "no rest for the wicked?"

Shrugging, he released her foot and slid his arms around her. He maneuvered Maggie across his lap so that she lay against him, her arms resting languidly around his shoulders. "Right now, my world, my existence, is centered on one red-haired lady. Black Dawn is crippled. We did some good work. The world is safe for a while, at least." Gazing into her sparkling eyes, he whispered, "I love you, Maggie Harper. And I'm going to keep loving you with a fierceness that will last until we draw our last breaths."

Framing his face, she smiled brokenly. Shep was a man of few words and she knew the gift he'd just given her. "You're one of a kind, darling. My kind."

"Even if we fight like cats and dogs?"

"Oh, I'm sure we'll have our moments." Maggie laughed gently. Moving her fingers tenderly across his flesh, she watched his eyes burn that darker blue color that warned her of how much he desired and loved her. It sent a wonderful tingly sensation up and down her spine.

"Partners can disagree without hurting one another with words and actions," Shep promised her.

"And we'll both give each other the respect and the space we need when we hit those bumps in the road, Shep. I know we will."

Sighing, he said, "I've been too long without you, brat. And if this mission did nothing but point that out, then that's enough."

Smiling tenderly, Maggie leaned over and grazed his mouth with her lips. "You're *more* than enough for me, Shep Hunter. The war between us is over. We're going to spend the rest of our lives learning peaceful coexistence with one another."

Moving his mouth against the sweet softness of her lips, he rasped, "And I'm going to enjoy learning from you, sweet woman of mine…"

* * * * *

Carol Ericson is a bestselling, award-winning author of more than forty books. She has an eerie fascination for true-crime stories, a love of film noir and a weakness for reality TV, all of which fuel her imagination to create her own tales of murder, mayhem and mystery. To find out more about Carol and her current projects, please visit her website at carolericson.com, "where romance flirts with danger."

Books by Carol Ericson

Harlequin Intrigue

A Kyra and Jake Investigation
The Setup

Holding the Line
Evasive Action
Chain of Custody
Unraveling Jane Doe
Buried Secrets

Red, White and Built: Delta Force Deliverance
Enemy Infiltration
Undercover Accomplice
Code Conspiracy

Red, White and Built: Pumped Up
Delta Force Defender
Delta Force Daddy
Delta Force Die Hard

Visit the Author Profile page at
Harlequin.com for more titles.

BULLETPROOF SEAL

Carol Ericson

Prologue

The sweat stung Quinn's eyes and he squeezed them shut for a second—just a second before he refocused on his target. Rikki's beautiful face swam before him in his scope, her red hair standing out like a burst of flame against the emerald green landscape. Quinn's hand trembled.

He shifted his sniper rifle to the two North Korean soldiers walking behind Rikki, prodding her forward. They had rifles pointed at her back. Quinn spit the sour taste out of his mouth, along with the mud from the hillside in the DMZ between North and South Korea.

Someone had misinformed the CIA. Rikki Taylor was no rogue operative working with the North Koreans. She was their captive…unless she'd set up this whole scene for cover.

Quinn knew better than anyone about Rikki's duplicitous nature. But this? Working with the enemy to damage her own government and put her fellow CIA agents at risk?

He had a hard time believing Rikki would endanger agents in the field. Quinn lowered his sniper rifle and swiped the back of his hand across his mouth.

The trio below him stopped, and one of the soldiers pulled out a bottle of water.

Squinting, Quinn scanned the lush land where the borders of North and South Korea met—a no-man's-land where hostility and mistrust haunted the verdant beauty—not to mention the scattered land mines. This mistrust permeated his pores, had him doubting his mission, a mission he should've refused once he'd discovered the target.

He would've had to have come up with a good reason to refuse an assignment from the navy—even after that untraceable text he'd received. He could've tried the truth, but then he would've come under suspicion. Then his pride had taken over and he had to prove that he could carry out the assignment, prove his professionalism and dedication.

He snorted softly, and the leaves on the branch tickling his nose stirred. Prove to whom? His old man?

The group on the ground was on the move again, and Quinn took up his position. His rifle weighed on his shoulder like a lead block. His breath came out in short spurts.

Usually before he dropped a target, a deadly calm descended on him. Now, his heart raced and his trigger finger twitched. In this condition he'd be lucky to hit that boulder twenty feet away.

He closed his eyes and took a deep, steadying breath

through his nose and blew it out through puckered lips. He swallowed. He shifted. He braced the toes of his boots against the rock behind him.

Then he refocused. He put Rikki Taylor in his crosshairs for the last time.

Rikki licked her lips, and Quinn could almost taste their sweet honey on his own tongue. She tossed her fiery hair over one shoulder.

Quinn blinked and, in the split second of that one blink, Rikki attacked one of the guards, going for his weapon.

Quinn needed no other proof. He tracked his rifle to the other guard, lined him up and took the shot. The soldier jerked once and dropped to the ground.

Quinn swung his scope back to Rikki's struggle with her captor, and his heart stuttered. The soldier had possession of his gun, and Rikki had fallen to the ground, out of sight behind a clump of bushes.

As Quinn watched through his scope, blood pounding in his ears, the North Korean soldier shot his weapon into the bushes.

In a fury, Quinn zeroed in on the man who'd just shot Rikki, but before he could even take aim, Quinn came under attack from a hail of bullets.

Taking down the other soldier had revealed his position, and now he was outnumbered and outgunned. He rolled to his back and scrambled down the hillside like a forward-moving crab. He scuttled behind a row of trees and started breaking down his rifle.

Dragging himself up and wedging his back against a tree trunk, he stuffed his gear into his bag and then swung it onto his back.

He lunged forward onto his belly and army-crawled

his way through the forest to the tunnel that would take him back to South Korea and the designated pickup point.

What would he tell his superiors? He did end up with mission success. Although it wasn't his bullet that had done the job, he *had* neutralized the target—Rikki Taylor.

They'd been wrong. They'd all been wrong. Rikki had not been working with the enemy.

And now that Quinn was responsible for her death, his life wasn't worth living.

Chapter 1

Sixteen months later

The footsteps echoed behind her on the rain-slicked pavement. Rikki stopped and spun around. Silence greeted her as she peered down the dark, narrow street.

With her muscles coiled tightly, she continued, and her tag-along followed suit. As she began to turn again, the footsteps, two sets, quickened and two bodies rushed her.

The glint from a knife flashed in the night, and Rikki finished her turn with her feet flying. She kicked the assailant with the knife in the gut, and he doubled over, his weapon clattering to the cobblestones.

The other man yelped in surprise and before he could recover, Rikki swept up the knife from the ground and wielded it toward her attacker's face.

"Get lost, or I'll slice you from chin to navel. Yu done know?"

The man's eyes widened so that the whites gleamed like two orbs. His friend groaned from the ground.

Rikki growled, "And take him with you."

He held up one hand and grabbed his buddy by the arm with the other, dragging him to his feet. "Eazy, nuh."

"You take it easy and get moving or I'll call the police."

The two hapless muggers took off, and Rikki pocketed the knife. The streets of Jamaica, even in the tourist trap of Montego Bay, turned deadly after dark, but Rikki had more to fear in her own country right now.

She slipped into the alley where an orange light swayed in the breeze, sidling along the walls of the ramshackle building. She ducked under a tattered blue-and-white-striped awning and rapped at the window.

A curtain stirred. Rikki stepped sideways into the weak light to identify herself.

A wiry man opened the door and hustled her inside as he poked his head into the alley and looked both ways. "Where's your ride?"

"I walked from the main street."

He shook his head. "Dangerous place for anyone to be walking, especially a girl like you."

Rikki hid her smile behind a covered cough. "I'm okay. Are you Baily?"

"The one and only." He double-locked the door behind them and twitched the curtain back in place.

"Do you have everything ready?"

"Come with me." He crooked one long finger in her direction.

Rikki followed him through a single room where an old woman sat in front of an older TV, the blue light flickering across her lined face. She didn't acknowledge Rikki's presence or even move a muscle.

Baily shoved a dark curtain aside and waved Rikki into a small room. He pointed to a green screen and said, "Stand in front of that. I'll get your picture first. Everything else is ready to go."

As she took a step toward the screen, Baily tugged on her sleeve. "Business first."

Rikki pulled a wad of cash from her pocket. Those thieves on the street would've hit pay dirt with her—well, except for the fact that they'd picked a CIA operative, trained in self-defense and street fighting, as their target.

She counted out the agreed-upon sum, and Baily got to work.

Thirty minutes later, Rikki had a Canadian passport and a birth certificate for one April Thompson. She studied the passport with the Jamaican stamp. "I heard you were good, Baily. These better not let me down."

"Never had a problem yet." He cocked his head in a birdlike fashion. "Girl like you in trouble with the Babylon?"

"Babylon?" She stuffed the documents into the manila envelope he'd handed to her.

"De law." He waved his hands in a big circle. "De system."

"You could say that." She stuck out her hand. "Pleasure doing business with you."

He shook her hand and then yelled, "Darien!"

Rikki jumped, jerking her hand from his grip and placing it over the newly acquired knife in her waistband.

Baily placed one finger against the side of his nose. "No worries. Darien just my boy. He'll take you back."

A skinny young man poked his head into the room, his dreadlocks bobbing and swaying. "Yeah, Daddy?"

"Take this young woman wherever she wants to go. Don't stop anywhere."

Darien grinned. "Sure ting."

After thanking Baily, Rikki followed Darien outside.

He turned sideways and scooted between two of the houses along the alley. A chain clinked and rattled, and Darien pushed a scooter out in front of him. "Hop on de back."

Clutching her fake documents to her chest, Rikki climbed on the back of Darien's scooter. He zoomed through the streets of Montego Bay as she shouted directions in his ear over the buzzing sound of the bike.

A block away from the resort, she tapped Darien's shoulder and pointed to the side of the street.

The bike sputtered to a stop, and he leaned it to one side as if it were a mammoth Harley instead of a puttputt scooter. Rikki slid off the back and handed Darien a folded bill.

His gaze darted from the outstretched money to her face. "Daddy would smack me in da head if I took that."

"Daddy doesn't have to know." She tucked the cash beneath his fingers curled around the handlebar of his scooter and twirled away. She made a beeline for the resort and didn't slow her pace until she walked through the front entrance.

"Good evening, Miss Rikki."

"Hey, George." She waved her manila envelope and scurried out the side door and across the pool deck, where drunken tourists had gathered for one last nightcap.

The damp foliage brushed her skin, and she inhaled the sweet, heavy fragrance of the white bellflower as she tromped down the path to the cottage. When she was inside, she leaned against the front door, closing her eyes and hugging the fake documents to her chest.

"Did you get what you needed, Rikki?"

Rikki opened one eye and dipped her chin to her chest. "I did. Thanks, Chaz."

Her stepfather winked. "I've been on this island a long time. I know important people in low places."

Her mother floated into the room behind Chaz, her long gray braid hanging over one shoulder. "Are you sure you want to do this, Rikki? You don't owe them anything, and as far as they know, you're dead. You and Bella could live here with us for as long as you like."

Rikki rolled her eyes. "I would go stir-crazy here, Mom. Besides, I have to do this. I have important information."

"They don't deserve it." Mom sniffed.

Bella cooed and gurgled from the other room, and Rikki dropped the manila envelope on a table and hurried toward the bedroom. She leaned over the crib and scooped up her baby girl, holding her close and breathing in her baby-powder scent.

"She's going to miss you."

Rikki glanced at her mom, who stood with her shoulder wedged against the doorjamb, and blinked the sudden tears from her eyes. "I'm doing it for her, Mom. I have to get my life back for both of us."

"Does that mean seeing *him*?"

"I have to start with him, see what he knows, maybe use his contacts."

"You don't have to tell him about Bella. She'll be

safe with us until you can return and reclaim her, re-claim your life."

Rikki bounced her daughter in her arms, burying her face in Bella's soft ginger hair. "I'll see how it goes. I plan to use him to get what I want, and if that means telling him we have a daughter, I'll do it."

"He doesn't have a right to know about her."

"Lizzie." Chaz had come up behind his wife and placed a hand on her shoulder. "Let Rikki handle this herself…and let her have some time alone with the baby before she has to leave."

Chaz ushered Mom out of the room and blew Rikki a kiss before shutting the door.

Rikki collapsed in the rocking chair, cuddling Bella in the crook of her arm. As she sang softly to her baby, Rikki let the tears spill onto her cheeks.

She didn't know what she'd do when she came face-to-face with Quinn McBride—the man who'd tried to kill her and had gotten her locked up in a North Korean labor camp.

The man she still loved.

Quinn stumbled into his apartment and made his way to the kitchen, rubbing his eyes. He banged his shin on the coffee table and scowled at it. "Who put you there?"

He yanked open the fridge door and studied the sparse contents as he swayed on his feet. Giving up, he slammed the door, and the condiment bottles rattled and clinked against the beer bottles.

His stomach growled. The taxi driver had refused to wait for him outside the restaurant where he'd wanted to pick up some food, and Quinn didn't want to get stuck walking home through the streets of New Orleans lugging a bag of food, especially without a weapon at his side.

And he didn't trust himself with a weapon right now—not in his condition.

He fumbled in his back pocket for his cell phone and scrolled through his contacts. If he couldn't get to the food, he'd make the food come to him.

His thumb swept past Rinaldi's Pizza and he backed up. Rikki's name jumped out at him, grabbing him by the throat. As he hovered over her name, his finger shook, and it had nothing to do with the booze coursing through his veins.

He'd kept her number on his phone and had even called it once or twice just to hear her low, sultry voice caress his ear. But the last time he'd tried to call it, the harsh tones of an automated operator told him the cell number was out of service, and he had no business trying to contact the woman he'd sent to her death.

Dropping his chin to his chest, Quinn smacked the cell phone against his temple. If only he'd shown more restraint out there on the DMZ. He could've taken out both of the soldiers holding Rikki. She would've responded in an instant, would've been able to take appropriate evasive action.

She'd been one of the best damned operatives in the field.

The CIA and navy had clouded his judgment, had accused Rikki of being a double agent, had sent him there to take her out. If he hadn't been so damned eager to please his superiors, he would've gone in with a backup plan.

He always had something to prove.

He wiped the back of his hand across his mouth. He

needed to stop playing back the incident in his head over and over every day. Rikki was gone. The CIA was happy. The navy had sent him out on another assignment, which had allowed him to stuff everything away as he'd concentrated on the mission, and now that he was home on leave, he could erase it from his mind another way—the old-fashioned McBride way.

He hunched over the kitchen counter, bringing the phone close to his face. Avoiding Rikki's number, he placed a call to Rinaldi's and ordered an extralarge pizza with everything on it.

When he ended the call, he smacked the phone on the counter and yelled out to the empty apartment, "That calls for another beer."

His stomach rumbled again as he stared at the fridge, and suddenly the effort required to grab a bottle and twist off the top overwhelmed him. He went into the living room instead and crashed onto the sofa, grabbing the TV remote on his way down.

He clicked through the channels, settling on a true crime show about some cold-case murder, and stuffed a throw pillow beneath his head.

The doorbell startled him awake, and the remote fell from his fingers, which had been dangling off the sofa. He ran his tongue around his parched mouth and swept his wallet from the coffee table.

He peered out the peephole at the pimply-faced kid on his doorstep and swung open the door.

The delivery guy's eyes popped open as he held out the pizza box. "Your pizza, sir."

God, he must look even worse than he felt. He handed the kid more money than he should've just to compensate for scaring the hell out of him.

When he collapsed back down on the sofa, Quinn rewound the show, since he'd dozed off during most of it—*dozing off* being a polite term for passing out stinking drunk.

Before digging into the pizza, he retrieved a bottle of water from the fridge and downed half of it before making it back to the sofa. Three slices later and no closer to figuring out whodunit, Quinn closed his eyes and tipped his head back against the sofa cushion.

This time, the click of a gun near his temple woke him up.

Other than blinking once, Quinn didn't move one muscle. Then he spread his hands in front of him and said, "Take what you want, man. Wallet's on the table. Anything you can carry out is yours."

The gunman behind him huffed out a breath and then purred in the low, husky voice that haunted his dreams, "You sure have gotten soft since trying to kill me, McBride."

Chapter 2

Quinn jerked forward and cranked his head around. He choked as he stared at Rikki—but not Rikki—behind the Glock. She always did prefer a Glock.

Her blue eyes had been replaced by a pair of dark brown ones, narrowed in rage. Long, straight strands of brown hair framed her face instead of the thick, wavy red locks that used to dance on her shoulders like tongues of flame, tickling his body when they made love.

"Rikki?" He held out a trembling hand and then clenched it, cursing his drunken state. Maybe this was all an alcohol-infused hallucination. "Is it really you?"

She stepped back, wrinkling her nose. "You smell like a brewery."

Then it hit him. Her presence two feet away sobered him up like a cold shower and a pot of coffee, and his blood hummed through his veins with elation. "How are you here? I—we thought you were dead."

She took another step back, her aim at his head never faltering. "Yeah, too bad for you the North Koreans wanted me more alive than dead. That shot the soldier took grazed me, nothing fatal, but at least it protected me from the bullet waiting up on that hill—a bullet from a deadly navy SEAL sniper."

"I wasn't going to do it. Why do you think I took out the other soldier? I realized you hadn't turned traitor the minute I saw you make a grab for your guard's gun. I couldn't get a clean shot at the soldier holding you, but I thought you might be able to take care of him yourself."

Her lashes dipped over her eyes once. Her mouth softened, and for a crazy minute he almost took that as a sign to kiss her. *Yeah, if he wanted a bullet between the eyes.*

"That's a good story. At what point during your prep for the assignment did you realize the CIA *spy* you were supposed to eliminate was your former lover?"

"Not right away."

"But even if you had known immediately, you never would've turned down the mission, would you?"

He lifted a shoulder. "I received an order. The CIA had proof."

His words, spoken aloud now to Rikki's face, sounded tinny and paltry to his own ears. How would they sound to hers?

She snorted. "And of course you would've had to reveal that you'd carried on a fling with a CIA operative while we were both on assignment in the Middle East."

"If I had doubted the evidence against you in any way, not only would I have owned up to our…affair, but I would've tried to convince them to call off the hit."

"Instead you charged right in like the good little soldier you are, all honor and duty." Her dark gaze flickered to the half-empty pizza box and the two bottles of beer on their sides at the base of the coffee table.

"All I needed to see was one shred of proof contradicting the CIA's story—and you gave it to me when you charged that soldier. That's why I shot the other one. I was trying to give you a chance."

"Are you sure you didn't kill him because you were afraid I'd already passed along secrets to him?"

"They were low-level grunts marching you along the DMZ. I didn't figure that was the time and place you were going to spill intel. Besides—" Quinn kicked the pizza box out of the way and braced his foot on the edge of the coffee table "—if I'd wanted to take everyone out, including you, I would've started with you first and then dealt with the two soldiers."

She flipped back her dark hair with a shrug of her shoulder. "Maybe."

"I had you in my crosshairs, Rikki. Had you there for a while. I could've dropped you at any time. I couldn't do it."

The corner of her eye twitched. "What does the CIA think? I know my name's not cleared, so whatever you told them, it didn't have much of an impact. Unless you told them nothing and took credit for eliminating a CIA spy."

He scratched his unshaven jaw. How did she know her name hadn't been cleared? How did she get out of North Korea? "I told the CIA and my commanding officers in the navy exactly what happened. Told them their intel must've been wrong, that the North Koreans had you as a captive."

"They didn't believe you?"

"They didn't care. I also told them the North Korean soldier had shot you dead. Case closed."

"Except it's not closed, is it? Here I am."

At least the gun had slipped a little from her grip. Even in his current muddled state, he probably could disarm her. Then again, nobody ever benefited from mistaking Rikki Taylor for an easy target.

"How'd you get out of North Korea? How'd you get here? Where have you been the past—" he counted on his fingers "—sixteen months? And can you get that gun out of my face?"

"If I do, will you take me down? Call the CIA and turn me in?"

He rubbed his eyes and pinched the bridge of his nose. "Do I look like I'm in any condition to do that?"

She cocked her head. "You do look pretty bad, but I'm not stupid enough to underestimate a navy SEAL sniper—even one I shared a bed with. Or maybe that should be *especially* one I shared my bed with."

"Ouch." He held his hands in front of him, wrists pinned together. "You can tie me up or cuff me if you want."

A light sparked in her eyes, and her nostrils flared, the heat between them still palpable.

Desire and need surged through his body, making him hard.

"Drop your pants." She waved the gun.

He swallowed. He'd been kidding, but he should've known better than to kid with Rikki—not in her current frame of mind. "You're serious?"

"Damn right. I can't check you for weapons, but at least if you're naked I can make sure you're unarmed."

"Rikki…"

"The last time we were together, if you want to call it that, you had me in the crosshairs of your sniper rifle ready to take me out." She steadied her Glock. "What's changed since then except I had the good fortune to escape from the labor camp?"

A knot twisted in his gut. He knew those North Korean labor camps, and the thought of Rikki confined to one of them made him sick.

"Drop 'em."

"Okay, okay." He pushed himself to his feet, feeling completely sober. He unbuttoned the fly on his shorts and yanked them down. The flip-flops he'd been wearing earlier were wedged beneath the coffee table, so the shorts dropped to his bare feet.

"Kick them off and stand away from the sofa where I can see you."

He rolled his eyes but complied, stepping out of his shorts and kicking them across the room. He could get into a tussle with her right now, but she did have the upper hand.

He stepped away from the sofa and the table and held his arms out to the side. "Nothing on me."

Except the raging erection she could clearly see bulging in his black briefs.

Rikki's gaze dropped from his face to his crotch, and her cheeks flushed. "Now the T-shirt."

Patting his chest, he said, "Do you really believe I have a holster on underneath this shirt? A knife strapped to my back?"

"I'm not taking any chances. Off."

He grabbed the hem of his T-shirt and peeled it off his body. He dropped it to the floor. "Happy?"

"Turn around."

Turning around for her inspection only made him harder. Maybe that would be enough to prove to Rikki that he was on her side—would always be on her side.

When he faced her again, he shoved his thumbs in the waistband of his briefs. "You want the rest off?"

"Don't be ridiculous." She reached behind her back and pulled out a pair of open handcuffs, dangling them from her fingers.

Quinn's mouth dropped open. "No way."

"I know you. I know who you are and what you're capable of. I've come this far, and I'm not taking any chances." She jingled the cuffs. "If you want any more information out of me, hold out your arm—your right arm."

He stretched his arm in front of him. Two more inches and he could touch her soft cheek, tell her everything he'd thought about this past year.

She snapped the cuff around his wrist and yanked on it, the metal cutting into his flesh. "Over here, by the radiator."

He would've preferred the bedroom, but he followed in her wake as she pulled him toward the window.

"Sit down and link the other cuff around this pipe."

He slid to the floor and hooked himself up to the pipe on the radiator. He crouched on his haunches.

Rikki let out a long sigh and placed her weapon on the counter that separated the kitchen from the living room. She dragged a stool from the kitchen and straddled it. "That's better."

"Rikki, I'd never hurt you."

"You were singing a different tune sixteen months ago."

"I explained all that to you. Now that I'm—" he rattled his cuffs against the pipe "—contained, are you going to tell me what happened? What were you doing in North Korea?"

"You mind if I have a beer? Scratch the request. What are you going to do about it?" She hopped off the stool, and he watched the sway of her hips in those tight jeans as she walked around the counter into the kitchen.

Before Rikki sat back down, she tipped the neck of the beer bottle at him. "You keep drinking like you were tonight, and you're gonna trade one six-pack for another…and wind up just like your old man."

He clenched his stomach muscles. She'd been checking him out despite all the tough talk. "North Korea?"

"My partner, David Dawson, got intel that Vlad was meeting with the North Koreans."

Quinn raised his eyebrows. "Vlad?"

"I knew that would get your attention." She took a sip of beer. "David had a way into the country across the DMZ and tagged me to go with him."

"Under the radar of the CIA. They didn't know why you were there."

"David didn't trust anyone, and it turns out he was right." Rikki sniffled and wiped the hand holding the beer bottle across her nose.

"The CIA didn't kill David. They thought you had a hand in his death."

"I know, but they were wrong. The North Koreans killed David and captured me. I had already been their…guest for several days before you spotted me marching along."

"They killed David and were sending you to a labor camp." Quinn bumped his manacled hands against his forehead. "If I had been faster, had taken out the soldier holding you first, you might've had a chance."

"I had no chance, not there. I figured I was a dead woman when I went for the soldier's gun anyway. The area was crawling with North Koreans. You saw that after you took your shot." She dragged her fingernail down the bottle's damp label, ripping a line through it. "I-I thought the person out there was trying to save me and I didn't even know it was you—not until later. And then I found out it was you and you were trying to assassinate me."

He clanged the bracelets against the radiator. "Not when I killed that soldier. I'd changed my mind already. I was trying to help you, Rikki, but I failed, and I've been punishing myself ever since."

Her gaze swept over his unkempt apartment, his tousled hair, the stubble on his face. "Maybe the navy punished you for failing in your duty, for failing to take out the rogue CIA operative."

"They didn't. They figured you were dead and one way or the other, I was the cause of your death." Closing his eyes, he lowered his backside to the floor and drew his knees to his chest. "I'd figured the same thing."

"That's why neither the CIA nor the navy can know I'm still alive." She pinged her fingernail against the bottle. "Not until I can sort all of this out."

"How did you escape from the labor camp?"

"The kindness of strangers."

"The kindness of strangers and a will to survive. I know you, too, Rikki."

"I had a lot to live for."

"Because you got information on Vlad?"

"Yeah, Vlad." Her eyelashes fluttered. "And now I'm going to bring him down and clear my name."

"I'll help you."

She chugged some beer, eyeing him over the bottle. "How do I know I can trust you? How do I know you're not going to run back to your commanding officers and tell them I'm still alive?"

Quinn lifted his hands. "Do you really think I couldn't get out of these if I wanted?"

She sputtered and slammed her bottle on the counter. "Try it."

"I don't want to." He hunched his shoulders. "That's the point. I want you to feel secure. I'm no threat to you, Rikki. I wanna help you."

Someone banged on the front door, and Rikki jumped from the stool, grabbing her weapon. "Who'd you call?"

"Nobody."

"Quinn? Quinn, buddy? You alive in there?"

Rikki took three steps toward the radiator, raising her brows and her gun in his direction.

Quinn whispered, "It's just a friend, an acquaintance from the bar."

Leaning over him, Rikki pushed open the window. As she clambered onto the sill above him, she said over her shoulder, "Get rid of him."

"You're crazy." Quinn tried to grab her ankle with his manacled hand, but she slipped out the window and onto the ledge outside the building.

"Quinn? I know you're in there, buddy. You left your hat at the bar."

A knock followed his words, and a woman's voice came through the door. "C'mon, sugar. Open up, and we can continue the party."

His hat. Damn it. He didn't care about the hat.

Alice's singsong voice continued. "Little pig, little pig, let me in, or I'll huff and puff and blow."

The doorknob rattled, and Quinn's stomach sank when the door started to ease open. He'd forgotten to lock it. He rose from the floor and stuck his head out the window. "Rikki. Give me those keys."

In response, she slid the window half-closed and left him to his fate.

Chapter 3

Rikki heard the door bang open all the way, and the woman with the Southern accent let out a whoop.

"Whatcha doin' there, sugar?"

The man, who seemed a bit more sober, said, "This isn't a burglary or anything, is it?"

Quinn rattled the handcuffs. "Just a little…fun that got out of hand."

The man swore and chuckled. "Is the little lady still here?"

Rikki held her breath as she pressed the palms of her hands against the rough siding of Quinn's apartment building.

"Long gone. Can I get some help here, Elvin?"

"I don't know about that, sugar. I like what I'm seein'."

Rikki didn't blame Ms. Southern Belle. She'd liked what she'd seen of Quinn, too. His slide into despair over her supposed death couldn't have been that dire, given the condition of his hard body. Hard all over. Hard for her.

Elvin grunted. "Alice, if you think I'm going to hang around while you torture Quinn here, you've been drinkin' too many Hurricanes."

"Who said anything about torture, and who said anything about you hanging around?" Alice must've walked toward Quinn, as her words carried right out the gap in the window.

Rikki shuffled a few steps on the ledge to the left.

"I finally got Quinn right where I want him, as soon as he loses that underwear."

Quinn cleared his throat. "Yeah, well, I think I've had enough fun and games for the night. Thanks anyway, Alice."

Elvin interrupted Alice's foreplay. "Do you have the keys, man?"

Rikki traced the outline of the cuff keys in her front pocket. At least Elvin seemed to be in a hurry to get out of there. A nearly naked man in handcuffs would probably give this good ol' boy nightmares.

The handcuffs jangled against the radiator. "She took the keys. Must've thought it was pretty funny."

"You want me to call a locksmith or something? Go home and get my saw?"

"God, no."

Quinn practically shouted, and Rikki couldn't help the smile that curved her lips. Served him right for leaving her for dead in the DMZ.

"Grab a paper clip from the drawer by the dishwasher. There should be a bunch of loose ones in there. That'll do it."

Rikki heard heavy footsteps and then heavy breathing near the open window.

Alice asked in a low, hoarse voice, "You sure you don't wanna give me a whirl, sugar? I know I could do you better than the girl who left you here."

"No offense, Alice, but I'm not sure you could. She wore me out."

Rikki clapped a hand over the laugh bubbling on her lips and teetered forward.

Finally, Elvin came to the rescue. "Will this work?"

"That'll do it. Right there."

A scrape and a click later and Quinn said, "That's better. Thanks, man, and thanks for picking up my hat. I could've lived without it."

"We'll get out of here. Maybe that little firebrand will return."

Quinn raised his voice. "I hope so."

"Can we at least take the pizza?"

Quinn answered, "Go for it, Alice. I'll see you guys around."

"Maybe another time, sugar, when you're not so… tired."

Quinn mumbled something incoherent, and Rikki closed her eyes and took a deep breath, thankful she didn't have to listen to some other woman having her way with a naked and chained-up Quinn.

The front door shut, and Rikki's eyelids flew open. Now Quinn was free, probably armed and most likely pissed off.

The window beside her slid open the rest of the way, and Quinn stuck his head out. "Are you okay out here? God, I had visions of you tumbling off my building."

Rikki tossed her head. "It's a wide ledge and it's so

humid out here, I'm practically stuck to the side of the apartment."

"Come here." He stretched out his arms. "And for God's sake, be careful."

She sidled along the wall and ignored his help when she got to the window. "I got this."

When Quinn stepped back, Rikki swung into the room, her gun in the waistband of her jeans. She drank him in, still in his briefs, a light sheen of sweat dampening his chest.

"Why did you do that? Why'd you leave me hooked up to the radiator?"

"How was I supposed to know your front door was unlocked? If I'd known that, I wouldn't have gone through all the trouble of breaking into your place through your bathroom window."

"You left me exposed to that...man-eater." He hooked a finger around one bracelet of the cuffs and dangled them in the air. "I should've taken her up on her offer and left you out on that ledge until morning."

"Why didn't you?"

Her question wiped the smile from his face. "Because you're here, standing in front of me, fulfilling every one of my wishes over the past year, and now I don't ever want to let you go."

Before she had a chance to blink, Quinn had her in his arms, and hers curled around his neck in a traitorous response.

His head dipped, and his mouth sought hers. The kiss he pressed against her lips tasted like booze and... desperation. Her muscles tensed. She wasn't here to be Quinn McBride's salvation.

The desire that pumped through her veins and

clouded her brain began to lift. As if waking from a dream, she planted her hands against the flat, smooth planes of muscle shifting across his chest. She pulled away from his demanding mouth, backed away from the prodding erection that promised a night of heaven and a morass of hell.

"Quinn. We're not doing this." And how much of "this" was a trick to lure her into trusting him?

Quinn's large frame shuddered. He dropped his hands from her shoulders and clenched his fists at his sides.

Rikki felt the loss of his touch like a cold wave washing over her. Tears ached in her throat. While she'd been locked up, she found out it had been Quinn behind that sniper rifle, and her hatred of him had kept her alive in the labor camp—that and his baby in her belly.

Without her anger, what did she have left but love? And loving Quinn McBride had only ever brought her heartache. That's all love ever brought.

Flexing his fingers, he turned away from her and plucked his shorts from the floor. He stepped into them and ran a hand through his messy hair. "I just hope you believe me, that I'd changed my mind about the assignment. You can't stand there and tell me that if the CIA had given you orders to take me down, you wouldn't have done it."

"I guess we'll never know." She shoved her hands in her front pockets to stop herself from reaching for him again and smoothing her palms against the muscles that bulged and dipped beneath his flesh. "It's not like we were...together at the time of your mission, anyway."

He sliced a hand through the air. "Don't put that on

me. I tried to follow up with you, but you'd disappeared and wouldn't respond to my messages."

"I had my own assignment going on. That's when David told me about Vlad and the North Koreans. At the end of our affair, I thought we'd decided to call it what it was."

"And what was it, Rikki?" He crossed his arms over his broad chest, the skin across his biceps tight.

She flipped the unfamiliar dark hair over her shoulder. "A fling—a dangerous, ill-conceived fling that defied all the rules of the navy and the CIA. A fling that would've gotten both of us written up and reprimanded."

"You really believe that shooting you offered me a way out, a way to keep our affair secret?" His dark eyes narrowed to dangerous slits. "What we did wasn't the brightest move on either of our parts, but it wasn't enough to get me court-martialed or ruin my career. And you spooks break the rules all the time to justify the means in the end."

Licking her lips, she took a step back. "I've never slept with someone to get intel."

"Neither have I."

"I didn't mean…" She waved one arm over his shirtless body. "I didn't think that's what you were doing here."

"Really? 'Cause you sure pulled away fast. The Rikki I knew wouldn't have been able to turn off her desire like that. The Rikki I knew ran as hot as blazes."

A pulse beat at the base of her throat, and tingles ran up the insides of her thighs. Their need for each other had been undeniable and unquenchable. Whenever he'd touched her, she'd responded like a feral creature, her hunger not satisfied until he'd taken control of her body and mind in every way, slaked her thirst, tamed her wild cravings. He'd been the only man in her life who'd understood what she needed—before she'd understood it herself.

Her nipples crinkled under her T-shirt, and the familiar wanting throbbed between her legs. Beneath half-closed lids, her gaze wandered to the handcuffs Quinn had let slide to the floor.

If he didn't ask now, if he didn't wait for her consent, if he restrained and ravished her body like he used to, he'd fill the need she'd carried with her since the day she left him in Dubai.

She cleared her throat and stuck out her hand. "Truce? You don't get in my way, and I won't kill you."

He ignored her outstretched hand. "I can help you. Someone must already be giving you information, since you seem to know a lot of what went down. One of David's guys?"

"You're right. Someone else is already helping me, so I don't need your assistance." She swept her weapon from the counter and shoved it into the back of her waistband. "I just needed to hear a few things from your own lips."

Her cell phone buzzed, and she pulled it from her pocket. She entered her code and swiped her finger across the text message that had come through. She read the words *Gator Lounge* and then shoved the phone back in her pocket.

When she raised her head, she almost bumped Quinn's chin. He'd moved in on her again, and the heat coming from his body seemed to find its way into her pores.

She stumbled back, crossing her arms over her chest.

He held up his hands. "Since you wanted to talk to me, does that mean you already suspected I'd changed my mind about assassinating you?"

She'd been hoping like hell he could convince her, and he had done so, but she still didn't think she could tell him about Bella—not yet.

"I was blinded by rage when I found out you were the sniper on that hill, but I'd already figured any navy SEAL sniper worth his salt would've been able to take me out before dropping those soldiers—especially you." She held up one finger. "But the fact that you took the assignment enraged me just the same."

"I'm sorry, Rikki. If I had to do it all over again..."

"You'd do the exact same thing. Duty and country." She crouched down and picked up the handcuffs, then snapped them in their holder on her belt. She had no intention of leaving them here for Alice.

"I won't be staying in New Orleans long, and you can get back to doing whatever it was you were doing." She wrapped her fingers around the neck of her beer bottle on the kitchen counter and tipped it back and forth. "But if you're getting deployed again soon, I suggest you clean up your act, sailor."

"Where are you off to next? You can stay here until you leave."

She snorted. "Not a good idea. Take care of yourself, Quinn."

She held out her hand for a shake again. This time he took it, but instead of squeezing her hand, he cinched his fingers around her wrist and rotated her hand around. He pressed his lips against the center of her palm. "I'm glad you're alive, Rikki. Makes the world a whole helluva lot more bearable."

She pulled away from him and crossed the room to the front door. As she grasped the handle, she tried to think of some flip, clever way to say goodbye, but her throat closed and her bottom lip trembled.

In the end, Rikki slipped out the door without another word or backward glance.

The sultry night air pressed against her as she loped along the streets not far from the French Quarter. She ducked into a clump of bushes in a park a few blocks from Quinn's apartment and pulled out her scooter.

Just after midnight, the bars would still be open, and Rikki had another appointment at the Gator Lounge before she settled her business in this city. Before she left Quinn—maybe for good this time.

She hopped on the electric scooter and motored back toward the lights and action of downtown.

One quick glance over her shoulder, and she let out a sigh of relief. Nobody had followed her. Why would anyone be following her? As far as the CIA knew, a North Korean soldier had shot her dead in the DMZ and a trustworthy navy SEAL had witnessed her death.

She could trust Quinn not to out her. Besides, if he did and the CIA brought her in, he'd be going down with her. She'd make sure of that.

Traffic got heavier as she got closer to the French Quarter. She kept her eye on the side mirror to monitor anything unusual behind her, and would slip between cars if someone seemed to be following too closely or for too long.

When she reached the streets of the French Quarter, still teeming with tourists, she located the bar and then stashed the scooter on a side street. She slid from the seat and ran her fingers through her hair. Her contact had indicated the bar had a casual atmosphere, but she didn't want to look like she'd just come in from a horse ride.

She ducked to peer into the side-view mirror and pulled a lipstick from the purse strapped across her body. She hadn't thought to primp before accosting Quinn in his apartment, but then she hadn't thought much at all about what she wanted to accomplish by seeing him.

To make sure the heat still blazed between them? Check. To see if he still had a body that could weaken her knees? Check. To find out if her presence would make him happy? Check.

She had to admit to herself that seeing him...disheveled had given her a small, petty sense of pleasure. It had also backed up his claim that he'd had a change of heart about shooting her. Quinn wouldn't be drinking if something weren't troubling him.

Now that she'd confirmed that, she'd have to tell him about Bella. He deserved to know about his daughter, even though he'd never mentioned wanting children to her.

She straightened up and pulled her blouse over the gun in her waistband. She didn't expect trouble from her contact, but she had to be prepared for anything. Ariel had vouched for him, and that was good enough for Rikki.

She'd know her guy by his blue Dodgers cap in a city with no pro baseball team. Rikki joined the throng of tourists still crowding Bourbon Street after midnight, and quickened her pace when she saw the street for the bar up ahead.

Someone plowed into her and she spun around, her

hand hovering at her waist. The drunk who'd bumped her gave her a sloppy smile and raised his drink. She stepped to the side and rounded the next corner. A green neon sign announced the Gator Lounge, and Rikki surveyed the pedestrians behind her before ducking inside the darkness.

She shivered as the air-conditioning hit her warm skin. She'd overdressed for the heat and humidity in jeans, a blouse and tennies, but shorts and a T wouldn't have worked for breaking into Quinn's place and carrying a weapon and cuffs.

Her gaze flickered across the small cocktail tables and then rested on the back of a man seated at the bar, a blue baseball cap on his head.

Rikki scooped in a breath and threaded her way through the tables. As she hopped onto the stool next to her contact, she waved at the bartender.

"What can I getcha?" The bartender slapped a napkin on the bar in front of her.

"Light beer, no glass." She slid a glance to her right to see if her words registered with the man in the Dodgers hat.

She waited for his prearranged response—a folding of all four corners of his napkin.

He picked at the label on his beer bottle with his fingernail.

She held her breath.

The bartender placed her beer on the napkin. "Three dollars. Running a tab?"

"No." Her eyes glued to her contact's cocktail napkin, she unzipped the front compartment of her purse and pulled out a five.

Finally the man beside her dipped his head. "I have what you want, but who are you?"

The question had her convulsively clenching her fist around the bill in her hand. That was not part of the deal. He wasn't supposed to ask any questions. He was supposed to hand over a flash drive with information— after folding the damned corners of his napkin.

She turned toward him and smiled sweetly. "You can't possibly have what I want…sugar. And who the hell are you?"

He jerked his thumb upward, hitting the bill of his cap.

Rikki's heart stuttered. None of this made sense. He had half of the plan right, and it couldn't be just a coincidence. Who else would be wearing a Dodgers cap in this particular bar in New Orleans at this exact time?

Her laugh tinkled as she creased her money and tucked it beneath a candle. "Sorry, I'm no Dodgers fan. In fact, I don't even like baseball."

Wedging one foot on the floor, she took a quick gulp of her beer. She needed to abandon this rendezvous— and fast.

As she shoved herself to her feet, the man grabbed her wrist and growled in her ear, "I have a gun pointed at your ribs. Make a move, and I'll take you down."

Chapter 4

Quinn plowed through the crowd of people on Bourbon Street, stepping on a few toes and upsetting a few drinks. The Gator Lounge occupied a side street, and he made for the corner of that street like a heat-seeking missile.

Before he stepped through the front door of the bar, he tugged his baseball cap low on his forehead. If Rikki made him as soon as he walked into the bar, he'd lose his chance to find out what business she had in New Orleans. He might lose his chance of ever seeing her again.

Shoving his hands in his pockets, he hunched his shoulders and dipped his head. Two steps into the bar, he scanned it quickly, and his heart jumped in his chest.

His gaze locked onto Rikki and a man in a blue cap heading for the back of the bar. Quinn had frequented enough bars in the past few months to know this one led to an alley running behind it. Rikki and her companion were headed either for the restrooms or out the back door. Either way, he'd be in the vicinity to intercept them.

He backed out of the Gator Lounge and jogged through a small courtyard between buildings. He hugged the side of the bar and poked his head around the corner into the alley.

The blood in his veins ran cold as he watched the man propel Rikki in front of him—by force. Every line in her body screamed that she didn't want to be in his company or be going anywhere with him.

Plenty of people had seeped into this alley off the main street, and Quinn joined their ranks, edging closer to Rikki and her abductor.

The guy in the cap seemed distracted. He didn't notice the pedestrians who passed by him and Rikki, wasn't expecting any kind of intervention—and that was the way Quinn liked it.

Quinn joined a trio of late-night revelers and as they walked past Rikki and the man, Quinn dropped back. He reached out and grabbed the man's arm, twisting it behind him before he could use the weapon gripped in his hand.

Rikki made a muffled cry and dropped to the ground.

Quinn gave the man's arm a quick yank and heard the crack of his bone.

The man howled, his legs buckling beneath him.

Quinn heard a shout behind him. "Hey, hey. What are you doing?"

Plucking the gun from the man's useless arm, Quinn kicked him in the gut for good measure.

Someone came up behind Quinn and grabbed his arm. "What are you doing?"

As Quinn shrugged off the stranger's hand, he slid the man's weapon beneath his shirt. "Dude was taking off with my girl. You're comin' home with me, Lila."

Rikki grabbed the sleeve of Quinn's T-shirt, glanced over her shoulder at the concerned onlooker and shrugged. "Jealousy."

Quinn hustled Rikki out of the alley before someone called the cops or an ambulance. When they hit Bourbon Street, Quinn whipped the hat from his head and clasped it against his side with his arm. "Are you okay?"

"I'm fine. How the hell did you know where I was?"

"Car?"

"Scooter a few blocks away."

"You wear a helmet with that thing?"

She poked him in the side. "You're concerned about helmet safety at a time like this?"

"Let's get that helmet from your scooter, and then we'll hop on my bike."

"If you see me to my scooter, I'll be fine."

"Oh, no, you don't." He gripped her upper arm. "I'm not letting you out of my sight. Some guy with a gun almost took you away—again. I wanna know what kind of danger you're in, and I wanna help. I owe you that."

"Really…" She tripped as he pinched her arm tighter. "Okay. My scooter's around the next corner."

Quinn loosened his hold on her and smoothed his fingers over the bunched material of her blouse. If he'd learned anything about Rikki during their short affair, he knew she didn't respond to halfhearted attempts at persuasion—or lovemaking.

She pointed to a small electric job with a white helmet locked to the back. "That's it."

"Let's grab it and go. You don't know if they ID'd your vehicle or followed you."

"No." She bent over the scooter and released her helmet. "I was not followed from your place—unless it was by you. How'd you know where I was?"

"Later. My motorcycle is back toward the bar." He patted his waistband. "I got the guy's gun, so unless he has a backup he's not going to be taking any shots at you."

"The way his bone cracked when you twisted his arm behind his back, I don't think he could handle any weapon right now." She crossed her arms over her helmet, hugging it to her midsection.

"When I saw him hustling you away at gunpoint, I wanted to do worse than break his arm, but I don't need to be charged with murder or even questioned at this point. Who was he?" He placed his hand at the small of her back and propelled her across the street.

"Later."

As they reached the other side of the street, Quinn ran his hand along the waistband of Rikki's jeans, sitting low on the curve of her hips.

She stiffened beneath his touch. "I don't think it's the time or place to be groping me."

"I'm not groping you, unless you want me to." He briefly cupped her derriere through the tight denim. "What happened to your gun and handcuffs?"

"He relieved me of them and dropped them in a Dumpster right outside the club."

Quinn muttered an expletive. "Maybe we can retrieve them tomorrow."

"We?"

"Here's my bike. Get that helmet on and hop on the back."

She placed a hand on his shoulder. "Are you okay to drive this thing? You were sleeping off a bender when I sneaked into your apartment."

"The events since that time have gone a long way to sober me up."

She held out her hand. "Doesn't matter how you feel, Quinn. Your blood alcohol level is probably still over the legal limit. You don't want to get arrested for murder *or* driving while under the influence."

He jingled the keys and glanced down at his Honda. "Can you manage a bike this size? It's not your little scooter."

She snorted. "Hop on the back."

Rikki handled the bike like she handled everything else—with confidence and ease. He did have to help her hoist the bike onto its kickstand, but she'd been right about taking the wheel—or the handlebars. He'd been an idiot to take a chance like that on the bike, no matter how sober he felt, but he couldn't stand to see her waltz right out of his life just after he'd discovered she'd survived the ordeal in North Korea.

How the hell had she escaped that torture?

As they approached his front door, Rikki hung back. "You didn't leave your place unlocked again, did you? We're not going to find Alice waiting in your bed, are we? Or worse?"

"I can dispense with Alice easily enough, but if that man who had you at gunpoint has any friends, we want to make sure he hasn't ID'd me and dispatched one of his cohorts to wait for us."

Rikki's brown eyes widened as if the thought had never occurred to her. If it hadn't, her spy skills needed some refreshment.

Where had she been since escaping from North Korea?

He tucked her behind him. "Wait here while I give it a quick check."

Her hand grabbed his side, and she lifted her abductor's gun from his waistband. "Now I'm armed, too. We'll take 'em on together."

"I forgot who I was dealing with." He unlocked his door and pushed it open slowly with his foot. When it stood wide, he entered his apartment with his weapon sweeping the room.

Rikki closed and locked the door behind them and crept in beside him, peeling off to check out the back rooms. She called out, "All clear."

Quinn peered over the counter into the kitchen. "All clear here."

Rikki joined him and blew out a breath. "How would that guy have ID'd you? He barely got a look at you before you took him down."

"If he knows who you are, he might make the connection from New Orleans to me and me to you."

"There aren't many people who knew what we did in Dubai." Her lashes fluttered, and she got busy putting away the spare gun. "I mean, that we…hooked up. I don't think some random person from intelligence is going to make that link between me and you."

"Intelligence? Is that who that was? You said it yourself earlier. The CIA thinks you're dead."

She raised her shoulders to her ears. "I don't know

who he was, and more important, he didn't know who I was."

"Are you telling me that was some kind of random abduction?" Quinn shook his head. "No common street thug is going to get over on you, Rikki, especially when you have a gun and cuffs on you."

"I didn't say he was a common criminal. The guy had mad skills himself and I'm not downplaying your heroic rescue, but he'd let his guard down by the time he got me outside the Gator Lounge. He wasn't expecting anyone to come riding to my defense."

"You think he was from the Company?"

"I don't know. We didn't get that far in our acquaintance, but he did not know who I was. He asked me."

"Maybe I am still drunk." Quinn massaged his temple with two fingers. "If he didn't know who you were and he was some kind of spy, why was he abducting you and why were you meeting him?"

Rikki hopped on a stool, straddling it, knees wide. "First, you. How did you know I was going to the Gator Lounge when I left here?"

"I didn't know you were going straight there when you took off, but I saw the text message come through." He clicked his tongue. "Careless, Rikki. I was looking straight down at your phone, but then maybe you wanted me to see that message."

She shot up on the stool, her back ramrod straight. "That's ridiculous."

"Now you. Who were you meeting at the Gator and why?" He held up one finger. "And don't even try lying to me."

She slumped, her shoulders rounding, her hands on her knees. "I don't know exactly who I was meeting. We had a series of clues for each other, a back-and-forth, starting with his Dodgers cap."

"That guy was wearing a Dodgers cap. What happened?"

"I spotted him at the bar, everything on track. I ordered a beer, using the agreed-upon language, but he didn't reciprocate. He went off script. My contact didn't know who I was and wasn't supposed to ask, but this guy…" She waved one hand in the air.

"You figured he wasn't your guy or maybe your guy had been replaced? What did you do?"

"I admitted nothing to him and was getting ready to abandon the mission. I must've telegraphed that because the next thing I knew, he had his gun poking me in the side."

Quinn crossed his arms, curling his fingers into his biceps. "Did he ask you any more questions at that point?"

"Nope. Started marching me away to God-knows-where." She captured the unfamiliar brown hair in one hand and curled it around her fist.

Quinn's gaze locked onto the dark, silky strands. Even without her wavy red hair and bright blue eyes, he'd recognized Rikki in a flash. Why wouldn't he? She'd been in his dreams nightly.

He tugged on a lock of his own hair, which he'd grown out since his previous deployment. "Is that a wig? It's so…different."

Her mouth formed an *O* and released a little puff of air. "I thought we were talking about my abductor."

"We are, we will, just wondering about the transformation." The warmth from his chest began creeping up his neck.

Even discussing a violent incident and a mystery, Quinn couldn't tamp down his attraction to Rikki. He could take her right now, across that kitchen counter, bent over that stool, and not give another thought to her mysterious meeting or the man he'd beaten down in the alley.

What did any of it matter with this woman back in his life, sitting right in front of him, inches away?

She tossed her head, and the dark hair flowed over one shoulder. "It's not a wig. I had my hair straightened when I had it colored. It'll last for several weeks—as long as I need."

Quinn ran both hands over his face as if waking from a long, drugged sleep. "As long as you need to do what, Rikki? What are you doing in New Orleans? What was that meeting all about?"

"The man I was supposed to meet had something for me, something that might help me clear my name. I need that. I need something before I can go to the CIA and reveal that I'm still alive—and no traitor." She blinked and rubbed her nose with the back of her hand.

The Rikki he knew, the woman who'd dumped him in Dubai, never cried. But that woman had been a trusted CIA operative at the top of her game and still on the rise.

When she'd succumbed to him, knowing her superiors would frown on her conduct, knowing she could be reprimanded, she'd spun out of control. Their desire for each other had been so great they'd both thrown caution to the wind. They'd made love in glass elevators high above the glittering city, coupled in the warm waters of the Persian Gulf in a place that frowned upon spouses holding hands in public.

And during all of it, the kick-ass CIA operative who could disarm a man without breaking a sweat and interrogate a suspected terrorist for twenty-four hours straight had relinquished control to him in every way. She'd waited for his commands, done his bidding, which was really her own. She could pretend to herself that he'd mastered her mind and body, but in reality he'd been the captive. She'd enthralled him. Still did.

Quinn launched forward and crouched beside her. His thumb swept her bottom lashes where a single teardrop trembled, although she'd willed it not to fall.

"You deserve that life back, and I'm going to help you reclaim it. What did your contact have for you?"

"A-a flash drive containing some information. I don't think he even knew what the info meant, but he was going to pass it along to me."

"On whose authority? Who's your contact at the agency? Who sent him?"

Rikki swept her tongue along her bottom lip. "Maybe it was all a setup. Maybe the goal of the plan all along included my capture. The flash drive a ruse to lure me out."

"Who sent him? Not some anonymous source? You didn't trust some anonymous CIA drone, did you?"

"It was Ariel." She hunched forward, her nose almost touching his. "You know Ariel, don't you?"

"The head of the Vlad task force. Several of my SEAL team members have been on assignments controlled by Ariel—and they trust her, or him."

"Her. Ariel is definitely female."

"How do you know that? I think one of my team members actually spoke to her, but we're not even sure it was the real Ariel." Quinn's eyes narrowed. "You know her?"

"Ariel was my mentor at the CIA when I started. You know, one female spy to another in a department dominated by men."

Quinn sat back on his heels. "You mean, you know the *real* Ariel? The actual woman behind the clever pseudonym? From what I understand, the Vlad task force is controlled by Prospero, Jack Coburn's black ops organization. Ariel, Prospero—from the Shakespeare play."

"Yeah, I remember my Shakespeare and yeah, Ariel is with Prospero now, recruited from the CIA several years ago."

"Her real name?"

Rikki ran her fingertip along the seam of her lips. "Ariel."

Quinn jumped to his feet and paced in front of the window. "You don't owe her anything if she set you up."

"I can't be sure she did. She's the one who discovered I was in the labor camp and not dead. She's the one who helped me escape, get back to…get out."

"Maybe she did all that so she could dial in the CIA and have them recapture you. Maybe she didn't want you hobnobbing with the North Koreans, possibly passing them intel."

"I don't believe that, not… Ariel. If that's what she wanted, my contact at the bar would've followed through with our assignment without alarming me, and then she could've sent the FBI to pick me up and arrest me." Rikki slid from the stool and edged around the counter into the kitchen. "That's not how this went down."

"Maybe the contact himself went rogue. Maybe he recognized you."

She made a half turn from the fridge, a bottle of water in her hand. She raised it. "In this getup? Just because you had me figured out immediately doesn't mean some CIA agent is going to recognize me from a photo in a briefing on spies within the Agency. Dark hair, dark eyes…" She patted her hip. "A few extra pounds. This is a damned good disguise."

When she touched her body, Quinn's gaze followed her hand. Rikki had always been long and lean. He tracked up the curve of her hip to the loose blouse draped over her form, brushing the ample swell of her breasts.

He swallowed hard. He'd always enjoyed Rikki's slim, athletic build—especially given their marathon lovemaking sessions in…unusual places and circumstances. But for the first time this crazy evening, he noticed the new softness of her body—the way her jeans hugged her derriere and thighs, the seductive sway of her hips when she walked, the way her blouse pulled tight across her breasts when she spread her arms or gestured. His erection pulsed again.

Then he blinked. Rikki hadn't just escaped from a North Korean labor camp. She'd been recuperating somewhere.

Quinn cleared his throat. "God, it's late. You're bunking here tonight, and I don't want to hear any arguments."

She snapped her mouth closed and chugged some water from the bottle. "Okay, but just so we're clear you're sleeping in the bed and I'm taking the couch."

Quinn's erection ached for relief, and he tugged on

the hem of his cargo shorts. "Yeah, of course, but I have a sofa bed in my office and you can have that." He opened his mouth in a pretend yawn. "We can try to figure out what happened to your contact tomorrow. If you still trust her, get in touch with Ariel."

Rikki sloshed some water in her mouth before swallowing. "Do you happen to have an extra toothbrush?"

"I'm on leave, and you're in luck because I just went to my dentist two weeks ago. I think he's under some misconception that the navy supplies me with one toothbrush every two years, because he loaded me up. They're in the second drawer on the right. This place has two bathrooms, so you're welcome to the other one."

"I'll take the water with me to bed." She swept her small purse from the counter. "This is good. I'll get a good night's sleep and regroup in the morning. I'm sure Ariel will have an explanation for me."

"If you think you can trust her."

"I do." She turned at the entrance to the hallway. "Thanks for your assistance tonight, Quinn. Maybe I *did* want you to see that text after all."

"You can always ask me, Rikki. You can ask me for anything."

A smile trembled on her lips, and then she disappeared down the hallway.

Cocking his head to the side, Quinn listened as she got a toothbrush from his bathroom and then shut herself in the other one.

He sprinted down the hall and ducked into the second bedroom. He pulled out the sofa bed, darted to his bedroom, snagged a pillow from his bed and tossed it onto the sofa bed. Despite his best efforts at a quick assembly, Rikki hovered at the door of the office as he dragged a blanket across the bed.

"Just making up the sofa bed. Did you find the toothbrush and toothpaste okay?"

"Yep." She ran her tongue along her teeth.

"Okay, then. Tomorrow." His gaze darted to Rikki still propping up the doorjamb. She didn't expect him to squeeze past her, did she? He couldn't handle that.

A few seconds later that seemed like minutes, Rikki pushed herself off the door. "Nice apartment. I had memorized your address from…before. I was hoping you still lived here."

He spread his arms. "Still here. Sleep tight."

He practically ran from the room, slamming the door behind him. Sleep tight? What did that even mean, anyway?

He brushed his own teeth and studied his reflection in the mirror. He needed a shave—and an attitude adjustment. Rikki didn't want him anymore. She'd made that clear before. And after he'd gone on a mission to assassinate her? Yeah, pretty much killed any thread of a chance he had left with her. Now if he could only send that message to his body.

He yanked the covers back from his bed and pulled off his T-shirt. He unzipped the fly on his shorts and hooked his thumbs in the band of his briefs as he started to take them down with his shorts. He usually slept naked, but maybe leaving on his underwear would protect him from lustful thoughts about Rikki.

He crawled between the sheets, rolled on his side, then the other side, and then flopped onto his back, one arm flung across his face. Briefs, no briefs, fully clothed, suit of armor—didn't matter. Rikki Taylor was in his blood, and now she was back in his life.

About an hour later on the edge of another feverish dream, Quinn bolted upright in bed, his heart racing. He paused and heard the noise that had awakened him.

Someone pounded on the door again.

Quinn rolled out of bed and grabbed the gun on his nightstand. He crept toward the front door and paused, holding his breath.

The pounding resumed, following by a groan and a shout. "Quinn? Quinn, you there?"

Quinn drew his brows over his nose and released the locks. He eased open the door, and a man fell across the threshold, bruised and bloody.

"Quinn, you gotta help me. They're gonna kill me."

Chapter 5

With her blouse pulled on over her panties, Rikki tip-toed to the office door, the gun Quinn had taken from her abductor clutched in her hand.

She opened the door a crack and sucked in a breath as the men's voices, Quinn's and someone else's, carried down the hallway.

Had he called someone to take her in?

She rubbed her eyes. If that were the case, the guy wouldn't be banging on the front door in the wee morning hours. She pressed her ear to the gap in the door, wrinkling her nose. She couldn't hear a damned thing.

With the gun leading the way, she edged down the hallway and tripped to a stop.

Quinn looked up from tending to a badly beaten man stretched out on his living room floor. "Put down that gun and soak some towels with water."

The authoritative tone of his voice had her jumping into action. She placed the weapon on the kitchen counter and scurried back to the hallway, where she rummaged through a few shelves, sweeping towels into her arms.

In the kitchen, she ran two of the towels beneath the faucet until they were soaked and dropped next to Quinn attending to the injured man.

As Quinn checked the man's injuries, Rikki dabbed the cuts on his face with the corner of a damp towel. "Who is he?"

"CIA."

Rikki dropped the towel and jerked back. "You called him?"

Quinn spit out between clenched teeth, "I did not. He just showed up on my doorstep like this. I don't know what the hell he's doing here, but he's a friend, and I'm not turning him away."

"O-of course not." Rikki grabbed the towel and continued cleaning the man's facial wounds. "What happened to him?"

"I don't have a clue. He appeared and collapsed."

The man moaned, and Quinn leaned in close. "Jeff, Jeff. What happened?"

Jeff peeled open one puffy eye, caked with blood. "Got the jump on me. Beat me up."

"Who? Street robbery? Do you want me to call the cops?"

"No." Jeff dug his fingers into the flesh of Quinn's arms. "On the job."

Quinn's eyes met Rikki's for a split second, and her heart flip-flopped. The CIA on the job in New Orleans?

She couldn't stay here. Couldn't stay with Quinn any longer.

Quinn tugged Jeff's shirt back down over his stomach. "I don't see any weapon wounds."

"No weapons." Jeff closed his eyes. "Unless you count the guy's fists."

"You need some ice." Rikki dabbed the last of the blood from Jeff's face. She gathered the bloodstained towels and wrapped them in a plastic bag. She loaded another plastic bag with ice.

When she returned to the living room, Quinn had helped Jeff onto the sofa. Without the blood smearing his face, Jeff no longer looked half-dead.

Rikki perched on the edge of the coffee table, facing Jeff. She thrust the bag of ice at him. "Here. Can you manage?"

"Yeah, thanks." Jeff grabbed the impromptu ice pack and pressed it against the lump forming around his eye.

Quinn started for the hallway. "I'll get you some ibuprofen and water."

As Quinn walked away, Rikki scooted off the table. "I'll get the water."

She and Quinn returned to Jeff's side at about the same time, and Rikki noticed Quinn had pulled on his shorts. That made two times she'd seen the man almost naked in one night, and she didn't have to use her imagination for the rest. They'd spent two whole days together in his hotel room sans clothing. Answering the door for room service had been the only times either of them had slipped into something to cover their nakedness.

Rikki tucked her hair behind one ear and held out the bottle to Jeff. "Here you go. Feeling better?"

She just hoped to God her disguise would see her

through and Jeff wouldn't recognize her, but then nobody in the CIA would be expecting to run into Rikki Taylor—the dead double agent.

"I feel a lot better." Jeff tapped his jaw and winced. "I'm really sorry about intruding here."

Heat prickled Rikki's cheeks. *If only.* "Oh, no, we…"

Quinn shrugged and dragged Rikki against his side with one arm, his hand resting perilously close to the under-curve of her breast, his warm skin soaking through the thin material of her blouse.

In her haste, Rikki had yanked on her top but hadn't bothered with a bra and Quinn seemed to be taking full advantage of that fact.

"Yeah, man, bad timing."

Rikki bit her bottom lip. Definitely taking advantage.

"I'll be out of your way tomorrow morning. If I can just stay the night, I think can get back on track."

"Are you sure you don't need medical care?"

"I could use some, but there's nothing urgent. Nothing that can't wait for tomorrow. I'm really sorry, Quinn."

"Don't worry about it. I'm just glad I was here. Can you tell me what you were doing in New Orleans?"

"Can't do that, man, not even for a badass navy SEAL, and especially not in front of your girl here."

"Me?" Rikki tried to wriggle out of Quinn's grasp, but he wasn't having it.

His fingers curled into the curve of her hip. "She can go into the other room."

Rikki nodded, anxious to escape Quinn's realm where she had zero discipline and even less self-control.

"Sworn to secrecy. You know the drill."

"I do know the drill. I wouldn't tell you about my

next mission, either." Quinn jerked his thumb over his shoulder. "I've got a spare room with a sofa bed all made up. I even have a few extra toothbrushes."

Rikki bumped Quinn's hip with her own. "Maybe Jeff would be more comfortable out here."

Jeff tilted his head from side to side, stretching his neck. "Honestly? Stretching out on a bed sounds like a sure cure for me right now."

"Make sure that bed's made up for Jeff, honey." Quinn gave her a little shove from behind, and Rikki clenched her fist at her side. He was milking this situation to the max.

She could raise a fuss in front of this CIA agent, someone who would recognize the name Rikki Taylor immediately, but why tempt fate on this crazy night? "Sure, of course. Why don't you find him a toothbrush and clean towel?"

"I owe you one, McBride, more than one."

Rikki scurried down the hallway and slipped into the office. She smoothed out the covers on the sofa bed and grabbed the rest of her clothes and her purse. Then she crossed the hall to Quinn's bedroom.

As long as he'd invited her into his inner sanctum, she'd make herself at home. She swung open the walk-in closet and dragged a T-shirt off its hanger. Still inside the closet, she pulled the blouse over her head and replaced it with Quinn's T-shirt.

Beneath the T-shirt, she skimmed her hands over her body. Would he be able to tell she'd given birth nine months ago? She cupped her breasts, which still felt heavy although she'd given up breastfeeding a month ago in anticipation of her journey.

Reaching around outside the closet, she flicked off

the light. Quinn McBride would not be getting a look at her naked body.

The bedroom door clicked softly as she stepped out of the closet.

Quinn's head jerked up. "Where'd you come from? I thought maybe you'd slipped out onto the ledge again."

She tugged at the hem of the T-shirt. "Thought I'd find some proper sleepwear."

His dark gaze scorched her head to toe, making her feel as if she were standing in front of him without a stitch on instead of in a baggy shirt.

"Sorry about that. Jeff deserved my full hospitality after what he'd been through. I had to offer him that bed."

She wedged a hand on her hip. "You're not sorry. You jumped at the chance to kick me out of that bed and lure me into this one."

A slow smile claimed Quinn's wide mouth. "I saw it as a win-win."

He crossed to the other side of the king-size bed and flipped down the messy covers. "Be my guest."

Rikki folded her arms, grabbing handfuls of the cotton material of the T-shirt, her gaze darting around the room. She leveled a finger at the floor. "You can sleep there for just one night. I'm sure you've slept on harder surfaces than that in your illustrious career as a navy SEAL sniper."

"Not happening." He set his jaw in a hard line. "The bed's big enough for the two of us. You stay on your side, and I'll stay on mine."

She looked him up and down—all six feet three inches of rippling muscle. "This bed is barely big enough for you."

"On my honor—" he drew a cross over his heart "—I'm not gonna lay a finger on you, Rikki. What kind of caveman do you take me for?"

Her eyes flickered across his broad shoulders. *The thoroughly delicious kind.* "Okay, okay. We both need our rest anyway."

Quinn returned to his side of the bed and dropped his shorts.

Holding her breath, she watched him out of the corner of her eye. Those shorts had better be the only piece of clothing he planned to shed. She eased out that captive breath when he slid between the sheets in his briefs.

As she positioned herself at the very edge of her side of the bed, Quinn punched a pillow and said, "At least we know your identity is still safe."

Her eyes flew open. "What do you mean?"

"Rikki."

The mattress dipped and she knew he'd turned toward her. "What? What does that mean, I'm safe?"

"You didn't figure it out?"

"Figure what out?" She rolled onto her back, her head falling to the side.

"Jeff was your contact person."

She hoisted herself up abruptly, banging her head against the soaring headboard. "No."

"Of course he was. Instead of meeting you at the Gator Lounge, he met up with someone who wanted to replace him. The man you saw in the bar, the man who marched you out at gunpoint, is the same man who beat up Jeff and stole his baseball cap."

Rikki covered her face with her hands. *Of course.* How could she be so stupid? Had she really believed two CIA covert ops were going on in New Orleans at the same time?

Motherhood had affected her brain in more ways than one. Or maybe she could chalk it up to the distracting presence of Quinn.

"You see that, right?"

"I-I-I do now. Of course, that's clear. I'm an idiot."

"Don't beat yourself up. You've had a rough night, a rough year." He smoothed his palm up her thigh, froze and then snatched his hand away. "Sorry."

His touch had sent goose bumps racing up her inner thighs. "You're right. I didn't register for Jeff at all except as your late-night booty call."

A laugh rumbled in Quinn's chest. "You say that like it's a bad thing. Look, Jeff doesn't know who he was supposed to meet or why. You were smart to stick to code words and exchanges instead of descriptions."

She wriggled up higher against the pillow. "But where's that flash drive? Do you think he has it on him?"

"Do you really think the guy who beat him up and stole his hat didn't search him? Maybe he didn't want to have the flash drive on him when he met you. Maybe he left it somewhere in case the meeting didn't come off—which it didn't."

"If he takes a shower tomorrow morning, I'm not above searching through his clothes."

"I'll strongly advise him to take a shower."

"Wait." She sat up straight, crossing her legs beneath her, under the covers. "Why did he come here?"

"For help. Jeff and I go way back. He knows I live in New Orleans. He's been to my place a few times. He came to me for help." A muscle ticked in Quinn's jaw.

"You don't think I had anything to do with his coming here, do you? I hope we're past that suspicion. If I'd wanted to turn you over to the Agency, I could've done it hours ago."

"We're past that." She grabbed the pillow and slid down again, pulling it beneath her head.

"Good. Get some sleep."

Still on her back, Rikki shifted her gaze to the right, taking in Quinn's large frame, positioned on his side, facing her. He'd pushed the covers down to his waist, although the air-conditioning had cooled the room down to a comfortable temperature.

Her eyes had adjusted to the darkness and she drank in the lines of his body, the hard muscles, even in repose, still etched beneath his smooth flesh.

Before she knew what she was doing, before she could stop herself, her hand shot out and she traced her fingertips around one of his brown nipples.

He sucked in a breath. "You don't want this, remember? Don't tease me, Rikki."

She snatched her hand back and rolled to her side, away from him and his irresistible body. "You're right."

Quinn released a long, shuddering breath.

She had teased him with her light touch, had made him hard. Sighing, she drew her knees to her chest, thrusting out her backside, the heat of Quinn's body inches away. Just inches.

She yawned and wriggled into place, her toes skimming his shin, the hair on his leg tickling her.

"Rikki."

She edged toward him, curling one arm around his waist. "Maybe just once, for old times' sake."

He hissed through his teeth. "You're sure about this?"

She pulled her body closer to his, her front flush against his, and breathed into his ear. "I'm sure."

She edged her fingers between the elastic of his briefs and the flat, hard muscles of his abdomen, dragging her nails along the tip of his erection, barely contained by the thin cotton of his underwear.

He shivered. "I've been imagining that all night, but nothing tops the real thing."

She plunged her hand deeper and cupped him with her palm while stroking his tight flesh with her thumb. Her voice, rough with desire, rasped in his ear. "Take me like only you can."

His erection throbbed in her hand, and she could feel her bones melt and her breasts soften in anticipation of his fiery touch.

Quinn hesitated for just a second until Rikki squeezed him and bit the back of his neck.

In one motion, Quinn rose to his knees and ripped the covers from them both. Towering over her, bulging from the confines of his briefs, he growled, "Take them off."

Tingles rushed through her body at his gruff tone of voice, and she started the game. Leaning forward, she took the band of his briefs between her teeth and dragged them down, over his erection. She continued pulling down his underwear with her mouth, past the flaring muscles of his thighs, down to his knees, buried in the mattress of the bed.

Closing his eyes, he plowed his fingers through her hair. "I can pretend it's the fiery red I love."

"Shh." She pressed the pad of her thumb to his lips.

His fingers dug into her scalp as he urged her down. "Take me in your mouth. Taste me."

She closed her lips around his girth, and he moaned in rhythm as she drew him in and out of her mouth.

He pulled away from her, sitting back on his heels. "It's been too long. I can't last like that."

She caressed his shoulders and kissed the spot right above his left nipple. "Tell me what to do next."

He grabbed a fistful of T-shirt. "You can take this off for starters. Why are you still covered?"

She clutched the edge of the shirt, suddenly shy. Would he notice the differences in her body? Would he know what they meant?

She'd been rail-thin when she escaped from the labor camp, four months pregnant. Undernourished and overworked, she'd feared for the life of her baby. If she'd been captive any more than the two months she'd endured, she would've lost Bella for sure.

Instead, she'd wound up in Jamaica with her mother and Chaz, and Mom had coddled her through the duration of her pregnancy, kept her in bed the first two months, well fed and stationary.

Rikki had put on more than enough weight for her pregnancy, and Bella, although born a few weeks early, had posted a healthy weight and length.

During the pregnancy and after, Rikki's breasts had increased in size and softened, her hips had widened, too, and she presented a much different figure than the taut, tight athlete Quinn had first bedded in Dubai.

Impatient with her reluctance, Quinn dragged the T-shirt from her body and yanked down her panties. "That's much better."

With her bottom lip caught between her teeth, Rikki watched Quinn study her new body. His eyes darkened to unfathomable depths.

Then he reached out and cupped her breasts. The thrill of his touch shot down to her belly and lower, creating an aching need. She arched her back, thrusting her chest forward.

He juggled her breasts in his hands as if testing their heft. "I like this new development."

He molded her waist with his palms and reached back to stroke her derriere. "And this. When you get your job back with the Agency, you should let them know you wanna lay off the PT because someone likes your new curves."

One side of her mouth crooked into a smile. He approved of her appearance, and more important, he'd dismissed it as the lack of rigorous physical training on her part. Not that she planned to keep Bella a secret from him forever. She just needed to get through this, get her life back, and then she'd tell Quinn everything—no strings attached.

He kissed her mouth. "What are you smiling about?"

"I'm just glad you like the difference."

"You're kidding. I wouldn't think you'd give a damn one way or the other." He eased her back onto the bed and straddled her on his knees. He lowered his body and squeezed her breasts around the tip of his erection. "But just in case you do give a damn and need proof? Here it is, baby."

He skimmed his tip down the length of her body, prodding between her legs.

Her knees fell open, inviting him in, inviting him home.

He stretched out on the bed on his stomach, between her legs, his own hanging off the foot of the bed. He placed his hands against her inner thighs and spread them apart.

Butterflies swirled in her stomach, and her legs shook.

Quinn dragged his scruffy chin over her soft flesh, drawing a gasp from her lips. Then he probed her with the tip of his tongue, searching out all her secret places.

She stretched her arms over her head, crossing them at the wrists, in total supplication and surrender. Raising her hips off the bed, she choked out, "More, please don't stop."

"Oh, I won't stop, my little Buttercup, but you wanted to play this game, didn't you?"

The teasing glint in his eye had her desperate laugh ending on a hiccup. Her job demanded that she be strong, in control, tough as nails, and she'd delivered. When she first met Quinn, he'd joked that she could scare the buttercups off their stems. So when she became soft and vulnerable for him, just for him, he'd started calling her Buttercup. It still made her weak in the knees.

But he hadn't forgotten the game they played, and he began in earnest. He removed his tongue from her throbbing, swollen flesh and nibbled on the insides of her thighs. He touched her everywhere in every way, except for the pleasure spot between her legs.

He set every nerve ending on fire, had her thrashing her head from side to side, digging her fingernails into his buttocks, wrapping her legs around his hips—until she quivered and begged beneath him.

"Please, Quinn. Please. I'm aching."

He sat back, his erection bobbing in front of him, his skin flushed, obviously experiencing the same frustrated, agonizing pleasure she was—but that wasn't their game.

"I need you. Only you. I'm begging you."

He gave her burning nipple one more tweak. "Since you asked so nicely, Buttercup."

He buried his head between her thighs, and two flicks from his tongue sent her over the edge.

Her orgasm roared through her, wringing the strength from every inch of her body, draining her, releasing her from every expectation, every responsibility, the sensations of her body taking over her mind, flooding it with pleasure.

She whimpered beneath him as he plowed into her, his hard desire eager and hungry.

Rikki wrapped her arms and legs around Quinn as he spent himself inside her.

After, he shifted from her body and pulled her back against his front, nuzzling the hollow of her neck. "I'm glad you're among the living. It's like I just had Christmas, my birthday and Mardi Gras all on the same day."

"Me, too." She pressed a hand against her stomach to calm the butterflies. Quinn wasn't the bad guy. He needed to know about Bella, however he felt about having a child.

"Quinn?"

"Mmm?"

"I have something to tell you. I-I hope, well, I hope you'll be happy about it." She paused and swallowed. In a hoarse whisper, she said, "I had a baby—your baby."

She waited several seconds while Quinn's breathing deepened and slowed. Twisting her head over her shoulder, she scooted onto her back.

She sighed as she took in Quinn, sound asleep, still blissfully ignorant that he was a father.

The following morning, Quinn woke her up by holding a mug of coffee beneath her nose. "He's in the shower."

"Who? What?" She rubbed her eyes. "Jeff?"

Quinn nodded, and she nearly upset the coffee as she bounded out of bed.

"Relax. I already searched his clothes, which he left on the bedroom floor. I didn't find a thing."

She tripped to a stop and pulled the T-shirt she'd been clutching to her chest over her head. "Do you think you can devise some story to get him to tell you about the flash drive without revealing who I am? Maybe I can just admit I'm the person he was supposed to meet."

"If you do, that'll connect you to me. He's gonna wonder what our relationship is all about."

She grabbed the edge of her T-shirt and twisted it into knots with her fingers. "Jeff didn't know why he was meeting me. Didn't know who I was. I'm sure he still thinks Rikki Taylor is dead, if he thinks about her at all. He sure as hell doesn't know you had a fling with Rikki once upon a time." She narrowed her eyes. "Does he?"

"It's getting cold." He held out the mug to her. "And no, Jeff doesn't know anything about my personal life."

"Then let's just tell him I was his intended contact last night." She took the mug from him and curled both hands around it.

"I don't like that idea, Rikki. The lower you keep your profile, the better. What if Jeff talks?"

"Doesn't seem like much of a talker. Pretty tight-lipped if you ask me." She took a sip of the black brew and rolled it in her mouth before swallowing it.

"He's discreet, a good agent, but what if he hears something about us from someone and puts two and two together? You've been doing a good job of keeping under the radar."

"We're going to have to reconnect anyway. I'm not letting that flash drive slip out of my clutches if it's something that can help me. He's going to see me then."

"Not necessarily. You can arrange a drop where you don't meet face-to-face. That'll be easy for you to insist on, since Jeff has already been compromised."

Rikki sank to the foot of the bed. What Quinn said made a lot of sense. She didn't want to reveal any clues to her identity to anyone.

"You're right. I'll arrange a drop with him." She curled one leg beneath her. "Who do you think ambushed him, us or them?"

"Since he's still alive, I'm betting on one of ours— FBI maybe. They could suspect him of being a double agent. The good news is that they were following Jeff and not you."

"All Jeff needs to do is get Ariel to vouch for him without revealing anything else. She's doing stuff not even the CIA knows about."

"Obviously, if she's helping you. Why is she helping you?"

"Let's just say Ariel is a kindred spirit."

"You mean another woman in a male-dominated field. You mentioned that before."

"Something like that." She pulled the T-shirt away from her body. "I'm going to take a shower."

As she brushed past Quinn, he grabbed a handful

of her T-shirt and pulled her toward him. "Any regrets about last night?"

"None at all." She kissed the edge of his chin. "You?"

"No, except that I feel like I kinda tricked you, I mean by inviting Jeff to take the extra room."

She snorted. "You didn't have me fooled for one minute, Quinn McBride."

Showered and dressed in the jeans and blouse from last night, Rikki joined the men in the kitchen with her empty coffee cup.

Jeff raised a piece of toast in her direction. "I was just telling Quinn how sorry I am that I barged in on you two."

Rikki squinted at Jeff's black eye and puffy jaw. "I'm glad Quinn was home. Do you need to see a doctor?"

"I might need some stitches." He brushed aside the lock of hair drooping over a bandage on his forehead. "But I'm okay."

Hopping up on a stool at the kitchen counter, Rikki placed her cell phone in front of her. "Then we don't mind at all, do we, Quinn?"

"Happy to help, bro." Quinn held up the coffeepot. "Refills?"

Rikki shoved her cup across the counter, and Jeff nodded as he pulled his cell phone from his pocket.

"Do you want something else to eat, Jeff?" He pointed to the fridge. "Eggs?"

"Nothing fancy. Toast is okay."

Her phone buzzed on the counter, and Rikki grabbed it. Jeff had sent her a text.

Slowly she raised her gaze to meet his. Understanding and acknowledgment flashed between them.

She'd been outed.

Chapter 6

A charged silence descended on the kitchen. Rikki held her breath as Quinn looked up from pulling slices of bread from a bag. His gaze darted from Jeff to her, understanding dawning in his eyes.

Rikki locked eyes with Jeff, his color high. Her chest rose and fell with each breath, her fight-or-flight instinct in high gear.

Jeff ventured first, turning his cell phone outward. "You're my contact, aren't you?"

She ignored the question. "What happened to you last night? You can tell me."

Jeff shifted his gaze to Quinn, his head down, busy with a bag of bread, whistling like an idiot—as if she and Jeff didn't know he was listening to every word they said.

Rikki waved her hand in Quinn's direction. "You can trust him."

Jeff tipped his head at Quinn. "Are you involved in this?"

"Who, me? I'm just making toast." Quinn held up two pieces of bread.

"Quinn's not involved." Rikki circled the edge of her coffee cup with the tip of her finger. "I know him, knew he lived here. Just like you, I went to him for help after things fell apart last night."

Jeff dropped his shoulders as if dropping his guard. "I'm glad to see you're okay. I didn't know what happened after that guy attacked me and took my cap. He was trying to get info out of me, but a cop came by and he took off. He knew where we were meeting but none of the details."

"That became obvious pretty quickly, since he didn't have the sequence of codes down."

"I'm sorry. I would've stayed around to warn you, but the cops wanted to question me. I had to get out of there, and then I passed out in a churchyard." Jeff traced the lump beneath his eye. "He didn't get anything out of you? Didn't hurt you?"

"I-I was able to get away, and that's when I called this guy." She leveled a finger at Quinn.

Quinn shrugged and snatched the toast from the toaster. "I guess I'm the go-to guy in New Orleans."

Rikki crossed her arms on the counter and leaned forward. "Do you have it?"

"Not on me." Jeff patted his pockets. "Thank God. That man would've snatched it in a second."

Quinn slid a plate in front of Rikki. "Do you have any idea who he was, Jeff? Was he one of yours?"

"CIA coming after one of its own? Maybe."

"Let's face it." Rikki pinged her cup with her fingernail. "You were not on official CIA business. You were on Ariel's business, and she flies under the CIA radar. Maybe someone at the Company picked up your actions and figured you for a double agent."

Jeff leaned against the kitchen counter for support. "I hope not. I don't want to have to do any explaining. After that whole Rikki Taylor thing with North Korea, our agency is on high alert."

Rikki's eye twitched and she rubbed it. "Rikki Taylor is dead."

"Yeah, but not forgotten." Jeff wiped his mouth with the back of his hand and then dumped his coffee into the sink.

She wanted to ask Jeff the meaning of those words but didn't want to show too much interest in Rikki Taylor. Quinn had been right. He wasn't one to kiss and tell, and Jeff didn't know of the connection between her and Quinn.

Now this second chance had fallen into her lap, and she had no intention of letting it slip by.

"Where is it?" Rikki had broken up her toast into several pieces but hadn't taken one bite yet.

Jeff narrowed his eyes. "Why didn't you tell me who you were last night when I staggered across Quinn's threshold? You must've made me right away as your contact."

"Quinn's a friend. I didn't want to expose him—not to you, not to the CIA. He's on leave trying to relax. Just because we both chose to drag him into our business doesn't give us the right to put a target on his back."

"Hey, what are friends for?" Quinn raised one hand.

Jeff nodded. "I get it. I wouldn't have come here if I thought I could get back to my hotel safely."

Rikki's heart flip-flopped. "Nobody followed you here, right?"

"I was careful."

Rikki pressed her lips together. Not that careful if he'd been found out before. "Anyway, I didn't want to pull Quinn into this and didn't want you linking me to him. I figured I could get you to drop the flash drive for me somewhere, and I'd pick it up and be on my way. Less exposure for you, too—you don't know who you met, what she looked like or why you were dropping the flash drive."

Jeff coughed. "I didn't even know it was a flash drive. All I have is a small padded envelope."

"My bad." She exchanged a quick glance with Quinn, who was pretending to clean up the kitchen. Rikki should've known Ariel would keep things as anonymous as possible. "So, can you get it for me now?"

"I'll do you one better. I'll give you the same information I meant to give you at our meeting."

"I'm ready."

"It's in the St. Louis Cemetery Number One."

Rikki's mouth dropped open. "You couldn't leave it in a safe-deposit box?"

"Who's going to suspect a cemetery?" Jeff lifted one shoulder. "It's in the entrance to one of those family mausoleums—the St. Germaines. Two steps down, loose stone six in on the right. Pull that out, and you'll find your flash drive...or whatever."

"Kind of a public place, and it's summertime with lots of tourists. Hope nobody stole it." Quinn crossed his arms, feigning disinterest no more.

"Honestly, I wasn't expecting it to be there overnight." Jeff pushed himself off the counter. "Now I'd like to get out of this city."

Quinn didn't budge from his position, and with his arms crossed and his biceps bulging, he looked large and in charge. "How and where do you think that guy picked up your trail?"

"I don't have a clue." Jeff licked his lips. "Nobody knew I was out here. I was thinking it must've been Ariel. Maybe someone is tracking her communications."

"Why would that be?" Rikki tried to keep the panic from her voice, and she slipped her hands beneath the counter where she twisted her fingers into knots.

"I'm not sure. Have you ever met her?"

Rikki relaxed the lines of her face into a smooth mask. "No."

"Nobody has. Do we even know if she's male or female? Ariel's a pseudonym."

"I'm assuming Ariel is she." Rikki lifted and dropped her shoulders quickly.

"She's a woman."

Rikki held her breath and swiveled her head around toward Quinn. He'd better not out Ariel. Rikki asked, "How do you know that?"

"One of my teammates actually spoke to her. She was going to help him out with an ambush but didn't have to in the end."

"If that's who he was really speaking to. All I know is Ariel is the head of the Vlad task force, and she has a lot leeway, including employing navy SEALs stateside in her efforts to stop him." Jeff wagged his finger at Quinn. "You'd better lie low, or she'll get you, too."

Quinn held up his hands. "I'm trying to, but you

never answered my question. Do you know when this guy picked you up?"

"I'm ashamed to say, I don't. He wasn't in a talkative mood while he was punching me in the face."

Quinn stepped aside, clearing the way for Jeff to leave the kitchen. "Take it easy, man, and get those stitches, and, Jeff?"

Jeff glanced down at the hand Quinn had placed on his shoulder. "Yeah?"

"You never came here, never saw me, never saw her here, never saw her period, right?"

"Yeah, yeah. Of course, man." Jeff ducked away from Quinn and nodded once to Rikki. "Good luck."

Rikki let out a long sigh when Jeff closed the door behind him. "What do you think?"

"I don't know." Quinn rubbed his knuckles across the dark stubble on his jaw. "I think Ariel could've picked a better agent to make the drop. Someone obviously followed Jeff from his hotel, from the airport, who knows? And Jeff didn't have a clue."

Rikki slid from the stool and stretched. "At least that guy last night hadn't been following *me*. It seems as if Jeff was the focus of that whole mess. Someone suspects him of double-crossing the Agency. Hopefully, once it's cleared through Ariel, he'll be off the hook."

"Ariel is currently not answerable to anyone in the CIA. I know guys who have been on her assignments. You're lucky she can act at will." He swept her plate with its crumbled toast from the counter and dumped it in the sink. "Why is she looking out for you?"

"I told you. It has to do with Vlad."

"And we know Ariel would move heaven and earth to bring down Vlad. Do you know why?"

Rikki shoved her hands in her pockets. She had no intention of outing Ariel. The woman had her back, and Rikki would do everything in her power to keep Ariel's secrets. "That's a dumb question. Vlad is building a terrorist network across the globe. He's involved in drugs, weapons, assassinations. He's the CIA's public enemy number one. Why *wouldn't* Ariel be hot to bring him down?"

"From what I've heard, it seems…obsessive."

"I don't know. All I can tell you is that David was on Vlad's tail when he proposed that North Korea trip to me."

"Talk about dumb." Quinn slammed his fist into his palm, and Rikki jumped. "David should never have dragged you along on that assignment."

"Why? Because I'm a girl?" Rikki wedged her hands on her hips.

"No, damn it." In two steps, he ate up the distance between them and grabbed her by the shoulders. "Because I was falling in love with you, and David took you away from me."

Rikki pressed a hand to her chest, above her fluttering heart. "That wasn't going to work, Quinn. It was hot and heavy sex in the heat of Dubai. I left because of my job, a job I couldn't do tangled up in the sheets with you."

He pinched her shoulders, his fingers digging into her flesh. "Don't pretend that's all it was between us. I'll admit, the sex was exciting, crazy—just like last night—but you know there was more than that."

She stroked his wrist. "Your libido can play tricks on you sometimes."

"I'm a man, not a boy." He softened his hold on her,

smoothing this thumbs across her clavicles. "I know the difference between sex and love. When you left me—" he thumped a fist against his chest "—I felt it here, not farther south."

"And when you got the assignment to kill me?"

"God, Rikki." He spun away from her. "Didn't we go through this yesterday? I didn't know it was you until it was too late to back out. They'd already convinced me of your guilt before I got the name and picture of my target. If it had been so easy to prove your innocence and call off the hit, where was your precious Ariel? How come she didn't do anything about it?"

"Like you said, the proof was there, but someone manufactured that proof against me and David. That's what I hope to discover from the flash drive—information about who double-crossed us. That's my starting point."

She backed up from the heat emanating from Quinn's body. She wanted to get on safe ground and away from Quinn's feelings. Had he really just mentioned love?

She'd always been afraid of hearing that word from any man. For her mother, it had been a magic spell, and she'd dragged Rikki around from man to man, giving up everything for that one little word. Rikki had a mission, a career, or at least she'd had one. Even if she did clear her name, she had Bella now.

Her stomach sank. She had to tell Quinn about his daughter. If she really did want to push him away, keeping his daughter from him would cement that. She couldn't do that. For all Quinn's sexy manhood, he had a big heart. He'd fallen for her, foolishly and disastrously, and here he was admitting it. Any other man whose lover had left him would never fess up, never make himself vulnerable to that woman again. And yet here he was.

Of course, he'd had a sniper rifle trained on her last year.

He dragged both hands through his hair. "Okay, your starting point is that flash drive. Let's go get it."

"You know where this cemetery is?"

"Of course I do. Every good N'awlins boy does. I'm not sure how we're going to march up there and remove a stone from a mausoleum in the middle of the day with tour groups wandering around."

"I am not going to a New Orleans cemetery at night."

"It's not deserted. There are tours at night, too. Those might be the more popular tours."

Rikki cocked her head. "Should we join one of those? Just two tourists on a cemetery tour at night? We could break off from the group to examine the St. Germaine mausoleum more thoroughly. That way, if anyone tracked Jeff there, we wouldn't stick out."

"You had the same thought I did." He swung his leg over the barstool, straddling it. "How long had Jeff's attacker been following him?"

"That's exactly what I thought. Maybe he hadn't been tailing Jeff closely enough to see him stash something at the cemetery, but he could've seen him go there." Rikki bumped her forehead with the heel of her hand. "I can't believe some of Jeff's actions."

"He would pick a cemetery." Quinn raised one eyebrow. "Sounds like Jeff was watching too many spy films."

"I guess he just never figured he was being followed. This wasn't a regular assignment for him. He probably jumped at the chance to do a favor for Ariel and the Vlad task force."

"Maybe." Quinn strode into the living room and slid his laptop in front of him on the coffee table.

"What are you doing?"

He looked up. "We're gonna book a tour of St. Louis Number One tonight."

They'd decided against the midnight ghost tour. The one after dinner in the dark would be creepy enough.

Rikki had wanted to get the grand tour of New Orleans with Quinn as her guide. She'd been to the city just twice before, but Quinn had a love of his hometown and would've been able to do it justice.

He'd put a stop to that idea, however. Although the chances were low, Quinn didn't want to run into Rikki's attacker from last night. They took a quick trip to Rikki's run-down motel to collect her possessions and check her out of the room, and then reclaimed her scooter from the French Quarter.

Quinn had insisted he could protect her better at his place, and Rikki didn't doubt that, but they both knew they'd wind up in bed together for as many nights as she stayed.

She needed to use one of those opportunities to break the news about Bella. Quinn hadn't wanted children, as his own mother had abandoned him, and his father never let him forget it. Even though Quinn's dad was an alcoholic and the adult Quinn knew his mother had run from him, the child within Quinn never stopped blaming himself. Then he somehow figured if both his father and mother had been uncaring parents, how could he possibly be any better?

Rikki couldn't imagine Quinn as anything but a loving, doting father. It was one of the things about him that had scared her off—his ability to feel deeply.

She thought she'd been getting into a relationship marked by kinky sex and a shallow appreciation of each other's bodies. But Quinn was right. It had started developing into so much more—and had scared the hell out of her. David's call had come just in time.

Later that night, Quinn emerged from the back rooms with his freshly washed hair slicked back and a towel around his neck. He eyed the sundress she'd changed into when they went to her hotel. "You're not going to change into all black for the occasion?"

"In this heat?" She fanned herself with her hand. "No, thanks. Maybe my floral dress will keep the ghosts at bay."

"Or maybe it will bring them out to force you to have some respect for their final resting place."

She pointed at his light-colored shorts. "I see you're dressing more for the weather than the occasion."

"It's almost July. I'm not crazy."

She combined the remains of their Chinese food into a couple of containers. "Thanks for dinner, but take-out Chinese is not exactly what I was expecting in New Orleans with all the fantastic restaurants here."

"We're not on vacation, despite the tour. We don't know where that guy is or even who he is. He could be lurking around waiting for you."

"Unless Jeff has already reported back to Ariel and gotten the all-clear."

"Nobody told you yet, so you're gonna lie low."

She poked her head around the refrigerator door while putting away the leftovers. "This is your dream come true, isn't it? To keep me captive in your apartment?"

He widened his eyes. "You're making me sound like a perv. I just wanna keep you safe."

"I know that." She slammed the fridge door. "I can't stay hiding out here forever, can I?"

"No. I don't expect that. I meant what I said that first night. I want to help you get your life back—even if that life doesn't include me."

She turned her back on him and dumped their dishes in the sink. That life would have to include him once she told him about Bella.

Thirty minutes later, Rikki climbed onto the back of Quinn's motorcycle and pulled on her helmet. Quinn had a small car he used while in town, but he always used his bike downtown for parking purposes. That was why she'd rented a scooter—she'd needed to get in and around the city quickly.

Quinn claimed a parking spot for his motorcycle at the edge of a small lot about a block from the cemetery.

Rikki slid from the back of the bike as Quinn tipped it to the side. She pulled the helmet from her head and shook out her hair.

"I'll take that." Quinn took her helmet from her and locked it on the back of the motorcycle along with his.

He took her hand, and they jogged across the street toward the rambling cemetery behind a wrought iron fence. He led her to a group of people hanging out by the entrance gates, and they joined the rest of the tourists, taking pictures with their phones and peeking through the gate.

Several minutes later, a tall African-American woman with long braids and a gauzy skirt floated up to the group. "Everyone here for the tour? I'm Aida, your guide. We'll take care of earthly matters first if you'll hand me your printed ticket or show me the ticket on your phone. Then we'll get to the unearthly matters."

One of the tour members, who'd had a few too many Hurricanes to drink, let loose with a ghoulish laugh.

Aida raised her brows at him. "Taunt the spirits at your own risk."

Despite the real ghouls Rikki had encountered over the past year, she sidled up next to Quinn and tucked her hand in the crook of his elbow.

Once Aida had checked all their tickets, she led them into the cemetery and stopped at a small grave site with an ornate cherub guarding it. She rested one hand on the cherub's chubby winged foot. "This is the sad resting place of AnaBella Lafleur. She died at the tender age of five, but her wealthy father forbade her burial in the family mausoleum because he never accepted her as his daughter. He had suspected his wife of cheating on him, and even after the child's death, he never got over it and ended up murdering his wife."

The warmth of the evening couldn't suppress the little chill that ran up Rikki's back. She tugged on Quinn's arm and whispered, "Jeff and his morbid ideas."

As the group moved past AnaBella's grave, Quinn brushed his hand over the headstone. "Poor Bella."

Rikki tripped over a crack, and Quinn steadied her. "Whoa."

She pulled him away from the group. "Once we find the St. Germaines, let's get out of here. I don't want to hear about any more dead children."

He cocked his head at her. "You okay?"

"Nervous."

"I don't blame you. It's gonna be okay."

He draped an arm over her shoulder, and she welcomed the heavy pressure of it. Why had he called that girl Bella? It must have been a sign.

Aida delivered the history and the atmosphere as the group moved from grave site to grave site, and Rikki might've enjoyed this tour another time.

A half hour into the tour, Aida stopped at a Baroque-style mausoleum with heralding angels on either side of the entrance and a profusion of flowers carved in stone and trailing down the columns.

Aida folded her hands in front of her. "This is the St. Germaine mausoleum, notable for its Baroque style and detailed stonework."

As Aida's smooth voice hummed in the background, Rikki elbowed Quinn, her mouth dry. She scooted closer to the steps, and someone asked if they were going inside.

Aida replied, "Not this one. There's a smaller one toward the end of the tour, and a few people at a time can duck inside."

Aida continued talking about the stone carvings as Rikki took one step down, pretending to study the writing on the side of the mausoleum.

The group began to shuffle off, and Rikki took the next step down, running her fingers over the rough stone on the right—six in, loose stone. Aida had better not catch her and Quinn defacing a crypt.

Aida's voice grew fainter, and Quinn joined her on the second step. "Did you find it?"

"Not—" her fingers scrabbled over the stone, looking for a gap or a give "—yet."

She crouched down and flashed the light from her phone on the wall.

Quinn crouched beside her, bumping her shoulder. "Is it loose right here?"

She shoved the heel of her hand against the spot he'd indicated with his middle finger, and the stone seemed to rock.

A scrape and a shuffle had her spinning around, knocking into Quinn as he straightened up, reacting to the noise.

Rikki's throat tightened as she looked up at the drunken man, not looking so drunk now, his face lit from below, his eyes narrowed.

"What are you two doing down here? And why don't you let me in on it?"

Chapter 7

Quinn instinctively stepped in front of Rikki. "Just doing a little historical investigation."

"Yeah, right." The man pulled a gun from his waistband, a silencer attached to the barrel.

Quinn's own weapon burned against his back, useless. He held up his hands. "Look, man. We don't want any trouble. We were just looking around."

"Looking around for something that spook left you?" The man laughed. "The CIA needs to do a better job of screening its applicants."

Rikki squeaked next to Quinn. "CIA? What are you talking about? I thought you were a cemetery ranger or whatever and thought we were defacing the mausoleum. You really are drunk."

The man glanced quickly to his side as laughter rose from the group. "Who are you?"

Quinn raised his hands higher, hoping Rikki might see the gun stuck in the back of his waistband, beneath his shirt, and hoping she might be able to get her hands on it. "Buddy, we're a couple of tourists on a cemetery tour. I don't know what your game is, but we don't have any money on us and you're not going to get too far with our credit cards."

Another laugh from the group had the man licking his lips and sliding one foot off the top step.

That was all Quinn needed. With the man off balance, Quinn charged him, knocking him backward. The gun tipped up and Quinn made sure it stayed that way by slamming his fist against the man's elbow.

The force and placement of the blow caused the man to drop the gun, and Quinn kicked it away. As the man came at him again, Quinn grabbed him by the throat.

"Now it's your turn. Who the hell are you?"

"Is there a problem?" The tour guide hovered several feet away. "Are you two fighting?"

Under the cover of the shadows, Quinn put the man in a sleeper hold. He slumped, and Quinn lowered him to the ground.

"I think this guy had a little too much to drink. He was bothering us, but no harm done." He jerked his thumb over his shoulder at Rikki, who'd been no help at all. "My wife's done with the tour, though."

Rikki stepped over the prone body and brushed off the skirt of her dress. "Yeah, I've had enough."

Aida put her hand to her heart. "Do I need to call the police?"

"If you want to report a drunk in public." Quinn slipped the tour guide a twenty. "Thanks. Great tour."

Putting his hand at the small of Rikki's back, he propelled her through the cemetery as if they had a couple of ghosts on their tail.

When they escaped through the gate, Quinn let out a breathy whistle. "How the hell did he pick us up? And what the hell were you doing back there? Didn't you see the gun in my waistband?"

"I saw it, but I was attending to more important business."

"Really? There's more important business than saving my life?"

She plunged her hand into her purse and pulled out a folded envelope. "I got the stone loose and grabbed the envelope Jeff left for me."

He pinched her cheek. "Smart girl, but I guess you answered my question."

"Your question?" She took one skipping step next to him.

"That envelope is more important than my life."

She gave him a shove from behind. "I knew you could handle that guy."

"Thanks for the vote of confidence." He pulled out his weapon. "Still didn't answer the first question, though. How'd that guy make us? He walked up a little later, after we met the group out front."

Rikki took a step back and wrapped her fingers around the bars of the cemetery fence. "There are at least two of them. The drunk in the cemetery and the guy who beat up Jeff and tried to hustle me out of the bar last night."

"There could be more." Quinn dangled his gun at his side as they started down the street. "The good news is that they don't seem to have a clue who you are."

"And they might not be CIA. Sure didn't sound like

he worked for the Agency, did it? If they did, wouldn't Jeff had already cleared himself through Ariel? The CIA must know by now that Jeff wasn't involved in any counterespionage. So why would they still be after the flash drive?"

He pulled her close to him. "Let's get home right now. We'll talk about this later. I'm worried that dude in the cemetery has a partner out here."

"We already know what his partner looks like. He tried to kidnap me last night."

"If it's just the two of them."

"Who the hell are they if not CIA? Why were they following Jeff?"

"I think we need to talk to Jeff again."

Quinn didn't let out the breath he'd been holding until they reached his motorcycle. Once on board, Quinn gunned the engine and took a different route back to his place, keeping an eye on his mirror.

They returned to his apartment unnoticed, and Quinn let Rikki off the bike before tucking it into his parking space next to his car.

They walked inside his place, and he fired up his laptop. "Let's see what's on this flash drive, and it better be worth all the trouble."

Rikki dug into her purse, pulling out the envelope. She ripped it open and dumped the flash drive into her palm. "Okay. I'm ready."

She sat next to him on the sofa and scooted in close as she reached past him to insert the flash drive into the side of his computer.

Quinn double-clicked on the device when it appeared on his display. He ran the cursor down the list of files. "Emails. Is that what you were expecting?"

"I didn't know what to expect. Ariel indicated she'd run across some files that might be useful to me."

Quinn opened the first email, and Rikki gasped beside him.

"They're David's emails."

"To you?" Quinn hunched forward and squinted at the addresses at the top of the message. "No. Who's Frederick Von?"

"I have no clue." Rikki grabbed the laptop with both hands and brought it close to her face, as if that would help her identify the recipient of David's email.

"It sounds like he's discussing his trip to South Korea."

"It does, but that's strange." She placed the computer back on the coffee table. "I thought the two of us, David and I, were the only ones in on that trip."

"He probably had to get approval from someone."

"That someone was Ariel." She tapped the keyboard. "Let's see the next one."

After Rikki opened four emails in a row, Quinn whistled. "Looks like David was two-timing you. He sent all these messages to Freddy, and they all seem to be referencing the trip to South Korea that he took with you."

"Frederick Von." Rikki drummed her fingers on the edge of the laptop. "That name sounds familiar to me."

"Another agent?"

"Not sure." Rikki clicked back through the emails, and then slumped against the sofa. "This doesn't tell me anything. These are mundane messages about a trip I was on. They make no sense to me. Why would Ariel think these would be useful, and why would those men following Jeff go to such great lengths to get them?"

Quinn squeezed Rikki's thigh. "Maybe there's something in the simplicity of the messages. Why would David be relaying insignificant details about his trip to someone—unless the details mean something else?"

She shot up. "Like a code?"

"That makes more sense to me than these emails."

She opened the first email again and read it aloud. "'Frederick, the trip to South Korea is on. We have intel about our man. I'll follow up with time and location.'"

"Time and location for what? Did the two of you meet anyone in South Korea before you crossed over?"

"Just our guide. I'm not sure what happened to him after David was murdered and I was captured."

"I'm assuming your guide wasn't Frederick Von."

"No. His name was Buddy Song."

He bumped her knee with his. "Let me have a look."

Jabbing his finger at the next open email, he said, "This email, which is the next one in the sequence, doesn't have any more information about the promised time and location. This one discusses car rental details."

"We didn't rent a car." She tilted her head to the side and caught her long hair with one hand. "Buddy picked us up and drove us around. This email doesn't even make sense."

"None of them do." He'd clicked open several more and bounced among the messages. "These are in order by date, but the subject matter isn't sequential."

"A code." She tossed her hair over her shoulder. "The emails are significant in another way, a way only Frederick understands."

"How'd you do in secret code class?"

"Secret code class?" She snorted softly. "No such thing."

"Yeah, right. I know you agents learn stuff like that. Hell, we reviewed it ourselves. Were you an A student in deciphering like everything else?"

She sucked in her bottom lip, clamping it between her teeth. "Something like this? It could be anything—position of letters, single words, and the entire message might be run across all the emails with different rules for different messages."

"But there are people at Langley who specialize in this, aren't there?"

Spreading her arms, Rikki kicked her feet up on the coffee table next to the computer. "Do I look like I'm in with Langley? They think I'm dead, and good riddance. Do you think Langley would appreciate learning that Ariel from a black ops organization got into one of their dead agents' emails? That ain't gonna happen, McBride."

He tapped one finger on the laptop. "That's all right. I have my sources, and they're not connected to the Agency."

"Like Jeff? No, thanks."

"I said my source is *not* with the Agency." He put his feet up next to hers and tapped them with the ball of his foot. "Are you giving up? You went through a lot to get this flash drive. Ariel must've understood the significance of finding a set of David's emails, and she went through a lot to get them to you."

"Who said I was giving up?" She draped her leg over his and wiggled her toes against his ankle. "I'll give it a try. I just don't understand why David was sending coded messages to someone about our trip."

"Maybe he had a different reason for taking that trip, one he didn't reveal to you."

Closing her eyes, she tipped her head back against the sofa, but she was anything but relaxed. Her hands curled into fists in her lap, and her eyelids flickered and twitched.

"What is it? He told you he had info about Vlad, right? Maybe that wasn't it at all. Maybe he just said that to get Ariel's support...and funds."

"Yes, he said we were on Vlad's trail, but that's not what I'm thinking of. David was...different on this trip. I thought about it after he died, and figured I was reading too much into his behavior because it was the last assignment we'd do together, but he was definitely in a different place."

"In what way? Do you think he was lying to you? Had he ever lied to you before?"

"Once." She opened one eye. "And it wasn't about work."

"What then?"

"Love."

Quinn raised his eyebrows. "He lied to you about love?"

"Yesss." The word came out like a hiss.

Quinn waited. If Rikki wanted to tell him, she'd tell him. She'd found the perfect profession for her temperament. She kept secrets like nobody else he knew...had kept secrets from him.

Rikki sighed and sat up, drilling him with her gaze so that he clenched the muscles in his stomach and prepared himself.

"David was in love with me...or at least he thought he was."

A muscle flickered at the corner of Quinn's jaw.

What man in his right mind *wouldn't* be in love with Rikki? "I thought David Dawson was a married man."

"He is…was. That was the problem, or at least one of them. I told him in no uncertain terms I didn't fool around with married men, and of course I felt guilty that maybe I'd led him on."

"You didn't. You're no tease." Quinn ran a hand over his mouth. "How'd he take it?"

"Not well—at first. He gave me all the old excuses married guys trot out—Belinda didn't understand him, the marriage was in name only, he thought she might be having an affair of her own, they were on the verge of divorce." She squeezed the back of her neck. "Then I dropped the other shoe."

"Which was?"

"Even if all those things were true, I wasn't in love with him, and I apologized for suggesting otherwise."

"How'd he take *that*?" Quinn didn't even have to imagine David's despair at the news, as he'd felt it himself when he woke up in that empty hotel room in Dubai with a white sheet of paper on the pillow next to him.

"Better than I expected. He didn't rant or rave or protest or even try to convince me I felt differently. Although it pained me, I suggested we work apart for a while, but he wouldn't hear of it. Insisted he could cope and keep our relationship on a purely business level— and that's when he lied to me."

"He kept up his protestations of love?" He could almost feel sorry for the poor sap, but at least Quinn had taken it like a man and never had contact with Rikki again—until it came time to kill her.

"David never mentioned it to me again, but I knew he still had feelings for me." She ran her hand down

Quinn's arm and threaded her fingers through his. "I could tell he did when you came onto the scene."

"Me?"

"David knew about us in Dubai, of course. David and I knew each other so well, he could tell. He got all fatherly on me and played the role of the mentor, which of course he was. He warned me about what having a fling while on assignment could do to my career." She pulled his hand to her lips and kissed his knuckles. "As if I could've stopped that wildfire between us even if I'd wanted to—and I didn't."

"Until the end." He disentangled his fingers from hers so that he could think straight. "Is that what happened? Is that why you left me high and dry? David's sage advice?"

Now he felt no sympathy for the man, but had an itching desire to punch him in the face—except he was dead.

"No." She brushed the hair from his forehead to torture him some more. "I realized our relationship belonged in the short and combustible category."

"You realized that without discussing it with me, then. I could've combusted like that forever."

A low chuckle vibrated in her throat, and he swallowed. The damnedest things about her could make him hard.

"Anyway, David's cautionary words didn't have any influence on my leaving you and Dubai."

"Maybe his cautionary words didn't, but his actions did." Quinn sat up on the edge of the sofa, making a half turn toward Rikki. "If you don't think he pulled you out of Dubai to go on this wild-goose chase in South Korea to separate us, you're naive—and I've never considered you naive before."

"I suppose there was that element to it, but David was hot for this mission and wanted me along." She shrugged.

Quinn snorted. "David was hot for you. He never did leave his wife, did he? That horrible, half-baked, failing marriage."

"No."

"So, that was the one time David lied to you. Said he'd accepted you two would never be more than colleagues but all the while harboring that fire down below."

She held up her finger. "Careful, you're talking about a dead man and a damned good agent who died for his country."

"You're right." He grabbed her finger and kissed the tip. "If he lied about that, how do you know he wasn't lying to you about other things, like this trip to South Korea?"

"Because he wasn't a very good liar, was he? He couldn't hide his feelings for me."

"A CIA agent who's not a good liar? He should've found another career."

Rikki cocked her head. "I mean, he was a good liar. If you could've seen him in action with our contacts… masterful."

"Then he could've been masterfully lying to you about Korea."

"Not to me." She shook her head, and her dark hair slipped over her shoulder.

Quinn wrapped his finger around one silky lock, missing her red curls. "Overconfident much?"

She bit her lip. "Pretty smug, huh? You're right. He could've totally been playing me, but why?"

"I can't tell you, but it sounds like David used you as a cover and put both of you in danger. Stupid move." Quinn stretched and then pointed to his laptop. "Are you going to look at these anymore?"

"I'm calling it a night." She pushed herself up from the sofa. "At least we have one thing to be grateful for."

He snapped the lid of his laptop closed and stood up next to her, resting a hand on her hip. He was just grateful Rikki was alive and back in his life—sort of. "I know what I'm grateful for."

Her lips formed an *O*, and a blush washed over her cheeks. "I-I meant that those people out there who were following Jeff don't seem to know who I am or what they're looking for."

"Yeah, of course." He pinched her hip. He didn't want to put Rikki on the spot. If she chose to fly away once she found whatever it was she was looking for, he'd let her go.

She'd gutted him the first time she left him, but her supposed death and rebirth had given him perspective. As long as Rikki Taylor was living and breathing in this world, he'd take that as a win.

Twisting his T-shirt between her fingers, Rikki leaned into him and kissed his chin. "Meet you in bed."

"You go ahead and get ready. I'll lock up."

Quinn checked his doors and windows and stopped to stare down at the dark street. Rikki had been right. They hadn't been on anyone's radar until Jeff had been compromised. One of those two men or both had been following Jeff before they even accosted him. They'd tracked him to the cemetery but hadn't been able to see what he'd done there.

The one guy had already ID'd Rikki as Jeff's contact, and the other man must've been keeping watch on that cemetery and spotted Rikki.

But they didn't know who she was, and if they weren't working for the CIA, maybe they didn't care. As far as the Agency knew, Rikki was dead. Did they want to keep her that way?

Quinn twitched the curtains closed and secured his apartment before sailing through the master bedroom to Rikki snug in his bed. "I'm just gonna brush my teeth. Don't steal all the covers before I can make it in there."

She looked up from some papers in her lap. "What is this Quinn, a book?"

He took a detour from his beeline to the bathroom and snatched the papers out of her hand. "Nosy."

"You're writing a book?"

"Nothing definite, just telling some stories—with the names and places changed. Just a collection of ideas at this point. Don't make a big deal out of it."

"It *is* a big deal. You'll have to run it by the navy, won't you?"

"Of course." He waved the papers. "It's in its infancy."

"Had me hooked right away."

He dumped the papers on his nightstand. "Definitely not bedtime reading, especially after the day we had."

Quinn went into the bathroom to brush his teeth and splash some water on his face. When he returned to the bedroom, Rikki had his notes clutched in her hands again, sitting cross-legged on top of the covers.

"Oh, come on. It's not that good."

"I think you've got something here, Quinn. I'd read this."

"Yeah, because you live it." He snatched the papers from her hands again and tossed them on the floor. "I'm looking at something a lot more interesting."

On his knees, he straddled her and buried one hand in her hair, pulling her close.

Her body, usually so pliant and willing beneath his touch, stiffened.

He kissed her mouth, but her soft lips didn't return the kiss. He opened his eyes and ran the pad of his thumb over the crease between her eyebrows. "Too wound up? I can fix that."

"Frederick Von."

"What? David's email recipient? Did you remember who he is?"

"Oh, yeah. I remember now."

Quinn shifted his body and lay on his side, propping up his head with one hand. "Who is he?"

"Frederick Von is a character in David's spy novel."

"That's not what I expected to hear. David wrote a spy novel?"

"He was working on one, and he shared it with me—yours is much better."

"That's a relief to hear, but mine's nonfiction. Why would David be sending emails to a fictional character—his own?"

Rikki crossed her arms and hunched her shoulders. "Frederick Von was the bad guy in David's book."

"I'm not following you, Rikki."

"Frederick Von was the bad guy—a traitor."

Quinn blinked.

"A trai-tor."

Rikki strung out the two syllables as if speaking to someone with a tenuous hold on the English language, and right now he felt as if she *were* speaking in a different tongue.

He shook his head. "You need to give me a break here. One minute I was ready to ravish you, and the next you're staring at me speaking gibberish about some fictional character in a bad spy novel—and it would have to be bad if it's worse than my drivel."

"I think David was being clever for the sake of being clever in those emails, just because he could and nobody would catch on…nobody but me."

"David *is* clever because I still don't understand the significance."

"Von is a traitor, Quinn—just like David."

Chapter 8

"Whoa, whoa." Quinn held up his hands. "How did you jump to that conclusion?"

"Why the secret emails? Ariel discovered these on a different server, a nonclassified server that wouldn't be under intense scrutiny after his death. There would've been no reason for David to send these emails. The only people who knew about the trip besides David were me and Ariel. David and I communicated in person about the trip. And what do those emails even mean? You said it yourself. They appeared to be cover for a code."

"A code. It doesn't mean David was a traitor just because he used the name of his character, who happens to be a traitor." Quinn slid back under the covers. "If it is true, what do you think David was doing in South Korea if not tracking down a lead on Vlad?"

"I'm not sure, but it all went horribly wrong. David

was killed, and I was captured by the North Koreans." She stretched out beside Quinn and rested her head on his shoulder. "The whole assignment was off. I saw the red flags but didn't trust my instincts, like David had always taught me."

"That's convenient. David taught you to go with your gut…until your gut was warning you against him."

"I never thought I'd see the day when I had to look into David Dawson."

"Look into him? How do you propose to do that?"

Draping her arm around Quinn's waist, Rikki nuzzled his neck. "I'm going to pay a visit to Belinda, David's widow."

"That's a dangerous idea. You want to stay anonymous for as long as you can."

"Belinda and I never met. She doesn't have a clue what I look like. She'd know the name, but I'm no longer Rikki Taylor, remember?"

"I think you'd better let me check in on the widow."

"You'd come along?" She fluttered her eyelashes against his face. "You don't even know where I'm going."

"Doesn't matter. If you're going to be doing any investigating, I'm coming with you." He combed his fingers through her hair. "Where *are* we going?"

"I'll have to check for sure, but they lived in Georgia—Savannah. She's from there, so I can't imagine she'd want to leave after David's death."

"We can drive, but I'm not sure what you hope to find out from her."

"It's a start. Besides, most agents confide in their spouses, whether or not they're supposed to. That's why…" She broke off and buried her face in the hollow between Quinn's neck and shoulder. That's why she'd never wanted to get married or have a serious relationship with someone. That's why she'd run out on Quinn without a backward glance. Her career always had to come first. She never wanted to follow in the footsteps of a man.

But now she and Quinn had a child together, and the longer she waited to tell him, the harder it was going to be to spit it out. What was she afraid of? Quinn would welcome the news, despite his own fears of being a bad father.

"Yeah, yeah." He wrapped her in his arms. "That's why you never wanted to get married. We don't have to get married, Rikki, but we can pretend for a few nights."

Then he made love to her in a way that no married man had a right to make love to his wife.

The following morning, Rikki searched for Belinda Dawson and found her in Savannah. She poked at the monitor displaying the address and said, "I think this is a different address from the one she shared with David, but at least she's still in Savannah."

"Then it's on to Georgia today. Map it out and see how far we have to go. It's about a ten-hour drive, if you're up to it. I think it's safer than flying right now, even though you have your fake ID."

"Driving is fine." She entered Belinda's address on the computer. "Will your car make it?"

"It's sturdier than it looks, and I just changed the oil. Let's get some breakfast, throw a few things in a bag and hit the road."

She tapped the print key and heard the printer in the

other room gear up. "That car may be sturdier than it looks, but I know it doesn't have a GPS."

"I'll use my phone's GPS, but we need a plan beyond showing up on her doorstep, especially if you're not going to out yourself."

"We have ten hours to think up a plan." Rikki hopped off the stool and circled into the kitchen. "Besides, we need to get out of New Orleans. You just disabled those two guys. You didn't eliminate them."

"Yeah, can you imagine me explaining two dead bodies in my hometown?"

"At least those two dead bodies aren't ours." She grabbed the coffeepot and raised it. "Eggs or pancakes?"

Two hours later, Quinn aimed his little junker car across the Pontchartrain bridge and they headed out of New Orleans.

Rikki dozed while Quinn drove the first few hours, and she woke up trying to hold on to the last wisps of dreams about Bella. Her heart ached, and she wanted nothing more than to call Mom in Jamaica and hear her daughter's coos and babbles.

She slid a sidelong glance at Quinn. He'd probably want to hear his daughter, too. She had to tell him, sooner rather than later. If she waited for the perfect time, she'd never tell him. There would never be a perfect time to tell him that she'd discovered her pregnancy while on assignment in South Korea and had spent the next few months of that pregnancy locked up in a North Korean labor camp, and then believing the father of her child had tried to assassinate her. Yeah, never a perfect time for that.

"Everything okay?"

"Sure, why?"

"You sighed like you meant it. Are you having second thoughts?"

"About this trip?" *About telling him about his child?* "No. I know this is the right thing to do."

He cocked an eyebrow while drilling the road ahead with his gaze. "The right thing to do? You make it sound like a moral decision. It's just a chance we're taking that Belinda knows something about David's activities before his death."

"I know that." She covered his hand clenching the steering wheel with her own. "It's nice being on the road with you. Do you want me to drive for a while?"

"I can go for another few hours. Then we'll stop for gas, get something to eat, and you can take the wheel."

"Just let me know." She stretched her arms to the roof of the car and wiggled her fingers. "A big guy like you needs a bigger car than this."

"Not the best for long trips, but when I'm home I don't drive it much. I stick with my bike."

"How much more leave do you have?"

"Less than a month, and I intend to help you wrap this up before my next deployment."

"I appreciate it, but that's not why I contacted you."

"I know." He turned up the air. "You looked me up to find out if I was really going to kill you. How did you find out it was me behind that sniper rifle?"

"Not telling." She clapped a hand over her mouth.

"Ariel. It had to be Ariel. What can you tell me about her? Are you close to her?"

With her hand still over her mouth, Rikki shook her head.

Quinn puffed out a breath. "Whatever. I know you

female spies stick together. She's risking a lot by keeping your secret and giving you classified information."

"David's emails aren't classified, and Ariel doesn't work for the CIA. She's Prospero and doesn't report to anyone."

"Yeah, Jack Coburn's black ops agency, but I didn't realize she had such free reign."

"Oops, then I guess I did reveal something about her. See how that works?" She snapped her fingers. "That's why we're paying a visit to David's widow."

"About that, now that you've had a nap, let's brainstorm. Who are we and why are we there?"

Rikki drummed her fingers on the dashboard. "We're with the Agency. If she tried to check up on our story, she won't be surprised if the CIA denies our existence. She and David had been married for twenty years. She knows the drill."

"Okay, we're with the Agency. How about from human resources? We're following up on some benefits? Or we're collecting some equipment."

"The second scenario is more likely, since HR would just call or send an email. If we were checking up on equipment, that would explain our in-person visit."

Quinn skimmed his hands over the steering wheel, warming to the task. "Maybe someone already confirmed that she had David's equipment for pickup. The fact that she doesn't know what we're talking about can be written off as bureaucratic red tape."

"Plenty of that, and your story might give us an excuse to look around."

He let out a short laugh and hit the steering wheel with the palm of his hand. "Would you let two goons from the CIA search your place?"

"After what they did to me?" She rolled her eyes. "I wouldn't let them set foot on my porch."

Quinn took a swig from the bottle of water in the cup holder. "I thought that was the point of this whole exercise. I thought you wanted back in at the Agency."

"I want my life back, my reputation. I want to be able to return to the States as Rikki Taylor without getting taken down at gunpoint."

"And you wouldn't go back to the CIA if they'd have you? Does that mean you're done with the spy business?"

"I don't know." She flicked the air vent away from her and rubbed the goose bumps from her arms.

They'd veered onto dangerous ground here. She didn't want to talk to Quinn about the future—hers, theirs. Right now she just wanted to clear her name and be with Bella without worry. And Quinn? She'd never wanted him more, but she had to tell him about Bella.

"Kids?"

She choked on the water she'd just sipped. "What?"

"Kids. Do David and Belinda have children?"

"They don't."

"Good. I mean, that makes things a little easier, and it makes sense."

"Does it?"

"Why would someone in David's line of work…or yours…want children? Just a complication."

Rikki stuffed her hands beneath her thighs. From the frying pan to the fire. "People do."

"Selfish people."

She reached forward and twisted the knob for the air. "It's cold in here. So, we're CIA paper pushers looking for government equipment. I'm going to use a different name from the one on my current ID. No need for anyone to link up April Thompson from Canada with a CIA agent. Who are you?"

"I'll think about it, but we'll probably need some badges in case she asks for ID."

"You're right." She pressed her fist against her forehead. "I'm sure David taught her to be cautious."

"Do you think you could have someone re-create that badge?"

"To pass someone's brief glance? Sure. Do you know Savannah? I don't. Where would we get these badges?"

"You know as well as I do, there are people in every city across the country who provide these services— for a price."

She patted her purse, thinking about Baily in Jamaica. "I sure do, but we're not going to have much time."

"Since you can't exactly call one of your former contacts, I can ask one of my teammates to look up something in Savannah for us."

"Your navy SEAL teammates? Would they know?"

"You'd be surprised what they know about covert operations, especially now. Your BFF, Ariel, has been dragging them in from deployment to do her bidding."

"Really?" Rikki folded her arms across her stomach. Had Ariel had an ulterior motive in directing her to stop in on Quinn when she arrived stateside? She hadn't needed much encouragement, as she'd wanted to square things with Quinn first…and tell him about Bella, but Ariel had initiated the idea.

"Why is Ariel using your sniper teammates for these assignments?"

"Because of Vlad. Because we know him. Because he knows us."

She whipped her head to the side. "Vlad knows you?"

"Who do you think nicknamed him Vlad?" He jabbed a thumb against his chest. "That was us, or more specifically I think it was my teammate Alexei Ivanov, the moody Russian."

"Why Vlad? He's not Russian, is he?"

"We don't know what he is. He's a man of many disguises. Just when we think we know what he looks like, he appears as someone else."

"So if he's not Russian, that you know of, why'd Alexei start calling him Vlad?"

"Because of his Russian sniper rifle—the Dragunov. Alexei uses the same rifle. Vlad was a sniper for the opposition forces, any opposition forces, before he started amassing his terrorist network. We came up against him many times. Sometimes we bested him, sometimes he bested us, but we never killed each other. Make no mistake about it, Vlad knows my entire team. I think he even reached out to the Russian mobster who killed Alexei's father just for that reason."

A chill claimed her body, and she'd turned off the air conditioner ten miles ago. "That's scary."

"Yeah, it's personal, so Ariel fights fire with fire. She's involved us in the battle to bring him down. I think I'm the only one who's escaped—and here I am."

"Yeah, here you are." Rikki nibbled on the end of her finger.

Quinn glanced her way and flexed his fingers on the steering wheel "What are you saying? Are you telling me it wasn't your idea to look me up?"

"It was my idea, but…"

"But Ariel was on board." Quinn twisted his head to the side and pinned her with a questioning gaze. "Ariel knows about us?"

Rikki dipped her chin to her chest. "She does. Sh-she knew before, before I even went on that assignment in Korea with David."

Quinn whistled. "I wonder if she knew you were my target before I did."

"I don't know why she would." Rikki traced the pattern on her skirt with her fingertip. "She's not CIA. Why would the Agency give Prospero a heads-up on their...assassinations? Especially of one of their own."

"C'mon. Prospero has ways of discovering things, even about other intelligence agencies. They're the best in the business."

He picked up his bottle and swirled the water inside.

"I can't believe Ariel knew about our relationship and knew about your assignment and did nothing to warn you."

"She did." Quinn slammed the bottle back in the cup holder. "She did, damn it."

"What are you talking about?"

"After the navy revealed my target to me, along with the evidence of your betrayal, I was sick. I didn't think I could go through with it."

"But the evidence was irrefutable." She twirled her finger in the air. "I believe you."

"When I was already in South Korea preparing for the assignment, I received an anonymous text on my secure phone. Just two words—*she's innocent*."

Rikki gasped and smacked her hand against her chest. "Ariel?"

"Who else? Of course, the text sent me into a tailspin, planted doubts in my head. I couldn't call off the mission based on an anonymous text. It could've been from the enemy. But it was enough. When I saw those soldiers marching you along, guns at your back, and saw your last, desperate attempt to get away from the very people you were supposed to be conspiring with, I knew the truth."

"You're here because Ariel wanted you here with me—looking into who set me up, looking into Vlad."

"Since it wasn't your own idea to contact me, I'm grateful to Ariel for intervening." His lips twisted into a bitter smile.

"She didn't have to do much convincing, Quinn. I wanted to see you. After the initial shock and anger and much reflection, I knew you'd changed your mind about that mission, about me." She rubbed her hand down his bare thigh.

"Where did you do all this reflecting? You haven't even told me where you were after the escape from North Korea."

She owed him. "Jamaica."

"Jamaica?" His thigh muscles tensed beneath her touch. "What's there?"

"My mother and stepfather."

"Ah, the former hippie, right?"

"They've been there for years. My stepfather runs the rental shop out of one of the resorts there—snorkeling equipment, skimboards, parasails. My mother met him there and stayed, which is no surprise. She'd follow any man anywhere, always did."

"I'm assuming the Agency knows about them?"

"Of course, but the CIA thinks I'm dead. No reason to question my mom. I felt safe there."

"If Ariel knew about us, knew you were alive and knew I hadn't gone through with the assassination, why didn't she tell me about you?" Quinn clenched his hands on the wheel, his knuckles turning white.

"She didn't know if she could trust you, Quinn. I didn't know if I could trust you." She ran her fingers over the ridges of his knuckles. "Someone had been actively working against me, planting false evidence. I didn't know how much of that you believed."

"I suppose I don't have room to complain. I *was* stationed on that hillside, ready to take you out." He rolled his shoulders. "I wish it had been someone else."

"I don't."

"You're happy a former lover had you in his crosshairs?"

"If it had been anyone else, I'd be dead."

Chapter 9

When they reached the outskirts of Montgomery, Quinn eased off the gas pedal. "Keep an eye out for a gas station and a few fast-food joints."

Rikki jerked her thumb over her shoulder. "I saw a sign back there listing a bunch of places. Should be right off the highway, convenient for travelers."

"We're making good time and should be in Savannah before eleven o'clock if we keep moving."

She eyed him up and down, and he felt the familiar ache under her gaze, even after five hours of driving, cramped in the same position. His attraction to Rikki knew no bounds.

"Are you sure you don't need to get out and walk around? We can wait for a rest stop."

"I'm used to hunching in the same position for long periods of time. Doesn't bother me."

"I'm still taking the wheel. You can nap, if you like. Your phone's GPS has gotten us this far, so I'm sure I'll be okay."

"I can sleep anytime, anywhere, even standing up."

"Like a horse." She rapped one knuckle on the window. "Two miles until services."

Two miles later, Quinn took an exit toward a clump of gas stations and restaurants. "Do you have a preference for food?"

"Chicken."

"I think we'll be able to find chicken in Georgia." He made a hard right turn into a gas station. "Let's fill up first. Bathroom?"

"I'd rather wait and use the restroom in one of the restaurants. I don't trust these gas station restrooms."

Quinn filled the tank while Rikki walked around the car with a squeegee, washing splattered bugs from the windows.

"Ugh, these bugs in the south are supersize."

"That's right. You've never spent much time down here, have you?"

"Back in Dubai, you promised to show me around New Orleans sometime." She dropped the squeegee in the soapy water and grabbed a couple of paper towels.

"What do you mean? I showed you a good time on Bourbon Street and we had a helluva cemetery tour."

She bunched the paper towels into a ball and threw it at his head. "You've got a sick sense of humor, Mc-Bride."

The nozzle clicked, and he pulled it from the gas tank. "Let's get you some chicken and get back on the road."

Rikki opted for a crispy chicken sandwich so she could eat and drive at the same time.

Quinn lowered the back of his seat and stretched his legs as far as they would go. He grabbed a sweatshirt from the backseat and bunched it between his head and the window. "I'm gonna catch a few hours of shut-eye if you think you'll be okay. You're going to head toward Atlanta and then veer east."

"Don't worry. I'm good at directions, especially when the nice computer lady spits them out."

"I trust you. You made it out of North Korea." Quinn adjusted his seat again and closed his eyes. At least he trusted her to get them to Savannah in one piece, but he didn't quite trust her to leave his heart in one piece.

Rikki woke him up twice along the way to pull into a rest area to use the bathroom. After the second time, he stayed awake for their arrival into Savannah. He pointed out a small motel outside the historic district where Belinda Dawson had a house. "Looks like there's a vacancy here."

"We should pay cash."

"Nobody's tracking me. I'm on leave, and I can do what I damn well please."

"But you're here under an assumed name, which you haven't chosen, by the way. What if Belinda checks you out?"

"You really think she's going to ask us where we're staying and call to confirm our names?"

"Humor me." She jerked her head toward her purse in the backseat. "I have enough cash in there to cover it."

"I'll humor you, and I've got it."

If the motel clerk thought it was strange that they

paid for two nights up front with cash, her bored face didn't show it.

When they got to the room, Quinn picked up a card on the desk. "Free Wi-Fi. Can you get on my laptop and re-create a CIA badge? That'll make it easier when we ask someone to produce a badge for us."

"Did you hear from your friends yet?"

He held up his phone. "Two suggestions from two different sources. It's gonna mean a trip to one of the seedier areas of Savannah."

"That kind of stuff always does."

"Yeah, you should know, Ms. Thompson."

"I'm going to use a different name for this identity." Her gaze tracked to the digital clock on the bedside table. "Not tonight?"

"We'll save it for tomorrow. Do you know if Belinda works?"

"She did. I don't know about now, since David's death."

"Nine-to-five job?"

"She's in marketing, and I think she went into an office. So we should pay her a visit at the end of the workday."

"Exactly, but not too late. We don't want to scare her by showing up on her doorstep in the dead of night."

"Poor woman has had enough to deal with. I almost feel guilty nosing around."

Quinn threw himself across the bed and toed off his shoes. "We're just there to look around and assess. We're not gonna accuse her husband of anything, but if we see anything that needs closer examination, I'm not gonna rule out making a return visit—while she's not there."

"I agree." Rikki yawned. "I'm tired."

He patted the bed. "Come on over here and I'll give you a massage."

"I know how your massages end." She put her hands on her curvy hips. "I said I was tired."

"I missed you, Rikki. I missed us, but I think I can control myself if you're too tired for sex. Hell, I'm just happy holding you in my arms." And as insincere as that sounded, he'd meant it. "Go brush your teeth and do whatever it is you do to get so beautiful and then I'll deliver a no-strings-attached massage to your aching body."

"Sounds like heaven."

When she returned to the bedroom, an above-the-knee cotton nightgown floating around her body, Quinn turned off the TV and jumped from the bed. "Stretch out. I'll brush my teeth and be right back."

While in the bathroom, Quinn washed his hands with warm water and plucked a little bottle of lotion from the counter. Squeezing the lotion into his hands, he walked back into the bedroom and winked at Rikki. "I was afraid you'd be sound asleep."

"Close to it, but I'm curious to witness this self-control of yours as I've never seen it."

"That's cold." He perched on the edge of the bed, rubbing his hands together. "No massage oils, but I found some lotion."

"That'll work." She stretched like a cat, pointing her toes off the foot of the bed.

"Um." He tugged at the hem of her nightgown. "Do you want to remove this?"

She twisted around. "I knew it."

"Come on. Even massage therapists who are complete strangers have you disrobe for a massage."

As she pulled the nightgown over her head, she said in a muffled voice, "But they usually have a towel or sheet for the naughty bits."

"Do you really want me to cover you with a towel?"

She tossed the nightgown over her shoulder, and he made a concerted effort to keep his gaze off her luscious breasts.

"Nope. Have your way with me, McBride. You always do." She lay back down on her stomach, her arms at her sides.

He started with her shoulders, digging his thumbs into the sides of her neck.

She let out a long breath of air between her teeth in a hiss. "That feels good."

"Did you forget about these magic fingers?"

"I remember the magic fingers. I just don't remember them plowing into the sore muscles of my neck."

"Shh. You talk too much."

She wasn't kidding about those sore muscles. He worked at the tight knots at the base of her neck until they disappeared, and then he squeezed her shoulders and pressed the heels of his hands into her shoulder blades.

Rikki's breathing had deepened, and Quinn continued massaging the smooth flesh of her back. He expected another sarcastic comment from her when he reached her buttocks, but she moaned softly as he kneaded her glutes.

Her new womanly shape enticed him as much as her fit, athletic build had, but he knew now his attraction to Rikki ran more than skin deep. He'd known it all along, from the moment he met her at that hotel bar in Dubai. He'd known it the minute he awakened in that same hotel all alone.

His loss had punched him in the gut then and had nearly brought him to his knees months after that when he watched that North Korean guard shoot her.

He'd had his next assignment to distract him after his second, more permanent loss of Rikki, but his leave had sent him spiraling out of control. How much longer he could've gone on like that if Rikki hadn't shown up on his doorstep two nights ago, he hadn't a clue.

This time, as he faced his third abandonment by Rikki, he'd be ready. She'd survived. That was all that mattered to him.

He caressed her outer thighs and whispered, "Do you want me to go on? I can do a mean foot massage that could put any pedicurist to shame."

Her only response was a long, drawn-out sigh.

He stopped, his hands hovering above her legs. He slid off the bed and crouched beside it, his face close to Rikki's, nose to nose.

Her long lashes fluttered, and her lips parted on a minty breath.

That was the first time he'd ever put Rikki Taylor to sleep…and it gave him a good feeling. He drew the sheet up to her shoulders and climbed into bed next to her.

She shifted onto her side, facing him, and he stroked the side of her full breast.

He murmured the words he'd never say to her out loud. "Love you."

She mumbled something, and Quinn's heart skipped a beat. Had she heard him and responded in kind?

"What?" He held his breath until he realized she was fast asleep.

She spoke in her sleep again, and this time he heard the word and repeated it. "Bell?"

Her mouth curved into a soft, sweet smile, and he kissed the tip of his finger and touched her bottom lip.

He didn't hear any bells, but he didn't have to. He knew how he felt about Rikki…even if she wanted to keep denying her own feelings for him.

And he'd do whatever it took to make her happy— with or without him.

They spent the following day getting two credible CIA badges and a handful of matching business cards with Quinn's temp cell phone number, shopping for some convincing clothes to wear and holing up in the air-conditioned motel room.

Watching TV from the bed, Rikki crossed her legs at her ankles and tapped her bare feet together. "The small glimpses I'm getting of the city make me want to see more of it. The architecture is incredible, and I'm itching to tour some of those homes."

"We'll put Savannah on your list the next time you come out to New Orleans and do a two-for-one. I'll even throw in Nashville."

"I'll take you up on it." She drew her knees to her chest and wrapped one arm around her legs. "That was some massage last night. Totally relaxing."

"I aim to please." He touched two fingers to his forehead.

"I'm sorry I fell asleep. I mean…"

"Proved you wrong, didn't I?"

"You did?"

"You didn't think I could give you a massage without jumping your bones."

She balanced her chin on her knees. "I didn't mean to imply you were a caveman with no self-control. It's that our relationship before…"

"Was purely physical?" He shrugged. "Maybe for you."

Her eyes widened. "We didn't have that much time in Dubai."

"It was enough time for me, Rikki. You don't think I know what I want in a woman? What qualities are important to me?"

The panicked look on her face stopped him cold.

"You know what? We should start getting ready if we want to greet Belinda Dawson when she gets home from work. We don't want to give her too much time to go out again."

"You're right, although I dread putting on that suit." She rolled from the bed and grabbed a jacket from the back of the chair.

"You and me both." He ripped the plastic from the cheap, off-the-rack suit he'd bought earlier that day. "Do you know you talk in your sleep?"

"I do?" She froze and clutched the jacket to her chest, her pale face a shade lighter than the light beige of the suit. "What did I say?"

"I honestly don't remember." He just knew it hadn't been his name or any form of endearment for him. "Okay, I'm gonna put this thing on—if you think you can control yourself while I change."

She laughed a little too loudly. "That's fair."

He dropped his shorts to the floor and pulled on the polyester slacks. "Are you nervous about this?"

"David and I used to do stuff like this all the time. It's a snap."

"I'm not David. Are you afraid I'm going to screw it up?"

"You'll be fine. You're a quick learner."

Forty minutes later as Quinn drove his car, which had developed a rattle, down the gracious streets of Savannah's historic district, Rikki poked him in the side.

"You're going to have to park this jalopy a few blocks away. There is no way David's wife is going to believe the CIA is paying her an official visit in this little death trap."

Quinn ducked his head and peered at the palatial homes behind the live oaks dripping with Spanish moss. He whistled through his teeth. "Either David was making a lot more money than you at the Agency or he had a ton of life insurance. Did you say this was a new address for Belinda?"

"Yeah." Rikki rolled down the window and took a deep breath. "Smells lovely out here."

"Where did they live before?"

"Not in this neighborhood. I looked up David's old address and it wasn't near here, so the widow purchased some new digs after her husband's untimely death."

Glancing at the GPS, Quinn said, "Her house is up ahead on the right. I'm going to pull up alongside this park. Can you check the signs?"

"Slow down." Rikki stuck her head out the window. "It's okay to park here."

Quinn pulled up to the curb and unfolded himself from the car. "Can you please grab my jacket from the back?"

Rikki joined him on the sidewalk, jacket in hand. "Here you go."

They walked the two blocks to Belinda Dawson's house. Quinn's hand swung at his side so close to Rikki's, they kept brushing knuckles. He resisted the urge to grab her hand.

What would they do after this dead end? What would Rikki do? Where else would she go to find answers? He wanted to send her back to Jamaica and continue the investigation on his own. He had sources at the CIA— better sources than the hapless Jeff. He might be able to track this down for her. It might even be a good idea for Rikki to turn herself in and cooperate with the investigation.

He slid a glance at her firm jaw and long stride. No way. She wouldn't go down that road, and he didn't blame her. If the powers that be at the CIA thought they had their woman a year ago, what would change their mind this time? The fact that she'd spent time in a North Korean labor camp wouldn't convince them.

"There it is." Rikki tugged on his sleeve. "And there's a Lexus in the driveway, so she's probably home."

"Home and livin' large."

She drove a knuckle into his back. "You act like she's happy her husband's dead and would rather have the money."

"David Dawson was a snake. You should know that better than anyone. He wanted to cheat on his wife... with you. You don't really believe that garbage he was spewing about how Belinda didn't understand him. That's the oldest line in the book."

"I know that."

"And if you were so quick to peg David as a traitor

based on the flimsy evidence of a fictional character, deep down you knew David was a snake."

"All right, all right." She put her finger to her lips as they approached the wrought iron gate ringing the house. "It's time to keep your thoughts to yourself."

Quinn pushed down on the handle of the gate. "Whew, not locked. Ready, Agent Reid?"

"Copy, Agent Miller."

Once on the broad porch, Quinn rang the doorbell, which resounded somewhere deep in the house. "I wouldn't be surprised if a maid in a frilly apron answered the door."

"Or a butler."

A soft voice with a honeyed Southern accent floated out to the porch over an intercom. "Who is it? Press the white button, please."

Quinn reached for the speaker to the right of the doorbell and jabbed the button with his thumb. He laid his own Nawlins accent on thick. "Good evening, ma'am. I'm Agent Miller and this is Agent Reid. We've come to collect Agent Dawson's equipment."

At first Quinn thought she was going to ignore them and shut them out. Then the soft drawl responded, "Equipment?"

"I'm sorry, ma'am. The Agency contacted you about some equipment of Agent Dawson's and you indicated you had it at home?"

"I don't remember that." The locks on the door clicked, and it inched open.

A petite woman with fluffy blond hair appeared in the doorway.

Rikki stuck out her hand. "Mrs. Dawson? I'm Agent

Reid. Sorry for any confusion. We were sent to pick up some equipment."

Belinda released a measured sigh. "Sometimes I wonder how the government functions. Please come in."

Quinn took the attractive woman's soft hand in his. "Sorry for your loss, ma'am, and sorry for the red tape."

"It's been over a year. I'm used to it." She closed the door and folded her hands in front of her. "Can I get you some tea? Lemonade?"

"I'd love some tea, ma'am." Quinn slathered on the Southern charm. A woman like Belinda Dawson would expect it. A quick glance around the lavishly appointed living room marked Belinda as a woman who spared herself no comfort or reward.

Rikki shook her head. "Nothing for me, thank you. You have a beautiful home."

"Thank you." Belinda started for the kitchen and glanced over her shoulder. "I'll get it for you myself. The help has gone home for the day."

When she entered the vast kitchen, Quinn exchanged a quick look with Rikki, who raised her eyebrows.

Belinda returned to the room, carrying two glasses of tea, the ice clinking softly. As she handed one glass to Quinn, she said, "Equipment, you say?"

"Yes, when we…lose an agent, we do an inventory of his equipment. A few pieces were missing from Agent Dawson's effects. Agent Reid and I received notification that you'd been contacted and had located the missing equipment."

"You know, it's completely possible." Belinda aimed her big blue eyes at Quinn over the rim of her glass as she took a sip of the very sweet tea. "There was so much…red tape when David died. Did you know him?"

"I did not have the pleasure, ma'am." At least Quinn could be truthful about something.

"Agent Reid?" Belinda had approached Rikki from behind, hovering over her shoulder as Rikki studied a vast array of framed photographs on a shelf.

Rikki cranked her head over her shoulder. "No, I never met Agent Dawson, but then our paths wouldn't have crossed. I'd heard he was an incredible agent, though. A real treasure to the Agency."

Belinda bowed her head. "That's nice to hear. It's too bad he was betrayed by the one person he trusted the most."

Quinn's heart hammered as he watched Rikki across the room. *C'mon, Agent Reid, keep it together.*

"Oh?" Rikki tipped her head and her dark pony-tail swung behind her. "I'd heard he was killed by the North Koreans."

"He was, but his partner made that happen. Rikki Taylor." She spit out the name as if it were poison on her tongue. "They were partners. He was her mentor. He taught her everything. She tried to seduce him first, and when that didn't work she betrayed him to the North Koreans. But she got hers. I heard she died, too. I don't know how or when, but it gave me some measure of satisfaction."

Rikki blinked. "I can imagine it would. We didn't hear that story."

Quinn ground his back teeth together. Dawson was worse than a snake if he told his wife Rikki had been trying to seduce him. Belinda probably found some evidence of David's infatuation with his partner, and he turned it around on Rikki.

Rikki picked up a picture from the shelf. "Is this Agent Dawson?"

Quinn had uncoiled his muscles enough to move toward the two women. He wanted a firsthand look at the snake himself. He'd only ever seen him at a distance when he first met Rikki in Dubai.

Belinda took the framed photo from Rikki's hands and traced a finger over the form of a fit, compact man in his midforties, with the build of a long-distance runner, shirtless and standing in knee-deep water.

Belinda almost whispered. "This is Davey. This is the last picture I have of him. We'd taken a brief vacation to the Bahamas before he left for Dubai, and then North Korea."

Rikki sniffed. "I'm so sorry, Mrs. Dawson. We didn't come here to bring up painful memories. If you don't have Agent Dawson's equipment, we can write it off as a misunderstanding."

"I can pretty much confirm I don't have any of Davey's work equipment here. I moved into this house about nine months ago—too many memories in the old place—and I would've remembered seeing anything of Davey's from work and moving it over with me."

"We'll report that, ma'am. Don't concern yourself." Quinn raised his glass before finishing off the tea. "That sure hit the spot."

Belinda placed Dawson's picture back on the shelf, caressing the edges of the frame. "If I do find something, is there a number where I can reach you?"

Quinn reached into his front pocket for his newly minted business cards and pulled one out. He pinched it between his fingers. "Here you go, ma'am. It's best to call my cell phone number."

"Well, I will certainly take a look." She made a half turn toward Rikki. "Are you sure you don't want some refreshment before you leave?"

"No, thank you. I feel bad that we troubled you on this wild-goose chase."

Belinda waved her hands. "Oh, Davey and I were married for over twenty years. I know how the Agency works."

A bead of sweat rolled down Quinn's back in his cheap suit, despite the chilly air in Belinda Dawson's house. Not only did this turn out to be a wild-goose chase for Rikki, she'd had to listen to David's slights and lies.

As Belinda walked them to the front door, she asked, "Are you taking any time to see the city? I do volunteer work at the Savannah Historical Society every week-day morning, and we have an incredible selection of artifacts and can give you some good sightseeing suggestions."

Rikki shook her head, her ponytail waving from side to side. "I'm afraid it's business only for us."

Quinn smiled. "Thanks again, ma'am."

Belinda opened the front door and turned to shake their hands again. "Have a nice trip back to… Washington."

They didn't say a word to each other as they walked down the pathway to the front gate and into the still night, light from the setting sun playing peekaboo between the trailing tails of Spanish moss.

When they hit the sidewalk out of sight of the house, Quinn took Rikki's arm. "Sorry about that."

"Sorry?" She turned toward him, her eyes alight with sparks. "I couldn't be happier with the results."

He tripped to a stop. "You enjoy getting trashed and vilified?"

"Small price to pay for the truth and the first big break in my investigation."

"You lost me."

"Quinn." She grabbed his lapels. "David Dawson is still alive."

Chapter 10

Quinn's eyes popped open. "What are you talking about? How did you come to that conclusion?"

Rikki looked over his shoulder. She didn't trust Belinda Dawson one iota. "Let's keep moving. She could be calling the CIA or your cell phone number as we speak."

Quinn continued on the sidewalk, excitement lengthening his stride so that she had to hold on to his arm to keep up with him.

With a slight pant, she said, "It was that picture."

"The vacation picture from the Bahamas?"

"That wasn't the Bahamas. Did you get a load of that water? Looked like some muddy rice paddy in Southeast Asia."

"You're saying that's a recent picture of David? One taken after his supposed death in North Korea?"

"That's exactly what I'm saying."

"How could you possibly know that? Because of an imagined rice paddy?"

"Wait for the car. I'm not blabbing this on the sidewalk, even if there is nobody else around."

By the time they reached the car, sweat was dampening Rikki's back. She ripped off her jacket, and Quinn did the same.

Once in the car with the engine and the air running, Rikki bounced in her seat and turned toward Quinn. "It's not the place. It's the man and more specifically the tattoo."

"That tattoo on his chest? He didn't have that before?"

"Nope. The last time I saw David, right before I witnessed his so-called murder at the hands of the North Koreans, he most definitely did not have a big tattoo on his chest—a tattoo of a phoenix, I might add."

"You've seen David Dawson's chest?"

Her cough turned into a laugh. "That's all you can focus on? Of course I've seen David's chest. You know how scorching it gets in Korea, and all the other hot spots we've been in around the world. You've been in some of the same hot spots. I've seen him without his shirt several times, and I can say unequivocally the man never had a tattoo. Why Belinda keeps that picture around is beyond me. Beyond stupid."

"You don't think it could've been one of those temporary tattoos, do you?"

Compressing her lips into a thin line, Rikki tilted her head. "Really? The man is forty-four, not eight."

Quinn pulled away from the curb, his brows creating a vee over his nose. "David set up this Korea trip for the two of you with the cover that he had a line on Vlad. That got him money and support from Ariel. He engineered his own death, while fingering you as a traitor at the same time. Why you?"

Rikki's knees bounced. "Because of just that—the Vlad story was a cover and if nothing came of it, I'd be a witness."

"If nothing came of it, he could claim his sources fell through. Happens all the time."

Quinn snapped his fingers several times. "This trip was David's opportunity to turn, to go over to the other side. He fakes his death so nobody is looking for him, and he sets up his partner so she takes the fall for being the traitor…and he gets his revenge."

"Revenge?" Rikki's stomach dropped. "What do you mean by that?"

"Because you rejected him, Rikki. He kills a lot of birds with those stones."

"Oh my God." She wrapped her ponytail around her hand. "It was David all along. He set me up. Why? Who is he working for?"

"This has Vlad's fingerprints all over it. This wouldn't be the first time he turned an agent or someone on the inside. My buddy Miguel Estrada had to deal with that. He was betrayed in Afghanistan and captured. Vlad is a master of manipulation. It wouldn't surprise me at all if he'd worked on David. Did you get the full effect of Belinda's house? Do you really think life insurance money and a government pension are paying for that? It sounds like she quit her marketing job, too, and is volunteering her time."

"She knows. Of course she knows her husband's alive. He sent her that picture—maybe as proof." Rikki smacked her hand against her knee. "I should've taken that photo. I need to provide proof that David's still alive—not in a North Korean labor camp, not held captive, not suffering from amnesia and wandering around South Korea—but alive and well and functioning as a traitor to his country."

"Taking that picture would've been risky. Belinda would've known it was missing and would've known it was us."

"I need to get some proof."

"The decoding. Let me get my guy, Donovan Chan, to work on David's emails. I think we can take it to the bank that those messages contain some incriminating information." Quinn wheeled into a parking lot and squealed to a stop. "And if Dawson's betrayal has anything to do with Vlad, we're going to nail them both."

"I want that picture, Quinn. I'm sure I'm not the only person who can testify to the fact that David Dawson didn't have a tattoo when he went to North Korea. If I can plant some doubt that he perished in North Korea, maybe the CIA can start looking into Belinda Dawson's finances. There might be an offshore account or some other irregularities, but it starts with that photo."

"We can't just steal the picture. We'll have to stage it as a break-in, and we'll have to do it at night. God knows how many butlers, housekeepers and gardeners Belinda has around the house during the day."

"Tonight. We do it tonight."

"She'll know it's us."

"I don't care. Let her suspect. I'm only too happy to strike some fear into her heart—and David's." Crossing her arms, she hunched her shoulders. "I can't believe he turned on me, after everything we went through together."

"You know what I think?" Quinn put the car in gear and drove out of the parking lot. "I think if he had been successful in seducing you, he would've tried to lure you to the dark side with him. As devastated as I'm sure he was when you rejected him, that's not what pushed him over the edge. Guys like that are bad seeds. He would've turned anyway if the price was right."

"You're probably right." She tapped on the window. "Where are we going?"

"I'm starving. We're going to get something to eat before returning to the motel and changing into something more comfortable for breaking and entering."

"Can we please go out? I doubt we're going to run into Belinda Dawson at dinner, since she seemed to have something simmering on her stove when we were there. Nobody else knows we're here. Nobody knows I'm anywhere...just like David."

"I'll meet you halfway. We'll pick up some soul food and eat at the hotel pool."

"I guess it's better than fast food in the room." She turned toward him with a tilt to her head. "What exactly is soul food?"

Quinn quirked his eyebrows up and down. "Allow me to introduce you to its delights."

The delights of soul food included lots of deep frying and lots of carbs. Rikki sucked down a big gulp of disgustingly sweet tea and curled her legs beneath her on the chaise longue by the pool. She yawned. "So, soul food is a sleep aid, because the only thing I want to do right now is close my eyes and drift off."

Quinn rubbed and then patted his flat stomach. "Pretty good, huh?"

"Delish." Rikki eyed his trim waistline.

How did he manage to put away all that food and still look like a Greek god? She'd pay him the compliment, but she didn't want to get caught up in a discussion of food and weight and start Quinn wondering about all her new soft spots. He seemed to like them, anyway.

She pressed her hands against her own belly and the butterflies taking wing there. She'd tell Quinn about Bella as soon as she got the proof on David. Maybe she'd even let someone else take over the investigation, as long as the CIA didn't want to take her into custody.

Rikki swept up the used napkins on the table between them and shoved them into one of the plastic bags. "I have my clothes all picked out—black leggings, black T-shirt and a pair of sneakers for a quick getaway."

"And I have all my burglar tools. Should be a cinch to break in there—as long as she doesn't have an alarm system. If she has one of those, it'll take a little longer."

Rikki clambered out of the chaise longue and dumped their trash in the bin by the gate. "I should be able to tell if she does have an alarm system and if it's armed."

"If it is, I got that covered." He held up a deep-fried ball of something. "Do you want the last one?"

"Knock yourself out."

They returned to the room and changed into their night-crawler outfits.

Standing before the mirror, Rikki wound the elastic holder around her ponytail once more. "Wish we had your motorcycle for this little assignment, or better yet, my silent electric scooter."

"We'll be fine. I'll leave the car by the park again. We'll get in there, swipe the picture and get out. Who knows? Belinda may not even notice it's missing for a day or two."

"Wait." Rikki spun around from the mirror. "I thought we were going to steal a few more things to make it look like a break-in."

"Do you really want to steal some woman's jewelry and small electronics?"

"You don't seriously expect me to feel some sympathy for a traitor and his wife, do you?"

"I'm not a thief."

"It would be extremely odd for a burglar to steal a framed photograph only. You're the one who made this point earlier." She wedged a hand on her hip. "Why are you having an attack of conscience now?"

"Okay, we'll take a few other things and then return them to…someone."

"Whatever you want to do. We should return them to the CIA for the secrets David probably stole."

"We'll figure it out." Quinn hitched a small backpack over one shoulder. "Are you ready?"

"Oh, yeah."

They didn't say much on the way over, and Rikki focused her private thoughts on David and his behavior their last year together. He had changed, had become less open with her. She'd written this change off to the awkwardness after his declaration of love for her and his anger when he found out about her and Quinn. Because he had been angry. Had that set him on this course?

No. He had to have arranged the North Korea trip prior to Dubai. Quinn was right. David already had the inclination to betray his country; whether that came from greed or disagreements with the country's policies, she couldn't tell, and it didn't matter anyway. There could be no valid excuse.

Quinn parked the car and cut the engine. "Do you think we should give it another hour? It's not much past midnight. What if she's a night owl?"

"She's not. She turns in early. I remember David telling me that—it was supposedly another point of contention between them, since he liked to stay up late and sleep in when he wasn't working, and Belinda preferred the opposite."

Quinn snorted. "Yeah, because that's a good reason to cheat on someone and end a marriage."

"That was probably all a lie. He probably just wanted to compromise me to use me. I'm sure he never loved me. If Belinda is okay with his deceit and is happy to spend his blood money, they're made for each other."

He clasped the back of her neck and squeezed it gently. "It's not you. Dawson would've betrayed any partner."

"Okay, let's do this." She dropped her head to the side and kissed his wrist.

The night air was heavy with the scent of magnolias from the park, and the sweet smell reminded her of the fragrant blooms in Jamaica and nights spent cradling Bella in the rocking chair in Mom's garden.

What was she doing here? She yearned to be back with her baby. She yearned to tell Quinn all about their daughter.

But she couldn't live her life as a dead woman.

It didn't take long for Quinn to break into Belinda's house. In an odd stroke of luck, Belinda hadn't enabled her alarm system.

They stepped through the side door and Rikki held her breath as she looked around the living room where they'd been earlier this evening. Low lights from beneath the kitchen counters gave a soft glow to the room, and they didn't even have to use their flashlights. What a nice welcome.

Rikki made a beeline for the built-in bookshelf and tripped to a stop. With her gloved fingers, she tapped the empty space that David's picture had occupied.

She gestured to Quinn, still hovering by the door.

He ducked next to her, and she whispered in his ear, "The picture is gone."

He swept the light from his phone across the photos on the shelves and swore softly under his breath. "I don't like this, Rikki. We need to get out."

Her heart jumped, mimicking the urgency in his voice. "Wh-why?"

"It's all too convenient for us—the alarm system, the lights and now the missing picture. It's almost like she expected us."

"Then why would she make it easy for us?"

"To lure us in." He grabbed her arm. "We're done here."

Rikki twisted her head around for one last, longing look at that bookshelf as Quinn pulled her toward the side door—the door that hadn't been double-locked.

What had Belinda done with that incriminating picture? Had she realized the stupidity of showing it to a couple of CIA agents? Belinda had probably figured nobody would do a before-and-after comparison of her dead husband's chest.

Quinn hustled Rikki through the side door, and eased

it closed. As soon as the door clicked, Rikki heard another click.

"Get your hands up where I can see them."

Chapter 11

A shot of adrenaline pumped through Quinn's body and he dropped to the ground, making a grab for Rikki's legs to take her down with him. But Rikki was two steps ahead of him, already on the ground and army-crawling toward the back of the house.

A beam of light swept the space above them, bouncing off the door they'd just passed through.

Staying low, Quinn lunged around the same corner where Rikki had just disappeared. His gun dug into his ribs. He left it there. Although any cop worth his salt would've lit up the scene by now with more than just a flashlight, Quinn couldn't be sure that the Savannah PD *didn't* have them at gunpoint. It could very well be some rookie cop on the other side of that click.

Whoever it was hadn't given them a second order. He probably couldn't see them with the clouds wafting across the crescent moon and no lights illuminating the side of the house. That was another convenience Belinda had afforded them. She might have lured them to the dark side of the house, but she'd also just given them an advantage.

Neither of them spoke, but Quinn could hear Rikki's short spurts of breath as she dragged herself up to a crouching position.

She jabbed his shoulder and pointed to the fence.

A semicircle of light awaited them on their way to that fence, but Quinn didn't want to give their pursuer a shot at them once he rounded the corner.

He shook his head at Rikki and jerked his thumb over his shoulder at the stealthy rustle behind them. A seasoned cop would've called backup by now, but Quinn couldn't be 100 percent sure that Belinda hadn't called the police, and he didn't want to risk tangling with a member of law enforcement—especially since he and Rikki had been caught red-handed breaking and entering.

A body of water to his left caught a glimmer of light from the slice of moon as it emerged from a rolling cloud cover. Quinn tugged on Rikki's pant leg and tipped his chin toward the pond. Even if they made a splash going into the water, the man with the gun wouldn't be able to get a clear line of sight on them—not like he would once he came around that corner with his flashlight.

Rikki didn't need any encouragement from him. On her hands and knees, she crawled to the edge of the pond and slipped in headfirst.

Quinn rolled in after her and kept his body flat. The pond had enough water to cover them, but only if they stretched out their bodies and kept low. Now all they needed was a couple of reeds to poke up above the surface of the water to breathe.

He and Rikki floated and bobbed side by side, submerged in the murky water until they reached the far end of the pond.

They'd have to head over the back fence and make a run for it if they hoped to get out of this situation. He squeezed Rikki's arm.

Again, she knew what had to be done.

She breached the surface first, emerging from the water like some slinky, primordial creature, and he scrambled over the slippery edge behind her. The noise of their escape broke the silence of the night, and the light from the flashlight made a jerky survey above the pond.

By the time the beam of light found Quinn, Rikki had launched herself over the fence. As Quinn grabbed the slats of wood to freedom, their assailant fired his first shot—from a silencer.

The bullet cracked the fence inches from Quinn's right hand. That was all the incentive he needed. He hoisted himself over and landed on the ground.

Rikki grabbed the back of his shirt at the collar. "Run."

"No kidding."

They'd landed in someone else's backyard, but Quinn couldn't even see the house from their position. Belinda had bought herself a place on a large lot, alongside other homes on equally large lots. The size of these yards would save their necks.

In a crouch, they ran for the fence to their left. The

clouds cooperated with them and drifted across the slice of moon again.

Rikki hit the fence with both hands. "I can't get over this without a boost. Can you?"

"Piece of cake, Buttercup." He laced his fingers together, and Rikki wedged the sole of her tennis shoe against his palms. "Ready?"

"Just hurry it up."

He launched her up, and she hoisted herself over.

His height gave him an advantage, and he swung over the fence with ease.

They made their way through a couple more lawns like that before hitting the street. Their shoes squishing with water, they kept to the shadows until they reached the park.

Rikki was panting by the time she grabbed the door handle of his vehicle. "It's a good thing we left the car down here."

"Yep, but I'm surprised Belinda Dawson didn't provide a getaway car for us."

Quinn started the engine before he fully sat down or closed the door. He left the lights off as he crawled into the street, checking his rearview mirror.

The cars on the streets of Savannah were few and far between until they emerged from the quiet residential streets into a boulevard dotted with bars and nightspots.

Quinn finally let out a pent-up breath, but still kept watch on his mirrors.

Rikki slumped in her seat, pressing a hand over her heart and the wet T-shirt that stuck to her chest. "That was close. He was no cop, was he? Did you get a look at him?"

"I didn't see him at all, but you're right. I don't think

Belinda called the cops on us." Quinn sluiced his wet hair back from his forehead and combed out a piece of moss.

"Then who did she call? Who was that? He had a silencer." Rikki crossed her arms over her midsection. "It must've been CIA. She called the Agency to check on us and discovered nobody had been sent for David's equipment."

"Maybe, but how did someone get here so quickly and why the subterfuge?" Quinn rubbed his palms, which the fence had abraded, against the steering wheel. "If she called the CIA, found out we were impostors and then reported us, why would she collude with the Agency to catch us in the act? The CIA would never use a spouse like that to lure impostors out of the woodwork. Especially a widow. Can you imagine the liability if the Agency did that and a spouse wound up dead?"

"It could've been someone from the Agency but not sanctioned by the Agency. Is that what you mean? Someone already out here looking after Belinda. Someone who's in on the joke and knows that David is alive and well and getting tattooed in Thailand, or wherever." Rikki grabbed her ponytail and twisted it to wring out the pond water.

"That's what I'm thinking, someone with the Agency—or not, but nobody official."

Rikki tucked a wet strand of hair behind her ear. "That's a scarier scenario than having an on-duty agent after us."

"Except—" Quinn wheeled into the parking lot of their motel and parked in front of their room "—if an agent had captured us, taken us down at gunpoint, the Agency would've wasted no time identifying you, unless you erased your fingerprints with acid, but I recall your fingertips being intact."

She wiggled her fingers in front of her. "The hair and the eyes are as far as I'll go for a disguise. I'm going to agree with you and bet our shooter was either a rogue agent working with David or someone involved in this traitorous network of David's jumping on any hint that someone believes he's still alive."

Quinn cut the engine and lights but didn't make a move to leave the car. "Which brings us back to Belinda."

"It sure seemed like she trusted us while we were there. What do you think set off her alarm bells?"

"Maybe the interest in the photo. She realized after we left that the picture was of David post-death and started to get worried."

Rikki leveled a finger at him, seemingly in no hurry to get out of the car and her wet clothing. "Or she called the number on your fake card."

He tapped the burner phone in his cup holder. "Except I didn't get any calls on this phone."

"Either I showed too much interest in that picture or she had orders from David to be wary of any outreach from the Agency. She called the CIA to check out our story."

"Our story didn't pass the test. She brushed it off with the Agency and then made a call to her henchman."

"And set us up." Rikki rubbed her chin. "How did she know we'd be back?"

"She didn't know for sure, or Dawson is so paranoid he orchestrated the setup just to be on the safe side."

"Do you think she called David after we left?"

"Makes sense, doesn't it? Isn't that something

David would do? Disable the alarm system, leave off the lights on one side of the house, disengage one set of locks on the door and have Belinda call in backup when we showed up. Hell—" he yanked the door handle "—she might've had a camera watching our every move down there."

Back in the room, Rikki peeled off her wet T-shirt and shimmied out of the jeans sticking to her thighs. "Ugh, that pond water was disgusting. I hope you didn't swallow any of it."

"My lips were sealed. I'm just glad we left our phones in the car. I would've had a lot of explaining to do to get my encrypted phone replaced."

Rikki kicked her wet clothes into a corner. "We need to get David's emails to Chan and decoded. I want to know what he was up to and what he was doing in South Korea."

"Other than setting up his own death and your entrapment? I'd say Dawson was a busy boy—and I already sent the emails to Chan."

"Why South Korea? There must've been a reason for him to pick that area instead of staging all this in Dubai, for example."

"That's a mystery those messages might solve." Quinn pulled his own damp T-shirt over his head and tossed it into Rikki's wet pile of clothes. "Right now I want to get this pond scum off my body. Do you want to help me?"

"I'd like nothing more than to rub pond scum from your body."

Quinn sprinted past Rikki to the bathroom before she could change her mind. He ran a warm bath and dumped some body wash in the water to create bubbles.

Then he stripped off the rest of his clothes and sank into the tub, as much as his six-foot-three frame could sink.

"That was fast—bubbles and everything." Rikki hung on the door frame in her underwear.

"Technically it's body wash, but it worked." He scooped up a handful of bubbles and blew on them.

"I knew navy SEALs were resourceful. I just didn't realize in how many ways." She stepped out of her panties and unhooked her bra.

Quinn opened his legs, patting the water between them. "I have a place for you right here."

Rikki dipped a toe in the water before stepping in and lowering herself into the tub. Leaning back against his chest, she said, "Don't get any ideas in here, McBride. We might both end up drowning."

"Ideas?" He cupped her breasts from behind and nuzzled her neck. "What ideas do you think I might have?"

She put one arm behind her, winding it around his neck. "The kinds of ideas you have every time we're within two feet of each other."

"Can I help it if I find you irresistible?"

And then he used all his resourcefulness to show her.

The following morning, Quinn got back to business. While Rikki looked through her old emails from David, Quinn contacted Donovan Chan again. If Chan wondered why Quinn was asking about a dead agent, he kept his questions to himself.

Rikki looked up from Quinn's laptop. "I don't see anything suspicious in David's communications, nothing to suggest that our mission to Korea was anything other than what he claimed—a lead on Vlad."

"Did he ever disclose how he got this intel?" Quinn tossed his phone on the cushion beside him.

Rikki wedged the tip of her finger between her teeth. "Not in the emails, but he mentioned a name when we were in Dubai, and it was the same guy we met in South Korea—Buddy Song."

"Was this Song in intelligence in South Korea? Why wouldn't Song go straight to the CIA or to Ariel and the Vlad task force?"

"I don't know." Rikki shrugged. "I didn't ask him. David had his contacts outside of our partnership, relationships he'd cultivated over the years before I even became an agent and started working with him."

"Do you know how to contact Song? Did anyone ever reach out to him after David's supposed murder and your capture?"

"My supposed murder, too." She raised her eyebrows. "You know that better than anyone."

Quinn clasped the back of his neck and squeezed. "Do you have to keep reminding me?"

"Like I said before, if it hadn't been you I'd be dead." She tipped the computer from her lap onto the bed and crossed her legs. "Ariel didn't tell me what kind of investigation was done into David's murder, but I doubt anyone knows about Song. David didn't even put his name in an email to me. We only ever spoke about him."

"I think Song is a good place to start. What do you remember about him? Where did you meet?"

"We met in Seoul, at a park. He spoke English very well. He helped us cross the border, and I got the feeling it wasn't his first rodeo."

"He was probably someone who facilitated border crossings between North and South Korea. Maybe that was his insight into Vlad. He probably helped him cross the border, too."

"Could be. Song got us to a tunnel between the two countries and said goodbye there. The rest is history. David and I crossed over and hadn't traveled five miles before I was taken and David killed—or so I thought."

"But now we know Song didn't set up David. David manipulated the entire scenario, with or without Song's knowledge."

"And definitely without mine."

Rikki rubbed her nose, and Quinn knew David's betrayal of her stung. He couldn't imagine any of his sniper teammates turning on him like that. For a while, the navy had tried to tell them Miguel Estrada had been working with the enemy, but he and the rest of the guys hadn't believed that for one second.

But Rikki had proof.

Quinn stood up and stretched his arms, almost brushing his fingertips on the ceiling. "Do you think Ariel can track down Song? Would she? She's deep undercover enough that nobody's following her movements."

"I can ask her. I never thought about him before, but that's when I believed our mission to Korea was something straightforward, or at least as straightforward as our missions ever were. Now that I know David pulled a scam on me—" she flicked her fingers in the air "—everything and everyone is fair game."

Quinn peered through the curtains on the window. "We can do all this on computers and on my trusty phone. We don't need to stay in Savannah."

"When do you have to report back for duty?"

"Three weeks." A sudden fear gripped Quinn's heart.

"If we can't clear you before then, you need to go back to Jamaica where you'll be safe."

Rikki's lashes dropped over her eyes. "Maybe. I vowed I wouldn't return there until my name was cleared."

"I can continue our sleuthing."

She widened her eyes. "From Afghanistan or Pakistan or Libya or wherever you're going? I don't think so, Quinn."

In two steps, he was at the bed and sitting on the edge. "Then we'll figure it out, and then maybe you don't have to go back to Jamaica. You can go back to your job and I can do mine and maybe we can be together—freewheeling and fancy-free, no strings, nothing to tie us down except each other."

Rikki sucked in her lower lip. "That's what you want?"

"That's what I always wanted. I don't understand why I scared you off in Dubai to the point you felt you had to run away. Yeah, I felt something deep for you, maybe deeper than you felt yourself, but that never meant I wanted to restrict you, make you give up the job you love. Hell, my job isn't exactly a nine-to-five, white-picket-fence deal."

"We have to talk this through first." Rikki twisted her fingers. "There's a lot I have to tell you."

"About your time in the labor camp and your escape?" He cupped his hand over one of her knees. "I do want to hear about that, Rikki. It'll only make me think you're more amazing than I already do."

"It's not just that, Quinn. Jamaica…"

"You're not going to tell me you have a boyfriend in Jamaica, are you?" He curled his fingers into her leg.

"I don't even care. I know I love you more than anyone else could."

She pressed her fingers against her bottom lip and whispered, "Quinn."

"So whatever it is…" He jerked his head toward the ringing phone on the table by the window. "That's not my regular phone. That's the burner, and nobody has that number except Belinda."

"Or random telemarketers."

Quinn pushed himself off the bed and lunged for the phone. "It's her."

He jabbed the button to answer and to put the phone on speaker at the same time. "Hello? Agent Miller."

"Agent Miller, this is Belinda Dawson."

"Mrs. Dawson, did you find some of your husband's equipment after all?" He rolled his eyes at Rikki, who'd followed him off the bed and had her hip wedged against the table.

"Let's cut to the chase, Miller, if that's really your name."

Quinn swallowed. "Pardon me, ma'am?"

"You can cut the Southern boy charm, too. I'm immune."

"I'm afraid you lost me, Mrs. Dawson."

"I almost lost you last night to that thug watching my house night and day."

Rikki grabbed his wrist, her eyes taking up half her face.

"You're going to have to explain yourself, Mrs. Dawson."

"You and I both know my husband is alive, Agent Miller, and I can give you the proof you need."

Chapter 12

Rikki clapped a hand over her mouth. Why was Belinda doing this? Why was she outing David?

Quinn braced his hands on the table and hunched over the phone. "Why would you give me proof that your husband is alive?"

"That's what you were sniffing around here for, wasn't it? You and your...partner seemed awfully interested in that photo of David—the one taken after his supposed death. When you zeroed in on that picture, I finally felt a glimmer of hope."

Quinn raised his eyebrows at Rikki, but all she could do was shrug. She had no idea where Belinda was going with this.

Quinn cleared his throat. "What do you mean by hope? Hope for what?"

"David swore me to secrecy about his betrayal. He

warned me that I'd lose everything if the CIA found out he'd been spying for the enemy. He sent people to watch me, to keep tabs on me."

"How do you know my partner and I aren't just two more watchdogs?"

Rikki nodded at Quinn. He knew all the right questions—the same ones she'd be asking.

"You were fishing. They don't fish. Your unexpected appearance on my doorstep yesterday told me that the CIA has doubts about David's story."

Rikki scribbled a question on a napkin and shoved it toward Quinn.

He gave her a thumbs-up. "Why didn't you just call the CIA yourself and report this?"

"You're kidding." Belinda gave a soft snort. "You work for the Agency, so you should understand. I don't know whom to trust over there. I didn't know who was in on it, or even if his fake death had been sanctioned by someone over there. I wasn't about to step out of line, but you two…"

Quinn cut her off and with a gruff voice asked, "If you trusted us so much, why did you call the dogs on us last night?"

Belinda released a long sigh. "That wasn't me."

"The alarm system, the lights, the door? You even took the picture."

"They ordered me to do all that. They knew you'd been there." She sobbed. "They bugged my house."

Quinn's gaze locked on to Rikki's. "And now? How do you know you're not being bugged now?"

"I bought a throwaway phone, and I'm at a restaurant waiting to have brunch with my friend. David taught me well."

Rikki couldn't contain herself anymore. "Why are you turning on your husband now, Mrs. Dawson?"

Belinda sucked in a quick breath over the line. "I'm tired of living this way. David was supposed to send for me, but he hasn't. I can't trust anyone. I don't want to get on the bad side of the CIA and be tried as a traitor. I'd be willing to…you know, testify against him to save myself."

Rikki avoided Quinn's warning looks and plunged ahead. "At the beginning of the call, you said you had proof that David is alive. Is that the picture?"

"That and other things. I'll turn them over to you so you can go after him and I can be protected. I *will* be protected, won't I?"

Clamping a hand on Rikki's shoulder, Quinn answered the desperate wife. "I think we can work something out. How do you propose to get us this proof if you're under such close watch?"

"There are ways. I have a lot of old friends in this town, and I socialize quite frequently. In fact, I'm meeting old friends tonight for cocktails. If Agent Reid were to stop by our table, just another Savannah socialite… or friend of my husband's, who would question that?"

Quinn shook his head at her, and Rikki put her finger to her lips. "Let's hear the plan, Mrs. Dawson."

As Belinda laid out her scheme to pass off proof that David had faked his death, Quinn peppered her with questions and Rikki took a few notes.

When she finished, Belinda said, with a hitch in her voice, "I really want to do this. I need to think about myself now."

"I'll be there, Mrs. Dawson."

Quinn ended the call and tapped the edge of the phone against his chin. "Why should we trust her?"

"Because her reasoning sounds plausible."

"What if it's a trick to get us on someone's radar?"

"If it is, we can outmaneuver them. We did it last night when we weren't even expecting a trap. This time we'll be even more on our guard and on our game. Besides—" she ran a hand down his tense back "—why would Belinda admit the truth about David being alive if she weren't on the up-and-up?"

Quinn's back got even stiffer. "It wouldn't matter... if she planned to have us killed."

Rikki's hand stopped midcircle where she was rubbing Quinn's back. "I need this proof, Quinn. Nobody is going to believe me, or worse yet, some anonymous tip that Agent David Dawson is a traitor who faked his own death."

"Ariel will believe you. Take this to her and let her launch an investigation."

"There's no denying Ariel is pretty untouchable in the intelligence community, but she has her hands full running the Vlad task force."

"You said it yourself, Rikki. We could make a good case that this *is* about Vlad."

"A good case? A string of undeciphered, coded emails and the word of a disgraced CIA agent, presumed dead?" She slid her hand down his arm and entwined her fingers with his. "I have to do this, Quinn. I won't be by myself, right? You'll be there to look out for me."

"I don't like it, Rikki. I know better than anyone that a sniper can pick you off at a distance and we wouldn't realize it until it was too late."

"Then you also know better than anyone that I can get in and out of that restaurant undercover. With you on my side, no sniper or shooter is going to get a chance at me."

"I think you're exaggerating my talents." He turned and wedged a knuckle beneath her chin. "I'll get you inside that bar, and then you have one drink or whatever Belinda has planned, get the proof and get out of there."

"I think it'll work, and it's not possible for me to exaggerate your talents."

"I'm just glad you decided to forgive me so that I could help you with all this. Not that you're not a kick-ass agent, but at least two people need to be doing this job and I think we make a great team." He raised her hand to his lips and kissed the back of it.

She rested her head against his shoulder. They *did* make a good team, and she planned to tell him just how much they were going to be a team to raise their daughter—as soon as they got past this danger.

A few hours after dinner, Rikki slipped on taupe sling-back heels and smoothed her beige skirt over her thighs. "What do you think? Do I look like a Southern belle born to privilege and debutante balls?"

"I don't know about all that, but you look beautiful." Quinn came up behind her and ran a hand through her hair. "I miss those riotous red curls, though, and how the sun would set them on fire. The last time I saw you…"

His fingers tightened in her hair, sending a tingle down her thighs.

Tipping her head into the curve of his palm, she whispered, "But that wasn't the last time you saw me. I'm here now. We both are."

He pressed a kiss against her temple. "Let's keep it that way. Are you sure you want to meet Belinda? It could be a trap. She could have someone waiting for us."

"I have to get my hands on this proof." She placed a finger over his lips. "Why would she want us out of the picture? She knows we don't have any other evidence that David is alive."

"Why did the guy last night taking shots at us want us out of the way?"

"Because if he's working with David, he doesn't know what we have. He doesn't know what Belinda told us. He was trying to eliminate a possible threat."

"Let's get this over with. I can see there's no talking you out of it. You might as well have that red hair on your head, because you're just as stubborn as a brunette."

"Red hair does not make you stubborn." She gave Quinn a playful push while a smile curved her lips as she thought about little red-haired Bella already trying to assert herself at nine months old.

Rikki grabbed a light sweater from the back of the chair and held it up. "Just in case they're blasting the air in the bar."

Before they left the hotel, Quinn called a car for her and saw her safely inside before heading for his own vehicle.

Rikki waved to him out the back window and settled in her seat with a sense of excitement buzzing through her veins. She'd been made for this work. If she could clear her name, how would she reconcile her career with motherhood? Bella meant more to her than anything in the world, more to her than a career—even this career.

And Quinn? How would he fit into it all? He'd been

the one talking about forever when they were in Dubai, and that had rattled her. Now he'd changed his tune and had suggested they could both pursue their careers and meet up all over the world when they could. Now she had to break it to him that they had a child together.

She sighed and pressed her fingers against the window. "Almost there?"

"Just about. Ever been to Savannah Joe's before?"

"Nope."

"Nice place. You gotta try the mint juleps—best in the city."

"I'll do that. Thanks for the tip."

The driver pulled up in front of the restaurant-bar, and Rikki thanked him and slipped out of the backseat. As Quinn had instructed, she ducked her head and made a beeline for the entrance. If someone had a rifle trained on the entrance to the restaurant, he'd have to recognize her first and set up a shot. She'd given him no time for that at all.

Stepping through the front door, she let out a breath. Belinda had explained the layout—a restaurant in front with tables behind large screened windows, and a busy bar in the back on the river.

As the hostess approached her, Rikki pointed to the back and then made her way to the large bar that separated the dining area from the cocktail lounge.

She rubbed her lips together, moistening her lipstick, and squared her shoulders as she stepped down into the bar area. She scanned the room, and Belinda's subtle wave caught her attention.

Quinn didn't have to worry about the setup. This bar, packed with people, didn't exactly lend itself to ambush and murder at the end of a sniper's rifle.

Rikki plastered a smile on her face and wended her way through the tables to reach Belinda and her two friends, crowded around a cocktail table.

Belinda half rose from her seat. "Here she is. Peyton, this is Melissa and Jordan. Ladies, Peyton, a friend of David's family."

"So nice to meet you." Rikki shared limp handshakes with the other two women and sat next to Belinda. "This is a great place. I heard the mint juleps are to die for."

"Have this one." Belinda shoved a tall glass with a spray of mint in front of Rikki. "I've already had one, and these two already ordered another round."

"Thank you." Rikki smoothed out the napkin beneath the sweating glass. She wanted to keep her wits about her tonight, get the photo and whatever else Belinda had, and get out. Quinn was supposed to be waiting at the back door of the restaurant to whisk her away once Belinda had handed off the proof in the ladies' room.

She'd let Belinda call the shots and make the move to the ladies' room, but this had to look like a legit social interaction in case anyone was watching Belinda.

"Looks refreshing." Rikki swirled the straw in her glass as the waitress delivered three more drinks.

The waitress raised her eyebrows at Rikki. "Can I get you something?"

"I'm good, thanks." Rikki tapped the glass and then almost choked when she glanced over the waitress's shoulder and saw Quinn sitting at the bar.

He had to see that she'd be safe here. She'd rather have him keeping watch outside, and she hoped Belinda hadn't noticed him.

"To friendships." Belinda raised her glass in the center of the table and the other two women held up their glasses, as well.

Rikki clinked her glass with theirs. "To friendships."

The women immediately launched into a discussion of some mutual acquaintance, ripping apart her parenting skills.

Rikki smirked. So much for friendships. She pulled the straw from the glass and sucked some liquid from the bottom of the straw—just a drop or two.

Rikki puckered her lips. She'd never had a mint julep before, and the tartness of the drink surprised her. The garnish on the drink didn't even include a slice of lime.

She stuck the straw back in the glass and took a tentative sip.

Rikki rolled the liquid on the surface of her tongue, and her nostrils flared as the sour smell reached her nose. The drink dribbled down the back of her throat, but Rikki froze, refusing to swallow.

David's voice floated across her consciousness, and she could picture him in the hotel room in Bangkok pinching a small vial between his fingers. "I discovered this here, Rikki, and it's very useful because it has an immediate impact but proceeds to incapacitate slowly and gradually. It also has a tart taste and smell that could pass for a citrus garnish on a cocktail."

Rikki convulsively clutched the hem of the tablecloth. The liquid had traveled too far for her to stop it unless she made a scene coughing it up.

So she allowed the poison to slide down her throat.

Chapter 13

Quinn studied the four women over the rim of his beer mug. Rikki seemed to be doing a good job of acting like the long-lost friend. She laughed, chattered and sipped her mint julep along with the rest.

Did she forget this wasn't a social call? She needed to nudge Belinda along for their meeting in the john—if Belinda planned to stick with the scheme. He didn't trust the woman for a second.

"Another beer, sir?"

He waved off the bartender and plucked some bills from his pocket. Then from the corner of his eye, he sensed a commotion.

He jerked his head to the side to see Rikki stagger to her feet, almost upsetting her chair. His muscles coiled. His head swiveled from side to side. Nobody else had noticed.

Belinda rose from the table and placed a hand on Rikki's arm. Maybe this was the ruse to get them to the ladies' room.

Rikki leaned against Belinda while Belinda laughed with the other women and curled an arm around Rikki's waist.

Quinn let out a breath. For a minute he thought Rikki might be injured, but the demeanor of the other two women didn't support this.

Belinda would take Rikki to the ladies' room, hand over the proof, and then they could get the hell out of here.

Quinn narrowed his eyes and followed their progress to the hallway at the back. His gaze shifted to Belinda's friends, still at the table.

He'd give Rikki and Belinda exactly thirty seconds before he went back there himself and hustled Rikki out of the bar. Just because she'd gotten in here without incident didn't mean they'd let her leave. Belinda could have someone waiting for them in the alley.

Quinn shoved himself off his barstool and strode to the back of the room. Turning the corner to the restrooms, he grazed shoulders with a man coming out of the men's room, and the hair on the back of his neck quivered.

Knots formed in his gut and he crashed into the ladies' room.

A woman washing her hands at the sink smirked. "Wrong place."

Quinn ignored her and peered under the first stall. Rikki hadn't been wearing short boots.

He pushed in the door of the next stall. "Rikki?"

A groan from the third stall answered him and he

gave the door a shove. The door just missed Rikki propped up against the stall, her face white and twisted with pain.

"What happened? Where's Belinda?"

"Follow her. Just left. Get her."

"I'm not going anywhere. What the hell happened?"

"I'm okay. I'll be okay." She pressed her purse into his hands, her own shaking. "Get the ipecac."

He dumped the contents of her purse on the tile floor and grabbed a small brown bottle. "This stuff?"

She nodded. "Open."

He twisted off the cap and handed it to her. She placed it at her lips and threw some back. Almost immediately, she heaved.

"Out." She pushed him out of the stall.

Another woman had come in and hovered by the first stall. "Is she okay?"

The sound of vomiting came from Rikki's stall, and Quinn shrugged. "She's sick."

The woman wrinkled her nose. "Probably too many of those mint juleps."

Several minutes later, Rikki emerged from the stall, shoving her hair back from her face. She gave the woman at the sink a weak smile. "Sorry about that."

"Oh, honey, it was those mint juleps, wasn't it? Bourbon, powdered sugar." She stuck out her tongue. "Vile."

"You could say that." Rikki ran water over her hands in the sink and splashed her face and rinsed her mouth.

Quinn yanked several paper towels from the dispenser and handed them to her. "Feeling better?"

"Lots." She dabbed her face and neck with the paper towels and ducked back into the stall, ripping off a length of toilet paper. While she blew her nose and did another round of hand-washing, Quinn gathered the items from her purse off the floor and stuffed them back into her bag, including the bottle of ipecac. How the hell did she happen to have that? He studied the sharpened nail file, a bit of rope and another bottle of a clear substance before dropping each into her purse. Travel kit for a CIA agent on assignment?

Two other women had come into the restroom and Quinn apologized, explaining that his wife had been ill, but the women's presence didn't give him and Rikki a chance to talk. And they needed to talk.

Quinn took her arm and hunched over her as they exited the ladies' room. He placed a hand on the silver bar of the back door. "Stay down, crouch forward, stay next to the building."

Rikki cleared her throat. "I don't think we have to worry about anyone else. Belinda was lying about being followed. Besides, I'm supposed to be dead—again."

"Don't argue."

Quinn sneaked Rikki out the back door of the restaurant as if they had a team of snipers taking aim from all four corners of the alley.

He'd wedged his car behind a waitress's after paying her forty bucks for the privilege to get as close as possible to the restaurant. When he handed Rikki into the passenger seat, he said, "Stay down."

She complied, arms folded over her stomach, and he hoped she wouldn't have another episode in his car.

Checking all mirrors, he pulled out of the alley and drove for several blocks.

Rikki finally piped up. "We need to go after Belinda, Quinn."

"Can you tell me what happened now?"

"She poisoned me, slipped it in my mint julep. As soon as I figured out what I was drinking, I stopped drinking it. I wiped my mouth several times and spit the drink into a napkin. One time, I was able to pour out a bit on the floor."

His hands gripped the steering wheel. And he'd been worried about shooters outside the restaurant. "So that and the syrup of ipecac saved you. How'd you know to bring it, or is it standard operating procedure for you spooks?"

"Actually, David saved me."

"What?"

"I'd never had a mint julep before, but this one tasted nothing like I expected. It had a tart taste and smell, and then I remembered David showing me a poison he'd discovered in Thailand. Fast-acting to incapacitate the victim, but slow enough to delay actual death for a few days. Belinda didn't want me dropping dead at the table, but she also had no intention of giving me David's picture or any other proof."

"Did she tell you this as she led you away to the bathroom?"

"She didn't say much of anything. She kept up appearances to the end, soothing me and sympathizing—up until the moment she abandoned me in the bathroom stall and took off."

"She admitted David was alive because she planned to kill you and never turn over any evidence. But why go through all this to kill you? Why not call out one of David's henchmen, like she did at her house?"

"That didn't work because you were there."

"And why just you and not me? Unless she has something else planned for me."

"She probably does."

"But now I'm on my guard."

Rikki smacked the dashboard with both hands. "It's time to strike. She thinks I'm dead and you're running scared."

"This makes no sense to me, Rikki." Quinn plowed a hand through his hair. "If she had called in one of David's associates to take us out in the parking lot, or even if she never contacted us at all after the failed attempt at her house, both of those scenarios would compute better. Admitting David was alive? Luring you out to kill you with poison? I don't get it."

She pressed her hands against her bubbling tummy. "We don't have to get it. We just have to get her. She thinks I'm dead. Part of my stumbling and staggering with her was an act to convince her of that fact. She's going to pass on the news of my demise to the men she has coming after us."

"I'm very much alive, and wouldn't I be coming right at the woman who killed my partner?"

"We'll take her by surprise, at her house."

Quinn tugged on his ear. "You're after the photo again. She's probably destroyed it by now. Maybe it's better if I set up a meeting with her. She knows I'm still alive."

"Then what? A meeting is not going to do any good if she doesn't bring proof that David is alive."

"Instead of a meeting—" Quinn drummed his thumbs against the steering wheel as he made the last turn to their motel "—I'll take her by surprise. I'll escort her someplace where we can have a private…conversation. You stay out of sight until the interrogation.

I want to get to the bottom of this. I want her to explain her actions."

"I want that picture."

"I know you do." He rubbed her arm. "But we have to expect she destroyed it. Let's get some answers from her first."

"Where are you going to catch her off guard?"

Quinn parked the car and released his seat belt. "Despite her subterfuge on behalf of David, Belinda seems to go on with her life. We know she volunteers at the Savannah Historical Society in the mornings. I'll catch her when she's leaving her shift tomorrow morning. Just a friendly little talk."

"You don't believe someone's watching her?"

"Why would they? She's on David's side. She proved that tonight by trying to poison you." As that fact hit him all over again, he reached out to grab Rikki's hand. "I think she has an associate or two of David's close by that she can call out when she needs help, like setting us up last night, but I don't think they're keeping tabs on her. I doubt there was anyone there tonight."

"Just her and her little vial of poison." She pounded her knee with her fist. "I can't believe I fell for the oldest trick in the book."

"You didn't fall for it. You recognized the smell and taste of the poison and you took action. Your instincts are still good, kid."

She smiled at him before opening the door and slipping out of the car.

When they got to the motel room, Quinn checked his laptop. "Hey, I got a message from Chan on the decoding."

Rikki leaned over him, her hair fluttering against his cheek. "Can he do it?"

"He's going to try. He has some programs he's going to use."

"Fingers crossed." And then she crossed them.

He closed his hand around her crossed fingers and kissed the tips. "We're going to solve this and get you back into action—where you belong."

Rikki's eyes flooded with tears. "Back where I belong."

As one of those tears slid down Rikki's cheek, Quinn kissed it away, tasting the salt on his lips.

Were those tears for him? If she didn't think she belonged with him by now, he'd have to up his game to convince her otherwise. And he'd start tonight.

The next morning, Quinn pulled on a pair of cargo shorts with big side pockets as he watched Rikki tuck her gun into a purse.

"It's times like these I wish I had a purse." Quinn grabbed his own weapon and slipped it into a pocket of his shorts where it banged against his thigh. "I'd like to carry bigger, but I don't want to be obvious."

Rikki held up her purse, swinging it from her fingertips. "I'd like to carry bigger, too, but I'm not going to lug around a suitcase."

"Remember—" he took her by the shoulders, his thumb nestling beneath the strap of her purse "—stay out of sight, even when I get her alone. She doesn't need to know you're still alive."

"Got it."

"Nobody knows Rikki Taylor is alive. There's no reason for anyone to know April Thompson is alive, either, or Agent Reid, or whoever you were for Belinda's friends."

He released her, and she adjusted the straps of her sundress. Then she crossed to the bed and swept up a big hat. "I'll be wearing this for cover, too."

"Once I make contact with her and show her my gun, I'll walk her to the park in the opposite direction of the coffeehouse where you'll be waiting. Stay there until I text you or come and get you. I'll only come and get you when I'm sure Belinda is on her way home and can't see you."

"But if she still has the picture of David, you'll be going back home with her to get it, right?"

"I'm hoping for even better proof he's alive, so don't hold your breath on that picture."

"Just don't drink anything she offers."

"Don't worry about that."

They would be arriving to the area separately, so Quinn left first with the car. Rikki would be taking a taxi later. He didn't want her anywhere near Belinda Dawson after what Belinda had tried last night, but trying to keep Rikki away would take more patience than he had. Also, he'd discovered that keeping Rikki away was not in his DNA.

Quinn parked a few blocks away from the Savannah Historical Society and waited in his car for almost thirty minutes. They'd checked the volunteer shifts for that morning, and five minutes before he figured Belinda would be leaving, he walked to the block that housed the building and sat on a park bench facing the front entrance. She couldn't exit to the rear, and if she came out a side door, she'd be forced to this street anyway.

He had it all sussed out—but the best-laid plans had a way of taking a twist.

He glanced casually to his right at the coffeehouse with its umbrellaed tables spilling onto the sidewalk, and his heart jumped when he spied a big white hat with a black-and-white polka-dot band around it—as long as she stayed out of sight.

Quinn shifted his focus back to the building that housed the Historical Society and his eyes narrowed as he picked out Belinda skipping down the two steps, her arm tucked around the arm of another woman.

Quinn shook his head. As far as Belinda knew, she'd poisoned a woman last night, and she looked like a sorority sister going to lunch.

He held his breath as he watched the two women. He hadn't planned on dealing with a second person.

When the other woman peeled off in another direction, Quinn let out his breath and pushed himself up from the bench. Go time.

Quinn ripped back the Velcro on his shorts' pocket and gripped his gun inside—not that he planned to use it, but he wouldn't mind putting a little fear into the woman who'd poisoned Rikki.

Belinda kept her eyes glued to her phone as she strode down the sidewalk.

Quinn moved behind her and quickened his pace. He lost the element of surprise as she swung her head around and then tripped to a stop.

"You."

He slowed his gait as he continued to approach her, his hand curled around the gun in his pocket. "You killed my partner, and I wanna know why. I wanna know where your husband is."

Belinda's eyes widened and she licked her lips, her gaze dropping to his pocket. "I-I…"

A zipping sound ripped through the air. Belinda's eyes bugged out of their sockets one second before she collapsed in front of him.

Chapter 14

Rikki squinted through the small binoculars she cupped in the palm of her hand. As Belinda turned to confront Quinn, Rikki whispered, "Shoot. You gotta have more stealth than that, sailor."

Then Belinda's body jerked, and she fell to the ground.

With her heart pounding in her chest and a voice screaming in her head, Rikki jumped up from the table, knocking over her glass of water. Clutching her purse against her body, she ran across the street toward the Historical Society.

Her vision blurred as she ran, and she could no longer see Quinn standing on the sidewalk. She panted and bumped into someone running from the scene.

Someone shouted, "Active shooter."

Rikki jogged toward the downed figure and as she got close, a hand shot out from behind a tree and grabbed her.

Quinn pulled her back behind the tree with him. "Someone shot her. He might still be active. I don't think she's dead."

"I need to talk to her." She broke away from Quinn and dropped to the ground. Sirens wailed in the distance, and most people had hit the pavement or had taken cover behind trees.

Rikki crawled toward Belinda, her hand stretched out and her fingers curled. She grabbed Belinda's hand and scooted toward her, nose to nose.

Quinn had followed her and crouched beside her, blocking her from the direction of the sniper.

Blood seeped out from beneath Belinda's body, but her eyes were open and she'd zeroed in on Rikki's face. Her lips parted and she croaked.

Rikki squeezed her hand. "I need to know where David is."

Belinda gasped and mumbled, and Rikki put her ear close to her lips.

"Not telling you. Did you think I didn't know you when I saw you? David's beloved Rikki."

Rikki's mouth fell open.

"Wasn't sure. Then you saw picture. You knew. 'Course you knew David's body. You were his lover."

"That never happened. He turned on me. Set me up." Rikki rushed her words as the sirens from the ambulance sounded louder.

"Revenge, you broke it off. When I told him you were alive, it gave him…life." Belinda's lips twisted, whether in pain or bitterness, Rikki couldn't tell.

"So I wanted to take your life again. Away from him."

"Who did this to you? Where's David now?"

"Davey did it. You don't cross David."

An EMT's voice shouted above them. "Ma'am, ma'am. I need you to get out of the way now."

"Tell me. We'll take him down together." Rikki gripped Belinda's wrist. "Where is he?"

The EMT physically pulled Rikki away from Belinda, but not before she choked out one word. "Song."

Quinn took her arm, and his head swiveled back and forth like a weather vane in a hurricane. "You put yourself in extreme danger. Was it worth it?"

"Her last word to me? *Song.* Buddy Song knows where David is. I'd say that's worth it. The sniper was long gone anyway."

He cocked one eyebrow in her direction as he practically dragged her across the street. "Because you're an expert on snipers?"

"Well, he wasn't a very good one, was he? He didn't kill Belinda."

"Not yet."

"She seemed pretty lucid for someone on death's doorstep. She could very well recover from this."

"Maybe that sniper didn't want to kill her. Maybe he just wanted to interrupt her conversation with me or teach her a lesson about going rogue and murdering random CIA agents."

"Wasn't he ready to murder random CIA agents the other night at Belinda's house?"

"We don't know what his intentions were that night. He could've just wanted to trap and question, like I planned to do with Belinda." He took her hand and led her into a small public parking lot. "I'm in here."

She ducked into the car and slumped in the seat. "At least we can now start with Buddy Song."

"We knew about him anyway, and Belinda could've been lying." He cranked on the engine and squealed out of the parking lot. "What else was she telling you? That conversation lasted longer than one name."

"Oh, yeah." Rikki slumped farther in the seat. "She knew who I was."

"What?" Quinn stomped on the brakes at the stop sign, and her body strained against the shoulder strap and then thumped back.

"She made me." Rikki twisted her fingers in her lap. "She suspected who I was when we first got to her house, and when I showed interest in the picture, that confirmed it for her."

"Maybe she won't recover."

"Quinn." She jerked her head around.

"I'm supposed to be rooting for a woman who called out a gunman on us, tried to poison you and now knows your identity?" He lifted his shoulders. "I'm sorry. I don't have much sympathy for her. I don't want her blabbing to anyone in the CIA about you before we're ready, and we won't be ready until someone talks to Buddy Song or Chan decodes David's emails."

"It's too late." Rikki pressed her hands against her stomach. In the shock of Belinda's shooting and getting info about David out of her, Rikki hadn't dwelled on the fact that Belinda had known who she was from the get-go. Now the truth of it punched her in the gut.

"She already told someone, and it's the reason why she tried to kill me."

"Back up. Who'd she tell? Did that person order her to poison you?"

"She told David."

Quinn uttered an expletive. "And David ordered your

death a second time? I can't wait to get my hands on him."

"I'm not sure it went down like that." Rikki dug her fingers in her hair. "Belinda told David I was alive, and apparently, he was a little too happy about it for Belinda's liking. She always thought David and I were lovers, and his reaction to her news seemed to confirm that for her."

Quinn's jaw tightened. "David lied to her, told her you came onto him. She told us as much."

"Probably." Rikki rolled her shoulders, but the stress just clawed its way up her neck. "His reaction to my being alive wasn't what she'd hoped for, so she decided to take me out—it sounds like to spite him."

He swung the car into a parking space at their motel and threw it into Park. "She thinks her own husband ordered this hit on her today because she tried to kill you? Does David really think you're going to forgive him for setting you up as a traitor?"

"I don't know what David thinks. It sounds like he's gone completely off the deep end, but it gave me a little leverage with her to give up some intel on David."

"Buddy Song's name is hardly intel. If David knows you're still alive, it won't be long before the CIA knows."

"He's not exactly going to call them from the dead, is he?"

"He'll use other methods to get the news out. You know he will." He stroked her arm from shoulder to wrist. "Do you want to take what we have now and go to the Agency? Do you want to turn yourself in?"

"Take what we have?" She snapped off her seat belt. "We have nothing. No proof. I don't even have that picture of David with the tattoo he never had before his supposed death."

Quinn lifted his hips from the seat of the car and dug into his voluminous pocket. He pulled out a cell phone and held it in front of her face. "I have this."

"Belinda's?" Her heart skipped in her chest and she pounced on the phone, snatching it from Quinn's hand.

"She was holding it when I approached her. When the bullet hit her, she dropped it and I scooped it up."

Rikki pressed the phone to her chest. "Quick thinking."

"Let's regroup and get your life back."

When they returned to the motel room, Rikki huddled in a chair by the window and tapped Belinda's phone to wake it up. "Ugh, it's password-protected."

"You know how to get around that, right? Isn't that CIA 101?"

"There are a couple of ways I can get in, although every time the manufacturers hear about another trick to bypass security codes, they change things up." Rikki tapped through several key sequences and let out a pent-up breath when Belinda's home screen popped up. "I'm in. This looks like her real phone and not the temp she used to call you."

"And which she probably used to contact her husband." Quinn circled his finger in the air. "She'll have her personal stuff on this one, though."

Rikki swept her finger through Belinda's photos. "Lots of pics of Savannah and her house. She must've done some remodeling lately."

"That's not gonna help."

"Wait." With a shaking finger, Rikki tapped an

image of a shirtless man. "It's here. The picture of David with that tattoo that he never had before he died."

"All right!" Quinn pumped his fist in the air. "Now, who can verify that the tattoo is a new acquisition besides you?"

"Anyone who did PT with David. If they changed in the locker room with him or even if he wore a tank top during PT, his chest would've been on display, and I'm telling you he never had that giant phoenix tattoo."

"You're going to send that to Ariel." Quinn leveled a finger at the phone. "What's your answer if someone tries to claim he got it in Korea?"

"Not enough time—and look at it." She jabbed her finger at the serious face in the picture, the face she used to trust. "It's not a brand-new tattoo. We weren't in Korea long enough for something like that to heal up. Hell, we weren't in Korea long enough before we were captured for him to even get a tattoo like that. Don't those tattoo artists take several days to create a work of art like that?"

"It could take more than one sitting. It looks like we might have Dawson dead to rights on this." Quinn rubbed his chin and gazed over her right shoulder.

"What? I don't like that look."

His gaze snapped back to her face. "Dawson knows you're alive."

"Y-yes?" She squared Belinda's phone on the table and clasped her hands between her knees.

"He might try to get word to the CIA—anonymously, of course."

"Why would the Agency believe a man who faked his own death in North Korea and set up his partner to take the fall as a traitor?"

"What if he already beat us to the punch? What if the CIA already got a tip that Rikki Taylor is alive and well and skulking around Savannah, and is taking action?" Quinn paced to the window and back to the TV, his long stride eating up the space in a few steps.

Rikki's eyes wandered to the window of their dumpy motel and fixed on a road sign across the street. "You mean like right now?"

"We need to get out of this town and back to New Orleans." Quinn stopped in midturn. "Does Dawson know much about me? Where I live?"

"I never told him anything. He knew we were...together in Dubai, and he probably knew your name and knew that you were a SEAL from asking around, but I doubt if he got any personal info on you, and I certainly didn't tell him anything like that."

"Navy's not going to give him any details about me, but then he's CIA. He can get those details his own way."

Rikki shook her head. "I don't think he would've done that, and he can't do it now."

"Let's head back tonight." He grabbed the remote from the bed. "You up for an all-night drive?"

"To get out of Savannah? Hell, yeah."

Quinn clicked on the TV. "We don't even know if Belinda made it or not."

"I'm sure she did. From the blood pooling, it looked like she got hit in the back. Although she was losing a lot of blood, she was conscious and the EMTs got right to work on her."

Quinn flipped through the channels until he settled on some local news. "We may have missed the story. It must've been the lead."

"The hospital won't tell us anything." Rikki pushed herself up from the chair and stood in front of the TV with her arms crossed. Even though Belinda Dawson had tried to poison her, Rikki couldn't help feeling sorry for her. She must really love David to keep his secrets, secrets that could get her charged with espionage, and then to believe the man you loved, the man you'd protected, was obsessed with someone else must be torture.

Rikki had watched her mother bounce from man to man, putting her faith in love time after time only to have her heart broken. No man was worth that kind of pain.

Rikki's gaze slid to Quinn, perched on the foot of the bed, hunched forward. He was different from any man her mom had followed around the world. Sincere. Loyal. Family-oriented.

And he didn't know he had one.

His head jerked to the side. "What?"

"Just thinking about Belinda." Rikki gathered her hair into a ponytail. "When do we get out of here?"

"As soon as you can throw your stuff together. We can eat on the road."

"Have you heard anything more from Chan about David's emails?"

"Not yet. Did you send that picture of Dawson to your phone?"

As she reached for Belinda's phone on the table, Quinn said, "Wait. Better yet. Send that picture to my phone, and I'll send it along to Ariel. My phone is untraceable and won't come up on anyone's radar. We don't want that photo leaking out. Dawson's not going to know we have it, and we don't want to clue him in."

Rikki cupped Belinda's phone in her palm. "David

knows I'm alive, but does he realize that I know he's alive?"

"I'm assuming Belinda told him, right?" He grabbed his phone and aimed it at her. "Send it."

"She didn't really say one way or the other. I guess if she told him about my seeing the picture, he'd know that I figured it out." She tapped the phone to text the picture to Quinn's number. "Why?"

"Just wondering if Dawson would try to contact you."

Heat prickled across her skin, and she dropped the phone. It clattered on the table. "Why would he?"

Quinn lifted one shoulder. "To make some kind of overture."

"Overture?" Rikki's eye twitched and she rubbed it. "What kind of overture could he make with me now after setting me up as a traitor to the CIA and arranging to have me killed? How do you start that conversation?"

He joined her at the table and rubbed her back. "I hope you don't have to find out."

"Let's get out of here." She held up Belinda's phone. "I'm taking this with me. Who knows what else I can discover on here?"

Quinn dragged his bag from the closet floor. "Any texts?"

"Just a couple with some girl talk." Rikki pocketed Belinda's phone. "I wonder what all of Belinda's good, good friends would think about her if they knew she ran around poisoning drinks and covering for her traitor husband."

"They're going to find out soon enough once we get this investigation in official hands. That woman's going to get hers for trying to kill you."

Rikki pressed her lips together as she started packing. Having Quinn on her side gave her a warm glow in her belly.

Quinn had given her something else in her belly eighteen months ago, and she planned to tell him all about that little miracle when they got back to New Orleans.

As they headed out of Savannah, Rikki dug Belinda's phone from her pocket. "I'm going to look through this while it's still working. Once Belinda realizes her phone is missing, she'll have it deactivated."

"We don't even know if she's dead or alive. The most recent report I saw on my phone was that someone had been critically injured in that shooting, nothing about a fatality."

"I think if she'd died it would've made the news. Nothing about a suspect?"

"He's not going to be caught, and if she survives, Belinda's not going to implicate anyone."

Rikki rolled back the seat and wedged her bare feet against the glove compartment. "Do you mind?"

"You can put your feet anywhere." Quinn reached forward and caressed her ankle.

She curled her toes and almost purred. Instead, she thumbed through Belinda's pictures. "No more suspicious photos. Either that's the only one David sent her, or she deleted the rest."

"We lucked out with that one."

"Yep." She squinted at the text messages as she scrolled through each set. "No new messages, either. It's creepy that there's a text here to one of her friends about drinks the other night. Funny she doesn't mention the poison."

"Yeah, that's just what you want to tell your old friends. Meeting for drinks, and by the way, don't mind the dead chick at the table."

Rikki tapped Belinda's contacts and swept her finger down the list. One name flew by, and she gasped.

"What?"

"One of her contacts." Rikki dragged her finger back up the names and stopped on the most important one. "Frederick Von."

"You're kidding." Quinn flexed his fingers on the wheel of the car. "Dawson should've trained his wife better in the rules of espionage."

"Who would know the name of David's villain in an unpublished work of fiction? Besides, I'm sure he believed Belinda would never come under suspicion, that *he'd* never come under suspicion."

"And yet here they are—under suspicion." Quinn cranked his head to the side. "What are you going to do about it?"

She held the phone between both of her hands as if in prayer. "You think I should call him?"

"I do."

"If I do, I'm going to play nice." She tapped her steepled fingers against her chin. "I'm going to pretend I don't know he set me up."

Quinn raised his eyebrows as he studied the road in front of him. "Do you think he's gonna believe that?"

"I'll make him believe it. Why would I think he set me up? I thought he'd been killed, I was captured by the North Koreans, and I don't know anything about the CIA trying to take me down as a traitor."

"Devil's advocate here." He tapped his chest. "If you don't know he set you up, why haven't you gone straight to the Agency? Why are you floundering around Louisiana and Georgia?"

She held up one finger. "I didn't say the CIA didn't think I was a traitor. I just don't know *why* they think I'm one."

"He's gonna be suspicious as to why you don't believe it's him. He faked his death, you were captured, there was no Vlad."

"I just *thought* he died and we were both played."

"Do you think he'll believe you?"

Rikki dipped her head to hide her warm cheeks behind a veil of hair. "I think I can make David Dawson believe anything if I put my mind to it."

The silence stretched between them, and Rikki peeked at Quinn's hard profile.

He cleared his throat. "Then do it."

She wiped the back of her hand across her forehead despite the air-conditioning blasting her face. With an unsteady finger, she tapped Frederick Von and then put the phone on Speaker, even though she really didn't want Quinn listening to this conversation.

The phone rang, and Rikki clutched the seat's armrest. It rang several more times before a pleasant recording told her the phone's owner didn't have voice mail set up.

Rikki snorted. "I'd like to hear that voice mail greeting."

"Try again later. We have no idea where he is or what time zone he's in." He hunched forward and rapped a knuckle against the windshield. "Let's stop for some food and knock out the rest of this trip."

Four hours later and halfway through the drive, Rikki poked through one of the bags from the fast-food restaurant they'd driven through for dinner. "Do you want the rest of these French fries?"

"Are you hungry again? We can stop. We're making good time."

"Not really." She stuffed one of the fries in her mouth and licked the salt from her fingers. "Just bored."

"Do you feel like driving?"

"Too tired."

"Take a nap."

Belinda's cell, which Rikki had tucked beneath her right thigh, buzzed to life. She grabbed the phone and felt the blood drain from her face. "It's him."

"Are you ready?" Quinn put on his signal to pull into a rest area.

Rikki licked her lips and nodded. "Hello?"

The man's voice, David's voice from the grave, started before the first word left Rikki's lips.

"Belinda, what the hell are you doing calling me on this phone? I don't care if you have me listed as Dr. Seuss. You don't use this phone, especially not now."

"David, it's Rikki."

He sucked in a breath across the miles. "Rikki? My God. It sounds like you. What was the name of the bartender our first night in Athens?"

"Gypsy Rose."

A noisy rush of air gushed over the line. "Wh-when Belinda told me you were alive, I couldn't believe it."

Rikki met Quinn's gaze and dipped her chin once. David would admit nothing, whether he thought she believed him or not. She could do this.

Squaring her shoulders, she pinned them against the seat back. "I felt the same way when I discovered you were alive."

"From the picture. You saw the picture. That's what Belinda said. You knew. You knew me so well, you could tell it was recent."

Quinn made a sharp movement in the driver's seat, and Rikki placed a hand on his thigh.

They'd have to both get through this. "It was the tattoo, David."

"Of course." He coughed. "What did Belinda tell you?"

"Tell me? She told me nothing, but I saw the picture."

"Who was the man with you when you came to the house?"

"A paid associate." She squeezed Quinn's knee. "He doesn't know anything about what I'm doing."

David paused for two beats. "What are you trying to do, Rikki? Why aren't you with the Agency...or are you?"

"As far as I can tell, the Agency thinks I'm a traitor. That debacle in North Korea pretty much torpedoed both of our careers." She paused herself. "Why aren't you with the Agency? Where are you?"

"Deep undercover. The Agency thinks I'm dead, and I want to keep it that way. But what happened to you? I'd heard from my guy in South Korea that you'd been killed."

David's voice actually broke, and Rikki had to grip the phone harder to keep from throwing it out the window.

"The North Koreans captured me."

"Oh my God. We both know what that means. How'd you escape?"

"I had some help and some good luck. Seems like we both did." For just a moment, the knots in Rikki's stomach had loosened and it felt like old times talking with David about an assignment.

She only had to glance at Quinn's tight jaw to remember it wasn't.

"What have you been doing, David? Where are you? What happened to your lead on Vlad? Was it all counterintelligence?"

"That's the thing, Rikki. I'm hot on Vlad's trail right now. This will be my ticket back to the Agency—mine and yours."

Quinn poked her in the ribs, but he didn't have to prod her to encourage David in this line of thinking.

"Your intel panned out?"

"Once I escaped from the North Koreans, I buckled down and burrowed in. I'm getting ready to bring down Vlad and I couldn't be happier that you're alive to help me do it." He cleared his throat. "Just like old times, Rikki, right? You want to do this with me, right?"

Quinn jabbed her again, and she didn't know if he approved or not, but Rikki refused to look at him—just in case he wanted to dissuade her.

"O-of course, David. I'm in."

"You sound hesitant. You believe me, don't you, Rikki? You believe I never meant our operation to go down like that—you captured, us split up."

"I… Yes."

"Of course things are a little different now, but we can work around all that."

"Different? You mean because we're rogue agents instead of official ones with support from the CIA?"

"There's that…and the other matter. Your personal issue."

Quinn jerked in the seat beside her, and Rikki's heart began to hammer painfully in her chest.

"My personal issue?"

"You know—the fact that you have a daughter now. You can't try to tell me that little redheaded baby in Jamaica with your mother isn't yours."

Chapter 15

The roaring in Quinn's ears sounded like a Mack truck coming up behind them in the rest stop. His gaze flew to Rikki's face, a white oval in the darkness of the car.

Quinn waited for the eye roll. The laugh. The denial.

She stammered. "Wh-what are you talking about? You're in Jamaica?"

The bastard's voice lowered, silky smooth. "I'm not in this alone, Rikki. As soon as Belinda told me the good news that you were alive and well and…snooping around Savannah with a big bodyguard type, I sent one of my associates out to Jamaica. You see how well we know each other? I remembered your mother was out there. I thought maybe we could get some information about you out of her, and my associate discovered something even better."

The only response Rikki could muster was a small

gurgle, and Quinn clenched his jaw so hard he thought his teeth would break.

No denial. It had to be true. A child? A baby? Did it happen in Korea? Good God, it couldn't be David's.

David's voice continued, and Quinn just wanted to punch the phone.

"Don't try to deny she's yours, Rikki. I've only ever seen that hair color on one other person." Dawson's voice had an almost dreamy quality, and Quinn clenched his fists. "That, and we asked around. The locals are talkative, especially when cash is involved."

Rikki's lips emitted small bursts of air, as if she couldn't take in enough air to breathe. "Better?"

"What?"

"You said better. Why is discovering my…daughter better?"

Quinn wanted to shake Rikki, but she hadn't even looked at him since Dawson dropped the bombshell. Had she been raped in the labor camp? Quinn's blood boiled in his veins.

David sucked in a breath. "Having a child is a happy occasion, and she's not a small infant. Although I don't know much about babies, I do know yours must've been conceived before we left for Korea."

A shaft of pain pierced the back of Quinn's head. He wanted to grab the phone and end the call. He wanted Rikki to look at him. He wanted her to explain.

"Of course it's happy." Rikki leaned her head against the window. "I just don't understand your interest in my child."

"Everything about you interests me, Rikki. Let's just say, I need your help on this Vlad assignment. I've always needed you, Rikki."

"I'll help you. Where are you?"

"We'll talk again later…partner."

"D-don't you want to hear about Belinda? How I happen to have her phone?"

"I don't really care. Just keep it."

Quinn had been building to the boiling point during that call and wanted to pounce on Rikki with a million questions and accusations. But when Dawson ended the call, he sat there, staring out the window at the Alabama trees guarding the rest area, feeling like he'd been steamrollered.

Rikki didn't move, but mewling noises started coming from the other side of the car where she was huddled against the window.

Quinn opened his mouth, but he couldn't form any words, would probably sound like Rikki right now.

He swallowed and tried again. "What's going on? Whose baby?"

Rikki sniffled, and Belinda's phone slid from her hand and dropped to the floor of the car. "She's yours, Quinn. Ours."

Quinn covered his face with his hands. He had a baby with Rikki. How did she manage to keep it from him all this time? She lied for a living.

Cool fingers encircled his wrist. "I'm sorry. I was going to tell you. I'd planned to tell you all along, but—" she waved one arm in the small confines of the car "—this all got in the way."

Rikki's voice had a tone he'd never heard from her before—pleading, unsure, frightened—and it shocked him out of his trance.

He dropped his hands from his face and rounded on

her, grabbing her shoulder. "You were pregnant before you were in Korea."

"Y-yes. Of course. Bella is yours."

"Oh God, Rikki." He cupped the side of her face, his thumb caressing her wet cheek. "You were pregnant while you were in that labor camp."

She dropped her lashes, sticky with her tears. "I was."

"You must've been terrified, not only for yourself but for the baby."

"I just assumed I was going to lose her, and even after I escaped, I was concerned she might suffer."

A fist squeezed Quinn's heart and his breath caught in his throat. "Did she? Is she...?"

Rikki met his eyes for the first time, and a soft smile hovered on her lips. "Oh, Quinn. She's perfect in every way. You understand, don't you? You do understand why I had to keep her a secret, even from you?"

"I'm sure it didn't help my case for fatherhood when you found out I was the one behind that sniper rifle."

Her eyes widened, and fresh tears began a path down her face. "But she's not a secret anymore. David knows. He has someone in Jamaica."

"He's not going to do anything." He threaded his fingers through Rikki's hair and pulled her in for a quick kiss. "The guy still loves you."

She choked. "He set me up to be killed or captured, ruined my career, and just threatened my daughter. That's love?"

"The twisted, obsessive, delusional kind." He took both her hands in his. "The kind that you can use. You're not above using David Dawson, are you?"

"Who, me?" She lifted her shoulder and wiped her nose on her sleeve. "Hell no."

Quinn chuckled. "That's my Rikki Taylor. Now you've got another four hours on the road to tell me all about our daughter, Bella, but first you need to call your mother in Jamaica and give her a heads-up. Do she and your stepfather have people they can trust out there? People to look after them?"

"Oh, yeah. Chaz, my stepfather, has been down there for years. The locals have adopted him, adopted Bella."

"Good. She needs everyone looking out for her." He reached into his front pocket and pulled out his phone. "Use this one. Will your mom be alarmed?"

"My mom is accustomed to my work, and Chaz will make sure she stays calm. She takes all her cues from him."

"That's a good thing right now."

As Quinn got back on the road, he half listened as Rikki explained to her mother the need to keep Bella safe.

She ended the call and heaved a sigh. "Mom had already noticed a couple of tourists eyeing Bella at the hotel."

"Maybe you got the spy gene from your mom. Did you scare her?"

"A little, but she got Chaz right on the phone and he assured me they'd take care of Bella. I trust him... and the locals."

Quinn rolled his shoulders. "When did you find out you were pregnant?"

Rikki's posture stiffened. "I swear, Quinn. I had no idea until I was in South Korea. I thought the food didn't agree with me."

"You don't have to defend your decisions, Rikki."

"Why not? I figured the longer I waited to tell you, the more furious you'd be with me for keeping it from you, and now...you don't seem furious at all."

"What right do I have to be mad? When were you supposed to tell me? The moment you discovered it was me on the other end of that sniper rifle waiting and willing to take you down?"

"You didn't."

"You've been through hell and back, Rikki, keeping our daughter safe through it all. I owe you nothing but gratitude. But you know what this means, right?"

She folded her hands and clasped them between her knees. "What?"

"You're never leaving me high and dry again."

"I don't want to, Quinn, ever."

He might be a fool, but he believed her.

"Now tell me all about our daughter."

By the time they reached New Orleans, Quinn had already carved out a place in his heart for his little Bella, a girl with her mother's ginger curls and her father's stubbornness, although he secretly thought that trait came from Mom, too.

As Quinn inserted his key in the lock of his front door, Rikki put her hand over his. "Do you think your place could've been compromised?"

"Dawson wouldn't be able to get any information on me."

Rikki chewed on her bottom lip. "I don't know. He found out your name in Dubai and knew you were a navy SEAL."

"Navy's not going to give him anything." He held up his hand. "And before you tell me Dawson's some kind of CIA superagent, the CIA isn't going to give him anything, either."

He studied Rikki's face—eyebrows drawn over her nose, lips twisted into a frown—and pulled out his weapon. "Stay back."

He pushed open his front door and swept his gun from side to side as he scanned the living room and kitchen. "Everything looks in order."

Following him over the threshold, Rikki took out her own weapon and crouched behind him as he moved toward the back of the apartment. They searched through both of the rooms and found nothing out of place.

Quinn double-locked his front door. "Feel better?"

Rikki sagged against the doorjamb of the bedroom. "Not really. David knows about you. He must know Bella is yours, and maybe he even figured out you paid a visit to Belinda with me."

"Then it's your job—" he touched Rikki's nose with the tip of his finger "—to convince him he's the only man in your life."

"He's not a fool, Quinn."

"When a man has feelings about a woman like Dawson has about you, he'll be only too eager to believe what you're puttin' down."

She quirked an eyebrow at him. "Speaking from experience?"

"One of many differences between me and Dawson." Quinn held up a finger. "I'm in love with you, not obsessed with you. That allows me to look at you realistically. That's why I let you go when you hightailed it out of Dubai and left me holding the sheets. For whatever reason, you couldn't handle the feelings between us. It cut me to the core, but you had to do what worked for you. If you could figure it out and come back to me, I would be there with open arms."

"I figured it out, sailor." She wrapped her arms around his waist and rested her head against his chest.

He stroked her hair. "Dawson doesn't want to let you go. He pissed off his own wife, the woman keeping his secrets, with his reaction to the news that you weren't dead. Then he probably tried to have her killed for attempting to poison you."

"We don't know if that was David behind the shooting. He answered that phone call from me as if he thought it was Belinda."

"Maybe the order was to shoot his wife, but not to kill her. When he saw the call from her cell, of course he'd act like he didn't know anything about the attempt on her life."

"That's so cold."

"He doesn't want Belinda. He wants you, Rikki, and you're going to give him what he wants." He squeezed the back of her neck. "Are you okay with that? We can do it a different way—bring in Dawson and find out his connection with Vlad."

"If you think I'm going to let this opportunity pass me by, there are a few more things I need to teach you about myself before you start professing your love for me again."

"I'm sure there are a lot of things you can still teach me about yourself, but none of that's going to change how I feel." He wrapped her in a bear hug and rested his chin on top of her head.

She spoke into his chest. "And I'm ready to give David what he wants."

Quinn tightened his hold on her. "But first you're gonna give me what I want."

"Always, Quinn McBride."

He swept her up in his arms to carry her to his bedroom, but his lust couldn't blot out the twinge of uneasiness in his heart.

She still hadn't told him she loved him. He wanted more than her body. He wanted more than Bella to bind them together.

He wanted her love, unconditional and unreserved. The following morning, they worked on a plan over breakfast.

Quinn stabbed a clump of scrambled eggs and shook it at Rikki. "Dawson wants to bring you into his scheme. He always wanted that. Whether he believes you're game because he has someone watching Bella or because you've realized you can't live without him, doesn't matter. But he'll be more open with you if he believes the latter."

"I think I can pull it off, but if he knows I'm with you, that's going to put a serious crimp in my game. He was so jealous of you."

Quinn squirted some ketchup on his plate. "You've got an ace in the hole."

"I do?"

"I was the sniper who tried to take you out. Everyone believes I did the job. Dawson has to know that." He swept a forkful of eggs through the ketchup and held it over his plate as a red drop fell into the pile of eggs. "How could a woman ever forgive that, even if the sniper is the father of her baby?"

Hunching forward, Rikki broke a piece of toast in two. "That's believable. I can make a story out of that."

"Make that case to Dawson. And you need to tell Ariel what's going down."

"I will. Maybe she can send reinforcements for whatever David has planned."

"I forgot to mention." Quinn wiped his hands on a napkin and pulled his phone toward him with one finger. "Chan is making progress on Dawson's emails to Frederick Von, thinks he found a pattern, one he can enter into his computer program."

"The more evidence I can present to Ariel, the better. I'll let her take it to the CIA. I'm not going to the Agency directly."

"Good idea." Quinn stacked his plate on top of Rikki's. "Does Belinda's cell phone still work?"

"It does. She doesn't realize yet that it's missing, she's too injured to care or…she's dead."

Quinn tapped his phone. "Latest story I could find on the incident still lists one critically injured, no fatalities. Unless the CIA is hiding her condition from the press, it looks like she survived."

"Then David wanted her to survive."

"If it was David who ordered the hit." Quinn took their dishes to the sink. "I hope he plans to contact you soon, before Belinda turns that phone off."

"I did write down the number for Von, so I can always contact him if he doesn't get back to me."

"Yeah, but we want him reaching out to you first. He needs to make the first move." Quinn ran some water over the dishes and it hit him all over again that he was a father. He grinned. "When do I get to see some pictures of my little girl?"

"As soon as we get past this and we know Bella is

safe, I'll have Mom text me some pictures to my temp phone."

"I can't wait." Quinn crossed the room to yank open the drapes. "I'm picturing those red curls and big blue eyes just like her—"

Rikki screamed, "Get down!"

Instinct had him dropping his head and jerking to the side. He hit the floor—but not before he felt the searing pain of the bullet slam into his body. And all this time he'd thought he was bulletproof.

Chapter 16

Her heart thundering in her chest, Rikki crawled toward Quinn bleeding on the floor. "Please, God. Please, God."

When she reached him, he groaned and spit out an expletive.

"Quinn, you're hit." She cupped his head with both hands, her fingers searching every inch of his scalp.

"It's not my head, damn it. It's my shoulder."

Quinn lay on his side, his knees to his chest, blood pooling beneath him.

"Thank God."

"Really? Because it hurts like hell."

A laugh bubbled to her lips, and she kissed the side of his intact head. "I thought… I thought, when I saw the blood… I thought…"

He rolled to his back with a low moan. "You need to come back to planet earth and tell me what it looks like."

She ripped off what was left of his shredded, blood-soaked sleeve and peered at the damaged flesh. "Hang on. This is going to hurt."

She probed the wound and tucked her hand beneath his shoulder. "Went clean through, Quinn. Stay right here. I'll get some towels to stop the bleeding."

He grabbed her ankle as she started to crawl away. "No 911. We'll handle this."

Cranking her head over her shoulder, she said, "No 911, but you're going to have to see a doctor at some point. You need that properly cleaned, maybe some stitches, and you'll need some antibiotics for infection."

"I have some old antibiotics in the bathroom and ibuprofen. I need something to dull this pain."

Rikki didn't stand upright until she got to his hallway, away from that window. David. It had to have been David. They had both underestimated David's obsession with her. While still in good standing with the CIA, David had probably gotten a complete dossier on Quinn McBride once he learned about her affair with him.

She gathered several towels, wet down a few of them, and then snatched bottles of ibuprofen and expired antibiotics from a drawer in the bathroom.

She crawled back into the living room, pushing her medical supplies ahead of her. A few feet away from Quinn, she came to a dead halt and gagged.

He peeled open one eye where it gleamed from his bloody face. "Does it look bad?"

"What did you do? What happened? Why is that blood all over your face?"

"Because I'm a dead man. I just got shot in the head and you're going to take a picture of me for proof."

"For David."

"That's right. That bullet was meant for me, to get me out of the picture and out of your life."

"Why am I not crazy with grief?"

He scooped a little more blood from his shoulder wound and dragged it through his hair. "Because I'm the sniper the navy and the CIA sent to take you out. You always knew that. You were using me to get information and to help protect you against the CIA. Now you have Dawson."

Rikki left the towels and bottles on the floor and scooted toward the kitchen to retrieve her phone. She yanked on the charger to bring down her phone and made her way back to Quinn.

He positioned himself to resemble a man who'd been shot in the head, and as a navy SEAL sniper with plenty of kills under his belt, he knew exactly what that would look like.

"Take the pictures."

Rikki swallowed, almost believing the proof before her eyes and imagining how destroyed she would've been if the sniper had hit his mark.

She loved this man. He hadn't even been angry that she'd kept Bella's existence from him. His only concern had been how she'd begun her pregnancy in a North Korean labor camp and its effects on their baby.

She could give herself completely to Quinn and he'd never use or abuse her devotion. He'd only return it tenfold.

She clicked several pictures of him and his bloody head, and then grabbed the towels.

Quinn rolled to his stomach. "Not yet. Get back on that phone and call Dawson. He'll expect it, either way.

His guy is probably still watching the apartment building. He's gonna wonder where the lights and sirens are."

"David would know I'm not in any position to talk to the police and then the navy."

"Whatever. You need to make contact now. What reason would you have to keep silent, other than a desire to hide from him and hide the fact that his mission failed?"

"I hate him."

"Use that passion." He wiped his hand across his bloody mouth. "And hand me a towel so I can stop gushing blood on the floor."

She threw him a wet towel and a dry towel. "Bunch that dry towel under your shoulder and get on your back to apply pressure."

Taking a deep breath, she grabbed her phone and tapped the number she'd saved for David.

He must've been waiting, because he picked up on the first ring. "Yes?"

"It's Rikki."

"I figured as much. You okay?"

"Oh, I'm just fine, but Quinn McBride is dead, shot in the head right through his window. Are you crazy?" Her fingers got busy texting him Quinn's death shots.

"Do you care that much about him? The father of your baby? I could tell you a thing or two about your heroic Quinn McBride."

"Nothing I don't already know, like he was the navy SEAL sniper sent to eliminate me, the traitor."

David choked. "You knew that already?"

"Why do you think I came to see him right out of Jamaica? I wanted to take care of business. You taught me that, David."

Rikki glanced at Quinn, who'd paused from stanching his blood flow to stick his finger in his mouth. She scowled at him.

"But you didn't take care of business. You stayed with him, took him with you to visit Belinda."

"I needed him as a protector. He's all muscle and brawn, but not too much brain."

Quinn kicked her foot, and she stuck out her tongue at him.

"I knew the two of you weren't meant for each other, Rikki. I'm sorry I had him taken out right in front of you, but he has to be out of the picture for us to move forward."

"Oh, he's out of the picture." She tapped her phone several times and sent the last of Quinn's death pictures to David. "Am I safe now?"

"The sniper? He's long gone." David clicked his tongue. "Got the pictures. Once he saw McBride fall, he disassembled and took off—just in case you went ballistic and called in the authorities."

Rikki snorted. "No chance of that. Do you think I want to talk to a bunch of cops? Once they found out Quinn's identity, they'd call in the navy. No, thanks. His death needs to remain a secret for as long as possible."

"Any chance of discovery there?"

"Nobody heard the shot. There's a bullet hole in the window, but the velocity of the bullet was such that the window didn't shatter. McBride's deploying in another few weeks, and I'm assuming that's when his body will be discovered. He has no family to speak of. Nobody's going to miss him."

Quinn kicked her again.

"Good. There's someone very important I want you

to meet. Plenty of people have already switched to his side. He pays well and he's loyal—unlike the Agency."

"Y-you don't mean who I think you mean, do you? I thought we were going out to Korea to provide information that would lead to his capture. Can't we still do that?"

"There's no need for it, Rikki. What he does is no different from what we were doing, but he's supporting different countries than we are. That's all. He's not interested in taking down the US, but he wants us to think twice before sticking our noses in other countries' business—countries he wants to control."

"I'm not saying I'm in, David, but I also won't betray you. I'm done with the Agency. Y-you were always my first loyalty anyway."

"We could do this together, Rikki—partners. I could provide your daughter riches beyond belief, and with those riches, safety and security."

Rikki pressed a hand to her chest. Hearing David talk about her daughter struck fear in her heart. His threats against Bella always simmered beneath the surface. "When is this meeting? Where are you, David?"

"I'm where it all began for him, Rikki. I'm in Berlin."

Her gaze flew to Quinn's face, and he lifted his good shoulder.

"You want me in Berlin?"

"You must have an ID that you're using or you never would've made it to the US from Jamaica undetected. Besides, nobody knows you're alive except me and Belinda. We don't have to worry about McBride anymore."

"What about Belinda? Did you have her…shot?"

"I did. I had no intention of killing her, or she'd be dead." David made a strange hissing sound before speaking again. "I found out she tried to kill you, Rikki. She knew I was always in love with you. I couldn't allow that to stand. I wanted to let her know I could get to her anytime, anywhere. And now that you and I are going to be together, we don't have to give her another thought."

Rikki rubbed the sick feeling in her stomach. "Who is he? Who is Vlad?"

"You'll see."

David spent the rest of the phone call giving her instructions for getting to Berlin, but wouldn't give her the meeting place with Vlad.

After his precise orders, David's voice softened. "I know you don't love me...yet. I know you're not on board with joining forces with the other side...yet. But I think you're halfway there on both, aren't you?"

"I think I've always been half in love with you, David." She glanced at Quinn, but he avoided her gaze in favor of tending to his wound. "The other... I don't know."

"I knew it, but I hope you understand, Rikki."

"Understand what?"

"If you don't join forces with our friend and do a really, really good job of pretending you love me, we'll take your daughter."

Chapter 17

A white-hot fury coursed through Quinn's veins. His head felt light. Two seconds later, Rikki's cool hand fluttered about his face.

"You passed out." She folded a clean towel and applied pressure against his gunshot wound. "Enough of this nonsense. You need a doctor."

Quinn blinked and squeezed his eyes. "I need to find out where David is taking you to meet Vlad. This is our chance, maybe our one and only chance."

"You heard David. He's not going to tell me in advance. He's meeting me at the airport and taking me directly to the meeting. If he gets a hint that anyone has come with me or is following us, it's over, and it could be over for Bella. I'm not going to risk that."

"I'm not either." He winced as Rikki got aggressive with the pressure. "Following you is not good enough.

We need to know the meeting place in advance so that we can set up."

Once she secured the towel against his arm and finished cleaning up his blood, Rikki scrambled to her feet and closed the drapes over the glass with the bullet hole.

"Let's get you up." She took his arm and helped him up.

He collapsed on the sofa, clutching the pill bottles in his hand. "Can you get me some water to down these?"

She took away the bloody towels and stuffed them into plastic garbage bags. She banged through his cupboards and returned with a bottle of water and a bottle of whiskey.

"Now that's a good idea, even at ten in the morning."

She shook the water bottle. "This first and then a shot of whiskey just so you won't pass out on me again."

"Yes, ma'am."

She twisted off the water bottle cap and handed the bottle to him.

He downed a couple of antibiotics and three ibuprofens. "You need to call Ariel now."

Rikki poured him a shot in a juice glass and thrust it at him. "Drink this first."

"You don't have to twist my arm." He threw back the whiskey, and the burning down his throat made his eyes water but cleared his senses. "Ariel."

Rikki got through to the head of the Vlad task force almost immediately, and Ariel's smooth voice almost purred over the line. "What do you have for me, Rikki?"

"Quinn McBride is listening in."

"I would expect that. Did David reach out to you?"

"You could say that. David hired someone to take out Quinn."

"Since Quinn's listening in on this call, I'm guessing the hit wasn't successful."

"Only because Rikki saw the laser and saved my life." Quinn laced his fingers through Rikki's. "Did I ever thank you for that?"

"You were in shock. I don't hold it against you."

Ariel sighed. "If you two are finished with your cute banter, what's the upshot?"

Rikki explained to Ariel how they faked Quinn's death and told her about David's proposal.

The pause from Ariel dragged on so long, Quinn exchanged a glance with Rikki. He thought Ariel would be all over this.

Finally she spoke, her voice strained and thin. "You're meeting with Vlad?"

"I am. I have to go through with it."

"And we need to be there to make sure it's the last meeting he ever has."

"Agreed." Quinn squeezed Rikki's hand before releasing her. "David Dawson is never going to fall for any surveillance. We have to know in advance and we have to be ready."

"It's yours, Quinn, yours and your teammates', all of them. I'm calling them all into Berlin right now, today."

Patting his shoulder, Quinn winced. "I'm not sure how much use I'm going to be with a sniper rifle right now. That shooter missed my head, but a bullet went clean through my shoulder."

"We have five other sniper rifles to back you up."

"Wait, wait." Rikki waved her hands in the air. "This all sounds wonderful, but we can't have six navy SEAL snipers roaming around Berlin looking for a meeting place."

Quinn rubbed his knuckles down Rikki's thigh. "I've been thinking about this. We have Dawson's phone number, Ariel."

"That's a start."

Rikki threw up another roadblock. "If you think you're going to put a trace on David's phone, he'll be way ahead of you. He's not going to take it with him."

Ariel said, "No, but he'll need to communicate with Vlad, and we can track those communications."

No wonder Ariel was leading this task force. Quinn snapped his fingers. "Exactly."

"Again." Rikki pushed the hair from her face and scooted to the edge of the sofa as if ready to do battle. "David and Vlad are not going to communicate in plain English or any other plain language."

"They'll use code." Quinn tapped her knee. "Like the code in those emails."

Ariel spoke up. "We're working on those."

"Ariel, I have a guy working them as well, and he's getting close."

"Berlin, huh?" Ariel's voice had a dreamy, far-away quality and Quinn raised his eyebrows at Rikki, who shrugged.

"I know Berlin is a big city, but this meeting won't be in a public place. Vlad would be too worried about plants among the crowd."

"The forest." Ariel's voice rose with excitement. "The Grunewald forest is in Berlin."

Rikki scrunched up her nose. "I suppose that would be a good place for him. They would notice any people wandering around, wouldn't they? I know there are some schlosses there that attract tourists, but it's a big forest. Why did that come to mind, Ariel?"

She coughed. "Seems like it would work for him, but we need to do our research. When do you leave, Rikki?"

"I have a flight out tomorrow, and the meeting is the following day."

"That's not much time, but I can get Quinn's sniper team into Berlin tonight. I think Alexei Ivanov is still in LA. Miguel Estrada is in San Diego at Coronado. Josh Elliott is already back in Europe, as is Slade Gallagher, and Austin Foley is in the Middle East. I'll get them moving today, military transport."

"Whew." Quinn raised his eyes to the ceiling. "You're way ahead of me."

Ariel cut him off. "The number. Rikki, give me Dawson's number. We have to start intercepting now and hope we're not already too late."

When they finished their plans with Ariel and ended the call, Quinn drummed his fingers on the coffee table. "She's a dynamo for sure. Why is she so invested in bringing down Vlad, and what made her think of the Grunewald forest?"

"It's her job." Rikki bounded up from the sofa. "I'm going to check in with Mom, and then I'm going to pack. You'd better start thinking about a disguise to get out of this apartment house in case it's being watched."

"Don't worry about me. I have a way out of here, and nobody ever has to know I left." He reached for his phone. "I need to get on Chan and tell him to expedite the decoding."

After sending a message to Chan, Quinn got on his own laptop and brought up Dawson's email exchanges with Vlad—he had to have been communicating with Vlad and Dawson had childishly given Vlad his own villain's name from his book. Hubris was one quality that usually brought people down, and Dawson was no different. He couldn't really believe that Rikki would fall in love with him, and yet here he was, making plans.

A sudden, piercing pain gripped Quinn's shoulder, and he grabbed it. He hoped he wasn't suffering from the same delusions as David Dawson.

Rikki charged in from the back rooms. "Bella's doing fine. Mom says there's a twenty-four-hour watch on their place by some tough dudes from Montego Bay. Nobody's going to get to her." She held up her phone. "And I just got off the phone with Ariel again. She's sending a doc around for a house call. I have his number. Maybe you can sneak him in."

"Better yet. We're sneaking out of here, or at least I am. You go out the regular way in case someone's watching my place."

"Where are we going?"

"I have a buddy who manages a hotel just off Rue Royale. I did him a…favor once and he lets me have a suite at the hotel whenever I want."

"The Fourth of July weekend is coming up. Is he going to have anything available?"

"He usually has a high-end suite up for grabs that they use for upgrades. I'm calling in my chips."

Two hours later, Quinn had sneaked out of his apartment through the basement and into a penthouse suite overlooking the French Quarter, and Rikki had followed him out the front door of his apartment and assured him nobody had followed her.

She stood next to him on the balcony, resting her head against his good shoulder. "This is going to work, Quinn."

"I have a backup plan in case we can't get your location in advance."

She folded her arms on the railing of the balcony and bent forward, surveying the street. "Shoot—or maybe I shouldn't be telling a sniper to shoot."

His lips twisted as he pointed to his bum shoulder. "I don't know when I'll be able to hoist my rifle again."

"There will be five other ones there to do the job, but what's the backup?"

"You're CIA, or you were. You must know about the internal GPS."

She dipped her head. "You mean the one that's swallowed?"

"That's the one. It's undetectable if they scan and search you, but we'll have your location."

"I can do that. I will do that, but it might be too late once I'm there. Vlad probably has lookouts. Hell, he's a sniper himself, isn't he?"

"That's the problem, but it's better than nothing. Even if we miss Vlad, we might be able to go in and get Dawson."

"Don't miss Vlad." She dug her fingernails into his arm. "Whatever you do, whatever happens to me, don't let Vlad get away."

He cradled her jaw in his palm. "Do you think nailing Vlad is more important to me than you are? I'm not risking your life to get Vlad—and I'm not going to let anyone else do it, either."

She turned her head to kiss his hand. "You know we'll never be safe as long as he's alive. He has a personal vendetta against you guys. That's probably how David knew where you lived in New Orleans. Vlad may be distracted now because you've disrupted his plans so many times, but he'll come back at you and the others again and again."

"Let him." Quinn spread out his arms and faced the Mississippi, feeling invincible—until an ache claimed his shoulder.

"It's not just you, tough guy." She traced the outline of his bandage. "You have Bella now. You told me Miguel has a little boy, and Josh's girlfriend has a son. Austin Foley's girlfriend is not going to live on his parents' ranch forever, and Slade's new love puts herself in danger all over the world. And if you think that crazy, intense Russian, Alexei Ivanov is ever going to give up on Vlad, you're as crazy as he is. It has to end now in Berlin, where according to David it all started for Vlad."

"Point taken. I shouldn't have updated you on all my teammates." Quinn scratched his jaw. "Dawson did say that, didn't he?"

"What?"

"That it all began in Berlin for Vlad."

"Y-yes." She dropped her lashes and shifted away from him.

"I'd heard that when Ariel was with the CIA, she spent time in Berlin."

"I think so." Rikki pointed across the rooftops to the river. "Are those barges always there?"

"Not usually. They're getting ready for the fireworks." He cocked his head at her, and she pushed herself off the balcony and spun around to the room.

"The doctor should be here soon."

Quinn wiped a bead of sweat from his forehead and followed her back into the air-conditioned room.

Ten minutes later the doc showed up, and he must've

come from Ariel's special list, but Rikki still made herself scarce.

Dr. Smith, as he called himself, peeled back the homemade bandage from Quinn's shoulder and slipped his glasses to the edge of his nose. "Clean gunshot wound right there. You're lucky."

With very little further conversation, the doctor thoroughly cleaned the wound, replaced the bandage with something more secure, and gave Quinn a new bottle of antibiotics and some painkillers.

Dr. Smith shook the bottle of painkillers. "These will make you sleepy, so you might want to stick with the ibuprofen."

Quinn picked up a sling and dangled it from his fingertips. "And this?"

"You'll want to hold your arm still and pressed against your body. That will help, but your shoulder is going to be stiff as hell if it isn't already."

Quinn rolled his shoulder back in a test and winced. "It's getting there."

"That's all I got for you." The doc snapped his black medical bag closed. "Take the antibiotics as prescribed. In the unlikely event the wound starts to fester, you'll need additional treatment. If you're still here, that'll probably be me, but I have a feeling—" Dr. Smith shot a glance at Rikki's bag in the corner "—you won't be here much longer."

Quinn got up and extended his hand. "I hope you mean I won't be in New Orleans much longer and not on this Earth."

The doctor chuckled. "With you guys, it's always a crapshoot."

When Dr. Smith left, Rikki sauntered in from the back bedroom. "Everything okay? You gonna live?"

"According to the cheerful doctor Ariel sent, that's debatable."

"What?" Rikki flew to his side and grabbed his hand.

"I'm kidding. He was referring to something other than the bullet hole in my shoulder. That's going to be just fine." He kissed the inside of her wrist. "How about you? Are you just fine with all this?"

"I've been fine with all this for almost ten years. It's my job, Quinn. I can handle David Dawson *and* Vlad."

"The stakes have never been higher, Rikki. You never had this much to lose—Bella."

"You." She brushed her knuckles across his cheek. "We're going to do this, Quinn. And then I'll introduce you to your daughter."

He squeezed the top of his shoulder. "I'm not sure I can do anything with this shoulder. How am I going to fire my rifle?"

"Your whole team will be there. It doesn't have to be you who takes out Vlad."

"After what we've been through with him, it would be a gold star for any of us. It might not just be Vlad. We might have to take down Dawson, too, although Ariel might prefer we bring him in for interrogation. Are you okay with that?"

"David is already dead to me. He turned, and he didn't even do it for ideology. He did it for money."

"And because he could—pride." Quinn toyed with the edge of his bandage. "You said you read his book, right?"

"Yeah, the whole thing." She rolled her eyes. "It was painful, and that was when I still liked the guy."

"Do you have it somewhere so I can read it?"

"You're not going to pick up any tips from it."

"Maybe not about writing, but there could be lots of tips about Dawson in there."

"I can get you to it." She stepped away from him and sat at the table with his laptop in front of her. "He put it up on a document-sharing platform for me to read. It's over a year old. I read it before we went to Dubai, so if he's made any changes they won't be in this draft."

"That's okay. Bring it up for me. I'll need something to read on my flight to Berlin. My military transport is not going to be as comfortable as your first class on a commercial airline."

Rikki spent several minutes at his laptop navigating to the shared document site. She scribbled something on a slip of hotel stationery and propped it up on his laptop's keyboard. "Here's my user name and password for this site."

Quinn stretched his arms over his head. "I'd better get packing. I leave tonight."

Rikki rose from the desk and returned to his side. She skimmed her hand down the front of his body and curled her fingers into the waistband of his shorts. "You didn't take any of those painkillers, did you?"

"No." When she touched him like that, he felt no pain at all.

"Because if you're leaving tonight, that means I have to spend the night in this giant suite in that giant bed all by myself."

His breathing grew shallow, and prickles of desire raced across his skin. "That would be a damned waste."

Sliding his hands down her back, he slanted his mouth across hers and kissed her hard and possessively. If she had to pretend to love Dawson, he didn't want her to forget what true love felt like.

She took his hand and led him into the suite's master bedroom.

Sometime later, with their legs and arms entwined around each other, when he didn't know where he ended and Rikki began, she kissed the edge of his jaw.

"I want you to know, Quinn McBride, before we go into this battle and risk everything, I love you. I loved you in Dubai. I loved you when I found out you'd had orders to kill me. I loved you when I found you again in New Orleans. And I love you now. I'm not afraid of love anymore, not your love."

He smoothed her hair back from her face. "That's all I ever wanted to hear from you."

Later that night, Dawson's words bounced on the screen as the C-5 hit an air pocket over the Atlantic. Quinn steadied his laptop.

The story dragged and Dawson's prose reeked, but Quinn couldn't shake the feeling that if Dawson used his villain's name for Vlad, there might be other hints in his work of fiction. Dawson must've been working with Vlad already when he penned this mess. In fact, Frederick Von seemed to be a thinly veiled reincarnation of Vlad.

Quinn plowed through the rest of the book, his eyelids drooping until a passage gave him a shot of adrenaline, a passage about Von's hideaway—a schloss in the Grunewald forest outside Berlin.

Chapter 18

Ariel's team had a full day to set up at Grunewald before Rikki's meeting with Dawson and Vlad. They'd located a schloss in the forest owned by a blind trust.

In case Vlad had his people in the area, the sniper team came in as construction workers, tourists and locals out for a stroll. But if Vlad's people were counting, they'd know not everyone who'd entered the area for work or play left.

That first night with his brothers, his sniper team, had been like a homecoming for Quinn. They'd been scattered for so long, but the teamwork and comradery returned like second nature.

Alexei stroked his rifle like he would a beautiful woman. "Who's going to get the final shot at Vlad?"

"If there is a final shot." Austin Foley, gung ho and still a little green, looked up from his laptop. "We don't even know if this is the place."

"It's the place." Quinn formed his fingers into a gun and aimed at Austin.

Austin tapped the keyboard. "Rikki's in the hotel. Are you sure Dawson won't be able to detect the GPS in her system?"

Slade Gallagher waved him off. "You worry too much, Austin. Dawson's not going to know, and if he suspects, he'll be confident that Vlad's people are not going to allow anyone to follow him and Rikki."

"We know who's *not* going to take the shot." Josh Elliott tipped his head toward Quinn. "You got yourself a bum shoulder, son. You're out of the running."

Quinn snorted. "I'm almost sure I still have better aim with my jacked-up shoulder than you do, Elliott. Hell, even skinny Miguel over there has you beat."

Miguel Estrada chucked a glove at Quinn. "Watch it. I may have dropped a few pounds, but I've got more reason than anyone here to make that shot count."

The door to the loft in the schloss a half mile away from Vlad's cottage burst open, and every last sniper reached for his weapon.

A woman with dark hair in a ponytail wedged her hands on her slim hips. "I'll make that decision when the time comes."

Quinn's jaw dropped. He'd had a vague picture of Ariel in his head, but this woman, whose face they all knew, wasn't it.

Alexei, the blunt Russian-American, voiced what was in all their heads. "You! Lauren West, the wife of Defense Secretary West."

"That's not who I am here." She crossed her arms and propped up the doorjamb with her shoulder. "I'm Ariel, and I'm still the leader of this task force."

Once they all got over the shock of Mrs. Shane West being the infamous Ariel, they dug in to discuss their plans.

They wouldn't all be stationed in this hunting lodge. They had visibility of Vlad's schloss from a few well-hidden treetops and a museum that would be closed to the public tomorrow.

Ariel instructed Austin to keep tabs on Rikki and to notify her immediately if it looked like Rikki was not headed in their direction.

Quinn clamped a fist against the knots in his gut. He had to be right about the location of this meeting. It made too much sense. It synced up with Ariel's belief that the meeting would be in this forest.

His gaze tracked to the vibrant brunette giving orders as well as or better than her husband ever did, and Shane West was one of them—a retired navy SEAL sniper. How had she known? What connection did she have with Vlad? Her husband had come up against him a few times, but nothing like how the team in this room had.

A few hours later, after a meal and talk about the assignments that had led them all to this forest on this night, Quinn's teammates began scattering again—this time to take down a terrorist who had threatened them all and the ones they loved.

The next morning, Quinn peeled a banana and made it his breakfast. He had stayed in the schloss with Ariel, the only two who had buddied up, and for the hundredth time he cursed the gunshot wound in his shoulder. But if he thought his close proximity to Ariel would get her to open up, he couldn't be more wrong.

Which one of them would Ariel choose for the honor? All of them were at the top of their game, even Miguel after his time in captivity. Alexei could be a hothead, but not in a sniper situation, and Slade was laid-back enough to step away and let others take credit.

He and Josh had the most experience, but given his current condition, it might fall to Josh Elliott to take out their nemesis.

It was anyone's guess at this point, and Ariel kept her lips sealed.

The radio crackled, and Austin's cowboy twang came over the airwaves. "Our subject is on the move. Leaving the hotel."

Quinn tossed the banana peel in their makeshift trash bag and wiped his hands on his jeans. He shouldn't have eaten anything. His stomach churned.

Ariel studied him through narrowed eyes. "Don't worry about Rikki. She can handle herself."

"I know that, but if this isn't the meeting place, I screwed up royally and we'll have to scramble to catch up to them."

"You didn't screw up, Quinn. This is it."

He ran his tongue along his teeth. "How can you be so sure? How did you know it would be Grunewald forest when Rikki mentioned Berlin?"

Fire sparked from her dark eyes, and her nostrils flared, giving her a completely different appearance from the sophisticated, put-together lady of Washington. "You're not the only one who knows Vlad."

Quinn's brain whirred for the best response to get Ariel to open up, but Austin's voice interrupted him.

"They're on the autobahn, leaving the city."

The knots returned to Quinn's gut, and his shoulder

throbbed. A jumbled prayer ran through his head that Rikki would head straight to the schloss, that she'd be safe, that Bella would be safe.

Austin's voice filled the room. "Headed this way. On track. The subject is on track."

The others hooted and whooped it up, but Quinn silently thanked God as his gaze met Ariel's.

Throughout the morning, strangers had wandered into the forest and along the lake, and the team had ID'd them as operatives for Vlad. They clearly had no clue that they were already surrounded by a team of navy SEAL snipers and a support group whose sole purpose over the past year had been to neutralize Vlad and his terrorist network.

None of them knew what Vlad looked like. He'd changed his appearance like a chameleon in every fuzzy, vague photo they had of him. But he'd be the one meeting with Dawson and Rikki. There would be no question about that, so they had to wait. They couldn't just start taking down people as they got out of cars or made their way to Vlad's hunting lodge, giving him a heads-up.

After the tense waiting of the morning, everything started unfolding faster than Quinn had anticipated.

Ariel started spitting out directions in the military manner she must've learned from her husband, the secretary. She had Quinn zeroing in on the car carrying Rikki and Dawson.

He'd had some painkiller injected directly into his shoulder, and the numbness prevented him from even feeling the heft of his rifle resting there. The car pulled up on the gravel drive of the schloss, and Rikki stepped out.

For the second time in less than two years, Quinn

lined her up in his scope. He whispered. "C'mon, Buttercup. We're gonna do this."

Rikki threw back her head, laughing at some quip from Dawson, but Quinn could almost believe she'd heard his quiet entreaty.

Another car pulled up, and several men exited.

Quinn held his breath. The tension coming off Ariel stifled the air in the room.

She'd joined him at the window, her own rifle, a sleek, deadly model, hoisted and ready. How long had she trained for this?

As the group began moving toward the house, Rikki paused and shook hands with a tall man, the sun glinting off his clean-shaven head.

With rapid fire, Ariel gave them their targets. Josh had the man Rikki had just greeted. He must be Vlad. Lucky bastard.

Quinn had the driver as his target, but they had to assume he was armed as well and would pose a threat to Rikki and even Dawson once the shooting ended.

Ariel gave the countdown before the group could even move inside. She must be sure of Vlad and that he wasn't waiting inside for them.

Three. Two. One.

Quinn felled his target and then swept his scope to the other fallen men. They'd left Dawson alive, and his mouth gaped in shock.

Then he reached for a weapon as Rikki backed away from him, and Quinn took his second shot.

Rikki stood amid the dead men, her face composed, her dark hair blowing in the breeze.

Slade, who'd been stationed in one of the trees, closest to the schloss, ran onto the scene and grabbed

Rikki and pulled her away. Vlad could still have reinforcements nearby, but the head of the snake had been
chopped off.

Josh cackled from the museum. "I got him, boys. I
got that bald-headed bastard."

Ariel winked at Quinn. "No, you didn't, Elliott. Vlad
was mine. He was always going to be mine."

Epilogue

Quinn held a sleeping Bella in the crook of his arm as he stood on the hotel room's balcony next to Miguel's son, Mikey, and RJ, the son of Josh's girlfriend, Gina.

RJ squirmed. "When are the fireworks?"

"Another half hour, buddy." Quinn patted his head.

Josh swept up the boy and put him on his shoulders. "You can watch from up here when they start."

Gina came up behind them and wrapped one arm around Josh's waist as she tugged on RJ's foot. "Patience. I'm going to get you and Mikey some more food."

Miguel scooped up Mikey. "You hungry?"

Jennifer, Miguel's wife, hovered next to both of them. "I think he's been stuffing his face with beignets all day. You need to eat something, too, doesn't he, Quinn?"

Miguel rolled his eyes at Quinn. "She thinks I'm gonna break."

Quinn slugged Miguel in the arm. "This guy's unbreakable."

He cuddled Bella against his shoulder and strolled into the hotel suite where the childless couples had gathered, drinking more than the parents and anticipating the fireworks less.

Austin's girlfriend, Sophia, sat on the arm of his chair, excitedly making a point by grabbing his arm, the diamond in the side of her nose catching the light.

Austin shrugged. "I think that's a good idea, Sophia."

Quinn grinned and elbowed Slade. "The kid might be young, but he catches on quickly."

Slade winked. "I taught him everything he knows about women."

"I don't think there's enough time in the world for that." He pointed at Slade's girlfriend, Nicole, deep in discussion with Alexei. "What are those two cooking up?"

"The mad Russian has Nicole convinced that she needs to do a documentary film on the crime families of Russia."

"Do you want me to stop him?"

"Nicole will do exactly what she wants, but Alexei's girl, Britt, can keep him in line." Slade waved at Britt, and she shrugged, a smile curving her lips, as she stroked Alexei's hair. "She even has Alexei on board for adopting the orphaned baby of his worst enemy."

Slade cranked his head from side to side. "Did you invite Ariel, or should I say, Mrs. West?"

"I did invite her, but she and the secretary are at the White House for the fireworks." Quinn checked his watch. "Probably already saw them."

"Did Rikki ever tell you how or why Ariel knew Vlad?"

Rikki swooped in on them and kissed the bottom of Bella's foot. "That's Ariel's business."

Slade raised his eyebrows. "But you know."

"I'm a CIA agent, sailor." Rikki drew her fingertip across the seam of her lips.

Slade laughed and crouched beside his sleek, polished girlfriend as she grabbed his hand and began to tell him about her new project in Russia.

Rikki patted the bandage on Quinn's shoulder. "Feeling okay?"

"It aches. My doctor was not happy when I told him about that shot I got that allowed me to hoist my rifle."

"But you nailed your target…and I'm glad you did."

"Dawson was going for a gun, Rikki. He was going to kill you for betraying him."

"I know that." She kissed his shoulder. "You don't have to defend yourself. I don't think Belinda Dawson was too upset by the turn of events, either. The CIA already talked to her, and they're going light on her."

"What about my buddy Jeff? Did Ariel tell you what was going on in New Orleans?"

"Purely bad luck. That *was* the Agency on his tail. They noted his suspicious movements and were tracking him. Seems after that Rikki Taylor turned, the CIA got jumpy."

"Can you blame them?" He tugged on a lock of her red hair. "Did you know which one was Vlad before we opened fire and Ariel killed him?"

"No. I was being introduced around. David never gave away Vlad's identity. I don't think I would've ever known. Each of those men at the schloss planned to join us for the meeting, so I never would've known which one was Vlad." She shook her head. "I still can't believe David was stupid enough to put details of Vlad's hideaway in his book. I'm sure he never told Vlad about that."

"Like I said, hubris. Dawson was the only one who'd come close enough to Vlad, outside of Vlad's inner circle, who even knew he had that hunting lodge by the lake."

"Tobias Bauer. His name is not Vlad." Alexei stood up and uttered some oath in Russian. "Let's not give him that power anymore."

Nicole asked, "But who was he exactly? Can you tell us that?"

Quinn glanced at Josh and shrugged. "The intelligence agencies are still figuring that out, but we know he was a child of about ten in East Germany when the Berlin Wall fell. He and his mother moved to the more prosperous cities of West Germany during the reunification, but she died soon after and Toby, as he was called, took to the streets—stealing, hustling, getting in trouble with the authorities."

Austin's girlfriend slid into his lap and said, "He had my friend killed. How did he become a terrorist?"

"And where did he learn how to shoot?" Jennifer, Miguel's wife, shooed the kids back onto the balcony with Rikki's mother and stepfather.

Slade answered, "He learned how to shoot in the forest. He became an excellent marksman and started hiring himself out as a mercenary."

"And a master of disguise." Miguel put his arm around his wife. "I may have even seen him when I was held in those caves. Nobody really knew what he looked like."

"Except Ariel." Austin cleared his throat and glanced at Rikki.

"As more is discovered about him, his terrorist network will be dismantled." Josh raised his glass. "To the fall of Tobias Bauer and the protection of innocents everywhere."

A boom echoed from outside and RJ dashed into the room from the balcony. "The fireworks. The fireworks."

Quinn tucked his sleeping daughter into a bassinet and took Rikki's hand. She squeezed his hand and they kissed before joining everyone on the balcony.

While holding on to the woman he loved, Quinn watched the exploding colors reflected in the faces of his teammates. One by one, he met their eyes and nodded, a silent affirmation among them all that they'd do anything to protect the people gathered here and to protect the red, white and blue.

* * * * *

IF YOU ENJOYED THIS BOOK
WE THINK YOU WILL ALSO LOVE

INTRIGUE

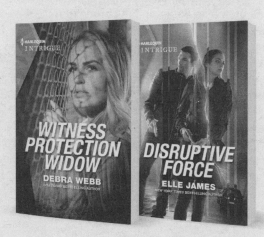

Seek thrills. Solve crimes. Justice served.

Dive into action-packed stories that will keep you
on the edge of your seat. Solve the crime
and deliver justice at all costs.

6 NEW BOOKS AVAILABLE EVERY MONTH!

Love Harlequin romance?

DISCOVER.

Be the first to find out about promotions,
news and exclusive content!

Facebook.com/HarlequinBooks

Twitter.com/HarlequinBooks

Instagram.com/HarlequinBooks

Pinterest.com/HarlequinBooks

You Tube YouTube.com/HarlequinBooks

ReaderService.com

EXPLORE.

Sign up for the Harlequin e-newsletter and
download a free book from any series at
TryHarlequin.com

CONNECT.

Join our Harlequin community to
share your thoughts and connect
with other romance readers!
Facebook.com/groups/HarlequinConnection

HARLEQUIN

HSOCIAL2021